SCARE ME TO DEATH

CJ CARVER

Print ISBN 978-1-913942-41-0

PRAISE FOR CJ CARVER

'A shocking, complex and beautifully written thriller and another cracker from the pen of bestseller CJ Carver'
Reader's Retreat

'CJ Carver can do no wrong. Fabulous. Extremely fabulous. Read this series. It's the best!'
Northern Crime

'A fast and ingenious thriller that pits the brilliantly addictive Forrester and Davies against a tense and chillingly real conspiracy... I'm full of admiration'
Isabelle Grey, author

'This is an extraordinarily tense, clever thriller. Don't expect to sleep, because this is unputdownable'
Frost Magazine

'A terrific page-turner. Heart-stopping action and a heroine with guile as well as guts'
Harlen Coben, author

'Anyone who is a member of a book club should be recommending (*Spare Me the Truth*) to their fellow readers with great gusto'
Book Addict Shawn

'Carver gives us strong heroines battling against the odds, fast-moving plots and a strong sense of place. She deservedly won the CWA Debut Dagger for *Blood Junction*'
Publishing News

"I'm so glad this is the first of a series: I want more... and I want it now!'
Julia Crouch, author

'Fast, smart and furious... it will have you clinging on by your fingertips. CJ Carver is one of the best thriller writers working today'
Tom Harper, former CWA Chairman

'A complex tale of betrayal and deception. CJ Carver writes with compassion about characters she really cares about'
Parker Bilal, author

'A top-notch thriller writer. CJ Carver is one of the best'
Simon Kernick, author

'A high-wire act of a thriller, with a plot as ingeniously constructed as a sudoku puzzle'
The Lady Magazine

'Powerful writing, a gripping plot and a unique setting... outstanding'
The Mystery and Thriller Club

ALSO BY CJ CARVER

THE HARRY HOPE SERIES
Cold Echo

Deep Black Lies

∽

THE LIA SHAN THRILLER
The Snow Thief

∽

THE NICK ASHDOWN THRILLER
Over Your Shoulder

∽

THE DAN FORRESTER SERIES
Spare Me The Truth

Tell Me A Lie

Know Me Now

Scare Me To Death

∽

THE JAY MCCAULAY SERIES
Gone Without Trace

Back With Vengeance

The Honest Assassin

For Steve, with thanks for the opening sentence.

SIXTEEN YEARS AGO

There was a girl in my seat. A teenager. Ripped jeans, red tassel top, bangles on both wrists. Auburn hair twisted into a knot. Her hands had been painted with geometric henna designs. She was absorbed in her paperback which, I saw, was the bestseller of the year, *The Da Vinci Code*.

'Excuse me,' I said. 'But I think this might be my seat.'

She didn't look up.

Even though I knew I hadn't made a mistake, I double-checked my seat assignment: 27C. Aisle seat towards the rear of the aircraft. Near the rear exits. The safest place to be.

'*Anna asif sayidi...*' I'm sorry, sir...

I backed up for the flight attendant wanting to pass, and tried again, this time moving so that I edged into the girl's personal space. 'Hello?'

She glanced up, obviously irritated at being interrupted. Her eyes were an extraordinary vivid green.

I showed her my boarding pass. 'Maybe we've been allocated the same seat. If that's the case...'

'No, no.' Her irritation immediately gave way to mortification. 'It's me, sorry.' She was already closing her book and getting up. 'I thought it might be free.' Sliding out of the seat she glanced over her shoulder. 'I was trying to get away from my extremely annoying little brother, that's all. Sorry.'

Her accent was clear-cut English, and I assumed the small boy with tousled hair the same colour as hers, who'd suddenly appeared over the headrest behind her, was the brother.

'Told you so.' His face was triumphant. 'Told you someone would come and kick you out. Now you'll *have* to play with me.' He vanished briefly to return with two toy cars which he proceeded to race along the headrest, making loud *vroom-vroom* noises.

'You're the Nissan. I'm the Ferrari.'

The girl gave a long-suffering sigh and rolled her eyes.

'You think that's a fair race?' I asked the boy.

He paused to look at me.

'I'm assuming you've got the Nissan 350Z,' I said. 'Three and a half litre six-speed manual, naught to sixty in 5.3 seconds?'

The boy stared at me, round-eyed.

'The Ferrari, however...' I bent and had a closer look, '...is a lot older than the Nissan. It's the 308 Dino. It does 7.7 seconds naught to sixty. If I were you, I'd have a rethink about which car you're going to race against.'

'Are you a racing driver?' he asked. His eyes were the same colour as his sister's and just as arresting.

'I have raced, yes.' I didn't think it wise to tell him that my last race had been in London's rush hour, chasing a terrorist suspect who'd been hell-bent on attacking the Underground with ricin poison.

The boy turned the Nissan over and looked at its underside. 'You'd have this one? Seriously?'

'It may not look as sporty, but the performance is actually pretty good.' I held out my hand. The boy put the Nissan in my palm. I don't know what it was, whether it was his solemn expression, reminding me of my own boyhood and my passion for cars, or if it was simply because I was exhausted after the past few days and needed a mental break, but I moved to take the empty seat next to him, raising my eyebrows at the girl to ask if that would be okay.

The girl looked astonished, then delighted. 'Be my guest.' She dropped into my seat fast, burying herself back in her book in case I might change my mind.

As I made to settle next to the boy, the woman on his right, sitting next to the window, sprang up. 'Bub, get back into your own seat *right now*.'

'But, Mum...'

'This gentleman shouldn't be hassled into doing what you guys want.'

'He offered!' the girl protested at the same time as the boy wailed, 'Mummy, but he *wants* to play! He's a racing driver!'

'Okay, Josh, Bubbles, just cool it. Both of you.'

Both kids fell silent. I turned to see the man I took to be their father studying me. Sandy hair, freckles and laughter lines edged a pair of eyes the same colour as his kids'. He had the seat across the aisle, which meant the family would have been in the same row if the daughter hadn't debunked.

'I don't mind,' I told him. 'Honestly.'

He stared a second longer before giving a shrug. 'Your funeral.'

'Yesss!' Josh punched the air as I sank next to him and gave him his first lesson in the technique of motor racing.

'What's the most important quality the would-be driver should have?' I asked.

'To drive really fast.'

I looked into his shining face. 'Absolutely. But it's more than that. And it's a quality you already have, which is great enthusiasm. Next, you need courage. And mastery over your nerves...'

As flight attendants began closing overhead lockers and preparing for pushback, we played with our cars, the boy asking me questions while I did my best to answer them, and after a few minutes I noticed the girl had risen and was watching us over the headrest. 'Are there any female racing drivers?'

'Some of the best drivers are women.'

'Ha!' The father snorted.

I ignored him. 'Check out Sabine Schmitz. She won twenty-four hours of Nürburgring. Twice. And what about Danica Patrick? She's one of the best NASCAR drivers around and the only woman to win an IndyCar Series race.'

'Girl power.' Bubbles grinned at me, raising a hand for a high-five. We clapped palms. Everyone smiled. Inside my chest, I felt muscles beginning to relax. This was just what I needed. To be part of a normal, happy world, with normal, happy people.

Usually I keep myself to myself. I blend in and make sure I don't do anything that anyone might remember. But I'd just finished an intense week and not having to think about it felt as good as a holiday on a tropical island. Eight bombers had bombed five places in Marrakech last week and I'd been brought in because one of those bombers had been British. The Moroccans hadn't taken my appearance kindly and although to my face they'd been perfectly polite, they'd been purposely unhelpful. Even though I'm known for being excessively even-tempered, by the end of the week I was anything but. I could have happily strangled the lot of them.

With a final check from the flight attendants making sure we were buckled up, our tables stowed away, we began rolling down the runway and lifting into the sky.

Minutes later – we were climbing through three thousand

feet or so – the plane fell suddenly straight down and gave a shudder.

Someone let out a small scream.

For a moment, I thought we might have suffered a bird strike but then the oxygen masks dropped and at the same time, I smelled smoke.

Quickly I snapped my mask into place. Checked that Josh and his parents had also put theirs on. I couldn't check on their daughter, Bubs, but since it appeared she'd pulled down her mask, I had to assume she was okay too. Josh looked at me, pale-faced and frightened. I winked.

Smoke began to fill the cabin. Acrid, filled with chemicals, it swept from the front like a black tidal wave. Somewhere, wires were melting. A fire was taking hold.

My pulse increased. *This didn't look good.* I forced myself to concentrate on my breathing. In. Pause. Out.

The intercom came on. A female voice told everyone to keep calm, assuring us that we were returning to the airport, that we would be landing safely and that the fire emergency services were already standing by. She sounded breezy and confident and I promised myself that if we came through this okay, I'd shake her hand because there was no way she'd know any of that. There'd been no time. She was improvising. Doing her job.

The smoke thickened until I could no longer see Josh's mum or dad, Josh or my feet. If the fire had started in the avionics bay, which I suspected, then the pilots would be in an even worse situation. They would have donned their full-face masks straight away, but if they couldn't see their instruments...

I willed myself to keep calm but my heart was hammering, sweat springing over my body.

I thought of my parents. Pictured us on the skiff sailing across Plymouth harbour, Mum's hair flying, Dad's eyes alight. I didn't want them to hear I'd died. I didn't want to die either. I was only twenty-four. I had my life ahead of me.

My mouth turned dry as the flight attendant began to tell passengers they needed to prepare. As everyone assumed the brace position I turned to Josh, made sure his seat belt was as low and tight as it would go. He couldn't reach the seat in front of him, which meant he had to put his arms around the back of his legs, his head on his knees.

Everyone fell quiet. Totally silent.

Seconds ticked past.

I checked Josh again, pushing his head down a little more, making sure his knees were pressed together.

Engines screaming, the plane made a sickening lurch to the side.

I leaned close to Josh. 'If anything happens, I want you to hold on to my hand and I'll get you and your sister, your mum and dad–'

My words were snatched from me as we ploughed into the ground.

1

PRESENT DAY

DC Lucy Davies stepped off the train at Bristol Temple Meads, one eye on the flow of passengers pouring along the platform, the other on the man in her peripheral vision who was walking four yards to her left. She'd first seen him when she'd boarded the train at Middlesbrough. Dark blue jeans and black leather jacket. Thickset. Strong-looking. She'd been walking along the platform when she'd glanced around to find him behind her. Their eyes had met for a split second. She wasn't sure if she'd imagined his flinch, but her nerves tightened when he came and sat in the same carriage. It was the studious way he avoided looking at her that made her spine tingle.

Was he a problem?

A biting wind cut her cheeks as she approached the stairwell leading beneath the tracks and to the exit. She wished she could have driven to Bristol – she would have felt safer in a car – but since her Corsa had a faulty water pump and was with the mechanic, she'd been forced to use public transport. As she walked, Lucy willed herself not to look at the man keeping pace with her.

You're paranoid, she told herself. Just because he resembles the man that kidnapped you last year doesn't mean anything. Yes, I know his family cursed you, that his mother swore to have you killed, but it doesn't mean that every solid-looking, dark-haired bloke is out to get you.

Does it?

Her shoulder began to pulse where her kidnapper had knifed her. She'd had twenty-five stitches and was lucky the knife hadn't lacerated any tendons or done any lasting damage. She'd been working a murder case last year and when she'd got close to exposing the killer, they'd kidnapped her, stuck her in a hole and left her to die. Thank God she'd been rescued or she'd be nothing but a pile of rotting clothes and bones.

Before she committed to the tunnel she brought out her phone, pretending she'd just received a text, and slowed her pace. The man slowed with her.

Nerves now shrieking with alarm, she kept hold of her phone and began pushing through the crowd, panic building. She had to get out of here.

'Sorry, sorry.' She barged ahead, her overnight bag banging into people as she passed. A quick glance over her shoulder showed the man wasn't far behind.

Lucy was almost running when she exited the station, her pulse pounding.

'Lucy!' Mac was waving but her attention was on the man, who'd followed her outside. He was walking straight towards her, eyes focused over her shoulder and then he was past her, and climbing into the back of a taxi...

Her knees went weak.

Definitely paranoid, dammit. When was it going to stop?

'Lucy?' Mac was by her side. 'Are you okay?'

'I just...' She made a vague gesture at the taxi, which was completing the loop in the station forecourt. 'Thought that man... but I was wrong.'

Mac looked at the taxi, then back at her, expression concerned.

'I'm fine,' she said brightly, even though her blood was still pounding. 'How are you?'

'Worried about you.'

DI Faris MacDonald. Mismatched grey eyes, curly brown hair and a serious expression. Her fiancé. They were to be married this time next year. A spring wedding. Some days she could hardly believe that the copper she'd met three years ago on a team-building exercise in Wales, the copper she'd fallen madly in love with back then, was going to be her husband. And she his *wife*.

They'd both been in relationships when they'd conducted their wild, out-of-control crazy love affair, which hadn't made Lucy proud, which is why she'd ended it. But then Mac turned up at Stockton-on-Tees Station as her DI. Each time she saw him it had taken every ounce of self-control not to think about the spectacular sex they'd had and even more willpower not to look at him longingly as a lover, but as a work colleague. She hadn't wanted to be professionally undermined by sleeping with her boss, but above all she hadn't wanted him to truly get to know her. She'd suffered from *moods* as her mother called them since she was a little girl and was scared that if he saw her at either end of her mood spectrum, he'd dump her.

She'd had to drag her courage from the bottom of her boots to open herself up to him, and even now it made her anxious. Especially since Mac had purposely left Stockton and taken up his old job in Bristol to give them space. If it hadn't been for her, he'd never have moved back.

'Please don't worry.' She reached up and kissed him. It still surprised her how soft his lips were and she closed her eyes briefly, absorbing herself in the feel of him, his taste. Anything to try and forget the fear that had flooded her.

'But if you're still...'

'I'm fine,' she repeated.

'...having flashbacks, you should see someone.'

'They're not flashbacks. I just get a bit on edge when I see someone similar, that's all.'

Lucy tried to make light of it. She didn't want to see a shrink. Yes, she'd had a few nightmares but she wasn't *that* bad.

'I know someone you can talk to.' He pulled her into his arms, held her close. Kissed the top of her head. 'She's a friend of mine. Really nice.'

Lucy leaned back in his arms. Sent him an arch look. 'A *friend*? What sort of friend?'

Mac looked baffled.

'Not this sort of friend, I hope?' Lucy wound her arms around his neck and twined her body close, sliding one of her thighs between his and taking his lower lip between her teeth, gently biting it.

Mac's eyes darkened.

'No.' His voice was hoarse. 'Definitely not that kind of friend.'

He practically carried her to his car. They didn't speak as he drove. Nor did they say a word when they reached his apartment. They made love with a silent, intense passion born out of separation and distance, and when Lucy came she curled her fingers at the nape of his neck and said his name. 'Faris.'

'Lucy.'

'God, I've missed you.'

'And I you, my love.'

Later, wearing one of his shirts, she poured them both wine and took the glasses into the sitting room where Mac had lit the fire. When she'd first seen the logs, twigs and branches ablaze she'd chastised him – Bristol was in a smoke control area – and he'd laughed. She'd been totally taken in by the faux gas fire.

They talked about their weeks. Mac had charged a suspect with murder after the body of a fifty-two-year-old man had been found earlier in the week. Lucy was in the thick of trying to track down a gang for a series of acid attacks in Middlesbrough.

'Thank God it's Friday,' she murmured.

They rang Hotline Thai Takeaway. Ate red and green curries, prawn crackers, jasmine rice. Lucy was scraping her bowl of black sticky rice pudding with mango – her favourite – when her phone rang. She looked at the display.

'Mum,' she told Mac. She wasn't sure whether to answer it or not. The last time they'd spoken, they'd rowed.

'Say hi from me.' He began picking up plates and moving them into the kitchen, making it clear he thought she should answer.

Lucy sighed. Mac was right. She couldn't ignore her mum. They may have quarrelled, but she still loved her to bits.

'Hi, Mum.'

'Lucy.'

One word and Lucy bolted upright, eyes wide open, her mind suddenly flaring with colour. She'd been diagnosed with a type of synesthesia where a cognitive pathway led to an automatic, involuntary reaction of colour when she was stimulated in some way. Usually, the colours became most intense when she was under duress or struggling to find a connection in a particularly complex police investigation. Right now, the colour was shimmering a warning amber.

'What's wrong?'

'It's, well... It's Rambo.'

'Rambo?' Lucy repeated, frowning. 'You mean Ricky Shaw?'

She'd gone to school with Ricky, otherwise known as Rambo because of his obsession with the fictional action-adventure hero. At twelve years old, Ricky had been the fattest kid in class but then he'd grown his hair long, donned a sweatband, a US

Army field jacket and combat boots. It had been his uniform until he'd left school and although he'd looked pretty daft – his stomach was a dough ball compared to Sylvester Stallone's six-pack – he was so earnest and endearingly polite that the nickname had been given out of affection as much as ridicule. Lucy guessed it was a good move on his part because it was certainly better to be called Rambo rather than 'that fat Asian kid'.

'He's murdered someone. A woman.'

The policewoman in Lucy knew that people were capable of anything but the kid in her reacted differently. '*What?!*'

'He's at Kensington Police Station. He wants to see you.'

2

'**K**ensington?' Lucy repeated in surprise.

'That's right.'

The last Lucy had heard, Superintendent Magellan had been promoted to Chief Superintendent and was now working out of the posh shop, as she thought of it. It had been Magellan who'd kicked her out of the Met, and it was only thanks to her old boss that she hadn't been fired, but 'voluntarily transferred' to Stockton. It had been a particularly traumatic and horrible time and Lucy had as much desire to see Magellan again as to swim in a vat of turds. In fact, she'd take the turd-swimming option any day. At least it would smell a lot sweeter.

'Why me?' Lucy asked her mother. 'I haven't seen Ricky for ages. And it's not like he was my best friend or anything.'

'You were at school with him.'

'Well, yes. He was in my year and we shared classes, but I never really *knew* him.'

'Come on, Lucy. He wants you to–'

'I can't see how I can help,' Lucy overrode her. 'It's not my jurisdiction, remember?'

'But I told Jaya you'd go!'

Jaya had been her mother's friend for as long as Lucy could remember. They'd become comrades at the school gates when they'd discovered they were both single mums. However, where Lucy's dad had buggered off to Australia with a yoga teacher called Tina, Jaya's husband had run off with another man. Even now, Lucy's mother reckoned she'd got off lightly in comparison.

'Oh, Mum...' Lucy rubbed her forehead.

'She's depending on you, you know.'

Lucy wasn't going to fold over any kind of emotional blackmail. She hadn't seen Mac for three weeks, dammit. Why should she have her weekend hijacked?

'I'm not with the Met any more, remember?' Lucy firmed her resolve. 'Tell her I'm sorry, but I can't help.'

Small silence.

'You're not saying that because of... well, our last conversation?'

Lucy blinked.

'I know I was a bit harsh,' her mother went on, 'but I don't think you should take it out on Jaya.'

Lucy sprang to her feet, suddenly furious. 'How could you say such a thing?! I'd *never* do something so shitty! I'm saying I can't help Ricky because I *can't*, not because you won't tell me where my father is! What sort of person do you take me for?!'

'Okay, okay. Sorry.' Her mother took a deep breath. 'We're just a bit upset over here, as you can imagine.'

'Right.' Lucy fought to rein in her temper.

'Would you like to speak to Jaya?' her mother asked.

'Sorry, but no.'

Lucy hung up.

Mac came in and topped up her wine. She gulped half a glass down in three swift swallows. He raised his eyebrows. Pushing her hair back, Lucy filled him in.

'I can't believe she thought I wouldn't see Ricky because she wouldn't tell me how to find Dad!'

'She's upset.'

'I know,' Lucy sighed, feeling her tension ebb, the colours in her mind settling to muted tones. She returned to the sofa, curling her feet beneath her until Mac sank down next to her and brought them onto his lap. Lucy wriggled her toes. 'I wish she'd tell me, though. I'm sure she knows where he is.'

It was thanks to her kidnapper that Lucy wanted to track down her father. Facing her own mortality had made her reassess priorities in her life. Priorities like Mac, and her dad, whom she'd last seen when she was eight, waving him goodbye as his taxi left for Heathrow Airport. At the time, it had been pretty awful – she'd missed him dreadfully – but after a while she got used to him not being there and her mum had been amazing, bringing her up on her own.

She hadn't wanted to find her father before, mainly because she felt she'd be betraying her mother by doing so, but when she'd looked death in the eye she'd pledged to track him down. Since then, her relationship with her mother had been shaky. Mum didn't want her to be reunited with Dad, but Lucy wanted to see her father, full stop.

They were halfway through one of Lucy's favourite movies, *Memento*, when her phone rang again. A number she didn't recognise. Knowing she could never resist answering the phone in case it might be an emergency, Mac paused the film.

'Hello?' Her voice was wary.

'Lucy, it's Jaya.'

Lucy squeezed her eyes shut, wishing she hadn't answered. She really was her own worst enemy sometimes.

'Look, we really need your help, okay? Ricky and me. We're at our wits' end... He didn't do it. I swear it. You know he wouldn't hurt a fly...'

Lucy had heard it all before in her job, but she didn't interrupt. Just listened until eventually, Jaya said, 'Please, Lucy. Will you see Ricky for me?'

'Jaya, I'm sorry.' Lucy was firm. 'I'm no longer with the Met, and–'

'What if I can tell you where your dad is?'

For a moment, Lucy thought she'd misheard. 'What?'

'If you see Ricky, I'll tell you how to find him.'

Lucy's brain fired bolts of colour, electricity fizzing. She felt a sudden euphoria. Was this for real? Was Jaya telling the truth?

'I promise,' Jaya added.

'That's blackmail.'

'I guess you could call it that. Yes.'

Long silence.

Lucy could feel Mac staring at her but her gaze was on the fireplace, the faux flames flickering.

'How do you know where he is?'

'I just do, okay?'

Lucy had asked around locally the last time she'd been in Southwark, her childhood patch, but aside from the fact he'd gone to Australia, nobody knew anything more. At first, she'd thought it was because her father had vanished so completely he'd left no trace, but after a while she came to realise everyone's silence was thanks to her mother threatening them with God alone knew what if they spilled any beans.

'He's in Sydney, isn't he?' Lucy pressed.

'No.'

'Melbourne?'

'I'll tell you after you've seen my boy. But no, not Melbourne either.'

Lucy considered Jaya and her mother's friendship. 'What about Mum?'

'She'll kill me,' Jaya said simply.

But it'll be worth it for Ricky, Lucy could hear her thinking.

'Okay.' Lucy caved in. She would zip up to London tomorrow morning, see Ricky, hopefully dodge Super-shit Magellan and be back at Mac's by teatime. And then she'd know where her dad was. And she'd see him. At last!

'Thanks, Lucy.' Jaya exhaled. She sounded close to tears. 'Thanks so much.'

When Lucy hung up, Mac gave a sigh. 'So, we're going to London tomorrow.'

'What do you mean, we?' She looked at him, startled.

'You don't think I'm going to sit here twiddling my thumbs while you have all the excitement of visiting a murder suspect, do you?'

'You don't have to come.' She frowned. 'I'll be back in the afternoon.'

He looked at her steadily. 'Even so, I'd rather be with you than sitting at home, alone.'

'Awww.' Lucy leaned over and gave him a kiss. 'That's really lovely.'

'I'll drive us up there.' Mac stretched before reaching for the remote to switch the movie back on. 'If we fancy it, we can always stay the night. Go to an exhibition or something.'

Lucy felt her spirit brighten at the thought of making a weekend of it. What had felt like a chore now had the potential to turn into a mini-adventure. She fell asleep wrapped in Mac's arms and for once, she didn't awake in the middle of the night screaming for help. She slept dreamlessly. Quietly. And when morning came, fingers of sunlight slipped past the curtains, indicating it was past nine. Mac was still fast asleep.

She was stifling a yawn, not wanting to wake him, when she heard her phone buzz. It was a text from Jaya.

Someone just tried to kill Ricky.

3

Dan Forrester half-read the BBC headlines on his phone as he queued to disembark from the aircraft at Heathrow. Same ongoing mess over Brexit. A gruesome murder of some poor woman in a London Airbnb.

'Goodbye, Mr Forrester.'

He looked up to see the smartly tailored flight attendant smiling at him. Mid-twenties, raven black hair, her face sharp and pale. Blue eyes and blush-pink lips, expertly made-up.

'I hope you have a good trip back to Chepstow,' she added in a smooth American drawl, professional to her last perfect hair and showing she'd done her job well by remembering something about him. He'd flown business class to and from a client meeting in Miami and had to admit he could see why the trip had felt so luxurious. Yes, the staff were attentive, the food gourmet, but what he'd valued most was the quiet provided in the airport lounges as well as on board, so you could hear yourself think.

'Thank you, Isla. I hope you enjoy your stay in London.'

Her smile was practised and bright as she nodded, her gaze already moving to embrace the passenger behind him.

As he stepped onto the passenger boarding bridge he felt a chill blast of March air. Spring may be around the corner but after spending half the week in balmy twenty-six-degree temperatures it felt unseasonably cold. He walked through the arrivals hall, people jostling alongside from earlier flights. Young mothers with babies, elderly people, backpackers. South Asian faces, African, Chinese. White skins, black and brown.

He rang Jenny as he walked.

'Hi, love. I've just disembarked. Everything okay?'

'Mischa's just started cutting his first teeth.'

He smiled. 'Lots of dribble, then.'

'Oooh, yes.'

'Aimee?'

'Squealing with excitement. She fully expects you to take her pony riding again. You do realise what you've started, don't you?'

'Everyone should learn how to ride a horse. And ski. And play tennis.'

'Dear God, Dan. You'll have your daughter going to private school next!'

'And what's wrong with that?'

'Apart from the expense there's the small fact that you hated it so much you ran away when you were nine.'

He gave a mental shrug. 'It made me an adventurer.'

'You can say that again.' Her voice was dry.

'Anything I can get you on my way home?'

'Just yourself. We've missed you.'

'Me you.'

It didn't take long to get through UK border control and into the car park. He beeped his BMW open, put his carry-on case in the boot. Inside the car he was about to start the engine when his phone rang. 020. A London number. He answered, thinking it was probably to do with work.

'Is that Dan Forrester?' a woman asked.

'Speaking.'

'My name is Sergeant Milton, from the Kensington and Chelsea Police. I'm making enquiries about Kaitlyn Rogers.'

'I'm sorry, who?'

'Kaitlyn Rogers.'

The name rang a faint bell but he couldn't think why and said so.

'Hmmm,' the sergeant said. 'Your number is in her contacts list. She rang you three times last week on Sunday afternoon, third of March, between three forty-five and five pm.'

Dan checked his phone. Out of the calls he'd missed, two had been from the office and one from Jenny. The other three were from a UK mobile which he had assumed was a phone scam. They'd all been made on Sunday. He recited the number recorded on his phone to find it matched the one the police officer was enquiring about.

'There's another number here.' As the sergeant recited it, Dan felt a chill in his stomach. It was his father's old number. Why did this woman have it? Dad had died last year.

'What's this about?'

There was a pause, then the sergeant said, 'I'm afraid I have to inform you that Kaitlyn Rogers was found dead last night.'

Dan frowned, half-watching an Asian couple wrestle a vast suitcase into the back of a taxi.

'What does that have to do with me?'

'I'm sorry... but Kaitlyn Rogers was murdered. This is a murder investigation.'

Abruptly, Dan remembered the headline on his phone. *Woman, 32, murdered in brutal Airbnb bloodbath.* She had been staying in Kensington. Sergeant Milton was from the Kensington and Chelsea Police.

'Are you talking about that woman in your borough? The one who was stabbed in her Airbnb?'

'I'm afraid so. Yes.'

When he didn't respond but remained silent, he heard her clear her throat.

'Is there any chance we could meet today?'

Dan flicked his gaze to his watch, and away. He'd promised to try and get back in time for lunch with the kids. Maybe take an afternoon walk, if the weather remained fine. 'No. Sorry.'

'Perhaps I can come to you? The address in Kaitlyn Rogers' contacts list says you're at 51 Churchfields in Dartmouth, is that right?'

Another chill. She'd recited his parents' address before his mother had died. 'It's my old childhood home. We haven't lived there for over a decade now.'

A pause, then, 'What do you do, Mr Forrester? I mean, work-wise.'

'I'm a global political analyst.'

From the ensuing silence, Dan thought he'd better expand. 'The company I work for specialises in advising clients on the potential risks and benefits of investing in a particular country.'

It didn't sound particularly exciting, but it suited him very well; not only did he meet a wide variety of people and travel the world, but a lot of it was investigative. He used to work for MI5, along with his boss, and although the information they gathered for their clients came from legitimate sources, they both had an unerring nose for tracking down an inside scoop or two.

'Could Kaitlyn Rogers have been a likely client?'

'No.'

'You sound very definite about that.'

'I've only been working there for the past fifteen months. I know every client and potential client on our books.'

Small pause.

'Where are you now?'

'Heathrow,' Dan admitted.

'Leaving or arriving?'

'Arriving. You?'

'I'm at Kensington Police Station. Earls Court Road.'

Dan pulled out his phone and went to the BBC website.

'I'd really like to see you,' the sergeant pressed.

Dan clicked on the news headlines. Scanned the piece on the murder of Kaitlyn Rogers.

'Why? Haven't you already arrested a suspect?'

'They're a suspect. Nothing more, nothing less.'

Dan leaned his head against the headrest. He didn't want to go into London, but he needed to know if this woman's murder was a threat or not. Had something from his past come to haunt him? Something he couldn't remember? His problem was that he'd lost great chunks of his memory when he'd gone through the trauma of witnessing his baby son being killed. Being unable to recall any information from the event was one thing, but it went further than that. Although all his childhood and university memories were intact, the ones of his old job in MI5 had vanished. It was as if he'd never worked there. What if this Kaitlyn Rogers knew him back then? What if she was bringing danger to his door?

'Okay, Sergeant. I'll be with you within the hour.'

4
___

While Mac drove off to find somewhere to park the car, Lucy trotted into the cop shop. She asked to see Ricky Shaw and was told to wait. One of the investigating officers would be right down.

'And who is that?'

'Sergeant Milton.'

'Not Karen Milton?' She felt a surge of dismay.

The receptionist blinked. 'Yes.'

Oh, shit. She used to work with Karen. She'd actually quite liked her but the sentiment obviously hadn't been returned since Karen had been one of the officers who'd stabbed her in the back, telling Magellan that Lucy was *abrasive*, *temperamental* and *difficult to work with*, which had ultimately given him the ammunition needed to kick her out.

'Great.' Lucy smiled weakly. She decided against sitting down while she waited. She didn't want to start off feeling disadvantaged.

'Lucy!' Karen swept into reception, hand outstretched. 'It really is you!'

'Yep, it's me all right.' She shook hands, hoping her dismay didn't show. It had only been a couple of years but Karen seemed to have aged a decade. Her waist had thickened and her hair turned wiry. She had lines around her mouth and eyes that were new. She looked closer to forty than the twenty-nine years Lucy knew she was.

'It's really good to see you.' Karen was positively beaming. 'I gather Stockton's treating you well. You've done great things up there.' She began ushering Lucy out of reception and into a corridor. 'I think leaving the Met was probably the best thing you could have done. Look at your last case! Global attention, or what?'

Not wanting to talk about it, Lucy desperately cast around for something personal to refer to as Karen ushered her into a corridor.

'How's your, er...' She couldn't remember any of Karen's family's names. Another of her failings, apparently. 'Little one? And your hubby?'

The lines seemed to deepen across the sergeant's face. 'We got divorced just after Christmas.'

Lucy's heart squeezed. No wonder she looked knackered. 'Oh, Karen. I'm sorry.'

Karen pulled a face. 'Yeah. You get married and although you know the divorce statistics, you never think it's going to happen to you.'

Lucy thought of Mac and getting married, having a baby, and abruptly a surge of panic washed over her. *Dear God. Did she want a child? What if they had more than one? A boy and a girl? Twins? What if she and Mac split up? Would she end up having a pair of latchkey kids who resented her? Would they turn to drugs, become drug dealers, die of heroin abuse?*

'Lucy?'

She hurriedly lassoed her stampeding thoughts as she realised Karen had opened a door and was waiting for her to step inside. *Don't panic*, she told herself. You can think about the kids thing another time. You're only twenty-six, after all.

'I was asking why you want to see Ricky? Is it connected to another case? If so, then I'll be–'

'No, nothing like that.' Lucy was curt. 'I went to school with him.'

Karen looked at her, startled. 'Really?'

'Yup.'

Karen closed the door behind them. She gestured for her to sit. 'Tea? Coffee?'

'No, thanks.' Lucy went to the window. A street sweeper was leaning against a lamp post, leg kicked out, smoking a cigarette. He was eyeing a woman walking her small white dog. She had high heels and fur on her collar. When he said something to her, she said something back. He smiled, showing gaps in his teeth. She scurried away.

Lucy turned to face Karen. 'What's this about someone trying to kill Ricky?'

A guarded look crossed the sergeant's face. 'I wouldn't say it was a murder attempt.'

'What was it, then?'

'His solicitor brought him a sandwich.'

'Aren't meals provided?'

'Well, yes.' Karen's mouth twisted. 'I know it's rare for a custody officer to allow food to be taken in, but it was professionally prepared by a supermarket and still sealed. The sergeant didn't think it would be a problem, but it had peanut butter in it.'

'Ricky's allergic?'

'Yep. Luckily, he only had a bite but it was enough to trigger a reaction. His mouth swelled up a bit, but he's okay. He'd brought an EpiPen with him, thank God.' She fixed Lucy with a cool stare. 'Who told you?'

'His mother.'

'I see.' Karen dropped the chilly demeanour and rubbed her eyes. 'Between you and me, Mrs Shaw has been, ah... somewhat vocal.'

Which meant Jaya was being a pain in the arse, no doubt hassling the police every minute of every day, but Lucy couldn't blame her. Not when her son had been accused of murder.

'And the vic?'

'Kaitlyn Rogers. Thirty-two years old, from Wiltshire, and–'

'Not that bloodbath in the Airbnb?' Lucy was aghast.

'The one and the same.'

Lucy couldn't help it. She had to sit down. 'Fuck.' No wonder Jaya hadn't said anything when Lucy had asked.

'It's gone ballistic,' Karen confessed. 'We've got every media outlet on our backs and even the Home Office has started shouting.'

'Why was she in an Airbnb?'

'She'd hired it for a week. Cheaper than a hotel in the same area. Nicer, too, in my view.'

'What was she doing in London?'

Karen looked at her as though weighing up whether to tell her something or not. Lucy held her breath, but then the sergeant blew out a breath and turned away. 'What can you tell me about Ricky?'

Lucy could picture the boy he used to be, sitting at the front of the class, the fat rolling over his too-tight waistband, his earnest expression, his eagerness to learn.

'He was good at maths. Sciences. Used to dress like Rambo. You know, bandana, combats, army boots. Glasses, acne. Shy. Polite. Helpful. The teachers and parents loved him.'

'But not the kids.'

Lucy thought back. 'We used to tease him about his weight, but when he started dressing up we teased him about being

Rambo. I guess it was a clever move to switch the attention from his scoffing doughnuts to dressing up as a super-hero... I can't say for sure if he was bullied or not. Personally, I never saw anything but that doesn't mean it didn't happen. How come you arrested him?'

'He was caught on CCTV, parking outside her property. We have him walking towards her place with a bottle of bubbly and a bunch of flowers, then he's out of view for ten minutes and when he returns it's at a run, no bottle, no flowers, and he's obviously stressed, covered in what looks like blood. He drives off.'

'Blood?'

'His car had her blood and DNA all over it. And he'd left his gifts behind.'

'That doesn't mean he killed her.'

Karen gave her a droll look that said, *yeah, right.*

'How did he know her?'

'She picked him up, apparently. In a bar.'

Lucy blinked. The photographs of Kaitlyn Rogers in the press had shown a strikingly attractive woman with a mane of chestnut hair and a smile that made you think of surfers and sunshine. Ricky, on the other hand...

'Quite.' Karen put her head on one side, considering her. 'If you find anything to help our investigation, you will let us know, won't you?'

'Sure,' Lucy lied, and at that moment, the door banged open and Chief Superintendent Magellan strode inside.

5

It was as though she'd stepped back in time. Where Karen's appearance had changed thanks to being knocked around by life, Magellan looked exactly the same. Same dyed black hair, same sharp suit and gym-fit body.

'Lucy!' He was feigning delight which simply made him look as though he had indigestion.

'Sir!' she exclaimed in the same tone but inside she could feel her blood begin to boil. This was the man who'd sabotaged one of her biggest cases. The idiot who'd ignored her when she told him time was of the essence, dragging his heels and allowing Mr Big to get away. And when she'd made it public it was his fault, he'd got shot of her. Far easier to send her packing than face his own shortcomings.

He was still grinning. 'Someone told me the Energiser Bunny was in the building, but I didn't believe them.' He knew she hated her nickname and in the old days she might have reacted but not today. She wasn't going to let him get to her. Coolly, she put out her hand.

'Good to see you, sir.'

His grip was over-hard and designed to crush her knuckles

and although it hurt like hell she didn't let it show. She felt a moment's triumph when she spotted his flicker of annoyance.

'Don't tell me you've come looking for your old job?'

I wouldn't take it if you paid me a million dollars.

'Gosh,' she beamed. 'Wouldn't that be great?'

His indigestion appeared to turn into fierce heartburn. Excellent. She was delighted to have rattled him. Holding her eyes, he spoke to Karen. 'Sergeant, if you could give us a minute.'

Karen hurried out.

The second the door closed behind her, Magellan stepped close, trying to intimidate Lucy's small frame with his powerful six feet two bulk. Lucy didn't relent an inch. Instead, she squared her shoulders a little and raised her chin, meeting his gaze dead-on.

'I know everyone thinks the sun shines out of your arse,' he hissed, 'but that's because they don't realise what a complete fucking nutcase you are.'

'Why, thank you, sir.' She gave him one of her prettiest smiles, making sure it warmed her eyes. 'I'd forgotten how one of your compliments could make my day.'

The skin around his nostrils turned white. 'The fact that Ricky Shaw knows you won't help him. I've got him for this and just because you think you're so fucking brilliant won't change shit.'

'So, you're not sure he's guilty,' she mused.

'Of course he's fucking guilty.'

She just looked at him.

He raised a finger and stabbed it into her face. It was so close she reckoned she could have darted her head forward and bitten it if she wanted.

'If. You. Fucking. Interfere. I will. Fucking. Destroy. You.'

She let her smile broaden. 'Oh boy, have I missed you.'

Before he could react, Lucy nipped around him and snapped

open the door. Karen was outside. As Magellan joined them, he fixed Lucy with an icy stare. 'Just remember what I said.'

She blew him a kiss as she turned and walked down the corridor, her mind humming a happy yellow.

Karen had arranged for Lucy to meet Ricky in one of their interview rooms. Two chairs and an aluminium table bolted to the floor. No windows. Like a lot of police interview rooms, it smelled of stale sweat, desperation and coffee.

'Ricky.' She stretched out her hand, trying to cover her shock. He wasn't just fat any more, he was obese.

His grip was soft and damp. It was like holding a bunch of damp sausages and she had to make an effort not to wipe her fingers on her jeans afterwards.

'Thanks for coming.' His words were slightly obscured thanks to his mouth still being swollen.

Despite his weight, he looked pretty good. His suit trousers were nicely cut, his white shirt tailored over his bulk. An orb emblem with a V in its centre was embroidered onto the chest. Versace? Vivienne Westwood? Whatever it was, it came from a high-end designer. She studied him further, noting his hair had been styled to curl just above his collar. His fingernails were buffed and manicured. He'd come a long way from the streets of Southwark and Poundland, and even without a tie or belt, or laces in his brogues, his attire shouted *money*!

'You should thank your mum.' Lucy thought she'd better be honest. 'It was Jaya who persuaded me.'

'They think I did it.' His voice trembled. 'They really do. But I didn't. I swear.'

'Who's your solicitor?'

'Ajay Pozo. Pozo and Partners.'

She took one chair while he took the other, settling his bulk carefully as though testing whether the chair would collapse or not. 'You need to be working with him,' she said. 'He's the one who'll get you released.'

'I couldn't hurt her. I'd never hurt her.'

'Any idea who did?'

He closed his eyes. Sweat beaded on his upper lip. 'No.'

Lucy let a silence pass before she spoke again.

'Tell me about Kaitlyn Rogers.'

He didn't move. Lucy waited.

Eventually, he opened his eyes. They were filled with tears and ineffably sad. 'She was beautiful.'

Lucy nodded. 'I saw her photograph.'

'You're probably wondering what she'd see in someone like me. Trust me, I wondered myself until she told me she liked having fun, and even more, she loved being spoilt...'

So, Kaitlyn had been turned on by money. Interesting.

'I didn't think twice. I bought her cocktails, an expensive dinner. I sent her flowers... I even planned to buy her a pair of diamond earrings we saw in a shop window but she d-died before I c-could.' He swallowed. 'Lucy, I had so many plans. I know we'd only just met but I was going to fly us to Venice. Verona, Paris, Tokyo, Sydney. She loved to travel. And even though I knew it probably wouldn't last, I didn't care. She was... wonderful.'

Somehow Lucy couldn't see Ricky killing someone he was so in awe of, maybe even half in love with. Perhaps he'd been obsessed with Kaitlyn? That could have been a dangerous state of mind, turning into jealousy, possessiveness and suspicion, which could drive emotions into previously unchartered territory.

'What happened last night?'

He took a deep breath. Brought out a handkerchief, crisp

white cotton, monogrammed. Mopped his lip and brow.

'She'd invited me to her place for dinner... I'd brought a bottle of Cristal Rosé and a dozen roses. She's vegan.' His gaze turned distant. 'I wasn't entirely sure what we'd be eating but I wouldn't have cared what she gave me. She was amazing. She made me feel as though I could conquer the world and I–'

He broke off when there was a knock on the door. Karen stuck her head inside. 'Your mother's here, Ricky. Shall I bring her in?'

'No!' Ricky seemed horrified. 'I don't think now is the right–'

'That would be great.' Lucy overrode him, her police instinct kicking in. She wanted to see why he was so dismayed, check out the family dynamics. 'Thanks, Karen.'

Jaya arrived in a flurry of vibrant silk and gold bangles. A cloud of touched-up black hair capped a plump, expressive face. High heels, dangling gold earrings and a huge orange handbag topped the ensemble.

Lucy rose and was immediately enveloped in an embrace that smelled of Clinique's light and floral Happy, taking her straight back to her childhood. It was the same scent her mum used to wear.

Jaya wept a little while Lucy muttered consoling words. She could see Ricky's jaw was tense, his body language closed. Eventually, take-charge Jaya said, 'Lucy, what's your plan? How are you going to get Ricky out of here?'

'That's just it, Jaya. I can't do anything except advise you to liaise with Ricky's solicitor, and hope things resolve themselves.'

'You can't really expect us to sit and do nothing!'

'Mum, please...' Ricky's tone was plaintive. He sounded six years old, not twenty-six.

'Quiet,' Jaya said sharply. 'I want to know what Lucy's going to do to find the murderer.'

'Seriously, Jaya, since I'm no longer with the Met, I really can't help. I have no jurisdiction. No authority.'

'Can't you find out something about this woman? What she was doing in London? The press say she lived on a farm in the Cotswolds, but what if she had an ulterior motive? What if she was connected to terrorists or something? And they had to kill her to keep her quiet? I'm just brainstorming here.' She turned to Ricky. 'What do you think this woman saw in you?'

'We just... got on.' Ricky's voice was small.

'Did she know you're an accountant?' She made it sound as bad as if she'd said *child abuser*.

'I'm doing very well, thank you.' Ricky drew himself up.

'Only thanks to Tomas Featherstone. Without him, you'd never have the client list you have.'

'Mum!' For a moment Ricky looked furious. 'Why can't you keep your mouth shut?!'

Lucy was startled. 'You don't mean Teflon Tom, do you? Who we went to school with?'

Ricky glanced away, seeming to shrink.

'You're Tomas's *accountant*?'

'He's a client, yes,' Ricky mumbled.

'Jesus, Ricky.'

Tomas Featherstone had been one of the cool kids, mainly because he lived on the edge. He stole cars, took his gang joyriding. He smoked. Took drugs. He was also charismatic and charming and quick-witted as hell. He'd been suspended several times, but the school never expelled him, convinced they could improve his behaviour. Although his teachers were tireless, never giving up on him, the second he left school he went into business with his father, selling chalets in the south of Spain which didn't exist. His dad ended up in jail for fraud, and how Tomas escaped being charged nobody ever knew, which is why he was nicknamed Teflon Tom. Nothing ever stuck to him.

'What's he into now?' Lucy asked.

'Lots of different things.' Ricky still wouldn't look at her.

'I bet.' Lucy's tone was biting. She wanted to say *I hope you're not helping him launder dirty money* but with Jaya there, she held her tongue. At least now she knew where Ricky had got his money from: criminals. Which opened Kaitlyn Rogers' case to all sorts of permutations.

'Did Tomas know Kaitlyn Rogers?' Lucy asked instead.

'Why should he?' Finally Ricky looked at her, expression puzzled.

'I don't know, but if you're doing business with the likes of Teflon Tom, I think you should take a serious look at your client list and–'

Ricky scrambled to his feet. His face had darkened. 'Don't be so sanctimonious. He's a *client*. That's all. I met Kat in a *bar*. I went to have dinner with her and when I got to her apartment...' He took a shuddering breath.

'Go on,' Lucy prompted softly.

'Well, the door was ajar and I called and called and when she didn't appear... I pushed the door open and took a step inside and I was thinking something smelled good, I was getting hungry, but then I got a whiff of something horrible... it turned my stomach, and then I saw her lying in the hallway, her throat had been cut... there was so much *blood*...' He began to sway.

'Sit down,' Lucy told him. He sat. His hands were trembling.

'I checked to see... if she was alive but... I couldn't find a pulse. She wasn't breathing...'

Lucy held out a hand to Jaya, stopping her from going to Ricky. She didn't want him interrupted.

'I was terrified. I thought the killer might still be there. I ran away... to my car. I drove off. I didn't drive for long because I had to pull over... I was sick. It was then I realised I hadn't called the police. I know I should have done it sooner, but I wasn't thinking. I just wanted to get away...'

Ricky's reaction wasn't uncommon. His fight or flight response had kicked in, producing a hormonal cascade, but where some people froze with fear, his body had made him flee the scene in order to survive.

Lucy released Jaya to swoop to his side, clucking like a demented chicken, but he pushed her away. 'Not now, Mum.'

Biting her lip, Jaya looked between him and Lucy. She was fighting tears.

'I wish I hadn't left her.' Ricky put his head in his hands. 'I feel really bad about that. I wish I'd held her until the police arrived.'

He looked stricken. Lucy sighed. She could no more turn her back on Ricky than a drowning puppy. Besides which, she would seriously *love* to prove him innocent to stick two fingers up to Magellan. Imagine his face! And if Ricky was guilty, well. At least she'd done her familial duty.

'Okay. I'd like to see your client list.'

He raised his head.

'And I'd like to see your diary.' She turned brisk. 'I'll contact Ajay Pozo myself. I'm not guaranteeing anything. I'll just have a look, that's all.'

'Thank you.' It was a whisper, but she couldn't miss the glimmer of gratitude in his eyes.

'Right, if you'll excuse me.' Lucy looked at Jaya. 'Your mum and I have some unfinished business.'

6

'Just through here,' Sergeant Milton told Dan as they walked down the corridor. At first glance, he'd thought she was in her late thirties but on closer inspection realised she was much younger, a tired twenty-something obviously exhausted given the bags under her eyes and her washed-out complexion.

Someone had left a box of posters to one side, exhorting parents not to tell their children that the police would cart them off to jail if they were bad. *We want them to run to us if they are scared... NOT be scared of us.* He and Jenny had taught Aimee that the first port of call if she was lost, or in trouble, was to always go to a police officer, or dial 999. He hated the thought of a world where his daughter wouldn't do that.

Milton led Dan into a meeting room. 'Have a seat.' The air was overly warm, muggy with heating, and Dan took off his jacket, hung it over the back of a chair.

'So,' said the police officer. She took the chair opposite him. Opened a folder. Slipped a photograph across. 'Kaitlyn Rogers.'

A young woman with a grave expression looked back. Black jacket over a white shirt. Auburn hair pulled back into a bun.

Freckles across the bridge of her nose. Generous mouth. Vivid green eyes.

For no reason he could think of, his heart hitched. He picked up the picture and rested his gaze on it as he'd been taught by his psychiatrist. Dr Simon Winter had told him to trust his instincts when he felt an old memory rising to the surface, and not to force anything. *Just let your subconscious swim where it wants and be alert as to how you feel.*

Dan touched the woman's face gently. He could sense sunshine and heat. Happiness. He felt tired, for some reason. Not now, but in this memory. As he sank into her eyes, a wave of anxiety washed over him, increasing until he felt real fear. She made him happy but filled him with fear.

He passed the photograph back and Sergeant Milton pushed over another handful of pictures showing the same woman standing, sitting, laughing, frowning.

The fear remained with him.

'I don't know,' Dan admitted. 'Sorry.'

The police officer then brought out a pair of vinyl disposable gloves and withdrew a small plastic envelope from her folder, opened it. She extracted a scrap of paper, slightly bigger than a business card, and folded into four. It was well-worn and tatty at the edges, indicating it had been around a while.

'We found this tucked in her wallet, between her driver's licence and a membership card. She obviously wanted to keep it safe.'

Carefully, the sergeant unfolded the paper and showed him a dried four-leaf clover that was no longer green but a dusty grey. It looked as though it might disintegrate at any moment.

Suddenly Dan felt like weeping. He didn't know why, but he felt devastated.

Sergeant Milton then opened the scrap of paper fully and showed him the writing there.

I found this on a walk with Dad at the weekend. It will help keep you safe. Dan x

He stared and stared.

It was his handwriting, no doubt about it.

'Yours?' the sergeant asked.

'It looks like my handwriting. Yes.'

'But you don't know her.'

'I think we'd better change that to: I don't *remember* her.'

He finally confessed his memory problem to Milton, but not that he'd been in MI5. He didn't want to open a can of worms that might come to endanger him or his family. If he thought the officer needed to know at any time, he'd tell her, but right now he was simply an ex-high-performance driving instructor who now worked as a global business analyst.

'You can remember your school and university days, but nothing afterwards?' She was frowning.

'Before my son died, there are blanks, but afterwards, everything is crystal clear.'

She raised her eyebrows but he wasn't going to say any more. Only five people currently knew the truth behind Luke's death: three of whom were in MI5 and two friends, one a GP, the other a cop, DC Lucy Davies. Not even his wife, Jenny, Luke's mother, knew. She thought Luke had been killed in a hit-and-run.

He'd been undercover, working the Albanian mafia, when his cover had been blown. Wanting to send a warning to MI5 against sending any more undercover officers, they snatched Dan's son and tortured him. They chained Dan to a wall and forced him to watch every second.

Luke had suffered multiple wounds all detailed in his post-mortem report: a broken back, gashes all over his head, a skull fracture, brain swelling, a lacerated liver, a fractured pelvis and a broken leg.

It was his fault Luke died.

His fault Luke had suffered, terrified and in agony, as the men slowly and meticulously smashed his tiny body.

It had sent him mad until he'd been given an amnesia drug. It had been in the research stage, but Dan hadn't cared. He'd signed the consent forms himself. Anything to stop the monumental pain.

When he'd been discharged from the hospital, he had no clue he'd ever worked for MI5. He believed he was suffering from dissociative amnesia after being unable to prevent Luke stepping into the road and being killed. Dan honestly thought he'd been a civil servant, a paper-pusher, before Luke's death, but he'd obviously craved some excitement from his old life because he'd taken up high-performance instructing.

Are you sure you haven't had any training? his driving instructor had asked as Dan powered the car through Quarry Corner at Castle Combe Race Circuit, a deceptively gentle left sweep over a blind brow hiding a sharp right.

Not that I'm aware of, Dan replied, concentrating so he wouldn't brake at the wrong time and compromise positioning the car for the turn.

In that case, you're a natural.

Then his old boss came to him out of the blue, desperate to track down a stolen weapon before it was used, and all the lies and deceits of the past five years were left lying as though beached as the tide went out. It was, he admitted, a miracle he and Jenny were still together, considering she'd been part of the cover-up. He'd walked out for a while, during which time the Director General of MI5 found him his current job with DCA & Co. It was, he explained, as close as Dan could get to his old job.

And here he was, in a grey office in a police station having fallen in love with his wife all over again, who'd given him his beautiful daughter, Aimee, and another baby son, and he would do anything, *anything at all*, to protect them.

7

'What membership card was Kaitlyn carrying?' Dan asked the sergeant. Over the next few minutes, he ascertained that Kaitlyn Rogers had been thirty-two, currently single, had never been married, or had any children. She'd been brought up in the West Country and lived on a smallholding in Wiltshire. Both parents were dead, her brother in a home.

'What sort of home?' he asked.

'For the disabled.'

'Was he born disabled, or did he become disabled?'

The officer frowned.

'Perhaps he used to be a soldier,' Dan offered.

'Perhaps.' The frown remained. She'd obviously just gone down the mental rabbit hole labelled *brother* to find it was empty.

'What membership card was she carrying?'

The policewoman ignored his question and asked one of her own. 'What did your father do?'

There was a sound of a jack hammer from the street outside. Dan waited until it subsided. 'He used to be with the marines. When he retired, he set up his own business, Tor & Associates

Ltd. It's a security and risk management company. He sold it five years ago. What job did Kaitlyn Rogers do?'

'She was a travel writer.'

'Which publication?'

'She was freelance.'

Dan raised his eyebrows. The sergeant looked stonily back.

'A versatile occupation,' he said neutrally. 'Useful, too, for someone who wants to present a legitimate job that enables them to travel freely across the world.'

The sergeant blinked.

'Was that all she did?' Dan asked.

'She had hobbies. Horse riding. Track driving. Flying. Diving. Skiing.'

His nerves quivered over the words *track driving* but he didn't let it show. 'A regular action girl.' He thought a bit further. 'Why was she in London? Why the Airbnb?'

Sergeant Milton considered him at length but didn't say anything.

'Why didn't she leave a message if she wanted to speak to me?' Dan wondered out loud.

The policewoman looked past him. 'You say your wife is an accountant.'

'Correct.'

'Would she know Ricky Shaw?'

Although he was pretty sure she was grasping at straws, he gave her credit for not giving up on her search to find some kind of link between him and Kaitlyn.

'I can ask her, if you like.'

She gave a nod. Dan rang Jenny. He'd already called her to explain what was going on and now he said, 'Hi, Jen. I'm at the police station, and they want to know if you know the suspect. Richard, aka Ricky, Shaw. I'm told he's an accountant.'

Jenny gave a snort. 'You're kidding me. Do they think that every bookkeeper in the country knows one another?'

'Apparently.'

'No, I don't know Ricky Shaw. Okay?'

'What about Kaitlyn Rogers?'

'That poor murdered woman? No.'

Sergeant Milton had been listening closely and now she gave a nod as he hung up. 'I think it's obvious Kaitlyn Rogers knew you but due to your memory trauma, you can't remember her. She wanted to speak to you, but it didn't appear urgent or any kind of priority, because she would have left a message, and would have kept calling. What do you think?'

He had, in fact, come to the same conclusion.

'Do you think she could have been an old girlfriend?'

Dan looked at Kaitlyn's photograph. Shook his head. 'Sorry. I just don't know.'

The policewoman stood up. 'Thanks for coming in. I appreciate it.'

Dan shook her hand and told her if he remembered anything about the murdered woman, he would call her immediately. She led him outside, and down the corridor. At the far end, he saw a middle-aged woman in a vivid silk kaftan appear from one of the interview rooms. She was talking to a slender woman with a messy side-ponytail. He only caught a glimpse of her before she vanished out of sight, but he couldn't mistake the lightness of her step or her attire: jeans, boots, tatty sheepskin jacket, big leather belt. Her uniform.

Lucy?

What the heck was Lucy doing here?

8

'Where is he? Where's my dad?'

Lucy and Jaya were walking down the corridor, behind an escorting PC. Lucy was desperately trying to keep her body language non-confrontational, her voice mellow, but she was struggling. She wanted to know where her father was, *now*.

Jaya looked away. She was chewing the inside of her lip, no doubt regretting her earlier promise.

'Blackmail works both ways,' Lucy hissed. 'If you don't tell me, I won't help Ricky.'

Still, Jaya didn't say anything.

'Come on,' Lucy cajoled. 'It can't be that difficult. Dad buggered off with that yoga teacher, Tina, and since you say he isn't in Melbourne...'

Jaya stopped walking. Looked around as though checking that she wasn't being overheard. When she spoke, it was a whisper. 'What if I said he never went to Australia?'

Lucy stared.

'What?'

Jaya just looked at her.

Lucy looked back.

'All right, ladies?' The PC had stopped and was waiting for them at the end of the corridor. Both Lucy and Jaya ignored him.

'Think about it, Lucy.' Jaya stepped close. So close Lucy could see the tiny clumps of eyeliner at the corners of her eyes. 'Did you ever get a postcard from him? See photos of him surfing on Bondi Beach? Walking across Sydney Harbour Bridge? Come on, hun. You're a copper. Work it out for yourself.'

Lucy felt as though she was falling. When he first got to Australia, Dad had written to her. Emailed her with his news. How hot it was, how blue the sky. How much he missed her. She'd read and reread his messages every night before she went to sleep. But he hadn't emailed for long. Two months, one week and two days, to be precise. The last email she'd received said he was going abroad on business and that although he might be out of touch for a while, she mustn't worry, and that he loved her very much. She'd cried herself to sleep for weeks after he'd stopped writing but eventually the pain began to lessen, proving a particular idiom true – *time is a great healer* – but back then it had been brutal, unforgivable.

'He's here?' Lucy suddenly felt breathless. 'He's in the UK?'

Jaya blinked, took a step back.

'I didn't say that, did I?'

'Then where?' Lucy's mind was spinning, filled with crimson light.

'The last I heard...' Jaya was biting her lip so hard Lucy wondered that it didn't bleed. 'He was in...'

Lucy held her breath. Her heart was beating fast. Her pulse roaring in her ears.

'Macclesfield.'

Lucy's mouth opened and closed.

'*Macclesfield?*'

If Jaya had said Vladivostok Lucy couldn't have been more surprised.

'Yes. But I don't know where. Just that he was there.'

'He's living there? Working there too?'

'Ladies?' The PC stood next to them, arms crossed, getting pissed off from the look of it, but Lucy held up a hand.

'One minute.'

'I'm sorry, but I really must ask you–'

'I said one minute,' Lucy snapped, hauling out her warrant card and shoving it under his nose. 'Now, fuck off.'

He turned bright red. 'I really don't think there's call for–'

She gave him her death stare.

He held up both hands. 'I'll wait just over here, okay?'

'Thank you so much.' She gave him a brilliant smile. One of her best. She could see him thinking *psycho*. Perfect. She swung back to Jaya.

'How do you know he's in Macclesfield? Who told you?'

'I can't–'

'Yes, you can.' Lucy was almost on top of Jaya, willing her to reply. 'Come on, a deal's a deal. I'm going to contact Ricky's solicitor, remember? Try and help you guys out.'

Jaya nibbled her lip. 'You could try Reg.'

'Reg?' Lucy repeated blankly.

'At the pub.'

'Reg the landlord, you mean? As in Mad Reg?'

'Yeah.'

'They're in touch, him and Dad?'

'Must be, I suppose,' Jaya mumbled. 'You won't tell your mum, will you?' She wouldn't meet Lucy's eye.

'Not if Reg can put me in touch with Dad. He can take the blame, if you like.'

'Thanks, love.' She gave a weak smile. 'And thanks for coming down and giving us a hand.'

Although it wasn't the best of circumstances, Lucy felt a wave of affection for Jaya. She could be in-your-face and

45

abrasive, but she had a good heart. She'd been one of the first people in the community who'd hosted a refugee family from Syria while they tried to get their lives back on track. Talk about generous, and in the most practical way.

She'd got on really well with Dad, Lucy remembered. He'd been treasurer for one of the leading anti-racist organisations in the area back in the 90s. Lucy could remember her parents, Jaya, and countless others sitting at the kitchen table plotting various campaigns in the aftermath of the murder of Stephen Lawrence, which involved not just ferocious passion for the subject but lots of laughter over communal suppers. Happy days, Lucy thought, filled with strong friendships and highly motivated causes. Until Dad had got arrested on a protest march, that was. She couldn't remember either of them getting involved in anything similar after that. It had probably scared the shit out of them.

She said goodbye to Jaya in reception, and with a lift in her heart that Mac was waiting outside, ready to sweep her off to a museum, an art exhibition or something out of the ordinary, she strode outside.

She'd just hit the pavement when a man called out behind her. 'Lucy!'

She glanced around to see a tall man with an angular face. Clear grey eyes. He had flecks of silver in his hair and was smiling as he approached, expression warm.

Her jaw dropped. 'Dan? What the hell are you doing here?'

'I might say the same.'

As he bent to kiss her cheek she reached up and hugged him. 'How's my godson?'

'Teething.'

'Say no more.' Lucy wasn't great with babies, but she'd been so honoured, so *thrilled* at being asked to be Mischa's godmother, she'd agreed. She'd been moved to tears in the church when little Mischa was baptised. What had Jenny said to her? *You're* smart, loyal and courageous. If Mischa grows up with half your qualities, he'll be a lucky boy.

'So?' Lucy gestured at the police station.

'I came in to talk through a murder investigation.'

Her eyes widened. 'Not Kaitlyn Rogers?'

'Yes.'

'Me too!'

It didn't take long to swap stories.

'Six degrees of separation,' Dan muttered. 'Who'd have thought it?'

He was referring to the idea that all people are on average six or fewer social connections away from each other, so that any two people could be connected via friends or acquaintances in a maximum of six steps.

Lucy mulled this over. 'If that's the case, then all we have to do is find the six people in the chain between Kaitlyn and the killer and ta-da! We'll have the murderer.'

'You don't think Ricky Shaw is guilty?'

'Not really, no.'

Dan was pensive. 'If we're two people in the chain, then we only have four more to go. But it's not going to be easy when I can't remember.'

Lucy pulled a face in sympathy. She'd first met Dan in an Albanian gang's junkyard. At first, she'd thought he was part of the gang but it turned out he was ex-MI5 and a bit of a hero. He'd saved her life that day. A gang member had been strangling her to death when Dan had loomed silently behind her attacker and belted him on his head. One blow, that's all it had taken. Her attacker's eyes rolled upwards and he crumpled into a heap.

Holding her throat, gasping, she'd looked at her saviour. He was covered in blood, a wreck. He held a small rock cupped in his hand.

For a second neither of them spoke. Then she said, 'Who the hell are you?'

Together, they uncovered the truth behind his son's death. Their friendship had been forged in the flames of survival and tempered by working together on two more cases. Both had been personal to Dan and both times Dan had called on Lucy to help him, the first when Jenny was kidnapped, the second when his godson died. He may be ex-MI5 but he couldn't go where Lucy could, or get the information she could either. He drove her crazy, pushing her to stretch legal boundaries when she was investigating on his behalf, half scaring her to death sometimes, but she trusted him with her life.

Now, agreeing to share information on the murder case, they moved aside for two uniformed PCs striding for the station.

'Do me a favour?' Dan said. 'Ask your friend Karen Milton to tell you where to find Kaitlyn's brother. He's in a home for the disabled.'

'Sure.'

He bent to kiss her cheek. 'Good to see you.'

With that, he was gone.

9

Isla had swapped her uniform for a little black dress and a pair of leopard knee-high boots she'd bought in the autumn. Sexy as hell. Mussed hair, hooped earrings and a mini velvet bag containing a miniature toothbrush and a pair of lace undies – you never knew your luck – a swift spray of Opium, and she was good to go.

As she walked through reception, she saw people look her way. She was used to being stared at in her charcoal-grey Egret Air uniform, her cap always perfectly placed, and now she was in casual wear, it felt gratifying that she could still grab everyone's attention. Outside, she stumbled a little, her vision blurring at the edges.

Boy, she hated jet lag.

It had been getting worse over the last few weeks, but even though she'd nearly dropped a passenger's wine glass in their lap thanks to her vision suddenly blacking out, she still refused to consider it. Yes, her headaches were getting more intense at the end of each long-haul flight, but she persuaded herself that suffering the odd migraine wasn't cause to panic.

She called a cab. Watched the glittering streets of London

slide past for a few moments before she turned to her phone. Posed with her boots up and pouting, she took a selfie and posted it.

London! I'm ready to party!

It was 11am in LA, her home base, and her best friend Emily responded with a photo of herself in her jogging kit on the beach. It was sunny and bright and Isla knew Em would go back and shower before heading out for brunch with a gang of their friends.

Missing youuuu babe!

Isla felt a stab of envy, and rolled her eyes at herself, recognising that she was a walking hypocrisy. When she was grounded, all she could think about was going back to her hectic, fun-filled flying life. On the flip side, when she flew, she craved routine, to wake up at a normal hour and to have normal eating and social habits. And to see her friends. And her parents. And not to have to keep waving goodbye, again. And again. Not that she was complaining. She wouldn't have her life any other way. But she had her moments, especially when she'd had such a good time hanging out with Em last week. She missed her friend. Simple. As the taxi began to slow to drop her off, she sent Em an emoji of a heart.

The cocktail bar was faux alpine with neon blue photos of ski slopes on the walls and sheepskin-covered stools. It had only opened a couple of months ago and was considered *the* place to be. Needless to say, it was packed, everyone drinking, chatting and laughing, having fun. Her gaze flicked across the room to see three of the crew were already there, waving at her to join them.

She knocked back a caipirinha and then another. The alcohol hit her system like a train, helped by the huge amount of sugar pounded into the fresh limes. She downed another couple of cocktails and she was just finishing her story about an emergency landing they'd made last month when the landing gear on both wings failed mid-air – even the most hardened air crew loved the odd scare story – when her phone rang. Her eyebrows lifted when she saw it was Captain Bob Brown from the Miami flight. No way could she ignore it. Waving her phone in apology, she weaved her way outside and onto the street to answer it.

'Bob? Everything okay?'

She didn't have any qualms using his Christian name. They'd flown together on several occasions as well as joined the same pool parties from time to time. He was an ex-US Air Force pilot with mischievous eyes and a talent for telling really good jokes that you could then tell your mother. No swearing, no smut, but hilarious just the same. He was married with four kids, two dogs and a house in Palm Springs.

'I was actually calling to ask you the same thing.'

She frowned. It wasn't like Bob to check up on her. Had she done something wrong?

'It's just that Grant and Liz are experiencing some pretty serious physical symptoms,' he told her. 'Nausea, exhaustion, blurred vision. Liz got really confused, apparently, and began slurring her speech. She's gone to hospital. Grant's sticking it out in his hotel room but he's in one hell of a state.'

'Shoot. That's terrible.'

'How about you? Anything?'

'No, I'm fine.' She wasn't going to tell him about her wobbling vision. She didn't want to be grounded.

'Have you been in touch with any crew members since we disembarked?' he asked.

'Yes.' She told him who she was with. 'They're all okay.'

'I'll keep ringing around the others. I want to make sure everyone's all right.'

Hesitantly, Isla said, 'You don't think it's aerotoxic syndrome, do you?'

Bob sighed. 'I wish I could say no, but between you and me, yes, I do.'

Bob had been struck by a mystery illness a couple of years back, experiencing flu-like symptoms, nausea and severe fatigue. After a while, he came to associate these symptoms with switching on the cockpit air supply. When he heard other pilots and aircrew were being similarly affected, and that their illnesses could be related to oil fume contamination of the air bled off from aircraft engines, he began a log, charting each incident when a crew member fell ill. He was now, he told her, convinced that aerotoxic syndrome was a real thing. When she'd asked him why he kept flying, he told her he loved his job. And that he possibly wasn't as sensitive to the air's toxicity as some others.

'Well, you don't have to worry about me,' Isla assured him.

'Good to hear. Have a great weekend.'

After sending crew members Liz and Grant a text each, offering help if they needed it, Isla returned to the bar. She told the others about Bob's call but didn't dwell on it. She didn't care if she was putting her head in the sand because so were the airlines. One day, she guessed they'd all face it together, but in the meantime, she was going to kick up her heels and keep enjoying her life.

Their number had increased to a dozen by the time they hit

their third venue, this one with music and a huge TV above the bar. When a photograph flashed up of a gorgeous-looking woman with auburn hair and a generous smile, one of the crew pointed it out.

'She was murdered two streets from our hotel. Someone slit her throat.'

'You're kidding.'

He told her the story.

When Isla eventually fell into bed after 4am, she fell asleep thinking of Kaitlyn Rogers surviving an air crash in Morocco only to get murdered sixteen years later. God, life could suck.

SIXTEEN YEARS AGO

The sound was incredible. A horrific crashing like a million metal dustbins being crushed together, a noise that didn't stop.

In the brace position, I squeezed my eyes tight shut. If by some miracle I survived this, I didn't want to be blinded by a piece of debris flying through the air.

Screams and shouts.

Oh God, oh God, oh God.

I felt a moment's weightlessness and realised the aeroplane had bounced and lifted into the air.

Bang! It hit the ground a second time and sunlight flooded inside. A chunk of the plane had broken off.

Another almighty *crash!* The plane bounced again, spinning, rolling and sliding. A wing was ripped away. My lungs became choked with dirt and dust.

There was a long shudder. Metal shrieked. I squinted my eyes open for a second. Saw objects flying past me. Luggage, bits of plastic, metal. I kept my brace position, crouched over with my head against the seat in front. I felt the ground juddering against the plane's underbelly and snatched my feet into the air.

I didn't want them torn off.

Fragments of things I couldn't identify fell onto me. Another quick glance, this time to my right, showed Josh curled up. His mother was screaming. I couldn't hear her above the sound of tearing metal. Through the window, I saw sand and dry grasses churning past.

Bang! The front of the aircraft vanished.

I waited for oblivion. I waited for death.

And then the plane came to rest.

Silence.

I knew I had to move. I couldn't afford to sit and thank God. I couldn't pause to take stock.

The fuel tanks would be ruptured. Wires would be sparking.

We had seconds to get out.

Fingers numb and shaking, I undid my seat belt. Reached across and snapped Josh's free too. On his forehead stood a blotch of blood, as though he'd taken a blow. His eyes were open but his expression was vacant. I stood upright. Scooped him up and wedged him against my hip.

Josh's dad was nowhere to be seen. Nor was his seat. His mother lolled, head hanging, unconscious or dead, I had no idea but I couldn't stop. I had to get out. Over piles of shattered metal and overhead bins I saw a jagged-edged hole in the fuselage. Wide enough for two people. I started to make my way towards it. Bubs's seat had been wrenched free of its floor bolts and lay on its side. Bubs was still strapped in. She was pulling at her legs, panicky. They were both broken.

I put Josh down. 'Don't move.' I unstrapped Bubs. Picked her up. She whimpered but didn't protest any more. Holding her in my arms I squatted down. 'Josh, climb onto my back.'

I felt him clamber up.

'Put your arms around my neck.'

He clung onto me like a limpet.

55

With an immense effort, I rose. Began to make my way forward. Clutching Bubs against my chest, I climbed over luggage and fibreglass. Scrambled across a man lying face up, his stomach drenched in blood. People shouted for help but I didn't react. I had to get myself and the kids out.

Two men pushed ahead of me and hurried through the hole. Another followed. Many more were trapped, faces rigid with fear, but I couldn't think of them. My arms and legs were starting to tremble. I tried to move faster.

Suddenly I heard a popping sound followed by a small explosion. A gout of black smoke swept past us. Yellow and red flames appeared. I felt a blast-furnace heat. My world was reduced to Bubs and Josh and the fire racing down the aircraft, straight for us.

'Hold tight!' I yelled.

I shouldered my way to the hole. I didn't look down, simply jumped. We landed in a scrambling heap. Bubs was screaming, a high-pitched sound of pain and terror. For some reason I was wet. Bubs was wet. We'd jumped into a lake of spilled fuel.

With Josh still clinging to me I picked up Bubs and ran. I ran like I'd never run before, all my senses on the aeroplane behind us, waiting for the explosion.

I ran towards a rocky knoll. A man raced past me. I tried to keep up but with Bubs weighing down my arms, Josh strangling me, I quickly fell behind.

The man vanished over the knoll. I kept running. I didn't stop until I heard an almighty *whoomph*. Gasping, my breath red-raw in my throat, I stopped and turned around.

Grasses burned outward from the fuselage. People were engulfed in flames from the waist down. Passengers were screaming and calling for help. Each piece of the aircraft was burning – the wings and tail, the nose cone. People ran and thrashed through the fire, tearing at their clothes.

I turned away, ran behind the knoll. Collapsed to my knees. I was shaking uncontrollably. A keening sound came from my throat. I couldn't stop it.

'Dan?'

A woman was soothing him. She had sheets of white-blonde hair and deep blue eyes.

'My love,' he heard her say. 'You're dreaming. Wake up.'

The smoke vanished. The weight of Bubs left my arms. Josh's grip eased.

I realised I was weeping.

'Dan, darling...' Jenny sounded distraught.

'I couldn't save them,' I gasped. 'Oh God. I wanted to. I wanted to go back...'

'Who couldn't you save?'

'Josh and Bubs's parents.' I closed my eyes as the horror of the crash returned with its full force. 'Bubs is Kaitlyn Rogers. I'm sure of it. I saved her and her brother's lives.'

10

Lucy had spent the rest of Saturday with Mac, exploring Camden Market. The sun had come out, making trawling art galleries and the like not half as attractive as sipping a beer on a roof terrace, watching the crowds seething below, drinking in the smells of crisping falafels, burgers and chips, sweet sugary churros. It felt like heaven to Lucy. She'd grown fond of Stockton, especially the team up there, but she couldn't help it, she was London born and bred and still missed it like crazy.

They were on their second beer, kicking back, eyes closed, faces raised to the sun, when Mac asked if she wanted to be seconded to Kaitlyn's murder investigation team.

'God, yes. But it'll never happen. They'll bring in locals.'

'What if I could swing it?'

Her eyes snapped open. 'Really?'

'I know the SIO. We were at Hendon together.'

Lucy felt a rush of excitement, her thoughts whistling past.

I'll be on a murder case again, I'll solve it within the week, get Ricky home and Reg at the pub will give me Dad's address and when I've found Kaitlyn's killer and put them behind bars we'll go to the pub and crack open a bottle of bubbly and celebrate, he'll be so proud of me...

Hurriedly, she brought her thoughts under control before they went stratospheric. A doctor once told her that her mood swings meant she was bipolar, frightening her into thinking she might lose her job, but when she got a GP friend of hers to run a test under the radar, it transpired she was *vulnerable at each end of the mood spectrum*. Which meant she had to be careful when she was high, not to be overconfident and think she was invulnerable, and when she was low, to make sure she ate and kept her fluids up to avoid a potential crash.

Having a medical professional tell her she didn't have a mental health issue that needed medication, or that she'd have to suffer some kind of psychotherapeutic intervention, had been an incredible relief.

Lucy looked across at Mac, feeling a rush of tenderness.

'You'd really do that for me? Get me on the case?'

'I'm not being entirely altruistic,' he admitted. 'London's a lot closer to Bristol than Stockton.'

'What about Wimpy?' She was referring to her new boss, nicknamed because rumour had it that the first thing he'd mentioned when he'd arrived at the station was that Wimpy Bars could be on their way back to Teesside.

'I'll talk to him too.'

By the time they'd finished sharing a plate of raclette – a gooey mess of melted cheese over potatoes and something you'd never get north of the Watford Gap – Mac had spoken to Wimpy and his Hendon pal, and put things into motion. Which was all very well, but she still hadn't told him about Dan. How he was connected to the case. The trouble was that although Mac respected the ex-MI5 officer on a professional level, and appreciated the fact that Lucy was godmother to his little boy, the last time Dan had called upon Lucy to help him out, she'd nearly died.

Mac was looking at her and smiling, his eyes crinkling at the corners and filled with warmth.

I'll tell him later, she told herself. *I don't want to spoil the day.*

She ducked inside to use the loo and as she returned, she saw Mac waving her phone at her. 'It's Dan Forrester.'

She took the phone, wondering if she'd conjured Dan up by thinking of him. 'Hello?'

'I knew the victim,' Dan told her. 'Kaitlyn Rogers.'

'What?'

'I saved her life.'

He went on to tell her an extraordinary story of an air crash in Morocco, and his bravery in saving two children's lives. He finished by saying, 'I'm going to ring Sergeant Milton now.'

Lucy put down the phone. Stared at the throngs of people shopping, eating, chatting, laughing.

'What is it?'

She took a deep breath. 'He knows the vic. Kaitlyn Rogers.'

Mac opened and closed his mouth. 'You're joking.'

'He saved her life.' She told him the story. How he'd played racing cars with Josh and talked to Kaitlyn about women racing-car drivers. The crash.

'Christ almighty.'

Mac looked as though he didn't know whether to tear his hair or punch someone. Lucy decided not to go into the six degrees of separation malarkey and kept quiet. He wouldn't backtrack on getting her seconded to the case, would he?

'Does he know Ricky Shaw?'

'No.'

Mac's eyes narrowed as he thought further. 'When did he last see Kaitlyn Rogers?'

'He doesn't know for sure, but it'll have to have been over

seven years ago because that's when his son died.' As Mac knew only too well, Dan's life was defined by Before Luke's Death and After. Before, his memories were unreliable. After, his memories were intact.

'And you say that Dan's father knew Kaitlyn too.'

Lucy nodded.

'His wife?'

'No. Jenny hadn't yet met Dan when the crash happened.'

Mac took a long pull of beer and set the glass down with more force than necessary. 'You know what I'm going to say…'

'Yes.'

He squeezed his eyes shut. His jaw was clenched.

Lucy held her breath.

When Mac spoke, his voice was strangled. 'The SIO's name is Jon Banks. Please, Lucy. Stay out of trouble?'

She exhaled. She could understand the effort it took for him to give her the go-ahead. Dan Forrester attracted danger like blood attracted sharks. Which was probably why she was attracted too. Life was never dull when Dan was around.

'Thanks.' She touched his face with her fingers and he caught her hand, turning it over to kiss her palm.

'You'd never forgive me if I tried to stop you.'

Which was true, but she wasn't going to say it. No point in rubbing it in.

He looked at her, expression intense. 'Ring in twice a day, no matter where you are.'

'Yes.'

'And if you're going off-grid, ring every hour.'

'Yes.'

They stayed in a hotel that night. They could have stayed with Lucy's mother, but since there was only a single bed in her old childhood bedroom, Lucy didn't hesitate to take the luxury option. Dinner was at a bustling tapas bar around the corner.

Breakfast, a full English near Paddington Station, where she kissed Mac goodbye.

'Remember,' he said gravely, 'try and stay safe.'

Lucy nodded but the second he'd vanished from sight, she practically sprinted to the Tube and Kensington Police Station, her mind firing a multitude of colours and fizzing with excitement at being on a big case again.

The SIO, Jon Banks, was a burly man with buzz-cut grey hair and a bulldog jaw. His handshake was strong, his gaze clear. 'Mac tells me you're talented, dogged, and like to work unusual angles on your own.'

Lucy began to preen at the word *talented*.

'Other reports say you're excitable, impulsive, unpredictable, and generally a pain in the arse.'

It was an effort not to say *I take it you've been talking to turdface Magellan* and hold his eyes with as much aplomb as she could muster.

'However, your track record can't be ignored. The media, in particular, will be delighted to hear you're on the case. I'm holding a press conference in half an hour and I want you there.'

Lucy felt a surge of dismay. She hated being in the spotlight and something must have shown on her face because he added, 'It's the price you're going to have to pay for joining my team.'

She lifted her chin. 'I will *not* talk about my last case.'

'Understood.' He picked up a stack of papers and aligned the edges. When he looked up, he seemed surprised to see her still there. Lucy scarpered.

11

The press conference went better than Lucy expected. Jon Banks kept a tight rein on proceedings and whenever a journalist tried to ask her about her last case, he slapped them down. She'd even managed to ignore the TV cameras which was a bit of a miracle. Usually she became horribly self-conscious, stumbling over every other word, but with Banks's support, she'd been surprisingly confident.

She met the murder squad in the MIR – Major Incident Room. No matter that it was the weekend, the whole team was there. Murder played hell with overtime budgets, but the dead couldn't wait until Monday. Grabbing a desk, she did her best to ignore the curious stares that reached past her jacket, trying to see the scars she'd collected when she'd faced her kidnapper. She was notorious now, and not just for being hot-headed. Picking up the phone, she rang Ricky's solicitor. When it went to Ajay Pozo's messaging service she left her mobile number and asked him to call her back.

Next, she rang her mum, who was over the moon that she was on the case. 'Jaya told me! Oh, Lucy. I can't tell you how grateful I am. If there's anything I can do...'

'Can I stay with you for a bit?'

'Of course! I'll make your bed up. You've got keys. Come and go as you like.'

'Thanks, Mum.'

'Love you, my darling girl.'

'Love you too.' Before her near-death experience she would never have said something so personal in the office but she didn't care who overheard. Life was too short for pissing about.

She rose and went to study the wall, a seeming mess of maps, photographs and multi-coloured Post-it notes that were the result of the investigation so far. Someone had traced the route Ricky had taken to Kaitlyn's Airbnb and then his erratic journey before he'd stopped his car to throw up. There were photographs of PJ's, the bar and grill where he'd met Kaitlyn, the table they'd dined at the following evening, the flowers and bubbly he'd bought. She blinked when she saw a photograph of Dan along with a printout of Kaitlyn's phone calls, which included three to Dan last Sunday. Dan had obviously spoken to Karen because there were copies of newspaper reports on the airliner crash.

Morocco plane crash:
jet was bombed in terror attack

A home-made bomb brought down the Air UK jet over Morocco's countryside, the Moroccan president has said, confirming that the plane was destroyed by a terrorist act.

The president vowed to find and punish those responsible for the attack that killed 214 people on board, including seven returning British holidaymakers. Thirteen people survived.

Morocco confirmed reports that two employees at Marrakech Menara Airport had been arrested in connection with the bombing. The final flights clearing British tourists from Marrakech left on Wednesday.

'She was in Morocco last week,' a voice said behind Lucy, making her jump. She hadn't realised anyone had come close.

'Sorry.' Karen looked at her curiously but Lucy wasn't going to explain that her nerves had been shot ever since her attack.

'She got back last Sunday. She rang him...' Karen tapped Dan's photograph with a finger '...after she'd landed back at Heathrow.'

'Dan Forrester,' Lucy said.

'Yes.' Karen nodded. 'He told me you've worked together.'

Lucy turned back to look at Kaitlyn Rogers' photograph. 'What was she doing in Morocco?'

'According to the API – Advance Passenger Information – she was on holiday.'

'Interesting choice.'

Karen turned her head to look at a photograph of the airliner's nose cone, buried in a sand dune. 'SIO's asked our counterparts over there for any intel, but they don't want to know. Too long ago. Plus, they don't want it all raked up so it scares the tourists away.'

At that moment, Lucy's phone rang. Ricky's solicitor. She mouthed *sorry* at Karen and moved away.

'Thanks for ringing me back.' Lucy quickly explained that although she was working with the Met on Ricky's case, she was also a family friend.

'Sweet.' He sounded pleased. He also sounded absurdly young. 'So, you saw Ricky yesterday. How was the man?'

Out of nowhere she felt a hot ball of anger lodge in her diaphragm. 'His mouth is still swollen.'

'What you talkin' about?'

'He's allergic to peanuts. You gave him a sandwich with peanuts in it.'

'What the fuck? I never gave him any sandwich.'

'Really?' Lucy was wrong-footed. 'I was told when you visited him on Friday, you brought him a sandwich.'

'No way! Seriously. Not me.'

'Well, who did?'

'No idea.'

'Maybe it was someone else from your office.'

'There ain't nobody here 'cept me and I saw the man once, at ten thirty pm.'

'Well, the records show someone from Pozo and Partners visited him again just after midnight.'

'Shit, man. That's someone lyin'. Nobody from here was there 'cept for me at ten thirty.'

A banner of lilac streamed across Lucy's mind, intensifying her curiosity. He didn't sound like your usual sort of solicitor. He sounded more like a rap artist. 'I'd like to see you. Later today, if possible.'

'Sure thing. How 'bout my office, four pm?'

She checked his address to see it was on Borough High Street, a ten-minute walk from her mum's. 'Can we make it after six?'

'Cool.'

They hung up. Lucy headed to reception where she tracked down the custody sergeant who'd been on duty when Ricky had been brought in. Read the paperwork.

'So...' She pointed at the form on the screen. 'Ajay Pozo attended Ricky at ten thirty pm, but who's this second person?'

The sergeant looked at the form. 'Chris Malone.'

'Can you remember what he looked like?'

She got a look that said, *you have to be kidding, do you know how busy it is here on Friday night?*

'Can I see the CCTV?' She made begging motions. 'Pretty please?'

He didn't jump at the idea but once she'd explained, his face tightened. 'Shit. You really think it was a murder attempt?'

'I'd like to say no, but maybe Ricky can shed some light. He's still here, I'm told.'

'Yup. The boss wants to keep him as long as poss.'

Which meant up to ninety-six hours, by which time they either had to let him go or charge him by Tuesday 9pm. The sergeant led her to the custody suite. Flipped open the hatch on one of the cell doors. 'Visitor for you, Ricky. Lucy Davies. Okay?'

'Yeah.' Ricky's voice was low.

The sergeant unlocked the door. Lucy stepped inside. Daylight filtered through a Perspex window, lighting the cheery yellow walls, the vivid blue chair and mattress. At the far end stood a WC and basin. A CCTV camera monitored every move.

'Knock on the door when you're done.' The sergeant locked the door behind her. 'I'll get the tape for you later.'

Ricky had been sitting in the chair when she came in, but now he stood up. His shirt was open at the neck, and he'd taken his shoes off. Now, he put them on, and buttoned up his top button.

'Hi,' he said.

'Hi.' She wanted to ask how he was but when she took in the way his fingers were trembling, decided it might be prudent to leave him with some dignity. 'Look, I just wanted to ask about the person who brought you the sandwich on Friday night.'

'Chris?'

'Yes. How do you know him?'

'Chris isn't a man. She's a woman. And I don't know her. Well, I do now, obviously. She's from Pozo and Partners.'

'Ajay says she isn't.'

'What?' He looked blank.

'Ajay says he's the only person from his firm to see you.'

The blank look remained. 'But Chris brought me something to sign. It was a client care letter, defining the work to be done, and how I'll pay for it. She said Ajay needed it before he'd represent me. She had his letterhead and everything. She was really nice.'

'She also brought you the sandwich that had peanut butter in it.'

Ricky stared at her.

'I wouldn't say that was particularly nice. Would you?'

At that, he paled. Sat down heavily.

'Have you considered that Kaitlyn may not have been the target? That it might have been you?'

His eyes widened so much she thought they might pop from his head.

'No.' His voice was hoarse.

'Make a list for me. Of anyone you think might benefit from your...' She'd been going to say *death* but hurriedly amended it to 'absence'.

The trembling in his fingers increased. 'But there isn't...'

'Just do it, Ricky.'

12

Dan drove along the A420, fingers unusually tight on the steering wheel. His mind was buzzing. He kept replaying the memory of Kaitlyn and Josh, their parents, worrying that if he thought about something else they would stop being real.

He'd spoken to Dr Simon Winter, his psychiatrist, first thing in the morning. Simon had been cautiously pleased that Dan had had a memory breakthrough.

'That's great news, Dan. But I'd be careful managing your expectations. You may not regain any more memories. Be prepared for that.'

Dan had checked his father's email history to see a fair bit of correspondence between him and Kaitlyn over the years. Dan's father had died last September but Dan, ever circumspect, had kept his father's computer, photographs and emails, in case they might be needed. It appeared that his father had helped Kaitlyn choose where Josh resided, and even went to visit the boy from time to time.

One of his father's emails to Kaitlyn explained why Dan hadn't known about her.

> I know you want to keep in touch with
> Dan, but his psychiatrist has advised
> against it. He's lost a lot of his memory
> due to the trauma over his son Luke's
> death, and the doctors are concerned if
> he remembers the air crash, anything of
> that period, it might tip him back into
> the abyss.

Dan knew he'd been a mess back then and although he could understand his father trying to protect him, today he found it immeasurably frustrating.

He was on autopilot, following the car in front until a dual carriageway appeared. He swept past the slower traffic until he came to the outskirts of Oxford, when he turned off to follow the satnav down a winding B-road. Twenty minutes later he came to a modern stone manor house surrounded by tranquil-looking gardens. He parked where indicated – next to a stone barn.

An impressive entrance hall with a sweeping staircase greeted him inside the house. A desk was set to one side, and with its softly glowing lamp and petite, navy-suited receptionist, it was more reminiscent of a five-star hotel than a nursing home.

'I'm here to see Josh Rogers. I called this morning.'

'Dan Forrester?' The receptionist rose and put out her hand. She had a cool, firm grip. 'I'm Gill Dix. Thanks so much for coming. As I said earlier, the police came to talk to him but even though I told them they wouldn't have any joy, they insisted. We're devastated over Kaitlyn's death. She visited Josh every week. We're all going to miss her dreadfully.'

Dan swallowed away the lump that threatened to form in his throat. 'I'm sorry too.'

Gill gave him a gentle smile. 'I'll ring for Ava. She'll take you to him.'

Ava was in her thirties, blowsy, with a kind round face. She expressed her commiserations over Kaitlyn and when Dan asked, told him Kaitlyn had set up a lifelong trust for Josh when their parents died. 'Thank the Lord,' she added. 'Because not everyone is so forward-thinking.'

She went on to say that Josh had sustained traumatic brain injury from the air crash. 'I'm sorry to say he won't know you. And I'd advise against trying to make him remember.'

Dan winced inside. It wasn't unlike what his dad had said about him, in his email to Kaitlyn. He recalled the four-leaf clover found in her purse along with his note, saying it would help keep her safe, and thought how sad it was that Kaitlyn hadn't been able to keep in touch with him, her rescuer.

Ava led him into a large lounge area with an inglenook fireplace and squashy sofas overlooking the garden. Paintings and bookshelves covered the walls. A young man sat at a table near the windows. His sandy hair was neatly brushed, his cheeks freshly shaven. He didn't move when they approached. He seemed to be staring at a bird feeder, the sparrows and blue tits flickering to and from the nearby bushes.

Ava bent and said, 'Josh? You've got a visitor. He's a friend of your sister's.' They'd already agreed not to mention Kaitlyn's death. He'd been told, apparently, but he hadn't responded. There seemed little point belabouring the fact.

'Hello, Josh,' Dan greeted him.

Josh rolled his head. Vivid green eyes looked at Dan but Dan wasn't sure they were seeing him. They didn't seem to be focusing at all. On the table were some children's colouring books and crayons. A spaceship had been covered in clumsy yellow scrawl.

'Nice colour. You'll be able to see it at night, no problem.'

Josh dropped his head. Drool swung from his chin. Ava brought out a tissue and wiped it away.

Dan had a look at the books. 'You've got a good collection there, but it's a shame there isn't one on racing cars.'

Reaching into his pocket, Dan brought out two toy cars. One a red Ferrari, the other a yellow Lamborghini. He put them on table.

'Sorry I couldn't find a Nissan, but even so, they're both pretty fast. Which one do you want to race?'

Josh straightened. Reached for the Lamborghini. Clutching it in his fist, he banged it on the table.

'Good choice. The Lambo's a lot quicker than the Ferrari. I think you've got a good chance of winning.'

Dan rolled the Ferrari around the colouring books. 'This is the warm-up lap.'

Josh's gaze remained unfocused as he banged the toy car up and down. When Dan placed the Ferrari in the centre of the spaceship colouring book, Josh suddenly lifted his eyes and looked straight at Dan.

Dan had no idea if he was seeing him, or remembering him, but as he held the young man's eyes he said, 'I'm so sorry this happened to you.'

He didn't stay for much longer. He couldn't bear it. He would have liked to have touched Josh as he said goodbye, squeezed an arm or his shoulder, but he'd been warned not to. 'Bye, Josh. I'll come and see you again soon.'

His emotions were all over the place as Ava walked him outside. He pictured Josh as a boy, his eyes alight, his energy and enthusiasm, his whole life ahead of him, and now? Dan felt like punching the wall. Grief mingled with sorrow, drenched in rage.

'Kaitlyn used to get angry too,' Ava remarked.

'Is it that obvious?' Dan was startled. Normally he was imperturbable.

'No. Don't worry. We're trained to notice.'

They came to his car. Weak sunlight lit the garden and for

the first time, Dan noticed the daffodils. Their cheery faces felt incongruous against the darkness in his soul.

'She tried to find out who was responsible, you know.'

After spending several hours on the internet that morning, Dan knew that although two airport employees had been arrested and thrown into jail for the bombing, there was still doubt over their guilt. Rumours abounded that they were just fall guys, that Morocco hadn't wanted its booming tourist industry to falter, and that the real bomber, or bombers, had never been identified.

'She never gave up,' Ava went on. 'People kept telling her to put it behind her, to move forward, but she couldn't. That's why she went to Morocco last week. She thought she'd found something new.'

Dan's attention sharpened. 'Like what?'

'She didn't say. But she was excited. Determined too. I told her to be careful but I knew she wasn't listening.' Ava gazed past Dan and back at the window where Josh sat. 'She would have done anything to get her family justice.'

13

D an headed for Kaitlyn's house. Thanks to Lucy, he had her address in the Cotswolds, and although neither of them knew why Kaitlyn had taken the Kensington Airbnb for the week, they'd agreed it wouldn't harm if he had a quick look at her home.

Fox Cottage was a large stone cottage set on the edge of Castle Combe, a quintessentially English village that was so ancient, so chocolate-box pretty, it was used regularly as a film location. A classic Audi Quattro stood in the driveway. Nice. Around the back, a Range Rover and horse box. Three immaculate stone stables, one of which housed a stunning red and black CBR600 motorbike. Behind that was a large paddock, where two bay horses were grazing. Even Dan could see they weren't your usual nags. Their conformation was elegant, thoroughbred, and they gleamed with health.

The front and back doors both had strips of police tape across them. *Do not cross.* Lucy had said the local police had been in yesterday, the day after Kaitlyn's murder, but reported they hadn't found anything of particular interest. But what had they been looking for? He peered through the windows to see an open fireplace, oak beams and wooden doors. Thick carpets, deep sofas. Traditional but luxurious.

Dan drove on to Castle Combe Circuit. Hadn't Sergeant Milton mentioned Kaitlyn was into track driving? He'd used Castle Combe himself from time to time, and although he hadn't been here for a couple of years it seemed that nothing had changed.

His spirits lifted when he saw a track day was in progress for Mick's Motorsport. Talk about perfect timing. Dan knew Mick and had driven for him regularly. As he walked to the office he paused to watch a handful of road cars popping out of Bobbies and tearing down Westway for Camp Corner: a couple of Golf GTIs, a Jaguar, Porsche and a Honda Civic. If it had four wheels and a current MOT, it was welcome.

He pushed open the office door.

'Dan!' a woman squealed.

'Well, bugger me,' a man added.

'Hi Julie,' Dan responded. 'Hi Mick.'

'Come for your old job?' Mick asked.

'Nope.'

'Bugger off then.' Mick, who sang Irish songs in a deep baritone, harboured a weakness for real ale that showed in the belly that hung over his belt. He came over and shook Dan's hand. It was like shaking a wrench. 'How's things?'

'Jenny's great, kids are great, job's great.'

'Awwww,' Julie said, eyes crinkling at the corners. 'Does that mean you've dropped in just to tell us how much you've missed us?'

Dan smiled. They were a good team and they'd looked after him for a long time. 'Not quite,' he admitted. 'I'm actually here because I'm helping investigate Kaitlyn Rogers' death.'

The atmosphere immediately darkened. Julie swallowed and looked away. Mick passed a hand over his face, noisily clearing his throat. Both were obviously battling the emotion suddenly rising.

'You knew her well.' It was a statement, not a question.

'She practically lived here.' Mick's voice was hoarse.

They were visibly upset so Dan took some time filling them in, letting them recover a little. He watched their eyes round when he told them how he knew her.

'You saved her?!' Mick exclaimed. 'Bloody hell. I didn't realise you were a hero.'

Dan looked away, uncomfortable. There was a lot Mick and Julie didn't know about him.

'The nurse looking after Josh said she'd been to Morocco, trying to find answers.'

Julie wiped her eyes with her fingers. 'She was a great person – we all loved her – but she was tormented. She lost her mum and dad, Josh, all in the space of an hour. The crash defined her…'

He listened as they told him about the girl he'd met, what she was like as a woman. Generous, fun-loving and kind, but with a shadow staining her soul. How angry she was about the crash. How she used cars and motorbikes to help release her rage.

'She was obsessed with the air disaster. She tried not to let it show but she'd had enough of people telling her to "move on" and "put it behind her". When you got to know her you soon saw she could no more forget about it than stop breathing.'

'Did she say anything about finding something new to do with the crash?'

'Yeah.' This was from Mick. 'She didn't say what, though. She didn't particularly want to go back to Morocco, but apparently there wasn't any other way.'

Dan's interest quickened. 'She hadn't been back before?'

'No. She hadn't flown since the crash either. This was the first time.'

'Brave woman.'

'One of the best.' Mick was grave.

Dan stayed for a coffee before heading back to his car. He was puzzled. How had Kaitlyn got a lead after sixteen years? Who had she been talking to? Had she found something on the internet?

He called Lucy before he started the engine.

'Any chance you can take a look at Kaitlyn's computer?'

'It's with the tech team. What should I be looking for?'

'Anything to do with the air crash, no matter how small.'

'Okay.'

'I'd like to see inside her cottage as well. Something triggered her trip to Morocco, I want to know what.'

'I'll see if I can get keys. Call you back.'

Dan waited in the car, half watching the vehicles on the track, half flicking through old reports of the Moroccan air crash. Looking at the photographs of smoking debris, metal and wreckage everywhere, he found it hard to believe he'd been there, let alone survived.

His phone buzzed. Lucy.

'The SIO's given me the go-ahead to check out the cottage with you. I'm getting the train to Chippenham. Can you pick me up? We can collect keys from the Wiltshire Police – they got them off a neighbour yesterday. The same neighbour's looking after the horses at the moment apparently.'

'Text me your train times.'

While he waited for Lucy, Dan went into the village and asked around about Kaitlyn. Everyone voiced shock at her murder. Some people were salacious, wanting gory details, but most were genuinely appalled. As Dan talked, he learned that Kaitlyn was a regular at the Castle Inn, especially for Sunday lunch. That she rode out with friends at weekends, took in friends' dogs when they went away, that she was bubbly and popular, and that although she had boyfriends, she'd never stuck with any for longer than a year or two. A serial monogamist, one woman called her.

'Anyone on the scene at the moment?' he asked the publican of the White Hart.

'She didn't bring anyone in for a pint, if that's what you mean.'

Two hours later, with Kaitlyn's keys in hand, Lucy let them into Fox Cottage. It was cold and smelled of an intriguing mix of wood smoke mingled with juniper and sage that came from a variety of scented candles dotted around.

Silently, they moved through the rooms. It was neat and orderly, everything put away. Just as Dan liked to leave his house before he headed overseas. Before he'd had kids, needless to say.

While Lucy started in the kitchen, Dan moved upstairs, looking up at the ceilings, down at the floor. He flipped through drawers and cupboards. He didn't find any evidence of male visitors. No shaving gear in the bathroom or male deodorant. Only one electric toothbrush. One set of towels. One bathrobe. In her study – a converted bedroom – he found nothing but investment valuations and tax returns. He was surprised to find nothing about the air disaster. Was everything on her computer?

Dan increased the depth of his search. He checked the undersides of wastepaper bins, felt the hem of each curtain, tested the edges of the carpets. Turned the sofa and armchairs upside down, fingered the stitching. Back upstairs, he opened the silver pine wardrobe and brushed some clothes aside. Immediately, he saw it.

A small handle set in the rear of the wardrobe.

14

D an pushed open the miniature door.
         'Lucy,' he called.

She arrived in a rush. 'What is it?'

With Kaitlyn's clothes now on the bed, he pointed at the tiny hidden room accessed through the wardrobe.

'Very Narnia,' she remarked. 'Have you been in?'

'Not yet. After you.'

While Lucy could bend her small frame double to go inside, Dan had to enter on his knees. Both of them straightened up and looked around, slack-jawed.

'Bloody hell,' said Lucy.

Sun streamed through a skylight above, lighting the miniature office. There was a desk with a computer and printer, a colourful rug on the floor, but it was the walls that took their breath away. They were covered in layer upon layer of papers and photographs. There were shots of the downed airliner, portraits of passengers alive and dead, newspaper clippings, printed-out letters and emails, and handwritten notes.

Police cover up! Corrupt! Defence minister, corrupt! GDNS, corrupt!

GDNS stood for Morocco's General Directorate for National Security, Dan knew. The interesting thing about his memory was although his old job was forever lost to him, the odd piece of information sneaked through. Like the words *ish jayyidan*, live well. They'd popped into his mind unbidden just now and he wondered who he'd spoken them to.

'Why hide away like this?' Lucy puzzled.

'Because people didn't understand. They wanted her to stop thinking about what had happened but she couldn't.' He looked at a photograph of a torn suitcase with a severed hand lying beside it. 'This way, she didn't have to explain herself.'

He moved further inside the room. Read the document nearest to him.

Initial hypotheses included determining whether the aircraft could have been hit by a ground-to-air missile...

Dan scanned down, his eyes taking in the investigator's name along with the on-scene commander's, the first responders' and the officer in charge of security.

Detailed photographs were taken of the bomb scene area before items of evidence were disturbed and before indigenous items of debris were moved to expose the forensically rich scene.

Both of them moved silently around the room. Newspaper headlines abounded.

Nightmare end for fairy-tale holiday. Air crash horror. Man proposes to girlfriend on plummeting plane. Passengers scream in terror. More than 200 feared dead. Final report on the fate of EG220.

'There's a system,' said Lucy. 'It starts here...' She pointed at the wall to the left of the wardrobe door. 'And works anti-clockwise to end here, at the desk. All this stuff's really recent.'

While Lucy rifled through the desk drawers, Dan gazed at the wall above the computer. What grabbed his attention was a piece of paper torn from a yellow legal pad and folded in two, stuck at head height with a drawing pin. Kaitlyn, he assumed, had taken a red pen and scrawled in large, slashing letters:

TASS! Fucking TASS! If it wasn't for TASS it would never have fucking happened!

TASS Russian News Agency? Or did she mean someone else? Dan looked up TASS on the internet to see it was an acronym for a variety of things which included the Talented Athlete Scholarship Scheme operating out of Bath in the UK. None looked as though it had anything to do with the crash.

He removed the note to find a photograph of a serious-looking, dark-skinned man. A phone number was scribbled over his forehead, along with a name. Hafid Khatabi. She had covered his cheeks with kisses and scribbled, *I love you for helping me. I love you love you xxxx*

Dan brought out his phone. Checked the code +212 and wasn't surprised to find it was the country code for Morocco. He dialled.

'*Shurtat Marakish,*' a woman answered.

He ignored Lucy staring at him. 'Hafid Khatabi, please.'

'Just one moment.'

There was a click, then a ringing tone.

'Khatabi.' A man's voice, curt.

'Hello,' Dan said. 'I'm sorry I don't speak Arabic. Perhaps you have a little English?'

'A little,' he said agreeably. Was he used to Western tourists?

'Thank you. I got your number from Kaitlyn Rogers' office. I'm a friend of hers.'

'Kaitlyn?' The man sounded astonished. 'I don't understand...'

'I was wondering what you were helping her with.'

'But...' The man fell silent.

Dan waited.

More silence.

'You see, I was on the same aeroplane. EG220. Like Kaitlyn, I survived–'

The man hung up. Dan dialled again.

'*Shurtat Marakish,*' the same woman answered.

'I'm sorry to trouble you, but do you speak English?'

'A little.'

'I wanted to know what organisation you belong to.'

'The Marrakech Police.' Her tone implied *what else?*

'And Hafid Khatabi?'

'He is one of our senior investigators.'

'How old is he?'

There was a short silence.

'You ask this, why?'

'I'm calling from the Kensington and Chelsea Police in London about an old case.'

He turned away so he couldn't see Lucy widening her eyes warningly at him.

'He is in his fifties. I'm not sure exactly.'

Which meant Khatabi would probably have been in his thirties when the plane went down.

'Would you like me to put you through?'

'Yes, please.'

Click. Ring tone.

'Khatabi.'

'Kaitlyn Rogers has–'

The man hung up again.

When Dan redialled the main number, the woman refused to put him through, and hung up. Khatabi had obviously told her to blank his calls.

'He knew Kaitlyn,' Dan told Lucy. He was staring at the man's photograph. 'He's a cop. He knows something. We just have to find out what.'

15

'And well done, Lucy.' The SIO wrapped up the briefing first thing on Monday with a nod in Lucy's direction. 'Kaitlyn's home computer is now with the tech team along with her laptop. Let's hope we get some joy from it.'

Lucy didn't look at Magellan but she could feel his killer stare drilling a hole in her forehead. He was hating every minute while she was loving it. Great rivers of green and gold bubbled happily through her mind, celebrating.

'Unfortunately,' Jon Banks went on, 'Hafid Khatabi has gone on leave for the next two weeks and is out of touch. Apparently, he's trekking in the Atlas Mountains.'

Lucy gave an audible snort. As if she believed *that*.

'The Marrakech Police say they know nothing about Kaitlyn and are being particularly unhelpful. The air-crash investigation was run out of the capital, Rabat, but the Marrakech lot were heavily involved. However, nobody in Morocco is interested in us, or our murder case, and even less interested in raking things up over the EG220 disaster. They've got their bombers rotting in jail and will do pretty much anything to keep them there, guilty or not. They don't want to be made to look stupid. Especially by us.'

The SIO went on to task the team over Ricky's client list. 'He has a hundred and twelve clients. He has three really big customers, one of which is Tomas Featherstone.'

There was a shifting movement through the room as people recognised the name. Teflon Tom's notoriety had obviously broken the borders of Southwark and seeped across London.

'Thanks again to Lucy for finding this little nugget...'

The bubbles turned to a joyful froth as the SIO praised her further. Lucy knew that if it hadn't been for Jaya, Ricky would have tried to keep Tomas out of the spotlight. The last thing Ricky needed was for the police to see him as someone who helped criminals, but it was too late.

Lucy scanned the list on the board. Ricky had told her how he'd struggled to get clients to start with. Just twenty in the first year, and even fewer in the second. But then Teflon Tom came on board and the referrals started.

'Lucy.' The SIO fixed her with a steely gaze. 'I want you to take Tomas. He's a difficult customer and you may have more joy since you knew him at school.'

Yessss! She'd bagged the biggie! She tried not to grin. She didn't want the rest of the team to resent her. Hoping she was keeping a straight face, she gave what she prayed was a cool and professional nod.

'Ricky's solicitor also represents Tomas Featherstone. They also share a racehorse, for what it's worth.' Another nod of approbation to Lucy. 'I want to know what else they share. Gambling, drinking, women. Was there some jealousy or competitiveness over Kaitlyn? If so, I want to know about it.'

Lucy gave another nod. It had been Ajay who'd told her about the racehorse. She'd met him last night, as agreed, in his office, a small and neat white and chrome space above a French bistro and with a view of The Shard from his windows.

Ajay had dreadlocks and wore a skinny fit, shiny grey suit that looked as though it had been made out of polished aluminium. He was loose-limbed, oozing Caribbean bonhomie, but his eyes were sharp and his intellect as shrewd as any top-notch barrister working out of Lincoln's Inn Fields.

He hadn't been impressed that Ricky had dropped Tomas Featherstone in the proverbial shit with the cops.

'Doesn't the man have any sense of self-preservation?'

'It was Jaya who told me.'

Ajay rolled his eyes, showing their whites like a frightened horse. 'Jaya.' With the one word he conveyed despair and exasperation in equal measure.

'She's a good woman.' Lucy couldn't not defend her mum's friend.

'I know that, man. She's as good as gold but I wish she'd back off and let me do my job.'

Jaya had been unrepentant when Lucy saw her last night. After Lucy had met Ajay, she'd walked to her childhood home where she'd found Jaya drinking tea with her mum in the kitchen.

'Poor Ricky,' her mother said gloomily. 'I know his clients aren't exactly snow-white but he really doesn't deserve this.'

Lucy listened to them lament and sigh for a while before she announced she was going to head to the King's Arms. Her mother looked surprised. Jaya swallowed and fixed her gaze on the teapot.

'I just want to see if anyone from the old days is around,' Lucy said, all innocence. Her mum would kill her if she knew she was going to ask Reg, the pub landlord, how to find her father – in Macclesfield, for God's sake. She still couldn't believe it.

Jaya jumped up. 'I'll walk with you, if you like.'

Thankfully the pub was on Jaya's way home so it didn't look odd when they left together. However, they'd barely reached the end of the street when Jaya stopped.

'I've your dad's number here.' Jaya brought out her phone. 'I'll text it to you now.'

Lucy felt her phone vibrate. She opened her messages and there it was. A mobile number. She felt disbelief descend. Was it really her dad's? Was it that easy?

'Look, Lucy.' Jaya's voice dropped. 'Don't mention to Reg I gave it to you, will you?'

'Why not?'

'Well, your mum made everyone promise... And you know what she's like...'

'Okay.' Lucy was staring at her phone. 'I won't tell anyone.'

'There's a love.'

Lucy didn't see Jaya leave. She was still staring at her father's number. She didn't have the guts to ring it straight away. She went to the pub and downed a vodka and tonic without talking to anyone. Walked back to her mum's in a state of disbelief. She was distracted all evening, which luckily her mother put down to working Ricky's case, and Lucy went to bed early where she lay awake for most of the night, rehearsing what to say.

Hi, Dad. It's me, Lucy. Yes, it's the daughter you abandoned when she was eight. Hi, Dad. It's your daughter Lucy here. How are you? What the fuck are you doing in Macclesfield? Why aren't you in fucking Sydney? Hi, Dad. It's Lucy here...

She'd read somewhere that cold calls went down best between 8–9am and 4–5pm, with the lunchtime period of 1–2pm being the absolute worst. She didn't think it would be particularly beneficial to ring first thing in the morning. He could be at work, or in a meeting. He'd also be distracted on a Monday, thinking about the week ahead.

She'd ring him tomorrow. Tuesday at 4pm, she decided. Meanwhile, she'd better call Dan and fill him in.

16

Dan was in his work office when Lucy told him that Hafid Khatabi had supposedly gone walkabout. They were definitely onto something. However, although he and Lucy had spent the previous afternoon scouring Kaitlyn's most recent notes and papers, nothing else had jumped out at them. Dan's mind kept returning to the photograph of the Moroccan policeman and Kaitlyn's scribble across his forehead.

I love you for helping me. I love you love you xxxx

'Marrakech is pretty nice at this time of year,' he told Lucy. 'Mid-twenties during the day. Cool at night.'

'Didn't someone say Khatabi's gone trekking in the mountains?'

'Trust me, he'll be at work. But if he *has* gone on holiday,' he contemplated, 'then I can have a break too. I can't remember anything about Morocco. I'd like to rectify that.'

'Well, bring me back a camel or something nice.'

'A camel?'

'Well, what else do they have out there, aside from marijuana?'

'Tagines. Teapots, carpets, slippers...'

'Stop right there. A bottle of duty-free vodka will do just fine.'

Dan hung up. Stared down the street where a man in a suit was climbing out of a black cab. Could he really go to Morocco? Should he? Curiosity aside, what did he really hope to achieve? If Khatabi continued to blank him the best he could hope for was a pleasant stroll around some souks and a traditional meal at the night market. He'd already been on the internet and had found a charming-looking *riad* to stay in, close to the centre. He was struggling to concentrate on his work, and if he didn't go to Morocco he'd have to be careful not to let his disappointment taint his mood.

A knock on his door snapped him out of his reverie.

'Dan.' It was his boss, Philip Denton. 'How did it go in Miami?'

Dan had been advising a British client whether to invest in a hotel chain in Florida, which was going for a rock-bottom price.

'I'm advising against it.' He talked Philip through his reasons, which included a tip-off through a CIA contact that the Russian mob were prohibitively active in the area.

'I can see your point,' Philip agreed. 'Copy me your report, please. Anything else?'

'Yes, there is.' When Dan started to explain, about Kaitlyn Rogers' murder and how he knew her, Philip closed the door behind him and came and sat in one of the chairs by the window. Folded his hands in his lap and waited for Dan to join him. Although Dan knew how busy Philip was, his boss looked as though he had all the time in the world. It was a quality Dan appreciated, the ability to switch priorities at a second's notice.

'So, the air crash occurred in your MI5 days,' Philip remarked.

'Yes. However, I have no idea if the EG220 disaster is connected or not to the firm.'

'But you'd like to find out.'

'Yes.'

Something in his tone made Philip's eyes narrow. 'I'd be careful about seeking a reprisal if I were you. It will only cloud your judgement.'

'I'm aware of that.' Dan's tone was stiff.

'Fill me in.' Philip waved a hand like a magician, and Dan did as he was told. He didn't see any reason to withhold anything. If Philip let him go to Morocco he'd need to be in the loop.

When Dan finished, Philip half closed his eyes, gazing at the building opposite. 'You have a nose for rooting out moles, fraudsters, imposters and liars – bad guys of every description – but you can also get into an awful lot of trouble.'

Dan remained silent.

Philip tapped a little tattoo on his knee before turning his head to survey Dan. 'I take it Jenny's okay with this?'

'I don't know,' Dan admitted.

'If she's on board, then I suggest you take the time you need. The last case you worked on with your policewoman friend proved excellent for business. The clients like your quiet style, your confidence, but what really works for them is seeing you performing so productively in the field.' His gaze intensified. 'You're good for business, Dan. Just don't get into any hot water this time.'

The first bit of hot water he was going to experience was talking to Jenny. Although they'd agreed he should feel free to follow any investigation he was involved in, wherever it may lead, he knew she hated it when he went overseas.

Procrastinating calling her, he looked up flights on the internet to see there was an easyJet departing first thing tomorrow, which would give him time to tidy his desk, go home and hopefully pack his bag. He'd leave work early, he decided. Have some time with the family.

~

He'd barely walked inside the house when Jenny appeared with a grizzling Mischa in her arms. His left cheek was a hot red from teething.

Jenny looked at Dan. He looked back.

'You're going to Morocco,' she said. It wasn't a question.

He raised his eyebrows. 'Have you just turned clairvoyant?'

'I can't see any other reason why you're home early.'

'Are you okay with my going?'

She looked down at Mischa. 'At least I'm not pregnant this time.' Her voice was wry.

'No,' he agreed. 'But even so...'

Jenny touched the ceramic pendant at her neck, which he'd given her last year. Her gaze was clear. 'I can no more stop you going on mad missions than fly to the moon. That said, please be careful?'

'I promise.'

The next morning Dan walked onto his easyJet aircraft with a sandwich, a bottle of fresh orange juice, and a spring in his step. He loved his life with DCA & Co, and loved his wife and children very much, but he needed an edge in his life, a quest as well as a challenge from time to time.

As the Airbus rose into the sky the corners of his mouth lifted. He never felt more alive than when on a mission.

17

Isla was dreaming of smoke. Not from a log fire or a stove, but great gouts of black clouds, dripping oil. She was trying to run from them but her feet were like lead, her legs as though they'd been filled with sand. A scream was building at the back of her throat when she became aware of a knocking sound, getting louder and louder...

She opened her eyes. At least she thought she had but she couldn't see anything. Was she still dreaming?

The knocking became insistent, followed by a woman calling, 'Room service. May I make up your room, please?'

Isla sat up in bed, heart thudding. It was daytime? She rubbed her eyes. Nothing. She could feel the sheets against her naked body, hear the air-conditioners rumble, smell the faintest aroma of bacon drifting from the hotel kitchen. But she couldn't see.

It wasn't night. She could tell by the sound of traffic outside, a rubbish truck's grinding, an aeroplane gliding overhead. There was an energy in the air too, that you didn't get at night.

She shook her head. Looked up and down, from right to left. Nothing.

She knew exactly where she was. Room 324 of the Park Grand London Kensington. She had an en suite double room and a mini bar. She knew the breakfasts were excellent. Earls Court tube station was at the end of the street. She'd stayed here countless times. Why couldn't she see?

Then came the sound of a key card being inserted in the door.

'Wait, wait!' Isla called. Panic threatened to erupt. There had to be an explanation. But what?

She wriggled to the edge of the bed. Put her feet on the floor. Rubbed her eyes again. Why couldn't she fucking *see*?

'Madam?'

'Wait! I haven't got any clothes on!'

'You want me to come back?'

'No.' Isla pulled the duvet around her. 'Please...' Her mind raced. Could she trust the maid? Her money and passport were on the side table... 'Yes, come back later. No. Sorry. Stay.' She changed her mind. Suddenly she didn't want to be alone.

'Madam?'

'I have a problem. I can't see. Can you fetch me my robe? It's in the bathroom.'

'I can come back if you like.'

'No! Please, just get me my robe.'

Soft sounds as the maid moved across the room. As she returned, Isla felt the woman lay it carefully on the bed. Cautiously, the maid said, 'Are you okay?'

Her voice was soft with an accent that was hard to place. Eastern European, maybe? Turkish? She sounded gentle, though. Helpful.

'I can't see.' Isla was amazed how calm she sounded. She wanted to scream. 'I could see last night. I fell asleep being able to see. But now I can't!'

'You are blind?'

'Yes.' A rush of horror. Was this aerotoxicity? Had the others gone blind as well?

'My phone. My phone...' She'd left it on the bedside table and now she clutched the duvet to her chest, reaching for it, fumbling through the detritus of eye shades, hand cream, tissues...

'I can pass it to you if you like.'

'Thanks.'

As Isla held out her hand a sob erupted. *I mustn't lose it*, she told herself. *Keep it together. There will be an explanation. You just have to find it.*

'Here.'

She felt the phone in her palm. 'Hello Charlie.' She greeted her intelligent personal assistant. 'Ring Captain Bob Brown for me.'

An electric voice intoned, 'Calling Bob Brown, mobile.'

In the brief silence, she could hear nothing but her heart hammering, feel sweat starting to spring all over her body. Dear God, what was going on? The sob rose and this time, it took an immense effort of will to swallow it down.

It rang three times before it went to Bob's message service. 'Hi Bob, just Isla here. I seem to be having a...' Her voice wobbled and she took a huge breath of air '...bit of a problem with my sight. I just wanted to know if anyone else was too. That's all. Bye.'

She held on to the phone. She was trembling.

'You say you lose your sight over the night?'

'Yes,' she whispered.

'You need a hospital. You must go.'

'I...' Isla put her hand to her face, ran her fingers over her cheeks, her eyebrows, her eyelids.

'Are you in pain?'

'No.'

'This is an emergency. My auntie lost her sight very suddenly one day. She had a stroke. I will ring the hotel doctor straight away.'

Isla heard the maid making a telephone call but she couldn't concentrate. A stroke? Oh my God, did that mean she might not see again? She'd never heard of anyone losing their sight overnight. What was wrong with her? Would she recover? Would she need an operation? Would her sight return as fast as it went?

'The doctor is coming. Now, you let me help you get dressed.'

Isla didn't see she had any choice but to trust her. Besides, the maid was incredibly gentle, and made murmuring soothing noises as she helped her, like she would to a panicky child.

'What's your name?'

'Zamira.'

'Thank you, Zamira.'

After the doctor had seen Isla, he agreed she should go to hospital. 'It might be a transient ischaemic attack but best you get to hospital quick smart. They can do ultrasonography and an MRI along with some blood tests.'

'It couldn't be connected to aerotoxicity, could it?' she asked him.

'I don't know enough about it, I'm afraid.' He was brisk. 'Now, Zamira tells me she'll go with you, is that okay?'

Isla realised she had to trust someone and since Zamira seemed the best bet of the day, she said, 'Okay.'

Twenty-four hours later all the tests had been done. She'd been questioned and prodded and poked, and she was still blind.

18

Tuesday crawled past. Lucy kept looking at her watch as if it would suddenly be 4pm and she could grab her phone and ring her father.

Hi Dad, it's Lucy here. Yup, your daughter. I'm fine, thanks, how about you? Oh, really? I'm so glad you've had such a fantastic life without us, you selfish bastard...

Desperate to distract herself, Lucy tracked down Teflon Tom's phone number through Reg the publican ('Just this once, love, I'm not a telephone directory, aw-right?') but when she rang it went straight to Tomas's messaging service. She dithered about leaving a message or not before deciding to be straight. She told him who she was and why she was ringing, and that although calling him was part of a police investigation it would still be great to see him.

Hanging up, still wanting diversion, she went to see the tech guy who had Kaitlyn's computer. Skinny, glasses, hoodie, he was the living stereotype of a computer nerd. Even his name was nerdish: Albin Kirk. With thoughts of Captain Kirk from *Star Trek* in her mind she almost asked if he was a Trekkie but decided not to go there in case he was insulted. *See?* she told an imaginary Magellan. *I can be as sensitive as the next person if I want to.*

'Any luck?'

'You have no idea how many emails the woman received.'

Apparently Kaitlyn had set up Google Alerts for anything to do with flight EG220.

'There's stuff about the bodies, survivors, witnesses, suspects, Boeings, assembly lines, twin-engine aircraft, flight recorders... you name it, she had it coming in.'

Curious, Lucy had a look over Albin's shoulder. 'How many in a day?'

'Ten years ago, maybe five hundred, but over time she refined her searches so today she gets around a dozen or so.'

'Like what?'

'Like...' He swivelled the screen round so she could see an email, a link to the BBC.

```
EG220   Morocco   plane   crash:   Dead
remembered amid tears.
```

It was dated Monday 11 February. The anniversary of the crash.

The next email alert was headed: `ARINC Standards are prepared by the Airlines Electronic Engineering Committee (AEEC).`

'Anything between her and Ricky?'

'No. They communicated through texts. Do you want to see?'

'Sure.'

Ricky's messages were practical, more about arrangements, but Kaitlyn's were flirtatious and fun and filled with emojis.

Hey you 😊😄 Loved last night. Blue is definitely your colour!

Lucy scanned further down.

Hello handsome. Would you rather work or come play with me?

Ricky had, understandably, said he'd much rather play, to which she'd replied, I'll pick you up from your office in half an hour, yippee!

Ricky obviously hadn't been particularly taken with this idea because he'd immediately responded by saying he'd pick *her* up and after a flurry of messages they settled on meeting at Nopi in Soho before they walked to Piccadilly Circus, where Kaitlyn wanted to take in sights like the Burberry shop and Karl Lagerfeld store.

'Anything from a guy called Hafid Khatabi?'

Albin pointed at an empty swivel chair. 'Park yourself.'

Lucy dutifully parked and wheeled herself to join him. She watched him search Kaitlyn's inbox, outbox, trashed files, cached files.

Nothing on Hafid Khatabi.

'What about Marrakech? Or the Commissariat Central?' Which was where Khatabi worked.

'Loads on Marrakech...'

Alvin continued to tap, his fingers flying, the screen flashing as it changed windows. 'Ah.' He paused. 'I've got a mention of someone called Jibran Bouzid here. She's red-flagged the alert.'

'Let's have a look.'

Albin turned the screen so that they could both read. Jibran Bouzid was mentioned in a blog that had come out of Indonesia on Monday 25 February, from someone called Budiwati, the Wise One. It was written in Indonesian and peppered with photographs of commercial aircraft taxiing, taking off and landing, passengers embarking and disembarking, luggage being loaded and unloaded.

'Can we translate it?'
'Sure.'

A day in the life of a dispatcher. My shift started at 04.30 this morning when I arrived at the inbound aircraft's stand and requested departures teams to start calling passengers to the gate at -30 minutes to departure...

Lucy continued to read, her interest piqued. She'd never appreciated the amount of effort that went into getting her backside onto her aeroplane seat and delivering her safely to her destination along with her baggage. It was impressive and it was also a huge time-waster.

Her gaze snagged on the word *bomb*.

Albin made to scroll the page down but she put out a hand. 'Wait.'

BEWARE FAKE BOMB DETECTORS.

Our security guy here tells me he's been conned. He bought a supply of bomb detectors from Morocco last month and every last one is fake. He's had to ditch them. So who's selling these things? I've heard talk of a man called Jibran Bouzid, but nothing's corroborated so don't quote me. Whoever it is, don't they realise they're putting innocent people at risk? In my opinion they should be strung up. It's my suggestion you test your equipment before implementing it and double-check its authenticity. Or people could die.

Lucy's mind filled with sparks of yellow and white. Using her phone, she searched the internet to find nothing on fake bomb detectors being linked to EG220. Next, she googled the name Jibran Bouzid, who immediately popped up as a Moroccan civil servant and politician, currently serving as Morocco's Defence Minister. Why had Kaitlyn red-flagged the alert?

'I don't suppose our blogger has a phone number,' Lucy said, then, 'not that that's much use if he doesn't speak English.'

'You can drop him an email.' Albin pointed at the little grey envelope at the top of the blog.

'Brilliant.'

Lucy quickly brought out her phone, opened up the blog, and shot off an email, conveniently translated by Google, to Budiwati, the Wise One, adding her phone number in case he *did* speak English. You never knew your luck.

She turned her wrist to see it was 3.53pm. Her stomach gave a lurch. Seven minutes until she called her father. She knew she didn't have to do it at precisely 4pm but if she didn't have some kind of deadline she'd only start procrastinating. She rose to her feet. Wheeled the chair back to where it had come from.

'Thanks, Albin.'

'Any time.'

Lucy decided on the privacy of the soft interview room for her call, as long as it was free, of course. Her heartbeat picked up as she approached the door. Ridiculous. She was only making a phone call but she felt as though she was preparing for her first bungee jump.

She was half-hoping the room was occupied and when she saw it was free, her pulse increased even further. *Come on, it's only a phone call for Chrissake.* She slipped in and shut the door behind her. A sofa, two armchairs, a coffee table, and a potted palm in the corner. She shouldn't really be here but where else was as quiet? Her fingers felt strange as she dialled her father's number.

Hi, it's Lucy. Your daughter.

It started to ring.

Lucy. It's Lucy. You're my dad. Remember me?

It kept ringing. And ringing. Eventually it rang out. No messaging service.

Deflated, she looked at her phone. She'd try him again later.

The door opened and a man walked into the room. Stocky, dark-haired. In one second her pulse went through the roof until she realised it wasn't her attacker from last September.

'You okay?' the man asked. 'You look a bit peaky.'

He was one of the murder squad, first name Simon, if she remembered correctly, and she only remembered it because it was her father's middle name. Carl Simon Davies.

'I'm fine.' Her voice was higher than its normal pitch and she hurriedly cleared her throat. 'I just needed a moment's quiet.'

'Don't we all.' He gave a sympathetic grimace. 'I was just checking the room was free...'

'It is.' She brushed past him, and even though she knew he wasn't her attacker her nerves still spiked. When would she return to normal?

The MIR was buzzing when she walked in, the atmosphere electric. She grabbed the nearest detective. 'What's happened?' God, she hoped she hadn't missed something vital. It would be just her luck.

'We've got CCTV of Kaitlyn scoping out Ricky's office last Sunday. It looks as if she flew in from Morocco and went straight there. She had her suitcase with her.'

'Scoping?'

'Yeah, she was checking it out. You know, looking up and down, peering in the windows.' The detective's eyes were alight. 'She then went to her Airbnb and changed, and guess where she went next?'

Lucy recalled where Ricky and Kaitlyn had met. 'PJ's?'

'Yup.'

'He was a mark.' Everything started to make sense. It wasn't romance, or even finding a rich man to spoil her. 'She targeted him.'

'It certainly looks like it.'

'How did she know he frequented–'

She paused when her phone rang, pressed answer and said, 'One moment...' She pushed her palm over the microphone.

'PJ's,' Lucy finished.

'Believe it or not, it's on his website. His bio. His interests are reading crime thrillers, eating out and going to the movies. He says when relaxing he can be found having a glass of fine wine at his local, PJ's. Apparently he's attracted several clients this way.'

'Because they can't be traced on the phone,' Lucy guessed. 'Ricky was using PJ's as an extended office.'

'That's what we reckon.'

Lucy nodded and turned aside to take her phone call. 'Yes?' she said.

'You called me.' A man's voice, sounding irritated. 'I'm calling you back.'

And she'd asked him to wait. He didn't sound as though he liked being told what to do.

'And you are?' She bet it was Teflon Tom and inside, she cringed. Nothing like starting off on the wrong foot.

'You first. You rang me, remember?'

So, he wanted to play that old game.

'DC Lucy Davies,' she sighed. 'Okay?'

'I'm sorry?' The man sounded startled.

'Lucy Davies. Detective Constable.'

Silence.

'Hello?'

'Lucy? As in Lucy Demi Davies?'

The skin at the back of her neck began to prickle. Nobody knew her ridiculous middle name, chosen by her mother who'd been star-struck by Demi Moore posing naked and pregnant on the cover of *Vanity Fair* just before she was also pregnant, with Lucy.

'Yes.'

'It's me, Lucy. It's your dad.'

19

Dan took a taxi from his *riad* to Commissariat Central. A twenty-minute trip which would have taken ten if a brick lorry hadn't broken down on the Rue el Gza. It was sunny and dry, the sky a clear blue. Twenty-three degrees or so. Not too hot, not too cool. He could see why it was peak season for tourists.

Palm trees lined the road, the green a vibrant contrast against the ochre buildings. He wound down the window. Inhaled a foreign country's scent. Dust and diesel with a hint of cinnamon maybe, but when a waft of dung sailed inside the car, he smiled ruefully. He'd probably imagined the smell of spices.

Three police vans were parked on a broad pavement outside the Commissariat when he arrived. Two cops stood outside, smoking. They watched him out of the corners of their eyes as he pushed open the swing doors into reception. Inside, it was cool. Air-conditioned. Lots of concrete and tiles. A metal double door on the right that was heavily dented from years of abuse. No chairs. No posters. A no-frills station. His footsteps echoed as he approached the desk sergeant. Her hair was scraped back tightly, her dark brown eyes made up to look huge and smoky.

'*Marhabaan*,' Dan said with a smile. Hello.

She nodded. No smile in return.

'Do you speak English?'

A sideways nod that meant maybe, maybe not.

'I have a meeting with Hafid Khatabi. He's expecting me.'

Her perfectly plucked eyebrows rose into peaks. 'And you are...?'

'Chief Inspector Bakkar. Attached to Sûreté Nationale, Rabat.'

She frowned and to his surprise she didn't challenge the fact that he didn't look Moroccan, or speak the language. Nor did she ask for any ID, just picked up the phone and spoke. He hoped she would simply tell Khatabi his name and rank, and that he'd come from the capital. And not mention that he was English.

The receptionist hung up. 'Please wait. He will be here soon.'

He kept his face perfectly neutral even though his nerves tightened. Had his ruse worked?

'*Shukraan.*' Thank you.

He'd downloaded a Moroccan phrase book at home and memorised a handful of words and phrases on his flight. Not much, but enough to be polite. He went and stood with his back to the wall. Kept his arms loose and relaxed.

A uniformed cop strode through the double doors. Flicked a look at Dan, walked outside.

The next person was Khatabi. Dan recognised him from the photograph on Kaitlyn's wall. He was bigger than he'd expected, over six foot, with the broad chest and thick thighs of a rugby player. Dressed in an immaculate uniform, he was staring at Dan as though unable to put the face against whatever picture he'd imagined.

'*Rayiys Almufatishiin?*' Chief Inspector? His voice rumbled loud as a truck.

Dan took a step forward. Put out his hand. 'Nice to meet you.'

The man didn't move.

'You're English?'

'I was on flight EG220. I saved Kaitlyn Rogers' life. And that of her brother. Kaitlyn was murdered four days ago. Friday. I'm working with the investigative team to find her killer.'

Khatabi stared at him some more.

'Murdered?'

'Yes.'

Khatabi's eyed darkened, but what with? Shock? Anger? Disbelief? Dan couldn't tell.

'We know you helped Kaitlyn–'

'We?' A look of alarm crossed the man's face.

'The Kensington and Chelsea Police. London.'

Khatabi gave Dan a long look as though he was committing his face to memory. Then he barked something at the receptionist who jammed her hand beneath her desk, eyes wide and riveted on Dan.

'We know you helped Kaitlyn in her search for justice. She was incredibly grateful. But I'm concerned about the information you gave her, because...'

The door burst open and two cops arrived in a rush. Khatabi snapped out what sounded like several commands, jabbing a finger at Dan. Dan didn't move. Not an inch. He let them take position on either side of him and grab his upper arms and wrists.

'...whatever it was, could have got her killed.'

Khatabi came over. Put his face close to Dan's. 'If you come near me again, I will have you arrested. Our cells are not nice. Not like a hotel. You may suffer some... how do you say it? Accident injuries–'

'Accidental.'

Khatabi's lips turned white. 'You will regret it.' He snapped something at the two policemen. Gripping his arms hard enough to form bruises, they marched Dan outside.

'You helped her,' Dan called over his shoulder. 'I need to know how. I want her killer caught and prosecuted. I'm betting you do too.'

Outside, the cops shoved Dan away from them so hard, the force almost brought him to his knees. He stumbled several times before standing tall. The cops gazed at him, stony-faced. Dan looked blandly back. He gave them a nod. They were only doing their job. He walked away.

He'd already studied the layout of Marrakech and headed south-east, aiming to return to the Medina. As he walked, he listened to the recording he'd made on his phone. Thanks to having kept his phone out of sight and in his jacket pocket, Khatabi's words were muffled. Not that it mattered since Khatabi had probably only said things like *Hit the emergency button* and *Get him the hell out of here*, but at least he had a recording of the man's voice for whatever it was worth.

He'd just stepped through the gates on the northern side of the ramparts when a boy, maybe ten or eleven, scampered up to Dan. Faded jeans, white T-shirt, a bright expression. 'You need help, mister?'

'I'm okay but thank you.'

'You are lost?'

'No. Not lost.'

'Maybe I can guide you? I know the streets inside out and back to front!'

'I'm sure you do.' Dan smiled. 'Do you know where the Tourist Police Office is?'

'Of course. You have been robbed?' The boy pulled a face. 'It happens. There are some scallywags in Marrakech. They give us honest Moroccans a bad name.'

'Scallywags?'

'I learned the word from an English woman.' The boy looked proud. 'I helped her with her travel insurance when her belongings were stolen.'

'That was good of you.'

'Six dirhams, to the front door of the Tourist Police Office,' the boy announced cheerfully.

Fifty pence. Which, considering the average Moroccan earned £70 a week, was a pretty high fee.

'Three dirhams.'

The boy's eyes rounded in horror. 'You're a thief! I cannot walk to the end of the street for less than four!'

Dan tried not to smile but the boy saw it. 'Ha!' he exclaimed. 'Four it is!' He put out his hand. Dan shook. The boy's grip was slim but strong. He was grinning.

'What's your name?'

'Naziha. It means pure, honest.' He puffed out his chest.

'Well, Naziha. Why aren't you in school?'

'School finished an hour ago.' His expression was affronted as if to say, *what do you take me for?! I'd never miss school!*

Dan fished out a five dirham coin. 'Do you have change?'

'Of course.' The boy took the coin and ran into a Maroc Telecom shop. Returned and gravely gave Dan a coin.

Dan liked Naziha, and he seemed to respond to this because as they walked, they chatted about each other's lives. Dan had had croissant for breakfast, but preferred eggs. Naziha had had fruit, but preferred ice cream.

'Ice cream for breakfast?' Dan looked mock-shocked.

'Chocolate is my favourite,' Naziha admitted. 'I would like to eat it for breakfast every day.'

His family lived in a two-room apartment in the Menara district, consisting of a bedroom and living room. They shared their kitchen, laundry and bathroom with his father's brother's family on the same floor. Dan's house sounded like heaven to Naziha.

'You can have your own television,' he said approvingly. 'You can watch whatever you want, whenever you want. You are very lucky.'

'Yes,' Dan agreed. 'I am very lucky.'

Twenty minutes later, Naziha stopped outside a single-storey peach-coloured building with sun-shaded benches beneath the windows and a red flag of Morocco flying from its rooftop. Two mopeds rested outside and a pair of dusty green olive trees flanked the building, giving it a cottagey air.

After paying Naziha for his guidance, Dan stepped inside the tiny police station. Dark and cool. Smells of incense and garlic. Two men in uniform. One was tapping on a computer keyboard at a metal desk while the other leaned against a paint-peeling wall, smoking a cigarette.

The policeman at the desk had grey hair and a weary face. He looked up at Dan without enthusiasm. 'Can I help you?'

A little metal nameplate on the desk read SERGEANT MEHDI.

Dan decided against any small talk about why he was there. He wanted to see their response first-hand, unfiltered. He simply brought out a photograph of Kaitlyn and laid it on the table. 'She was here two weeks ago.'

The second the sergeant's eyes went to the photograph, a tension fell over him.

Dan put another photograph down, and another.

'Do you recognise her?'

Mehdi began to put out a hand, maybe to touch the photographs, or pick them up, but stopped when the other policeman came over and had a look. Broom-thin with a wispy moustache, he ignored Dan. He snapped something in Arabic to the sergeant, who flinched and looked away.

The broom-thin cop swept up the photographs and shoved them at Dan. 'No.'

Dan held up one of the photographs to face Mehdi. 'Her name is Kaitlyn Rogers. I rescued her from flight EG220. I was on board.'

Mehdi's eyes snapped to Dan's. 'You were on the flight?'

'Yes. I saved her life. And that of her brother.'

At that Mehdi stood up. His face was filled with emotion as he came around the desk. He put out his hand. Dan was about to take it when the skinny policeman knocked his colleague's arm aside and, at the same time, spat a stream of angry-sounding Arabic at him.

Mehdi spat something back. Colour rose in his face.

More arguing. Skinny cop flung his cigarette on the tiled floor, crowding Mehdi who refused to back down. Their voices rose until suddenly, they fell quiet.

Skinny cop studied Mehdi for a few moments. The silence dragged on.

Mehdi said maybe five words before the other cop cut him off, making a chopping motion with the edge of his hand.

Another silence fell as the two police officers stared at one another. Repressed violence filled the air. Dan tensed, preparing himself to intervene when suddenly Mehdi made a disgusted sound and spat on the floor. He returned to his desk.

'Sorry,' he said then, firmly, 'good day.'

Dan was dismissed.

20

Naziha was sitting on one of the benches, throwing a stone from hand to hand, but when Dan appeared he sprang to his feet and bounded to Dan's side.

'You were on the aeroplane that was bombed?' He was agog.

Dan looked down at him, then at the window above the bench, which was wide open. 'Yes. What else did you hear?'

'Six dirhams!'

'You've already had five. Two.'

The boy's face fell.

'And a chocolate ice cream,' Dan added.

'I shall tell you everything!' Naziha beamed. 'If you tell me about the crash first!'

Dan gave the lad a brief overview of what had happened. Swapping information seemed only fair.

'You were very brave.'

'I don't know about that. I just did what I did.'

Naziha nodded sagely. 'It was a very bad thing. My grandmother was in the field when it happened. She remembers the tail coming away and a little girl tumbling out. She was still strapped in her seat. She was dead but she had no marks on her.

My grandmother stayed with her all day and through the night while the police and doctors came. She watched over her until she was taken away by the authorities. She called her *almalak alsaghir*. Her little angel.'

The Marrakech bombing had had far-reaching effects, Dan agreed. Kaitlyn and Josh had been orphaned and it was well-documented by the press that Kaitlyn would have given their £8 million inheritance away in an instant if it meant they could have their parents back.

'This girl, the one you saved, is now the woman you are asking about? Kaitlyn Rogers?'

'Yes.'

'Eight million pounds is a lot of money,' Naziha observed. 'But I think she is right. I would miss my mother and father very much if they died.'

Dan bought Naziha his ice cream which they took to a low brick wall surrounding a large date palm. Two tan-coloured kittens played in a patch of sun, coating their fur with dust. Naziha devoured his treat before he proceeded to give Dan a blow-by-blow account of the police officers' quarrel.

'He lied, the first policeman.'

'Mehdi.'

'Yes, Mehdi. He knew the woman in the photographs you showed him. The other man, he didn't want him to tell you this. He got really angry because they had been told not to talk about this woman to anyone.'

Dan didn't ask a question or interrupt. He wanted Naziha to tell the story his own way. He kept his eyes on a man cutting coloured leather with broad scissors in the window of the shop opposite but his attention was totally on the boy.

'Mehdi wanted to help you. The other man, he was shouting that it didn't matter how many people died, it was a long time ago, couldn't he just forget it? Mehdi said no, he couldn't, but the other man got even angrier. He said Mehdi was foolish. He was endangering them both. How dare he?!'

The man in the shop window laid the leather flat and started on another piece.

'That's all.' Naziha kicked his feet.

'Were any names mentioned?'

The boy looked away, biting his lip.

'Naziha?'

'I don't like to say it.' His voice was small.

'Why?'

Naziha was watching a donkey walking past, its male rider sitting side-saddle. 'Because he can be an animal and overhear us.'

'Who?'

'Shaitan.'

Dan waited.

'Shaitan is a bad djin.'

'Ah.'

Dan had heard of djins, the most terrible of supernatural creatures in early Arabian mythology. Able to assume human or animal form and exercising psychic influence over people, djins were revered and feared in equal measure.

'He is evil,' Naziha whispered furtively.

'And the police mentioned this name? Shaitan?'

'Yes.'

'Did the policemen say why they had been told not to talk about Kaitlyn?'

Naziha shook his head.

Dan watched a man in a long striped robe greet the leather cutter who nodded, then reached behind him and brought out a pair of shoes.

'One more thing,' Dan said to Naziha. 'I'd like you to listen to this and tell me what you can hear.' He brought out his phone. Played the recording he'd taken earlier at the Commissariat.

The boy listened intently. 'It's not very clear.'

'I know.'

'Can I hear it again?'

Naziha listened to it three times before he nodded. 'The woman is on the phone saying there is a senior police officer for Inspector Khatabi. Then I hear your voice and a man replies... then the same man orders someone to sound the alarm, that you must be ejected from the building...' Naziha's eyes were wide. 'The last thing he says is that he wants one of them to watch you. He wants to know where you go and who you see.'

He was being followed? Dan fought the urge to look around but with the great throngs of people jostling past with robes disguising their body shapes, hoods their faces, it would be almost impossible to know.

'Thank you.'

Naziha bit his lip. 'You are in trouble?'

Dan sighed. 'I'm asking questions that are making them uncomfortable. I think Kaitlyn, the woman who visited them recently, believed there was more to the air crash than is generally known. I'm trying to find out what.'

Naziha digested this. 'This is a good thing to be doing,' he said decisively. 'Perhaps I can be of more help?'

Dan didn't think having an interpreter was such a bad idea. 'Perhaps tomorrow. After school.' Dan told him where he was staying.

'I will be there!' Naziha raised his hand, palm out, for a high-five.

Dan watched the boy go, half-walking, half-skipping and full of beans. Only when Naziha was out of sight did he go in search of a rental motorbike. Within the hour, Dan was astride a Yamaha Ténéré in pretty decent condition, although the engine wasn't the smoothest. Nor did his helmet fit particularly well, but he wasn't going to quibble.

He rode to the Tourist Police Office and took up position on the opposite side of the road. Both motor scooters were still outside, which he hoped meant that both policemen were still there. Pulling off his helmet he checked his watch: 17:10. He settled to wait. A woman in sun-dulled clothes tried to sell him a tray of eggs. Another offered him a woven basket and when he declined, offered him a plastic bucket.

It was past six o'clock when the shutters of the little police station were closed and the officers stepped outside. Mehdi locked the door while his colleague climbed aboard his scooter and buzzed away. Dan put on his helmet. Mehdi brought out his phone and spoke into it while he pushed his scooter off its stand and mounted. Dan started his Yamaha at the same time as Mehdi started his own engine. The policeman was still talking on the phone as he rode.

Mehdi headed south and out of the Medina. It wasn't difficult to follow him. The road stretched itself into a dual carriageway busy with trucks and buses. Donkeys and carts trundled along the inside lane. Dan tried to see if anyone was following him but couldn't be sure. Too many vehicles, too much dust.

The policeman eventually turned into a quiet street lined with date palms. Square houses with roof gardens and satellite dishes glowing pink in the lowering sun. Dan looked in his rear-view mirror to see a decrepit Mercedes turn after them. Mehdi turned right at the next street and, halfway down, slowed to pull off the road and onto the pavement.

Dan rode straight past. He didn't turn his head or look at Mehdi. He kept going to the end of the street, where he turned left decisively and kept going until he reached the next intersection. Only then did he return.

The Mercedes followed him.

Dan had considered shaking off his tail, but since Khatabi was unaware that Dan knew he was under surveillance, he thought it prudent if it stayed that way. He might be able to use it to his advantage later.

As he slowed to pull off the road, the Mercedes rattled past, its driver staring straight ahead. Nobody else in the car that Dan could see. The man had black hair. Wrap-around sunglasses. Black shirt. Thirties. No distinguishing features. He acknowledged it would probably be difficult to recognise him again.

Dan parked his motorbike outside Mehdi's house. Saw the Mercedes turn around at the end of the street and park on the same side of the road. Dan took off his helmet. Walked to the front door. He raised his hand to pull the bell to one side of the front door but he needn't have bothered because the next second, it opened.

A woman in a brightly patterned over-shirt and jeans said, 'You must go from here.' Her gaze flicked to and away from the Mercedes.

'I want to see Sergeant Mehdi.'

'The night market tonight. Eight o'clock. Stall a hundred and two. Do not come here again.'

21

For a moment, Lucy was so shocked, she couldn't speak.

'Lucy? Are you still there?'

It was her father's voice all right. Strong, masculine. No regional accent. Just straight middle English. It sounded the way it always had.

'Yes,' Lucy croaked. Her mouth had gone dry.

'Hello, love.'

Out of nowhere a memory erupted. She'd been four years old. They'd gone camping in Devon. In a tent, in a field near a beach. She'd gone to the shower block to spend a penny, as her mum called having a pee. When she got there, there was an empty stall but when she went to walk inside it, a girl, older than her, stopped her.

'You can't go in there.'

'Why not?' Lucy started to wriggle. She was desperate to pee.

'Because I say so.'

'But I've got to go!'

'You'll have to do it in your pants.'

Lucy had tried to push past the girl, but she was bigger and forced her back. 'Go in your pants, go in your pants,' she chanted.

Lucy felt a trickle of urine slip down her leg, then a flood. She started to cry.

Suddenly, her father was there, scooping her up, roaring at the girl who went quite white.

Lucy was sobbing into his neck as he carried her back to their tent. 'Why was she so mean? I didn't do anything to her!'

'There are some nasty people in our world, Lucy. I'm sorry you had to meet one quite so soon.'

She had snuggled deeper into his embrace. She felt so safe, so secure. Nothing could harm her when Dad was around.

'Lucy?' Her father's voice on the phone brought her back.

Her throat had closed up. She wanted to cry like she'd done when she was four and have him scoop her up and hold her. She wanted to yell at him, shout herself hoarse with invective.

'I'll call you back.' Her voice was stiff.

'I understand.' His voice was gentle. 'Call me whenever you like. And I'll pick up straight away.'

Lucy hung up. Walked into the corridor and burst into tears. Memories crowded her mind. Dad lifting her from her bed – or was it her cot? – when she was a toddler and carrying her downstairs to show her off to his friends. Teaching her to ride a bicycle without stabilisers, showing her how to tie her shoelaces, collecting her from school, reading her a bedtime story. She could hear his laughter, see the way his eyes crinkled at the corners, the way he'd held her gaze while he lied about why he'd been away all week, why he was leaving them, why he was going to Australia... except he hadn't gone to sodding Australia, had he?

A torrent of crimson abruptly poured through her synapses, dousing her memories with fury. She rang him back.

'Lucy,' he said warmly.

'You didn't go to Australia,' she snapped.

'Who told you that?' His voice was sharp.

She wasn't going to dob Jaya in. Or Reg, for that matter.

'You're in Macclesfield.'

'Not quite,' he said cautiously.

'Why did you lie? I thought you were in Sydney!' The crimson deepened into ruby red and at the same time, her pulse soared. 'Where the hell have you been? Where did you go that day? You left for Heathrow! I saw you! You just about crucified me, you know! And what about Mum? Do you know what you did? How much damage you caused? I guess not, since you swanned off without a backward glance, marching into your sparkling new future, turning your back on your wife and daughter, abandoning them like so much rubbish and–'

She jumped when a hand touched her upper arm. It was one of the constables. He held a finger to his lips. 'You're shouting.' He glanced back at the MIR. 'We can all hear you.'

Shit.

Lucy hauled her temper back. Took a huge breath. The tips of her fingers were tingling. She took another breath. Her father was talking. She nodded at the constable, turned back to her phone.

'...love, I can't tell you how sorry I am.' His tone was penitent, heartfelt. 'I thought it was the best thing, I swear it.'

'The best thing?' She was incredulous.

'It was complicated,' he admitted.

'Because of Tina?' Her pulse was still pounding and her voice began to rise once more. She couldn't seem to stop it.

'Tina?' He sounded baffled.

'The yoga teacher you ran off with!' she yelled.

'Ah.'

There was a small silence. Lucy began to pace up and down, trying to keep some form of control. Then he cleared his throat. 'How are you?'

'How the fuck do you think?'

Another silence.

'So, you're a police officer.'

'No thanks to you.'

'I remember your mum making you police epaulettes after you sat in that patrol car. How old were you?'

'If you don't know, I'm not going to tell you.'

'You'd just turned seven.'

The year before you left us.

'You loved listening to the police radio, I remember. You were fascinated.'

'It's lost its magic by now, trust me.' Her voice was like acid.

He chuckled, seemingly unperturbed at her vitriol. 'I'm not surprised. Did I hear you say you were a DC earlier?'

'Yes,' she reluctantly admitted.

'A detective, no less.' He whistled. 'Congratulations.'

A picture of her mum at her passing out parade flashed across her retinas. She'd sat there on her own as usual, beaming. She'd been so *proud*. Lucy had spent the last twenty years picturing her father on a beach or having a barbecue, doing yoga or whatever the fuck, in the Aussie sunshine, and was having trouble readjusting.

'Didn't you go to Australia *at all*?'

'I think we should have this conversation face-to-face, don't you?'

Lucy hesitated, her mind suddenly darting sideways like a startled fish. What would her mother say?

'I can be wherever you like,' he added.

The words were out before she could stop them. 'I want to

come to you.' *I want to see what you've been up to, if you're living with anyone, what kind of house you're living in…*

'When?'

She took a breath. She didn't want to put it off. She'd go crazy in the meantime. 'This weekend?'

There was a pause. 'Hell. I'm sorry. I'm flying out to America tomorrow. Heathrow.'

She was shaken at the strength of her disappointment. 'For how long?'

'I've got an open return… I do business there a lot. Look, this is such bad timing…' His voice reverberated with frustration. 'How about I call you when I'm back and set something up then?'

Suddenly, she had to see him. Look him in the eye. Kick him, slap him, hug him, she *had to see him. Now.*

'What time's your flight?'

'Eighteen-ten. It means I get in late into New York and can grab some sleep before all the meetings start the next day.'

'Which terminal?'

'Three.'

Lucy nibbled her lip. 'What if I came to Heathrow tomorrow? And we met for a coffee?'

'You'd do that?' He sounded surprised.

'Yes.'

'Lucy…' He sounded overcome. 'That would be seriously great. I would so love to see you.'

Me too, she thought, but didn't say so.

'How about if I find the perfect café and text you where?'

'Okay.'

'Lucy.' His voice softened. 'I can't tell you how much it means that you contacted me.'

Realising she was beginning to soften, she hung up.

Lucy wandered back into MIR in a fog of disbelief. She was going to see her father tomorrow! Then she remembered her mother. She couldn't tell her, could she? Wouldn't it be better if she met with Dad and saw how it went and then... Lucy couldn't imagine how Mum would react. She'd hit the roof, probably, but Lucy couldn't not tell her. Could she?

She was gazing unseeingly at the exhibits desk when a gravelly voice permeated the fog.

'I've got the CCTV for you.'

It was the custody sergeant.

She followed him into a side room where four police officers were studying CCTV footage. These were the guys who'd spotted Kaitlyn scoping Ricky's offices and they were still hard at work, looking for further clues.

The sergeant settled Lucy in front of a computer and screen. Tapped a few times on a keyboard. A grainy picture appeared but it was clear enough to see a slender mixed-race woman, tall, with swishy dark hair scraped into a ponytail. Skirt suit. Whitish ruffled shirt. Briefcase. The woman who'd called herself Chris Malone.

'She looks the part,' Lucy commented. 'But she's an imposter.'

'Who gave Ricky a sandwich with peanuts in it.' The sergeant grimaced. 'I'm not letting anyone, and I mean *anyone*, bring any food inside again.'

Lucy ran the tape several times, trying to commit the woman's face to memory. Chin sharp and narrow. A fine nose. Upper lip fuller than the bottom. She was attractive. Smartly dressed, she wore the suit and heeled brogues as though she was used to them. Perhaps she *was* a solicitor, just not with Pozo and Partners.

'Can I have a couple of prints?'

'Sure. I'll send them to your phone.'

She was studying the way the woman moved – she seemed to favour her right leg slightly, had she had an accident? – when her phone gave a buzz, telling her a text had come in.

I'm at the King's Arms. Join me.

Teflon Tom had summoned her.

22

Lucy nipped home to change before she headed to the pub. Her nerves had got the better of her today and she wanted to shower the stress away, brush up before facing Tomas.

'Hello, love.' Her mother greeted her. 'How was your day?'

Weird. I spoke to Dad.

'Okay, thanks. Yours?'

'I lost one.' Her mother's face lengthened.

'Oh, Mum.' Lucy went and gave her a hug. Her mother was a nurse at St Thomas' Hospital and had been for the past twenty-five years. She was pragmatic, rational, and experienced as hell, but when someone she liked and had cared for died, she really felt it.

'I'm sorry.'

'He was only forty-two. He had three children and a lovely wife... It was an aneurysm.'

Lucy held her for a while.

'You'd think I'd get used to it,' her mother said, pulling back and wiping her eyes.

'I hope you never do. It would mean you'd turned into

Zombie Nurse, lumbering around the wards groaning unintelligibly.'

'No change there, then.'

Lucy gave a snort of laughter.

'Cup of tea?' her mother asked.

'Sorry. I'm on a QTA. Quick Turn Around. I'm seeing Teflon at the pub... Mum, can I borrow a shirt or something? I only planned to spend the weekend away and I'm running a bit short.'

'Sure. You know where my wardrobe is.'

Not for the first time, Lucy was grateful they were the same size and that Mum didn't dress her age: jeans, shirts, leather jackets, scarves, boots. Lucy filched a Metallica T-shirt and a butter-soft tasselled black suede jacket. A quick shower, upside-down blow-dry of her hair, a lick of mascara and she was good to go.

'Thanks, Mum.' She blew her a kiss.

'Say hi from me.'

Teflon was propped against the bar with Ajay when she arrived. Both wore sharp, skinny suits and fitted shirts, but there the resemblance ended. Tomas was pasty white with mousey hair and water-grey eyes, contrasting sharply beside Ajay's dark skin from his Caribbean heritage and his plentiful gold jewellery.

'Hey, DD!' Tomas called. His face split into a grin. 'Lookin' good as usual!'

She was glad she didn't blush. Not like ten years ago, when he'd found out her middle name and called her Delicious Demi, DD. She'd flushed beetroot then, making him and his cronies hoot with laughter. It could have been worse, she supposed, and she was glad she had relatively small boobs, taking the sting out of a nickname where people might assume the DD was for a double D cup-size.

'Vodka and tonic, please.'

'Reg!' he called. 'You heard the lady!'

He pulled out a stool for her but she chose to stand. She nodded at Ajay, who nodded back. 'Any news?' he asked.

She just looked at him.

'Sorry,' he said without looking repentant. 'We're all friends here. At least I thought we were.'

I'm not your friend, she thought. *I'm a fucking policewoman investigating a murder.*

'Sure,' she said, and smiled.

'DD here's one of the sharper pencils in the box,' Tomas told Ajay. 'She won tickets for *Pirates of the Caribbean, At World's End*, for getting the answer first.'

Lucy blinked.

'Don't you remember?' He was grinning. 'Three missionaries and three hungry cannibals have to cross a river using a two-man rowing boat. If on either bank cannibals outnumber missionaries, the missionaries will be eaten. How can everyone cross safely?'

'Good God,' she said. She'd forgotten all about it.

'I really wanted to go.' His gaze turned distant. 'But I was crap at maths. It was the only time I regretted slacking off. Christ, I was jealous...'

She turned her palm out in a commiserating gesture but didn't apologise. She'd been thrilled, and so had her mum. It had been a great movie and a real treat, considering how expensive the tickets had been.

'Eleven one-way trips,' Ajay announced.

'Sorry, mate,' Tomas said. 'You're twelve years too late.'

'But you can always rent the DVD,' Lucy added. 'Or catch it on Netflix.'

Both Lucy and Tomas cracked up.

'On that note...' Ajay was dry. 'I'll see you later, pal.' He bumped fists with Tomas, flicked a salute at Lucy.

'Later,' she said.

She stirred her drink, took a sip. 'So, both you and Ricky have the same solicitor.'

Tomas shrugged. 'We share a racehorse and like bagels too.'

'What about Kaitlyn Rogers?'

'Nah.' He shook his head. 'Never even met her.'

'What about other girlfriends? Did you meet any of them?'

His gaze turned cool. 'You're wearing your cop hat, aren't you?'

'Tomas,' she sighed. 'I'm investigating a murder. What hat would you like me to wear?'

At that, he smiled. His teeth used to be discoloured and crooked, a product of his poor diet and lack of dental care when he was a kid, but now they were strong and straight and bright white. They must have cost a fortune.

'Fair enough,' he agreed. 'You'll get Ricky off, though, won't you? I can't have him inside. Not exactly convenient.'

'Get him off?' She stared at him.

'Poor choice of words. Find him innocent, I meant.'

'That's why I'm on the investigative team.' She slowed her words purposely, as though she was talking to an idiot. 'To find the truth. Bring the killer to justice.'

He saluted. 'Yes, ma'am.' Then he sobered. 'Seriously, Lucy. He's a pal. We're like this.' He twisted his fore and middle finger together. 'Like brothers. Tell me what I can do.'

He was, she thought, just like his dad, with his own sense of justice. She remembered when Stan was jailed, nobody dwelled on the fact he'd swindled dozens of people because just before he was arrested, he'd returned the money to anyone who said they were in financial difficulty. Lucy had read an article on him titled 'Lovable Rogue or Rip-off Merchant?' Stan was both, and she guessed Tomas was cut from the same cloth.

She took a sip of her drink. Thought for a moment. 'When did you last see Ricky?'

'Friday before last. We had a Chinese before we played a game of pool.'

'Where were you?'

'My place.'

He gave her an address in Southwark, in a new residential tower that had spectacular views over Blackfriars Bridge.

'Two bedrooms?' she enquired, ever nosy.

'Three.'

Ten million plus, then.

'Nice,' she said.

He nodded. She liked that he didn't crow over his ill-gotten wealth, or rub it in.

'Did he mention Kaitlyn to you?'

Tomas shook his head. 'Not a word.'

Lucy raised her hand and twisted her fore and middle finger together, eyebrows lifted.

'He met her on Sunday. He only knew her for five days.' His face was surprisingly sad.

Lucy asked him about Ricky's clients.

'I brought most of them to him,' he admitted. 'He was fucking terrible at getting new business but he's a shit-hot accountant and anyone who uses him once, sticks with him. He's good value too. Trust me.' He gave a sigh. 'I'm having another beer. You?'

As they drank, the place began to fill up. Their conversation drifted between Lucy asking questions and Tomas having sudden reminiscences. Including the time he'd hot-wired the head's car and taken it for a joy ride.

'God, his face!' Tomas started to laugh. 'He looked as though he was going to have a heart attack.'

Lucy didn't join in with the laughter. She didn't want to be prissy but she didn't want to condone illegal behaviour, no matter that he'd done it when he was fifteen.

'Sorry.' His eyes were alight, teasing. 'I'd forgotten who I was talking to for a moment.'

'Look, off the record, is there anyone who'd want to stitch Ricky up that you know of?'

'Seriously?' He sucked his lips as he thought. 'Not off the top of my head. But I'll ask around. Let you know. Another?' He nodded at her glass.

'No thanks. Look, before I go...' She brought out her phone and showed him the photograph of the woman who'd called herself Chris Malone. 'Do you recognise her?'

He would never normally have shown a flicker of emotion but today, drinking with an old school friend, he'd dropped his guard. His face contracted. He knew her.

'Who is she?'

She could almost hear the gates being slammed shut, the drawbridges being drawn up. But it was too late. He'd given himself away.

'Dunno. Never seen her before.'

'Come on, Tomas. It's me here. I know you're lying. You *know her*.'

'No. I Do. Not.' His eyes chilled, turning the colour of dirty ice, and for the first time she saw the hard man he was behind the old schoolboy bonhomie.

'She tried to kill Ricky.'

Lucy could have announced she was going to be the next woman in space for all the response he gave. He was cold and unapproachable. She watched him down the rest of his pint.

She'd left her phone on the bar with the photograph of Chris Malone open but he was taking care not to look at it.

'Aren't you interested in why she poisoned him?'

He put his glass down with more force than was necessary.

'No.' But he didn't move.

'I think it's because Ricky knows something dangerous. Maybe he saw the killer. Maybe one of his clients wants him out of the way. He's in a trusted, confidential position as their accountant. He might have information someone doesn't want shared.'

Tomas turned his head. Looked her, expression cold. 'I'd be careful, if I were you. You dig too deep, you might not like what you find.'

She could feel her eyes widen. 'Are you threatening me?'

At that, he deflated. Ran a hand over his head. 'Fuck, no. I just don't want you to... *fuck*.'

She watched him with interest. He was conflicted. Angry. Anxious.

'What's wrong?'

'It was nice to see you.' His tone was stiff.

'You too.'

'But I don't think we'll be doing it again.'

He threw a couple of twenties on the bar and stalked outside without looking back.

When Lucy got home, her mother was in front of her laptop in the kitchen, frowning. A glass of wine sat at her elbow.

'You're not working, are you?' Lucy asked. 'It's getting late.'

'I'm trying to help a friend with a diagnosis in Chelsea and Westminster...'

As her mother picked up her phone, Lucy walked to the fridge. Had a look to see what she might have for supper.

'Claire?' her mother said. 'I wouldn't think it's aerotoxicity. You can get blurred and tunnel vision sometimes, but going blind overnight? I'd look for something more logical, like a stroke or TIA, or maybe a retinal detachment...'

Lucy's stomach squirmed. She'd always been a bit squeamish about eyes, and the thought of her retinas detaching made her feel slightly sick.

23

Isla was waiting for her evening hot chocolate to arrive with Emily, her best friend who'd dropped everything to fly over from LA on Sunday. She didn't think she would have got through the last couple of days without her. Em had been with her every step of the way as each test was undertaken, and by her side when the results were reported. Nothing had shown up on the CT scan or the PET. Now, they were waiting on the MRI results.

She had her earbuds in and was listening to Radio 4 on her phone, a First World War drama based on the lives of real people. She'd never listened to the radio like this before and found it not just absorbing but immensely comforting. While she listened to a live broadcast, she felt that the world was a safe place to be, people still walked to work, took buses, went to a pub, a cocktail bar at the end of their day.

How was she going to cope doing normal things if she couldn't see? She'd have to get a white stick... What about a guide dog? How did you get one of those? How the hell did you feed it, or pick up its poop if you couldn't fucking *see*?

'Isla Hanson?' a man called, interrupting her increasingly panicky thoughts.

She pulled out one of her earbuds, tapping her finger over the face of her phone, trying to find the pause button.

She heard the squeak as the door opened further. Thanks to the airline's health scheme, she had a private room. She didn't think she could have borne being in a ward with strangers.

She tapped some more, but the radio continued to play. She heard him step inside the room.

'Can I help?'

'I'm okay, thanks.' He might run off with it for all she knew.

'Charlie,' she snapped. 'Switch off the radio.'

Silence. Thank God for voice commands. She pulled out the other earbud. 'Yes?'

Her pulse had picked up, her heart beating faster than normal. Without her sight, she was constantly being put under pressure. She'd never felt so vulnerable before, so *helpless*. She lifted her chin, fixing her gaze on the space where she guessed he would be.

'My name's Nykko. I'm from the *London Herald*. I spoke with Grant Newman and Liz Moss this afternoon. They told me about your situation.'

Her colleagues had been really ill over the last few days, with severe physical symptoms that had kept Liz in hospital and Grant in his hotel room. They'd suffered nausea, fatigue, blurred vision and tremors, but they hadn't lost their sight.

'We talked at length about aerotoxicity. Have you been tested?'

She didn't think so but was reluctant to say anything. He'd said he was a journalist. She wasn't sure if she should trust him.

'Bob Brown told me to come and see you. He's really concerned for you. For all of you.'

'Captain Brown?'

'Yes. He's convinced you're all suffering from aerotoxicity. Have you had your blood tested for auto antibodies?'

'I'm not sure.'

'Oh.' He sounded taken aback. 'Are they biomonitoring your blood?'

'Er...'

'What about your urine? It could show 2-Hexandion or acetone, o-Kresol. This could indicate aerotoxic syndrome.'

Isla plucked at her bedsheet.

'I'm sorry.' He sounded genuinely regretful. 'It must be really weird having me ask you about this, but having seen Liz and Grant, I'm a bit concerned that you're not being tested for the same things.'

Isla bit her lip. 'I don't think they're looking at aerotoxicity in my case. I'm being tested for cancer, brain tumours, that kind of thing.'

'Oh.' He sounded taken aback. 'Perhaps they're unaware how horrific breathing contaminated air can be.'

Isla's anxiety rose. 'I did mention it.'

'But they didn't take you seriously.'

'Well, I wouldn't say that...' She wished Emily would get here. Or a nurse. She wasn't comfortable with the conversation.

'Most physicians have never heard of the term aerotoxic syndrome.' He sighed. 'I've known them diagnose sufferers as having psychological or psychosomatic disorders. One doctor told a Flying Bear flight attendant it was all in his mind. His condition worsened because it wasn't treated properly. He died in August.'

She didn't know how to respond to that, so she remained silent. She heard him move to one side of the room. He wore soft-soled shoes, slightly squeaky. She turned her head to follow him.

'It makes me so angry when this happens,' he went on. 'The

supposed experts closing their minds to reason. You must tell them it's the toxic chemicals in the fumes that attack the central nervous system, which consists of the spinal cord and the brain. That's neurological, isn't it?'

She grew alarmed. 'Yes.'

He moved back to the centre of the room. 'Get them to test you, okay?'

'Okay.'

'Whether it's aerotoxic syndrome or something else, I really hope you get better soon. You're a beautiful woman, you shouldn't have to have your life sabotaged like this.'

24

Dan sat with a glass of mint tea on the balcony of the Café Glacier, looking down at the bustling open square of Djemaa el Fna. There were dancers, acrobats and musicians. Orange juice sellers and snake charmers playing hypnotic melodies on flutes to make their cobras dance. Women offered henna tattoos while others sold souvenirs, candles, leather bags and baskets from where they squatted on the ground.

He checked his watch: 19:45. Lots of time.

He studied the square for a while, making sure he'd get his bearings amid the chaos before committing himself. Finally, he descended to ground level and immersed himself in the turmoil. Long rows of dining stalls were lit by strings of electric lights, everything blurred by great clouds of smoke wafting from cooking fires. Cumin, garlic, ginger. His mouth watered.

Stall 102 looked identical to all the others and was crowded with locals as well as Western tourists. A man in a white chef's coat invited Dan to sit on a stool and enjoy some koftas. Olives and bread were put in front of him. Dan ordered some spiced tea.

19:55.

CJ CARVER

People jostled past, occasionally bumping into him, apologising at the same time as they walked on. He pretended to watch a beggar working the table, selling packs of tissues, but his attention was all around, senses alert and aware of the sound of chattering, oboes playing and drums beating, the strong smell of hashish.

An uneasy movement in the crowd caught his interest. He wasn't surprised to see it was Mehdi, looking over his shoulder, expression apprehensive. When he caught Dan's eye he smiled, something in him relaxing. He was an ordinary-looking man of average height, dressed in ordinary trousers, a striped shirt and leather shoes. Someone you wouldn't look at twice except for the steadiness in his eyes that spoke of an inner strength, hinting he might be an individual you could depend upon.

Dan rose to greet him. Mehdi offered his hand. Dan shook it but the man put out an arm and hugged him.

'For saving those children,' he said, his voice thick with emotion. 'I remember it so well. You were a hero.'

'You were there?'

'I was one of the first responders. It was terrible...' He shook his head. 'I still dream about it. The devastation... charred remains. A toilet seat here, a guidebook there. Suitcases, shoes, magazines, clothes. Entrails, body parts everywhere. It was like hell.'

'Did we meet back then?'

'No. But we all knew who you were. You looked after those children, became their unofficial guardian. You flew back to the UK with them.'

MI5 wouldn't have liked that, Dan thought. He'd obviously felt responsible for the children, taking them under his wing. And having seen his father's emails to Kaitlyn over the years, his father had obviously helped too.

The chef came over and Mehdi rose. They kissed cheeks,

greeting one another affectionately before Mehdi turned to introduce Dan.

'Dan Forrester,' he said, 'this is my good friend, Mohammed.'

Dan shook the man's hand.

'Sit, sit,' Mohammed said. 'I will bring the food.'

They sat back down. Mehdi broke some bread and dipped it in olive oil. Dan did the same.

They made small talk. Mehdi had two grown-up children and three grandchildren, all toddlers. His wife was called Anisah and they'd been married for twenty-eight years. As he spoke of his family, the sergeant's eyes softened.

When dishes of sardines and calamari were placed before them, Dan thought it was time to open the subject. 'You saw Kaitlyn recently.'

'Just over two weeks ago. She walked in from the street. She wanted to make a report.'

Dan heard a motorbike approaching. He hadn't seen any motorised vehicles in the market and its presence made him look around, but he couldn't spot it through the crowds.

'I told her we were Tourist Police, that we couldn't help. I directed her to the Commissariat.'

'She went?'

'Yes, she made her report to Commissaire Hafid Khatabi.'

Hafid Khatabi had helped her, Dan thought, but didn't want to be involved any more.

The motorbike was closing in. Dan twisted sideways, trying to peg it. 'What was she reporting?'

'She'd met with a man called Commandant Jamal Azoulay.'

'In the army?' Dan raised his eyebrows.

'An officer. His rank is equal to your British major. Not so high.'

'Which division?'

Mehdi frowned as he thought.

Dan caught the flash of the motorbike's headlights and turned his body, nerves tightening, and at the same time there was a flurry of movement from the beggar and Mehdi gave a groan and fell sideways. The beggar had dropped his tissues and to his horror, Dan saw he was withdrawing a long, broad blade from Mehdi's shoulder. It had been pointing downward at a forty-five-degree angle. Straight at Mehdi's heart.

Dan leaped up, shouting, 'Mohammed!'

Images came to him like photography stills. Mohammed lunging for his friend. The motorbike roaring into view. The beggar springing back, trying to hide his knife in his robe. People's faces, slack with shock.

Dan launched himself at the beggar but the man was fast and slipped behind a pedestrian, raced for the motorbike.

Ignoring the beggar Dan went for the bike, barging people aside. He fixed his eyes on the rear tyre, just yards away, saw the beggar swing his leg over the back of the bike and as the engine lifted, preparing to accelerate, Dan flung himself forward in a messy, flailing rugby tackle. Right shoulder down, he crashed into the bike, taking down several pedestrians as well as his prey.

Shouts and yells. Someone screamed.

He swarmed over the bike, going for the beggar, but the man was already up and running away. The driver of the bike was kicking at Dan, yelling at him. He was just a kid, maybe sixteen or so, but Dan grabbed him and hauled him upright, and punched him hard on the side of the chin, where the jaw was attached to his skull. The boy's eyes rolled upwards. Dan let him drop to the ground unconscious and tore after the beggar, following the sounds of shouts and protests ahead, praying the man would continue to flee and not drop to walking pace and blend in with the crowd or he'd never find him.

Dan charged forward, elbowing his way past the crowds,

ignoring the protests, and then suddenly there was a clear patch of ground and dead ahead, the beggar running flat out for the souk.

Dan sprinted after him.

He tore across the entrance walkway lined with old men in robes, sitting silently. Their heads turned to follow him as he ran past.

A sea of colour enveloped him as he dived into the souk, tearing past stalls selling jars of olives, silver tea sets, ornate lamps, carpets. At the next junction, the beggar ducked right and for a moment Dan thought he might lose him – he'd know the rabbit warren like the back of his hand, wouldn't he? – but when he tore around the corner he realised he was gaining on him.

Dan increased his speed.

Their footsteps hammered on the ground. People stared as they flashed past. And then the beggar looked over his shoulder. A fatal mistake. He faltered, nearly tripped, and Dan was on him as fast as a leopard, piling into him and slamming him to the ground.

The man was smaller than Dan, light-boned, and Dan hauled him upright. Put his hands around the man's throat and squeezed. He was panting hard, the man gasping.

'Who sent you?'

The man's eyes were wild, terrified, his mouth open.

'*Who sent you?*' Dan roared.

The man kicked at Dan, tried to hit him, but Dan was far stronger. He shook him like a terrier would a rat. The man's face darkened as the blood filled his face. He plucked at Dan's arms. Turned puce.

Dan released his grip a little. The man took a gulp of air.

'Jibran,' he choked. '*Wazir aldifae–*'

His words were snatched away when Dan felt something hit

him very hard between the shoulder blades. Dan's grip on the man's throat slipped. He tried to grab the beggar again but someone punched him on the back of the head and suddenly there were three men attacking him.

The beggar turned and ran.

Dan tried to follow but the men stopped him, hitting him, slapping him and shouting. One of them was wielding a walking stick, another a tea tray.

Dan threw a jab at one man, felt it connect. Kicked another hard on the knee. A gap opened up and Dan went for it, pelting past the men and after the beggar, but his attackers had given his quarry the advantage and when he came to the next corner, the beggar was nowhere to be seen.

Dan didn't give up. He quartered the area, watching out for anyone taking more-than-usual interest in him, any abnormal movement or behaviour.

Nothing.

The beggar, the assassin, had vanished.

25

Dan headed back to the main square. As he walked, he thought of the decrepit Mercedes that had followed him from Mehdi's to his *riad*. Since he was under surveillance, he assumed he'd been followed to the night market but he then realised the beggar, the assassin, had been selling packs of tissues at the table when he arrived.

His apprehension grew as he thought further. It was a professional hit, he was certain. Knifing someone like that to reach the heart from behind was very difficult to pull off. How had they known Mehdi would be there? Or was it an opportunistic move? Kill anyone who met Dan that night? That would be ridiculous. Mehdi had been the target. When he'd visited Mehdi's house earlier, had the Mercedes driver been able to hear what the woman in jeans had said?

The night market tonight. Eight o'clock. Stall a hundred and two.

If so, it would mean a listening device of some sort. Something sophisticated and extremely sensitive. The only other explanation would be that the woman – Dan had assumed she was Mehdi's wife – had betrayed him, but it didn't feel right.

She'd been protective, shielding her husband. Angry too that he'd come to their house.

Mohammed was nowhere to be seen when he returned to the stall, but when the second chef saw Dan, he came over.

'They go in the ambulance. Mehdi...' His face lengthened. 'He is dead.'

Dan felt his heart hollow. 'I'm so sorry.'

'Mohammed wanted your telephone number.'

Dan gave it to the man. He saw no reason not to, not when Mehdi had been killed.

'Please, also... He tells me, do not go to the police. Not until Mohammed calls you. Okay?'

Dan thought it over, and since the cons far outweighed the pros, he agreed. Plus, the last thing he felt like was spending the night being interrogated. 'Did the police get the boy I knocked out?'

The chef shook his head. 'I was trying to help Mehdi and didn't see the boy wake up. He took off on the bike.'

You win some, Dan thought with a sigh, you lose some.

He walked to his *riad*. Now the adrenaline had gone, he felt peculiarly weak, and his knees were trembling. He was also ravenously hungry, another sign of the adrenaline draining from his body. He bought a double kebab wrap from a street seller and ate it as he walked. The streets had quietened. He checked for a tail but nobody appeared to be following him. Probably because they already knew where he was staying. He entered the *riad* courtyard with a sense of relief. A tray of welcome drinks was set on a table and Dan picked up a glass of orange juice, drank it, then picked up another and took it to the padded seat that encircled the large palm tree. He stared up at the sky, surprised to see so many stars. Slowly, he felt himself relax. His shoulder began to throb. His fists ached. Gradually, he let his mind drift.

Kaitlyn had gone to the police station wanting to report her meeting with Commandant Jamal Azoulay from Rabat. Why not lodge her report with the Rabat Police? Was it because she didn't trust the police there, or was it because the army was involved in the bombing? If so, why? He let his mind drift further. Had flight EG220 been the target, or someone specific on board?

'Hello.' A shy voice broke into his reverie.

Naziha stood just outside the door, looking in.

'Hello.' Dan beckoned the boy inside. 'Why aren't you at home?'

'They're watching something boring on TV so I came here to see you. Can I help you? Maybe find somewhere to eat?'

'I've eaten but thank you.'

'You are tired,' the boy observed.

'Yes.'

'I will come back tomorrow.'

'After school.'

Naziha nodded.

In his room, Dan rang Jenny. Told her about the night market, the Barbary macaques, an endangered species of monkey being paraded by photo-touts for money.

'That's awful. Poor monkeys.'

'It's a different world out here. But it's beautiful. Ancient. You inhale history on every corner. You'd love it.' He didn't mention his mission and Jenny didn't ask. After he'd spoken to Aimee, he hung up. Lay on the bed with his hands behind his head, thinking. After a while, he checked the BBC website. Checked his emails. Showered, went to bed. He slept restlessly, disturbed by images of knives and blood, the sound of Mehdi's deep groan of agony.

The morning call to prayer washed over him in waves. Soft light bathed his room in buttery tones. He reached for his phone to see nobody had rung, and that none of his emails needed an immediate response. He clicked on the BBC News website. Flicked through the headlines and paused when he thought he recognised someone. A woman, mid-twenties, raven black hair, her face sharp and pale. Blue eyes and blush-pink lips, perfectly made-up.

He stared at the photograph, momentarily shocked. It was Isla, the flight attendant from his Miami flight.

EGRET AIR FLIGHT ATTENDANT BLINDED BY AEROTOXIC SYNDROME DOCTOR SUGGESTS

Isla Hanson, from Los Angeles, went blind overnight in her hotel in Kensington, London, on Saturday 9 March.

Initial tests failed to find the cause of her blindness and when asked if she'd been tested for aerotoxic syndrome, she said she 'wasn't sure' but that she wanted more tests done after learning that James Matthes, aged 31, a long-serving Flying Bear Air steward, may have died from toxic air syndrome in August last year, as a medical examiner in the United States indicated yesterday.

Isla had been blinded overnight? She'd be terrified, poor woman. He read on to learn that although her parents couldn't fly to be with her – no reason was stated – her best friend Emily was there.

After scanning the rest of the news, Dan rose, got dressed. Went to the roof of the *riad* where breakfast was served. The sun was already hot and he chose to sit in the shade. Breakfast was brought to him: a plate of fresh fruit, eggs and croissant, a coffee carafe. Sounds from the streets below drifted around. Pots banging, people talking, the put-put of a motorbike. His phone vibrated on the table. He didn't recognise the number.

'Hello?'

'It is Mohammed.'

Dan started to open his mouth to say he was sorry, how saddened he was about Mehdi, but Mohammed immediately added: 'We must meet.'

'Okay.' Dan was cautious.

'You go to my brother's shop.' Mohammed gave him an address as well as directions. 'In one hour. Say you are looking for a gift, an embroidered fez. Okay?'

'Okay,' Dan repeated.

Dan checked the internet to see the shop sold traditional men's clothing. Set inside the city walls it wasn't far, so Dan finished his breakfast. Legs stretched out, drinking the last of his coffee, he texted Jenny and Aimee. Jenny texted back. All was well at home, releasing him to concentrate on the job in hand. Finding Kaitlyn's killer.

He took a long, roundabout route to the shop, doing his best to try not to be followed, but it was almost impossible to discern a pattern or remember a face in the constantly moving crowd of assorted races and dress.

The shop was quiet inside. Men's shirts lined one wall, along with shelves of fezzes, hats and scarves. Djellabas lined the other, some plain, others striped, some with hoods, some without. A man stepped forward, inclining his head in greeting.

'*Marhabaan.*'

'*Marhabaan,*' Dan responded, looking around the shop. 'I am looking for a gift, an embroidered fez.'

'Please.' The man walked to the rear of the shop and pulled back a curtain. 'Come this way.'

Dan followed him into a backroom where two women were sewing, a young man tapping figures into a calculator which he immediately put aside when they entered. Rising swiftly, he moved into the shop, to cover the older man's absence, Dan assumed.

'Here.' The man took a grey-striped djellaba from a hook and passed it to Dan, gesturing for him to put it on. Dan did as he was bidden. The man then signalled for him to pull up the hood and beckoned him to follow.

Outside, in a narrow alleyway, a youth sat astride a motorbike. He nodded at Dan, twisting to point at the seat behind him. Hitching up his djellaba, Dan climbed on board. As soon as he was settled the youth started the bike and headed down the alley. At the end, he turned left into a street busy with traffic and pedestrians, then right, and left again, weaving his way expertly through the Medina, dodging scooters and shoppers, bicycles and hand-drawn carts, until finally they nipped through the orange-red clay gates of the old Medina and were buzzing down a main road with buses and Mitsubishi trucks for company.

They rode for over an hour before turning off the main road and onto a rough, pitted dirt track. They passed a man on a donkey, riding side-saddle. A couple of scooters. Gradually, they began to climb. Stones spat beneath the tyres. Goats grazed the verges. They came to a concrete house. Bright blue sky swept over a bowl of hills, leading to a wall of white-capped mountains in the distance. After the dust and bustle of Marrakech, the air felt clean and pure.

The youth pulled the bike to one side. Stopped the engine. Dan looked down the hillside. Nobody appeared to have followed them and if they had, they would have had to have dropped well back to avoid being seen.

The young man gestured for Dan to dismount. Together, they walked to the house, stepped inside.

'*Alab!*' the youth called. '*Nahn huna!*' Father, we're here!

His voice echoed across the tiled courtyard. Dan took in the ornamental waterfall, the heavy wooden chairs and benches, the bright wall hangings, the faint scent of incense.

Mohammed appeared. He kissed the youth on both cheeks before sending him away. Then he said to Dan, 'Come.'

Dan followed Mohammed through the house. Ochre walls, ornate mirrors, colourful rugs. Nerves alert, but not in overdrive – he didn't feel threatened – he entered a room painted a peaceful blue, which overlooked a tiled terrace. A woman sat beside a bed, reading. She looked up at him, then at the bed.

Dan walked across. Looked down.

A pair of brown eyes looked steadily back.

'Dan Forrester,' the man said.

Dan felt a euphoric rush of relief. 'Mehdi. Thank God.'

26

'We've charged him,' announced the SIO. 'But be warned. The CPS want us to seal this. Watertight.'

Jaya would be devastated, Lucy thought. Thanks to Ricky being their only suspect, the chances of him being allowed out on bail was infinitesimal. He'd be with them for a while yet.

'There are still lots of questions unanswered and I want every base, every angle covered.' Jon Banks's eyes clicked to Lucy. 'I want Lucy to keep on top of Teflon Tom. Find out how he knows Chris Malone. *Who* Chris Malone is. Why she tried to kill Ricky with a sodding peanut butter sandwich... Revenge for killing Kaitlyn? And who knew Ricky was allergic? His family, his friends... I'm still not convinced that Tomas didn't have a hand in this...'

His eyes roved the room as he doled out tasks to the team. 'I want every one of Ricky's clients answered for. I want to know which ones Tomas knows, what nasty little deals they've been doing. I want to know everything about Ricky, what makes him tick, if he has a temper on him, if he's ever threatened a woman, a girl, a school friend...'

Once again, his gaze landed on Lucy. 'I want to know if Tomas moved in on Kaitlyn, did Ricky see red?'

Anyone could see red, given the right circumstances, but in this case, Lucy wasn't convinced. Even if Kaitlyn had a relationship with Tomas, would Ricky have killed her for it? Wouldn't he have gone for Tomas?

As the SIO wound up the meeting, her phone buzzed. Her stomach gave a lurch when she saw it was a text from her father.

Caffè Nero, terminal 3 arrivals hall, midday. OK?

Lucy checked out the café on the net then checked the journey times out to Heathrow. Lastly, she checked her watch: 9:25. She'd catch the Heathrow Express later in the morning, and link to Terminal 3 on the tube.

In two and a half hours I get to see Dad! Will he look the same? Of course he won't, you idiot, he's fifty-one now, not thirty-three... will he have gone grey? Put on weight? What's he been doing if he hasn't been in Australia? Why America? What business is he in?

Questions buzzed around Lucy's head like a swarm of bees, the colours confused, rioting rainbows. Excitement warred with apprehension until she began to feel nauseous.

Desperately needing a distraction, she grabbed a desk and tried to immerse herself in Ricky's list of clients. They ranged from scrap-metal merchants to car dealers, a chain of pharmacies, engineering and chemical firms, food processing plants, but by far the biggest were the property developers, one of whom appeared to have struck a deal with one of the car dealers to buy their land for an exorbitant price. Planning permission for two blocks of flats was apparently being sought. Lucy thought of Tomas's luxurious millionaire's pad overlooking the Thames and sighed. Fingers and pies. Money laundering. Favours rendered. How to unravel things?

She went and fetched a good old-fashioned pad of paper and a pen and started drawing a diagram of which companies did business with which. Charles Tyne Associates seemed to be involved quite a bit along with a manufacturing company in Wolverhampton.

As she drew lines and made notes, she still couldn't help looking at her watch. Time couldn't crawl any slower, could it?

'Got to be somewhere?'

It was Jon Banks, the SIO.

She looked at her watch again and saw that, thank God, it had staggered to 10.30am. It would probably only take an hour to get there, but she didn't want to be late.

'Yes.' She jumped up, nerves crackling. 'I'll be back two-ish.'

He raised his eyebrows.

'An old school friend,' she lied. 'To see if Ricky has a temper on him.' She grabbed her bag and scooted outside before he could ask anything further. She didn't like lying but needs must. She was going to see Dad!

She spent the journey gazing unseeingly down each train carriage, her nerves winding tighter and tighter, until she thought she might start screaming. Christ knows how she was going to react when she saw him. Shout? Fall speechless? Faint? And what about Dad? What was he going through? He'd sounded really keen to see her, really pleased. Why hadn't he kept in touch?

Lucy galloped off the train and into the terminal. Shiny floors, bright lights, echoing spaces. She found the café. Checked the time. Half an hour early. She didn't care. She walked up and down the terminal, heart beating fast, trying to keep calm and stop her mind from going crazy. Impossible. Her emotions were at fever pitch and when her phone rang she snatched it out of her bag. *Please don't let it be him cancelling. Please please please...*

But when she checked the display it wasn't her father's number, nor was it her mother's. International.

'Hello?'

'DC Davies?' a man asked. 'Lucy Davies?'

His voice was accented, what with she couldn't say. It was very foreign, the inflection unrecognisable to her ears.

'Yes. I'm DC Davies.'

'My name is Osbert Rahmat.'

Lucy frowned. She didn't recognise the name.

'I am head of security at Soekarno-Hatta International Airport. A dispatcher here runs a blog under the name Budiwati out of Indonesia. You sent him an email?'

Lucy nearly dropped her phone in amazement. Budiwati the Wise One was making contact!

'That's correct.'

'I am sorry that Budiwati only has a basic grasp of English. Which is why it is me who is calling.'

Lucy moved aside as a burqa-clad woman walked past with two massive suitcases the size of wheelie bins.

'In your email, you ask about the blog he wrote about the false bomb detectors.'

'That's right. He said they came out of Morocco.'

'Correct. I had to destroy them. It has cost us a lot of money. It was a scam… a very dangerous scam, selling equipment that doesn't work. I am very concerned, very angry. You must find the person behind this and stop them. Prosecute them.'

Lucy thought fast. It wasn't her jurisdiction but she didn't want to say so and piss him off. 'I'll do what I can. Do you have any shipping paperwork?'

'I shall email it to you.'

'Thanks.' Lucy thought of Kaitlyn red-flagging Budiwati's alert and said, 'Can I ask, did anyone else contact Budiwati from England about this?'

'Please, wait a moment. I shall ask him.'

She heard men's voices. Behind her eyes, colours ran vivid orange and yellow. The head of security and Budiwati. How brilliant was that?

'Yes, he tells me a woman called Kaitlyn Rogers emailed him. She was on the EG220 flight that was bombed sixteen years ago. Do you know it?'

'Yes.'

'She wanted to know the name of the company that sold us the defective detectors.'

'Did you give it to her?'

'Yes. It is on the shipping document. Tazi & Company, Rabat. I also told her that when we investigated, we found the company doesn't exist. They took our money and vanished.'

'Did she ask anything else?'

Again, the head of security spoke to Budiwati.

'No. But we will forward the messages to you for your investigation.'

'That's fantastic. Thank you so much.'

'We will do it straight away. Please, catch these people. It is not just the money we have lost, but we are concerned the fake detectors are being sold elsewhere.'

He was winding down the conversation and for a moment, she hesitated to mention Kaitlyn's murder. But what if the killer came after the Indonesians? She couldn't see why, but since connections were strengthening between the aircraft bombing and Morocco, now Indonesia, she told him. Predictably, he was shocked.

'This is a murder investigation?' said Osbert, sounding disbelieving.

'Yes.'

She heard Osbert talking fast to Budiwati. Their voices grew in pitch, urgent and anxious.

Finally, Osbert returned. 'Do you think this shipment has anything to do with her death?'

'I'm not sure.'

He left her for another chat to the Wise One. While they jabbered excitedly, Lucy paced, her mind bouncing here and there like a pinball. Had Kaitlyn found Tazi & Co? Uncovered who was selling the fake bomb detectors in Morocco? She couldn't think how this was connected to Kaitlyn's flight catastrophe. Morocco wasn't a half-baked country who'd use sub-standard bomb detectors. Their security organisations were top-drawer professionals, it just didn't seem possible.

Why had Kaitlyn contacted Budiwati? Lucy abruptly recalled Kaitlyn's email alert. It hadn't been for fake bomb detectors, but for someone called Jibran something... what was his name? She'd just checked the notes she'd made on her phone – *Jibran Bouzid* – when a man said behind her, 'Lucy.'

It was her dad.

27

He was smaller than she remembered. Not that he was small by any means, being five eleven or so, but in her memory, he was a giant. He had grey speckles through his hair and lines on his face. Laughter lines and of stress, of life, but the wicked twinkle in his eye was the same.

He was beaming ear to ear.

Any thoughts of hitting or hugging him no longer existed – she was totally focused on the phone conversation, the lead she was chasing.

She pointed at her phone and turned away.

A wailing child forced Lucy to duck her head and put her left hand over her ear when Osbert came back to her. 'Miss Rogers' murder is deeply unsettling... Please can you keep us informed?'

'Of course. But there's one more thing. Budiwati mentioned someone called Jibran Bouzid in his blog. Can he tell me anything more?'

Brief hiatus as Osbert conferred. When he returned his voice was cautious.

'Jibran Bouzid is the Defence Minister of Morocco. There

were rumours he might be involved in selling the defective detectors, but that's all they are. Rumours.'

Lucy made another promise to keep the Indonesians in the loop before she hung up. Turned to her father who was shaking his head slowly, gazing at her as though unable to believe his eyes.

'Lucy.'

Thanks to being on the phone when he'd arrived, her emotions were more settled and she could look at him now with a degree of self-control.

'Dad.'

He opened his arms and waggled his fingers just as he used to do to encourage her to leap into his embrace.

She felt a rush of affection – love? – but took a step back.

'Oh, come on,' he teased. 'Can't you give your old man a hug?'

The child in her was begging to be hugged, but the adult was resentful and bitter until she remembered why she was here. *You nearly died last year. You made yourself a promise...*

'You bastard,' she said, but her tone was tempered. She was shaking her head as she stepped into his embrace.

He held her close, a proper hug, and she felt him press a kiss on the top of her head. She shut her eyes briefly. Squeezed him back. It felt strange and slightly weird – the only men she'd hugged in the past twenty years had been Nate, her ex, and then Mac – but it also felt absolutely right.

'You're beautiful,' he told her.

'You're older.'

'Thanks a bunch!' He stepped back and for a moment she thought he was insulted but the beam was still there. 'Glad to know you haven't changed. You're just as forthright.'

They stood looking at one another for a moment. He'd nicked himself shaving and out of nowhere she remembered standing in the bathroom doorway when she was a kid, hearing him curse, watching him reach for a piece of loo paper, sticking it on top of the nick, his eyes going to hers and saying *occupational hazard*. He'd winked and she'd trotted off, probably to have a bowl of cornflakes before school.

Her throat closed up. She didn't want to cry and as she lifted her chin he glanced away, clearing his throat. He pointed at the coffee bar. 'So, what's your poison? Cappuccino? Or are you a latte girl? Or... dear God. Are you into herbal teas?' He reared back in mock-horror.

The lump in her throat immediately began to dissolve beneath an involuntary chuckle.

'What's wrong with herbal tea?'

He widened his eyes. 'Please, don't tell me you're one of those vegan crazies.' He made it sound scandalous. 'My own daughter...' He put a hand on his chest as though he might be struggling to breathe. He was, she realised, giving her emotional space.

'Not vegan,' she assured him. 'Not even vegetarian. My favourite food is steak and chips, and second to that, curry.'

'That's my girl.' He looked proud.

Together they walked to the coffee bar. Two cappuccinos. Both sprinkled with chocolate. Both ordered chocolate puff pastry twists. Without conferring, both of them moved to stand at the bar rather than take a table.

'So...' she started, at the same time as he said, 'How on earth ...'

They both stopped. Gave half-embarrassed laughs.

'What's in America?' Lucy decided on something less incendiary than *where the fuck have you been for the last eighteen years?*

He gave a shrug. 'I'm a salesman. I sell.'

She waited.

'I'm in the stamped components trade. The company I currently work for is a specialist manufacturer of non-metallic strips and sheets. Things like washers, gaskets and seals. Exciting, huh?' His mouth gave a self-deprecating twist.

'I don't know, is it?'

'Well, since I'll be meeting the sales director of General Motors tomorrow, I guess it could be worse...'

Had he always been a salesman? She couldn't remember him doing anything else when she was a kid. He could sell anything, from an idea to the plastic carrier bag you were currently holding and didn't know you wanted to buy all over again. Jaya used to laugh: *Your dad could sell curry to us Indians!*

He'd been salesman of the year several times. Whenever he reached his sales targets he'd blaze into the house waving tickets to a concert, a weekend away, shouting about his success and wanting his girls to help him *splash the cash!* Once he'd even swept her and Mum off to Disney World in Florida. They'd stayed in a really flash hotel with a balcony overlooking a savannah which had antelopes, giraffes and zebras grazing, safari-style. Being addicted to *The Lion King* at the time, Lucy had thought she'd died and gone to heaven.

While they ate their pastries, he told her about his job and she told him about hers. Both gave rough outlines. Few details. Anyone listening in would have thought both of them had the most boring jobs in the world. We're being cagey, Lucy thought, which isn't surprising after so long, but we really should get a bit personal. He's my dad, after all.

She'd already clocked he didn't wear a wedding ring but now she said, 'Did you get married again?'

He pulled a face. 'No.'

She took a breath, steeled herself for the next question that had been burning in her oesophagus. 'I don't have any half-brothers or half-sisters?'

He held her eyes as he said again, 'No.'

'What happened to Tina?'

'The yoga teacher?' He sighed. 'It was all a mess. Your mum went nuts... she turned into a crazy person.' He shuddered. 'I hadn't wanted to leave. You girls were my world... Christ, I loved you, I loved your mum – but she gave me no choice.'

Lucy stared. This wasn't the story she'd heard.

'She threw my belongings out onto the street, remember?'

No, Lucy couldn't remember. She only knew he'd left one day for the airport. That her mother had been furiously angry, then upset, then angry, then upset again. She'd heard her crying, sobbing her heart out in the middle of the night. She'd seen her reddened eyes in the morning. Watched her put her shoulders back and set her chin and head to the divorce solicitor.

'Including my vinyl collection. It was raining. She left them out all night... the covers were destroyed. She knew how much those records meant to me and overnight, they became just about worthless.'

Lucy could feel her mouth tighten. If he was looking for sympathy, it was in the wrong place.

'Your mum... Jesus.' He was shaking his head as though baffled. 'It was as if I'd turned into the devil incarnate. She didn't understand my life was *you*. You were my world. I wanted to keep you safe. Protect you. It was all I ever wanted, to be with my beautiful girls, but she wouldn't listen to reason.'

A rash of sparking red and black flashed across her vision. 'I wonder why?' Sarcasm dripped.

He surveyed her for a long time. Cautious, watchful. He reminded her of a defendant who was weighing up what to say next to make them appear in the best light. Finally, he gave a bitter half-smile. Looked away.

'Why didn't you go to Australia?'

'I never *was* going. It was your mum's idea to lie. She wanted you to think I was on the other side of the world.'

'What?' Lucy was shocked. 'I don't understand. Why would she do that?'

'It wasn't anything to do with you.' His voice was gentle. 'Your mum simply didn't want us to have any contact. I had to fight tooth and nail to email you after I'd gone, but then, seventy-one days later, she shut even that contact down. She blocked me from your contacts list. Blocked my emails. When I tried sending you something by post she returned it, unopened. I kept trying, you know, for ages. It was horrible having presents I'd taken such care over returned without acknowledgement and, rightly or wrongly, I finally gave up.'

Lucy knew her face had gone rigid. Had her mother really done that? If so, why had she let Lucy believe it was her father's fault he'd stopped emailing her? The red and black rash expanded in her mind to form long pulsing rivers.

'You didn't know.' He said it as a statement.

'Of course I didn't bloody know!' she said hotly. 'The last message I got, you said you were going abroad on business and that I shouldn't worry. That was it!'

'You blamed me. You thought I'd abandoned you.'

'Got it in one, mastermind.'

He suddenly looked tired. 'She did a good job, didn't she, keeping us apart.'

Lucy didn't want to diss her mum. Not after she'd brought her up on her own. He was either lying – which he was extremely good at – or there was something more. Her mum couldn't be *that* vengeful, could she?

'How did you find me?' He put his head on one side, appearing genuinely interested.

'Jaya. She had your number.'

Something in him stilled. 'Jaya, as in Ricky Shaw's mum?'

'Yes.'

'And she had it because...'

'She got it off Reg.'

He blinked, making her think he was surprised. 'As in Mad Reg, at the pub?'

'Yup.'

A small silence fell.

'I heard about Ricky,' he said.

'He was charged last night.'

'Was he?' Interest sparked.

'I'm one of the investigating officers.'

This time, he was definitely surprised. His mouth actually opened and shut. 'You're kidding me.'

'No. Ricky asked for my help. Actually, that's not true. It was Jaya who asked me.' Since he appeared to have fallen speechless, she added, 'And in return for my help, she said she'd put me in touch with you.'

He continued staring at her. 'Bloody hell. You're saying if Ricky hadn't been arrested for that woman's murder, then you and I wouldn't be here?'

'I guess so.'

'If I was religious,' he mused, 'I'd say that the Lord works in mysterious ways.'

'Amen to that,' Lucy agreed.

28

The road to Rabat ran through a vista of dry-baked, dusty countryside before it reached the coast. A wind was blowing hard off the Atlantic when Dan stepped outside Mohammed's car, and the air smelled salty. Above the sound of traffic, he could hear the shriek of seagulls.

He'd spent the journey filling Mohammed in on why he was in Morocco, and when he'd finished answering his questions, he mulled over Lucy's emails, putting together what they'd both learned. He'd told her that Kaitlyn had gone to the Moroccan police and spoken to a policeman called Mehdi after meeting a man called Commandant Jamal Azoulay. Mehdi had told her to take her report to the Commissariat, to Hafid Khatabi. Mehdi was then threatened to keep him quiet about what he'd learned, and when he went to meet Dan – who'd turned up asking the same questions as Kaitlyn – an assassin was sent to murder him.

In turn, Lucy told him about a possible link between Morocco and Indonesia and forwarded him copies of shipping documents for what had transpired to be fake bomb detectors. Dan was puzzled. Did this have anything to do with flight

EG220? Or was it something else? He couldn't imagine Morocco being taken in by such a scam.

Mehdi hadn't been so certain. 'Everyone has their price,' he'd said. His skin was pale, his eyes sunken and drawn with pain but Dan couldn't remember when he'd last been so pleased to see someone. Apparently, the knife had missed Mehdi's heart and it was only thanks to Mohammed's quick thinking, putting pressure on the wound and getting him to hospital quickly, that he survived.

'Mohammed's wife... works at the hospital,' Mehdi told Dan, his words coming in painful gasps. 'It's private, but even so... we were scared that another assassin might come... and finish the job.'

Which was why Mohammed and his wife smuggled Mehdi out of hospital, putting out the rumour that he'd died.

'However, Jibran Bouzid will soon find out I'm not dead, and then–'

Dan blinked. 'Who?'

Mehdi's mouth tightened. 'He is the Minister of Defence. After I sent Kaitlyn to see the Commissaire, Hafid Khatabi, he sent his men to me and my colleague. Told us to forget we had seen her.'

A coldness crept into Dan's stomach. The head of the armed forces as well as the Gendarmerie had warned Mehdi off. He couldn't imagine a more formidable enemy. Did Bouzid have something to do with Kaitlyn's death? And what about the army officer Kaitlyn had seen?

'Where can I find Commandant Jamal Azoulay?' Dan asked.

'I don't know. Sorry.'

The trail seemed to dry up at that point, which made Lucy's email a godsend when it came in later that day. Tazi & Co may not exist, according to the head of security at Soekarno-Hatta International Airport in Indonesia, but there was an address on the shipping invoice, in Rabat. This meant the two companies were separate. A quick internet check told him the shipping company was still in business. Mohammed offered to drive. Dan tried to dissuade him.

'It could be dangerous. Look what happened to Mehdi.'

'I have known Mehdi since we were children.' He ran a hand up his jaw, rasping the bristles. 'We are like brothers. Our wives are best friends, our children too... I must protect him because by doing so, I also protect my family.'

Now, they stood outside a group of warehouses on the Avenue Zarbia, a stone's throw from the Aéroport international de Rabat-Salé. Across the road stood a complex: Cité Militaire. Dan felt his senses quickening. Had Kaitlyn been here?

He glanced up as a Royal Air Maroc aeroplane roared overhead, flaps and gear down as it approached the runway. Together, Mohammed and Dan headed for the warehouse office, set behind a docking area where four trucks were parked. A man in brown overalls sat at a desk inside, smoking. Dan let Mohammed do the talking. When he mentioned the name Commandant Jamal Azoulay, the man's expression grew guarded.

'He knows the Commandant,' Dan stated.

'Yes,' agreed Mohammed.

'Where can we find him?'

When Mohammed asked, the man shook his head.

Dan stepped close, towering over him. He held the man's eyes. He spoke softly. 'I'll only ask once. Where is he?'

The man swallowed. Looked at Mohammed then back at Dan. He swallowed again before some tension left his face, then his shoulders. Dan guessed he was thinking, *it's no skin off my nose.*

Mohammed translated as the man spoke. 'The

Commandant, he used to be based here in Rabat at the army logistics centre, but he's retired to Marrakech.'

'His address?'

The man turned to his computer. Tapped a while. 'Here.' He swivelled the screen around and pointed at an address. Dan committed it to memory. Next, Dan brought out his phone and showed the man the shipping invoice. Yes, the man said, he remembered the shipment. Yes, it contained highly sensitive, top-of-the-range bomb detectors bound for Indonesia. No, he didn't know that the company Tazi & Co didn't exist. He was surprised, because he'd been paid, after all... his words trailed off and at the same time his facial expression changed. Grew guarded once more.

'How were you paid?'

The man looked at the ground when he spoke.

'Cash,' Mohammed translated.

'How much?'

At that, the man's eyes narrowed. 'Does it matter?'

Dan wasn't sure that it did since the man appeared to be nothing more than a shipping agent.

Another aeroplane engine thundered overhead. Dan waited until the noise had abated before bringing out a photograph of Kaitlyn and putting it on the desk.

The man stared at the picture. He gave a nod.

'She was here on Friday, two weeks ago.'

'The first of March?'

Another nod. 'She asked the same questions as you. She went to Marrakech to meet the Commandant.' A look of anxiety crossed his face. 'I was happy to help her. She survived the air disaster, you know. EG220.'

'So did I,' Dan said.

The man blinked. 'May Allah be praised.'

Back in Marrakech, the two men headed straight for the Commandant's address to find a modest house with a flock of sparrows dust-bathing on the front path. Dan could feel the sun on his head and shoulders, hear the sound of a game of football on a flat area of dirt on the other side of the road, but his attention was on the Commandant's front door.

Mohammed knocked. Dan stood back, body language carefully neutral, belying the fact his pulse was up and that his weight rested on the balls of his feet, ready for anything. This was the man who'd sold defective bomb detectors to the Indonesians. A man who might be implicated in Kaitlyn's murder.

The door opened. A short rotund man with speckled grey hair answered. Small brown eyes behind spectacles, snub nose, a fleshy mouth. He wore an open checked shirt and jeans. He smiled at Mohammed. Said something that Dan guessed was along the lines of, *can I help you?*

'Commandant Jamal Azoulay?' Mohammed asked. His tone was grave.

The man answered. The two men talked very briefly until Mohammed turned to Dan and gave a nod. It was his signal.

Dan strode forward. Put a hand against Azoulay's chest and propelled him inside his house. The man started to yelp but Dan put one hand over his mouth, his arm around the man's neck, and lifted him off his feet.

'Quiet,' he hissed.

He had no idea if the man spoke English, but Azoulay got the message and fell silent.

'Who else is in the house?' asked Dan, easing his hand from the man's mouth.

Azoulay started to tremble. '*Je ne comprends pas.*' I don't understand.

Mohammed hissed something at the Commandant. The man stammered something back.

'He has no English,' Mohammed stated. 'I translate for you.'

'Ask him if he's alone.'

Terror stood in Azoulay's eyes. 'My w-wife and children are here. P-please don't hurt them.'

Dan hauled the man into a side room. Tiled floor, sofas, coffee table with two tall bronze candlesticks. Dan pushed him against the wall, hard enough to smack his head against it. He heard Mohammed shut the door behind them.

'How many children?'

'Th-three. P-please, I'll d-do whatever–'

'You supplied false bomb detectors to Indonesia.'

The colour left the man's face so fast Dan was surprised he didn't faint.

'Didn't you?'

Azoulay just stared at him, ashen.

Dan brought out Kaitlyn's photograph. Held it in front of the man's face. His voice was low and filled with ice-cold rage. 'She was murdered last week. She died because of *you*.'

'No, no, no.' Azoulay's voice was thick with fear and rising hysteria. 'No, this isn't possible–'

'Her throat was cut.'

Azoulay gasped for air. 'This has nothing to do with me, I swear it!'

'When did you see her?'

'No, no. I don't know her. Please, believe me...'

Dan stalked across the room and picked up one of the bronze candlesticks. Swung it from side to side. It was the size of a baseball bat but three times as heavy.

'If you don't tell me what I want to know, I am going to get one of your children and break their feet. Do you know how many bones are in a foot?'

'P-please...' The Commandant started to weep. 'No.'

'Twenty-eight. Which means I'll be smashing fifty-six bones in total. They'll never walk without a limp again.'

Azoulay's trembling increased. Tears ran down his cheeks.

'When did you see her?'

'N-no... I c-can't...'

Dan looked at Mohammed. 'Get one of the kids.'

29

Mohammed looked at Dan, appalled.

Dan looked back.

This hadn't been part of the plan but Azoulay was obviously more terrified of someone else. Dan had to make the retired Commandant more terrified of him to get any leverage.

'Now!' Dan snapped.

Steps uncertain, Mohammed headed for the door. He was turning the handle when a little girl called out.

'*Baba, Baba!*' Daddy, Daddy!

Footsteps scampered up the corridor.

Dan raised his eyebrows at Azoulay.

'Don't hurt her,' Azoulay begged. 'Not Salma...'

'Get her,' Dan commanded Mohammed.

As Mohammed began to open the door, Azoulay cracked.

'Okay, okay.' He began to sob. 'I'll tell you, but please don't hurt her...'

Mohammed closed the door in a flash. Sweat beaded his forehead and trickled down the sides of his cheeks.

'Tell me,' commanded Dan.

'The woman in the photograph,' Azoulay gasped. 'She came here last Saturday... she accused me...'

'Of selling fake bomb detecting equipment.'

He nodded. He was panting as though he'd run a marathon.

'Where did you get the equipment?'

'I took delivery of it a long time ago.'

'How long?'

He closed his eyes. When he spoke, it was in a whisper. 'Seventeen years.'

Dan held his eyes as he said, 'I was on flight EG220.'

'*Iilhi aleaziz,*' Azoulay whispered. Dear Lord.

As he looked at Dan, something seemed to collapse inside him. He stopped gasping. He closed his eyes briefly, took a deep breath. He stumbled to a chair. Sank into it. Head hanging, he began to speak.

'We didn't know they didn't work. We thought the BSS184 was a highly advanced system. Innovative. Pioneering. When the flight was bombed, and we arrested the two men responsible – airport employees – I had my suspicions. One man was a ramp agent. The other a baggage loader. They should never have been able to bring explosives into the airport with the detectors in use. We scan *everyone*.'

Dan stared. 'You're saying the right people were arrested?'

'Yes.'

'There were rumours they were scapegoats...'

Azoulay looked weary. 'They were terrorists. They'd already bombed Marrakech. They wanted a bigger target.'

A car door slammed outside. Dan flicked a look through the window to see a woman in a djellaba walking away from an SUV, bags of shopping in both hands.

'I tested twenty machines myself. I didn't tell anyone. Not a single one worked.'

He was staring at the floor, eyes focused nowhere. 'I took one apart to find it contained no electronics whatsoever. It was nothing but an empty plastic box. The antenna on the outside of the box wasn't attached to anything, nor were the wires. I wanted to run away. I wanted to pretend I knew nothing about this, but soldiers and police officers were using these machines all over the country at checkpoints, to detect ammunition, roadside bombs...'

He gulped.

'What did you do?'

'I made a report. I went over my boss's head. I was risking my career, my family... but I took it in person to the *Général de division*. I could tell he was very disturbed by my revelations. He promised to investigate. Immediately, I felt better. I knew I had done the right thing. But then, five days later, the *Général* was dead. Killed in a car accident.'

He was shuddering with the memory.

'The next day I was called to my boss's office. Inside was a man I didn't recognise. A junior civil servant called Jibran Bouzid, from the Defence Department. When my boss left us alone, Bouzid casually asked me how the brakes were on my car. Whether it was mechanically sound. He didn't want me to suffer the same fate as the *Général*. It was at that point I knew my life was in the balance.

'Bouzid told me that the BSS184 had been used at dozens of military checkpoints across the country and had managed to prevent and detect more than two thousand bombs that could have killed many people, and that a hundred and fifty-four car bombs had been defused. I wanted to *shout* at him that he was a liar, but I couldn't. He made it clear he could have me disposed of as easily as he would a cigarette butt.

'Then he asked how many of the devices were still in store. I told him there were four hundred. He said, "Do you know how much they cost?" I said no. He said, "A hundred and twenty-five thousand dirhams. Each.'"

Dan did the maths: twenty-four thousand pounds per machine.

'He said the purchase price had been sixty-two thousand and that the balance went on training and middlemen. I was now one of those middlemen, and I would receive twenty-six thousand dirhams per machine.'

Dan blinked. Which made a total of around four hundred thousand pounds. It was a massive bribe.

'He told me I was to keep the machines absolutely safe, in a place where nobody could damage them. If any were requested, I was to make sure the job it was assigned to offered good value for money, and if I didn't think it was, to refuse to supply them.'

'You were told to lose them.'

'Yes. I put them at the back of an old warehouse full of disused and defunct military equipment. This is where they sat, undisturbed, until the service had a shake-up.'

Dan waited.

'Bouzid came to me once again. He was now the Defence Minister, one of the most powerful men in the country. He told me the defunct equipment in the warehouse had to be disposed of, permanently.'

'You sold them.'

Azoulay nodded glumly.

Dan checked the shipping document on his phone. 'How much did the Indonesians pay for the machines?'

Azoulay named a price that came to a tidy half a million pounds.

'And your cut?'

'I didn't get anything. I didn't *want* anything.' Misery filled his face. 'I tried to persuade the minister to destroy the machines, not to endanger people's lives, but he's not that kind of man. He takes opportunities where he can find them. That's what he said.'

Dan thought for a moment.

'Who sold the machines to Jibran Bouzid?'

'A British company. I don't know its name. But I do know the owner is named after Shaitan...' he glanced over his shoulder as though scared the djin might be behind him '...because of his ability to disappear. He exists on the borderline between light and darkness and is as ruthless as a crocodile and as cunning as a snake.'

'He's Moroccan? Or British?'

'I do not know this.' Azoulay shook his head. 'Just that he is as greedy as the Atlas Mountains are high.'

Dan held up Kaitlyn's photograph once more. 'And you told all this to this woman?'

'No. I didn't tell her anything.'

Dan thought over everything Azoulay had said, the way he hadn't backtracked or deviated in any way. It wasn't, Dan realised, the first time he'd told the story.

'Who did you tell?'

Azoulay looked bone tired. 'Commissaire Hafid Khatabi.'

Things began to tumble into place. When the trail Kaitlyn had been following from the Indonesians suddenly stopped dead, she'd made her report to Commissariat Central and then gone home. Hafid Khatabi had taken up her investigation.

I love you for helping me. I love you love you xxxx

Which meant Khatabi had probably been warned off by the Defence Minister as well. No wonder he'd thrown Dan out.

Dan looked around the room, at the relatively simple furnishings. 'What did you do with the minister's money?'

'It's in the bank. I wanted to give it away, but my wife told me to keep it for the children.'

By the time Dan and Mohammed made it to the Medina, the sun had set and the streets were lit yellow, making the city glow as if it was made of gold.

'What will you do next?' Mohammed asked when he pulled the car over.

'I'm not sure,' Dan admitted. 'I'd like to find this Shaitan, though. It wouldn't surprise me if he's still selling fake bomb detectors.'

'It would be good to stop him,' Mohammed agreed.

As Dan stepped out of the car, Mohammed leaned across. 'If you need more help, call me.'

Dan nodded. 'Thank you.' As he headed for his *riad* entrance, he half watched Mohammed's little Toyota beetle down the street. The street was busy with people heading home, people heading out to eat, shoppers bustling, friends laughing. It felt soft and benign and later, he realised he'd made the mistake of letting tiredness get the better of him, not checking the street as he neared what he perceived to be his sanctuary, or he might have taken in the grey sedan cruising slowly behind him, slowing down and stopping, two men climbing out and falling into step behind him.

The first he knew that something was wrong was when he felt the hard nose of a gun barrel pressed into the small of his back, against his spine.

30

'No, I haven't told Mum yet. I've only just left work.'

Lucy was walking down the street, her phone pressed against her ear as she headed for the tube.

'You're planning to, though?' Mac asked.

'I don't know.' Her voice wobbled. Her emotions were all over the place having seen her father. She couldn't believe how different her parents' stories were. Neither matched up in any way. How was she going to find the truth? She didn't want to hurt her mother, not after everything she'd done for Lucy over the years, all the sacrifices she'd made, but Mum had *lied*. Hadn't she?

In her job Lucy was only too aware that some people lied to try to control people. Or to protect themselves. Or protect the people they cared about. But even if their intentions were good, lying wasn't the solution because it was vital that people were able to make free decisions. Like Lucy wanting to be reunited with her father.

'I wish I was there with you,' Mac sighed. 'I'd give you a great big hug, make you a cuppa and bring you a slice of coffee and walnut cake.'

All three were pretty much at the top of her list of favourite things but right now, she reckoned a hug followed by a double shot of vodka might be more appropriate.

'I'll take the hug when I get to see you. Maybe Sunday.'

'How's the case going?'

'Well, now we know that Kaitlyn targeted Ricky, we're focusing on his clients...'

She quickly filled him in. She didn't tell him about Dan's email, the attempt on Sergeant Mehdi's life. He'd only worry himself senseless, and besides, she comforted herself, it had happened in Morocco, not the UK. Miles away. As she approached the tube entrance, she began to wind up their conversation.

'Mac, sorry, I've only got another minute... is everything okay with you?'

'Nothing a night of hot sex wouldn't fix,' he sighed. 'God, I miss you.'

Lucy sped past an elderly woman tottering along with a walking stick. 'What if we get too old to fulfil that side of our wedding vows?'

'I think that's highly unlikely.' Amusement threaded his voice. 'I have every intention of jumping your bones until I'm a hundred.'

'Ewwww. What will we look like?' She laughed.

'I don't know about me, but you'll always be gorgeous.'

Lucy was still smiling as she pattered down the steps to the tube. Only a year to go until they tied the knot. She'd secretly bought a wedding magazine last week and read the list of Things To Do. Which started now. Like setting their budget, making an appointment to see the registrar, booking the transport, start looking for a dress...

Her mind abruptly slammed to a halt. A dress? She could count on one hand when she'd worn one. She was a jeans and boots gal, leather jackets and belts, no jewellery... what kind of dress should she be looking for?

This question kept Lucy's line of thought nicely diverted from family lies until she exited the tube, when it switched to her mother, and whether to tell her about seeing her dad or not. Heartbeat picking up, Lucy let herself into the house filled with apprehension, and the moment she stepped into the hallway her body slumped in relief. Mum wasn't back from work yet.

Dumping her handbag on the kitchen table, she pulled out her laptop. Fired off an email to Dan, telling him that she'd spent the afternoon investigating Ricky's clients, two in particular: Charles Tyne Associates and HBS Property Developers. The latter was one of Teflon Tom's companies which appeared to be involved with the former through a land agency of some sort. It was like trying to disentangle a woollen cat's cradle but she was determined to unravel it so Tomas's dealings were clear in her mind. Knowledge was power, as Dan always said.

She was looking at a new company, formed just six months ago and given a start-up loan from HBS Property Developers, when she heard the front door bang. The million-pound factory – built in Wolverhampton – looked state of the art.

'Hello, lovely.'

Lucy looked up as her mother walked into the kitchen. She wore her staff nurse uniform with rubber-soled black shoes, her hair tied into a knot at the back of her head. She looked tired, the same as she usually did after a long day, and as Lucy watched her put her handbag next to her backpack on the table, a wave of emotions swept over her and the colours in her mind became a confused jumble of black, red and green.

'What's wrong?' Her mother's tiredness had gone. She was watching Lucy carefully.

'Nothing.' The word sat like a dark slug on her tongue.

'Lucy...' Her tone was soft. Kind but warning. 'I know that look, and it's–'

'I saw Dad.'

She hadn't planned to say anything. She'd thought she'd sleep on it first, but it had just blurted out.

Silence fell.

Lucy heard the wall clock ticking, a couple of cars driving past outside. Her heart was beating fast. She felt as though she was perched on a cliff edge.

'What?' Her mother's tone was blank.

'I saw him for a coffee at Terminal 3. He was flying to America. It was the only time we could meet as he'll be gone for at least a week.'

Her mother stared at her as if she'd never seen her before. 'You *what*?'

'I saw Dad,' she repeated.

Her mother reached out a hand and pulled out a kitchen chair. Sank into it. 'Fuck.'

Lucy didn't think she'd heard her mother swear before but she supposed now was as good a time as ever.

'He said you threw all his stuff out on the street.'

Her mother continued to stare in her direction. She didn't seem to be looking at Lucy, but at something in her own mind.

'He said it was your idea to tell me he'd gone to Australia. But he's in *Macclesfield*!' Anger began to rise, hot as molten lava. 'He said he didn't want to leave, but you forced him. That he loved us... and when he emailed me, you blocked him. You sent back all his mail and–'

Her mother rose so abruptly, her chair crashed to the floor. She didn't seem to notice. Her gaze was still fixed on Lucy.

'Stop right there. Stop repeating his shit.' Her voice was trembling, furious. 'Because that's what it is. *Shit*.'

'Is it true?'

'I can't believe you went behind my back.' Her fists were clenching and unclenching. 'Why did you do that, Lucy? Why didn't you tell me first?'

'Mum!' Lucy got to her feet. 'Is it *true*?'

'Which bit?' Her tone was like ice.

'That he tried to contact me and you stopped him. You sent back all his letters and presents to me, unopened.'

Her mother's lips pinched. 'It's true. And if you stopped to think why I'd do such a thing, you'd know why.'

'So he had an affair!' Lucy cried. 'So what? Millions of people have affairs! Why were you so unforgiving?'

A quick flash of dismay, before her mother's eyes flicked away. 'Is that what you think? That I'm unforgiving?'

'What am I supposed to think?'

'You're meant to *trust me*.'

'I *have*!' Lucy shouted. 'All my life I've trusted you but I had to see him, don't you understand? He's part of me, my DNA, and whether he's an unfaithful git or a superstar, he's my dad!'

'I'm sorry, Lucy, but this isn't going to happen.'

'You can't stop me.'

'Watch me.'

Her mother snatched up her handbag and pulled out her phone. Dialled.

Lucy felt as though she'd been pushed out of a top-floor window. Her stomach swooped, her skin chilled. Her ears were filled with a rushing sound.

'Carl? It's me.'

Her mother held Lucy's eyes as she spoke.

'No, I don't care. You could be boarding an aeroplane or the space shuttle for all...' Her eyes suddenly narrowed. 'Shut up.' Her tone was like a slap.

'Lucy told me you met today. Yes, you spun quite a tale...

well, I suppose it's true, but as you know, it's only half the story...'

Her mother listened for a while. Then she said, quite firmly, 'No.'

Lucy watched as her mother's face hardened.

'No. That wasn't the deal, remember?'

Lucy heard her father squawk, his voice tinny through the microphone.

'*Do you remember*?' her mother roared.

Silence.

'I want you to speak to Lucy. You know what to say.'

Her mother held out the phone.

Shaking inside, unsure whether it was anger or fear, Lucy took the phone.

'Dad?' Her voice was small.

'Sorry, sweetheart. She wins, okay? It was nice to see you, though. Lots of love.'

He hung up.

Fingers trembling, Lucy called him back but he didn't answer. She looked at her mum. 'What did you say?'

Her mother turned so Lucy couldn't read her expression.

'*What did you say?*'

'The same thing I said eighteen years ago. Leave. Us. Alone.'

31

Her mother didn't say another word. She simply walked out of the kitchen and headed upstairs to the bathroom. Lucy dogged her heels, shouting, begging and pleading, but it had no effect. It was as though she didn't exist. Her mum was blanking her and from past experience, Lucy knew she'd keep blanking her until Lucy changed her behaviour.

Sitting at the top of the stairs, listening to her running a bath, Lucy recalled the last time this had happened. She'd been fifteen and wanted to go to a party. She'd been invited by one of the seniors (who she'd had a crush on even though she was seeing Nate then) and needed something to wear. She'd been coveting a gorgeous Andrew Pax dress, red roses on a black background, short and silky with spaghetti straps, but her mum refused to buy it even though it was amazing value. And she looked stunning in it. And much older too. At least eighteen.

'It's too tight,' her mother told her, mouth pursing. 'I think the blue dress is perfect.'

'But it's hideous!' Lucy was appalled. 'I may as well wear a bin bag! I'll be a laughing stock.'

'It's the blue dress or you don't go at all.'

Lucy had gone ballistic at that point – hormones and temper getting the better of her – but her mother had simply remained silent until Lucy caved in and they'd bought the blue dress.

Her mother was the most stubborn person she knew. Lucy sighed. At least she knew where she got it from.

'Mum?' she called, getting up from the step. 'I'm going to the pub. I'll see you later.'

'See you later,' she called back. It was as though nothing had happened. Which is what she wanted, no doubt. For things to go back to how they'd been before. Without Dad. Just the two of them. But she was getting married next year. Shouldn't Dad give her away? And what about when she had kids? They'd want to see their grandfather, wouldn't they?

As she walked, she brought out her phone. Rang the number Jaya had given her for her father. Somehow, she wasn't surprised when it gave one ring and went straight to his voicemail: the standard response when a number had been blocked. No heart-warming *the caller cannot be reached* to indicate he was in the air. Just one ring.

He hadn't hung around, had he? He'd been almost unseemly in his haste to disengage with her. What had her mum said?

That wasn't the deal, remember?

What deal? If it was the last thing she did, she decided, she'd find out what had gone on before. She had a *right*, goddammit. She was their child. She had to know the truth, no matter how tough it was.

The pub was packed and noisy and for a moment she was taken aback. Realising she wasn't in the mood, she walked home, stopping at a Tesco Express to buy a couple of bottles of wine and a beef lasagne. Mum loved lasagne.

It was quiet when she let herself in. Then she heard the TV.

She put her head around the door to see her mum sitting on the sofa. Tears shone on her cheeks.

'Oh, Mum.'

Lucy dumped the shopping and went and sat next to her. She held her mother's hand. It was cold and she rubbed it gently between her own, trying to warm it.

'I bought lasagne.'

Her mother nodded.

'And two bottles of that Aussie Chardonnay you like.'

Her mother squeezed her hand. 'Thanks.'

Lucy took a breath. 'You can understand why I did what I did, can't you?'

A nod.

'Is whatever happened between you two really that bad?'

Another nod.

Lucy felt an anxious lurch in her gut. 'He's not a paedophile or anything, is he? A rapist?'

Her mother looked at her. Her lips twitched. 'No.'

'Well, what is it? I mean, I know he had that affair–'

'He lied.'

'But that's what cheaters do. They–'

'He lied about who he was.'

Lucy stared. 'What?'

'He told me one thing, and then I discovered he was something else. Our marriage was based on nothing but a lie.'

Laughter came from the TV, raucous and loud. Lucy barely heard it.

'What do you mean?'

Her mother looked at her. Her eyes were red-rimmed and filled with pain. 'I'll tell you, okay? But not tonight. I have to think about how to tell you, if that makes sense. It's complicated.'

Lucy wanted to know *now*, drag the story out of her straight away, but she also knew she didn't want her mum to clam up and go back to blanking her. She leaned over and kissed her mother's cheek, damp with tears. 'Thanks, Mum.'

32

'Get in the car.'

Dan glanced at the grey sedan that had pulled up alongside. The driver wore police uniform. His eyes were on Dan.

'There are three of us,' the man added. 'Only one of you.'

Still Dan didn't move.

'Don't think I won't shoot you.'

The gun nudged hard against his spine. Dan knew he didn't have a choice, not unless he wanted to have his spine turned into mush. He walked slowly to the rear of the car, the gun connected every step of the way. He bent down, looked inside.

'Commissaire.'

'Mr Forrester.'

Dan slid onto the back seat. 'You didn't have to use a gun.'

'I thought it best not to take any chances. You are a difficult customer, I've been told.'

'Who by?'

The policeman ignored him, instead barking an order at the driver. Immediately the car accelerated down the street.

Khatabi put out a hand. 'Your phone, please.'

Dan handed it over. The policeman put it in his jacket pocket. Stared outside. He could have been executing an everyday chore except for the tension in his neck and jawline. Dan turned to look out of his own window, deciding to keep silent until he knew where they were going. He didn't want to give something in his favour away.

To Dan's dismay, they headed out of the city. The busy ochre-coloured streets fell away. Darkness had fallen and all Dan could see from the headlights was a scrubby, brown countryside dotted with olive and argan trees and virtually no cars. Stones clicked against the bodywork, the tyres rumbling.

In another situation he might have been fearful they were taking him somewhere remote to shoot him, but since they probably had a file on him from his last visit, they wouldn't dare. There would be more than hell to pay if an ex-MI5 officer went missing.

They drove north-west for just over an hour. They were on a single-track dusty road when the driver eased off the accelerator, letting the car cruise to a halt. He put on the handbrake and although he switched off the engine, he left the lights on. A herd of goats drifted past, a small boy trailing them with a stick. The boy glanced at them curiously but didn't stop. After a minute or so, two pairs of headlights approached from the opposite direction. Both vehicles pulled over. Not too close, not too far. Maybe fifteen yards between the two. Dan's nerves were quivering, his senses alert.

'What are we doing here?'

'We are meeting someone.' Khatabi brought out a pistol from his holster. Checked it was loaded. Then he opened his door and climbed outside. 'Come.'

Dan climbed into the cool evening air. He could taste the dust kicked up by the goats and something sharply antiseptic, like rosemary. He studied the area covertly, where he might run if needs be, the knolls he'd head for, for cover. His pulse was up, his breathing shallow.

The first vehicle disgorged two soldiers who took up position next to the car. The second vehicle disgorged two more. All were armed with AK-47s. All stood on alert.

A stocky man in a suit climbed out of the first car. Walked to the space between Khatabi's vehicle and his own. He beckoned to Dan to join him.

Dan walked across, Khatabi at his side.

'Dan Forrester,' the man said.

Dan recognised him from his searches on the internet. Jibran Bouzid, Morocco's Defence Minister. But he didn't say so.

'I'm sorry,' he said politely. 'But who are you?'

The man's eyes gleamed flat in the headlight flares. 'If you don't know, then you're more stupid than I thought.'

Dan kept his gaze carefully neutral. He didn't say any more.

'My name is of no matter.' The man shrugged. 'My message is a simple one that even you will be able to understand. You see, I want you to go home, and stop meddling.'

Dan held the man's gaze. 'Why?'

Without taking his eyes from Dan, Bouzid called out something in Arabic. One of the soldiers next to the second vehicle spoke to someone inside. Two men appeared. They were dragging something with them. It was a boy, maybe ten or eleven. Faded jeans, white T-shirt. Normally his expression was bright and curious, but tonight his skin was chalky, his eyes wide with terror.

'What is this?' Dan asked. His veins felt as though they'd been filled with ice.

Bouzid didn't reply. He called out to the men, who stopped in the middle of the road. Naziha was pinned in the men's arms but it didn't stop the boy from flailing, lashing out with his legs.

'He's just a boy,' Dan said. 'What do you want with him?'

Bouzid turned his head and surveyed him. Dan kept his expression absolutely level, absolutely bland but his mind was darting from side to side, trying to work out if he could somehow pelt for Naziha and snatch him, make a run for it… but with four AK-47s against them he wouldn't stand a chance.

Still holding Dan's eyes, Bouzid clicked his fingers.

'Hafid.' He made the word a command.

The Commissaire hesitated.

'*Naima*, Hafid.'

The Commissaire swept up his pistol and pressed it against Dan's temple. His face was drawn and pale. Sweat beaded on his forehead.

'Hafid will shoot Dan Forrester if he causes any trouble. Won't you, Hafid?'

'Yes, sir.' His voice was loud and firm. Not what Dan wanted to hear. From the man's troubled demeanour he'd been hoping for a thread of doubt, some humanity, but there was none. He sounded like a robot for all the emotion in his voice.

Bouzid called out again. Another man appeared. For a second the two men holding Naziha were distracted and immediately the boy swung round, lashing at the nearest man's groin. He missed but still caught the man's inner thigh, making him curse.

'Let the boy go.' Dan's tone was tight.

Bouzid didn't respond. He was watching the third man as he came over, carrying what looked to be a can of kerosene, and a funnel. Immediately Naziha started bucking and kicking wildly, like a calf arriving at the slaughterhouse and sensing its doom.

'No,' said Dan.

The men worked quickly now, pinning Naziha to the ground. He watched in horror as one of the men bent over and pinched the boy's nostrils shut until he was forced to open his mouth to take a gulp of air. Immediately the man forced the funnel between Naziha's teeth. The third man stood ready to pour the kerosene down the funnel and into Naziha's throat.

Dan's head went light when behind them, one of the soldiers stepped forward. He lit a match.

'Whatever you want,' Dan said. 'I will do it. But leave the boy alone.'

Bouzid called out.

The men stilled.

'You will leave the country?'

'Yes.'

'Today?'

'Yes. Just let the boy go.'

'Not until I have confirmation that you have upheld your end of the bargain.'

'I will leave on the first flight.'

'And you will stop your meddling.'

'Yes.'

'When you get home, you must remember that I can find this boy any time. I also want you to remember that it won't just be little Naziha's safety you will be responsible for. You have your friend Mohammed, and his family, to think about. And Sergeant Mehdi. I don't know where he is at present, but unless he leaves the country, he will resurface. He has three grandchildren, did you know?'

Dan looked into the flat black eyes of a man driven by greed and now fear. Fear of being found out for hoodwinking his country, for providing his troops, the police and airport security with bomb detectors that didn't work and lining his pockets with his countrymen's money. He wouldn't just be thrown out of government, he'd be torn limb from limb if the public found out.

'How will I know,' Dan said, 'that you are keeping your side of the bargain?'

'Commissaire Khatabi will be our go-between. Won't you, Hafid?'

'Yes, sir.'

The last Dan saw of Naziha was him being thrust back inside the minister's vehicle.

33

D an sat in the back of the car. Both feet on the floor, back upright. He'd locked down his emotions. His fear for the boy, Mohammed and Mehdi was shut off deep inside. He couldn't win this particular battle. Not with so many vulnerable people he had no ability to protect.

'There is a flight to Heathrow at ten o'clock,' Khatabi said.

Dan didn't respond.

'We will go via your *riad* to collect your passport and belongings.'

There seemed no point in saying anything.

An hour and a half later, with his bag in the back, passport in his pocket, they returned to the car. To his surprise, the Commissaire returned Dan's mobile phone. Then he dropped his driver and the second man at the Commissariat.

'I will drive you myself.'

Dan nodded. It didn't matter who took him. He would have walked barefoot to the airport if necessary. Anything to keep Naziha safe.

It was only when they passed a large mosque with a lit

golden dome that Dan realised they weren't on the road to the airport.

'Where are you taking me?' His voice was calm but inside, a sense of unease crept through him.

Khatabi didn't answer, simply kept driving.

Dan concentrated on keeping his breathing regular. No point in thinking about the fact Khatabi worked with the corrupt minister, and that he had a gun. He would remain alert and ready, and only act if necessary.

The Commissaire made a right turn on the other side of town, passing a scooter carrying a family of four, the wife in her djellaba perched side-saddle. He parked in a busy street lined with restaurants and bars. They hadn't been there long before a striking woman, smartly dressed, approached. She came to the car and tapped her fingers on the bonnet, waving her red-lacquered fingernails at the Commissaire as she strutted past. She had glossy shoulder-length hair and a beautiful smile.

'That is my daughter,' Khatabi said. 'Naima.'

Dan watched Naima go, her hips swaying and her leather handbag swinging. He could hear the minister's voice in his head, commanding Khatabi to cover him with his gun. '*Naima*, Hafid.' It had been a threat. Little wonder Khatabi had done the minister's bidding. His family was at risk too.

'Naima is a real-estate agent.' His voice was proud.

At the airport, Dan checked in his bag and then joined Khatabi at a snack bar in the terminal hall.

'What will you do?' Khatabi asked.

Dan thought of Lucy's investigation but he wasn't going to trust Khatabi with anything. His daughter may be at risk from

Jibran Bouzid but that didn't mean they were now friends. 'Go home.'

Khatabi frowned. 'You don't want to find Shaitan?'

'Of course I do, but I also want Naziha to stay alive.'

Khatabi leaned forward, expression intense. 'Bouzid knows nobody in the United Kingdom. He has no influence there. You can investigate and he will never know.'

'How can you be sure?'

'He only has power here. Over people like me.' He sent Dan a stare filled with challenge. 'You will be free to continue the investigation. Just not in Morocco.'

'Like Kaitlyn did?'

The policeman had the grace to look away.

Silence fell.

'You must find Shaitan,' Khatabi murmured.

Dan didn't respond.

Khatabi raised his gaze to Dan. His eyes burned with desperation, anger, fear. 'Please. Help me. I want the truth to come out. Then I will be free of him and my family safe.'

Dan considered the Commissaire. His beautiful daughter. The note Kaitlyn had made and stuck to Khatabi's photograph.

I love you for helping me. I love you love you xxxx

'What lead did you give Kaitlyn?' Dan asked. 'She'd made a note that you helped her... she was really grateful. I think it was information you gave her here that sent her to London.'

'And which got her killed.'

'Yes.'

Khatabi held Dan's gaze. 'I gave her the name of the company that sold Bouzid and the Moroccan government those so-called bomb detectors.'

Dan felt something inside him quicken.

'Tactical Advanced Security Systems Ltd.'

Dan was suddenly taken out of the airport building to Kaitlyn's hideaway office. He was gazing at the wall above her computer. The piece of paper torn from a yellow legal pad and folded in two, stuck at head height with a drawing pin.

TASS! Fucking TASS! If it wasn't for TASS it would never have fucking happened!

'Now, you will go and find Shaitan?'

Dan gave Khatabi a long look. 'I'm sorry. But no. I have a family too.'

As he queued to board the aeroplane, Dan caught up with his messages. A particularly demanding client was, apparently, giving Philip a hard time, so Dan called the client direct and set up a meeting for the following morning. He'd spend the night in London, he decided. Return home when the client had, hopefully, been pacified.

The flight was only three and a half hours but it felt much longer thanks to the turbulence. Several people were wearing breathing masks, which Dan put down to the panic creeping across the media over the rumours that bled air, particulate pollution from jet engines, could turn you blind. Isla's picture was everywhere. She was young and beautiful and it was a tragedy she'd fallen blind, but Dan wasn't about to buy a mask. Not until the story had some real science behind it, anyway.

34

Using a pool car, Lucy drove to see Dan at his place on Saturday. She hadn't been able to see him earlier thanks to his having to mollify what sounded like an exceedingly difficult client, and although he'd told her not to bother coming all the way to Chepstow, she'd demurred. She wanted to see him face-to-face. Her boss agreed. Hence the pool car.

She knew they could have held the debrief over the phone or any one of the video chat apps, but it was never the same. Dan was pretty unreadable emotionally and body language-wise, but she'd known him for a while now and could read more into what he said by being with him.

What she hadn't told the boss was that Bristol was on the route to Chepstow and that she had every intention of returning via Mac's and, hopefully, spending the night with him. There had to be some perks in this investigation. She needed that double vodka as well as that hug, especially this particular Saturday. Usually on a weekend morning, she and her mum would sit at the kitchen table reading the newspapers but today, Mum hadn't appeared. When Lucy had called out, 'See you!' she'd just called back, 'All right, lovely. See you when I see you.'

Which wasn't very satisfactory, considering everything that was going on. She'd had a crap night's sleep, tossing and turning, remembering her father's defeated tone.

She wins, okay? It was nice to see you, though. Lots of love.

At least her mother had promised to tell her the truth. When she'd sorted out what to say. *It's complicated.* Or would she be trying to create another collection of lies? Last night, Lucy had brought out the old shoe box from under her bed and flicked through the photographs of her father. There were a couple of him before he'd married Mum when he'd had long hair and skinny jeans, a Malcolm X T-shirt. She'd studied the photos at length but struggled to put the angry-looking twenty-something Carl Davies together with today's clean-cut salesman. Talk about chalk and cheese, but then she supposed he'd had to sharpen up when he'd married Mum and Lucy came along. She liked the fact he'd been so passionate about real issues, though. It gave him a depth of character and gravitas she admired.

As Lucy drove up Dan's hill, she wondered why he lived somewhere so remote. It may be near Chepstow but it felt secluded, almost isolated, thanks to being surrounded by moorland, with nothing but the odd sheep and rabbit for company. She slowed when she spotted the thick clump of trees that heralded the Forresters' place and swung left, into the drive. Parking next to Dan's BMW, Lucy climbed outside, stretched. The air was clear and bitingly cold, holding none of the pollutant tang you could taste in London or Bristol. Grabbing her handbag, she went to walk for the front door but stopped when she heard a rasping sound behind her.

Her heart just about stopped.

Slowly she turned to face the Rottweiler. The dog was standing at the edge of the drive, lips pulled back over twin rows of gleaming white teeth. Trails of saliva oozed from its jaws.

'Hey Poppy,' she said as soothingly as she could with her heart hammering like a road drill. 'Remember me?'

She knew she shouldn't move or she might trigger an attack, but if she sprinted like buggery, she might just make it to the front door before the dog did.

'Poppy,' she said again and at the same time the Rottweiler relaxed. Strolled forward like nothing had happened. She shoved her nose into Lucy's palm, seemingly unaware that she'd just scared the crap out of her. She patted the dog's head, the size of a fridge door. She still found it hard to believe Dan had rescued the dog, but that was Dan for you. Surprising and heart-warmingly altruistic. Together the dog and Lucy walked towards the front door, which opened as they arrived. Aimee shot outside like a rocket.

'Lucy!' Aimee collided with Lucy's thighs, hugging them tightly.

'Hi, Aimee,' she greeted Dan's daughter.

'Can you stay for lunch? Please, please? We're having sausages and mash. Mum said to ask you but only after you've seen Daddy. He's in the study. He got home really late last night. He was in Morocco and then he had to stay in London. I was asleep but he still woke up before I did. He brought me a camel back. Not a real one, a toy one...'

Aimee took Lucy by the hand and led her inside the house, still chattering.

'Tell your mum I'd love to stay for lunch,' Lucy said when Aimee paused for breath. 'How's my godson?'

'He cries a lot.' Aimee pulled a face.

'That's what babies do when they're teething,' called Dan. 'Come in, Lucy. I've got a fresh pot of coffee here...'

Settled in an armchair by a window overlooking rolling hills of heather, grass and bracken, Lucy sipped her coffee, studying

Dan. He looked pretty okay, well rested, no injuries that she could see.

'How was it?' she asked. 'Remember much?'

'Absolutely nothing.' He poured himself some coffee from the cafetière. Came and sat on the chair opposite while he drank. 'It was strange, knowing I'd been there but not recognising anything. The odd phrase or two returned, but otherwise it was as though I'd never been.'

'I'm sorry.' She didn't know how he coped having his memory so fucked up. It would drive her insane.

He looked surprised. 'Don't be. I don't let it trouble me, as you know. So, what's new on the case? You said Ricky had been charged...'

He already knew about the Indonesians, so she ran him through meeting Teflon Tom and Ajay, her interest in Charles Tyne Associates and HBS Property Developers. She sent him a photograph of Tomas by email, along with Ajay's details.

'Tomas definitely knows Chris Malone. The woman who tried to poison Ricky. But he wouldn't tell me. He's a bit of a hard bastard...' She told him about Tomas's history.

Dan fell quiet, obviously mulling everything over before he told her about his trip. When he got to the part where Naziha had been threatened, Lucy found herself sitting forward, struggling to stay silent and not curse loudly. *Let him finish his story*, she told herself. *Don't distract him.*

Dan ended by telling her about Tactical Advanced Security Systems Ltd.

A single vivid-red rocket fired through Lucy's synapses. 'TASS? They sold the Moroccans those duff bomb detectors?'

'Yes.'

'Kaitlyn was after TASS.'

Dan nodded. 'She would have blamed them a hundred per

cent. If the detectors had worked, the bomb would never have boarded our flight.'

Energy flooded her body. She had to force herself not to jump up and race to her car, the MIR, and start tracking TASS down. 'I'll get onto it straight away.'

'And I'll have a chat to your Teflon Tom. Try and find out about this Chris Malone. Send me her photo, would you?'

Dan's phone pinged seconds later as Lucy sent him the picture. Although his manner was casual, Lucy knew he'd have more luck than she could hope for. As a police officer she couldn't threaten Tomas, but Dan could. He was good at that stuff. Teflon Tom wouldn't stand a chance.

When the doorbell rang a few minutes later she followed Dan into the hallway, thinking about nothing more than it was time to see Jenny and Mischa, and that she probably wouldn't stay with Mac tonight. Not with the huge fucking clue Dan had just given her. TASS! They were closing in on Kaitlyn's killer at last. The Indonesians would be pleased.

As Dan opened the door, something in her came alert. She wasn't sure what it was, but she paused. Turned her head to see who was there.

It was a man. He wore a boiler suit, obscuring his physique. His body language was open and friendly. He looked perfectly innocuous but there was something about him...

She realised there was something wrong with his eyes but she couldn't work out exactly what. He was half smiling as he passed a piece of paper, an envelope – she couldn't see exactly what – to Dan.

Lucy slipped along the hall, edging closer for a better look, and with a lurch, she saw what was wrong with the man's eyes. They were set inside a latex foam mask.

35

L ucy stared at the mask. A realistic mask that moved with the man's facial expression, and looked utterly convincing until you were close.

All the hairs rose on the back of her neck.

With a friendly wave, the man retreated. Dan stood in the doorway, watching him. Lucy scurried to his side.

'What the hell?' she said.

Dan showed her a single piece of paper upon which was printed in bold capital letters:

JUST TO REMIND YOU. JIBRAN BOUZID'S HAND REACHES BEYOND MOROCCO'S BORDER.

Lucy made to go after the man but Dan stopped her.

'Wait.'

He closed the door. Raced into the kitchen with Lucy hot on his heels. Together they watched the man saunter down the drive and vanish around the corner.

'I'll follow him,' Lucy said urgently. 'He didn't see me. He won't know I'm tracking him.'

'What's going on?' Jenny was by the sink, peeling potatoes. Now, she put down the peeler, anxiety flooding her face.

Lucy saw Dan glance at his wife, then back at where the man had disappeared. Lastly, he looked at Lucy.

'I don't like being threatened,' he snapped. 'Go after him.'

Lucy tore through the kitchen and utility room. She was yanking open the back door when Dan yelled, 'Take Poppy! You can pretend you're on a dog walk!'

'Okay!' she yelled back. She grabbed Jenny's Barbour and a dog lead. As it jingled, the Rottweiler appeared, looking expectant.

Lucy bolted outside. Poppy cantered steadily at her side as though they did this every day. Not wanting to be seen exiting the driveway, Lucy headed for the trees. Crashed past branches and through leafy mulch, the dog crashing happily alongside, obviously thinking it all a great game.

Half a minute later she could just see the pale grey of the road through the trees and at the same time, she registered a car's engine running. It sounded large. Powerful. It also sounded as though it was stationary. She heard a car door slam. She ran harder. The car was put into gear. With a deep growl, it began pulling away...

Lucy pelted past an oak tree, ducking a low branch, *sprinting*, desperate not to miss it... nearly there... She grabbed Poppy's collar as they erupted onto the verge. She didn't want the animal to get run over. 'Wait,' she commanded. To her relief, Poppy stopped immediately. Lucy saw a big 4X4 accelerating up the hill. A red Range Rover. It was already too far away for her to read the number plate. She yanked out her phone. Took a hurried photograph, then another. The car crested the hill and disappeared.

When they returned to the house, Dan uploaded her photos

to his computer, expanded the images. They were horribly blurred.

'Is that an 8 or a B?' Lucy squinted. 'Or a 5? A 3?'

'Could be anything.' Dan sighed. 'But at least we know it's a red Range Rover Sport. Base price eighty thousand.'

'I'll get the tech guys at work to have a look. They might get something.'

'That would be good.'

'You ruffled some feathers in Morocco,' she remarked.

'The same ones Kaitlyn did.' His expression hardened. 'But I can't have my family threatened, Lucy. Not again. Find whoever it is, will you? And shut them down.'

'I'll do my best.'

'I'll pretend to go to work as usual. Keep up the pretence I'm dropping the whole thing.'

She wanted to say *be careful* but kept quiet. If anybody could hoodwink the masked man it would be Dan.

'Is Jenny okay?' she asked.

'Not really. She doesn't like it that he knows where we live, but she's a tough cookie. And if things get hairy, she'll take the kids somewhere safe.'

Lucy knew Jenny hated doing that, *loathed* it. But luckily she wasn't stupidly stubborn and would hide if needs be, which was good news.

Dan surveyed her briefly. 'You'll stay for lunch?'

'As long as it's bangers and mash.'

36

Lucy bypassed Bristol that afternoon, thanking God she hadn't told Mac she might drop in. She hated getting his hopes up then disappointing him, but that was a cop's lot, especially when on a murder case. Mac understood that, but even so. They missed one another like crazy when they were apart. She rang him after she'd passed Reading and filled him in, including Dan's getting warned off.

'Hell, Lucy. Take care, will you?'

'The man didn't see me. I made sure of it.'

'Even so. I know what you're like. And they sound like a nasty lot...'

'Eyes in the back of my head. Promise.'

Come 5pm she was settled in MIR. As usual on a murder investigation, you wouldn't know it was a weekend. Every desk was occupied and the atmosphere intense, with detectives checking alibis, CCTV, statements from neighbours, people who knew Kaitlyn, who knew Ricky. Forty dedicated officers in the office and outside, creating not just leads to follow but tons of paperwork.

She'd given the photo of the red Range Rover to Albin but he hadn't been able to enhance the image much. As Dan had said, at least they knew the make and model of the car, so all wasn't lost.

Lucy started trawling for information on TASS. Wikipedia gave her an outline which she used to start nailing down some facts. Firstly, that it was a private limited company established on 15 June 1995. TASS made one product: an explosives detector known as the BlackShark Sniffer, priced between £5,000 and £50,000 per unit. The BlackShark Sniffer had been sold to twenty-five countries from Mexico to Lebanon and Thailand. The Saudi government was said to have spent £62 million on the devices.

Lucy whistled. This wasn't just big bucks. It was *huge*.

She read on to see the BlackShark Sniffer's inventor Helen Flowers, a former saleswoman, had been previously employed by the MoD – Ministry of Defence – one of the biggest public procurement organisations in Europe...

Lucy stared at the name *Helen Flowers*. She hadn't expected it to be a woman. Did that make her sexist?

Helen Flowers had apparently made millions of pounds from the sales of the BlackShark Sniffer, with which she'd bought a £4.5 million house in the Golden Triangle in Cheshire, where all the footballers lived. She'd owned holiday homes in Spain and Florida, a £1.5 million luxury yacht that she kept in Puerto Banús, a stable of Porches and Mercedes, and two racehorses called Black Shark and The Barracuda.

Lucy made a note of the racehorses before she returned to read that Helen Flowers was eventually brought down by a whistle-blower who said everyone at TASS knew that the devices were nothing more than a 'glorified tin can with a length of string'.

In 2001 export of the device was banned by the British government. A warrant was issued for Helen Flowers's arrest on suspicion of fraud. She vanished overnight. The police impounded her cars, raided the Watford factory, put traces on her phones, watched her house. Interpol put a warrant out for her in Spain, but nobody saw her again. There were rumours she'd moved to Florida, but nothing was corroborated and the FBI soon gave up searching.

Lucy asked Google for a picture of Helen Flowers. There weren't many since Flowers had vanished before the existence of smart phones, just a handful of her at the races, at the parade ring. Mid to late twenties. High heels, lots of bling. Take away her jewels, her highlighted blonde hair and red fingernails, she wouldn't be particularly memorable. Her features were soft and bland. No freckles or moles. A slightly narrow mouth, perhaps. Eyes a little small. She was one of the plain Janes of the world. And nothing like Chris Malone, the sinuous-looking woman who'd tried to poison Ricky.

Lucy enlarged the photos, studying the angles of the woman's face, trying to get something to fix in her mind. It was almost impossible, the woman was so bland. She put a phone call through to the SFO – Serious Fraud Office – forgetting it was Saturday. Could it wait until Monday? She drummed her fingers on the desk, thinking. Not really, she thought, but she didn't want to piss anyone off, so she went and saw the SIO.

'No, it can't wait,' he agreed. 'I'll get you someone to talk to. Give me ten minutes.'

It actually took him twice that long to get hold of the chief investigator, Colin Pearson, who headed up the SFO intelligence unit, during which time Lucy had found two more photographs of Helen Flowers. One was of her at a fundraising party in Mayfair, the other a charity event at London's Guildhall, supporting members of Her Majesty's Armed Forces and veterans who'd served in Iraq and Afghanistan. She didn't seem to be accompanied by anyone and Lucy wondered if she'd ever had a partner or boyfriend.

'Pearson says he'll see you at the SFO at seven,' Jon Banks told her.

37

C olin Pearson wore jeans, a button-down shirt beneath a woollen jumper and big mud-spattered Timberland boots. He'd been returning from a walk with his family when Jon Banks had rung. Lucy apologised for interrupting his Saturday but he waved it aside.

'I've been after Flowers for twenty years. Some might say another day or so wouldn't matter, but Jon told me there's been a murder?'

Lucy filled him in on everything she knew, including Dan's experiences in Morocco, and being warned off in Wales.

'Nasty.' Pearson frowned. 'But I'm not sure it's our girl. She was a bit of a cold fish, money-obsessed, but that wouldn't necessarily make her a killer.'

'Perhaps Kaitlyn found out where Flowers was? That would be motivation enough, wouldn't it?'

He was still frowning. 'I suppose so.'

'Did she ever have a male partner? A husband?'

'There was a man, but he was more a business colleague. Neil Greenhill. She used him to sell to countries who wouldn't deal with a woman. Like the Middle East. It infuriated her that she couldn't do it herself. She was the epitome of a feminist.'

'Where's Greenhill now?'

'Disappeared.' A look of frustration crossed his face as he brought out a file, bulging with papers and photographs. 'Both of them vanished like puffs of bloody smoke.'

'Together? Or separately?'

He mulled it over. 'I honestly don't know. But they were lucky to run during a time when CCTV wasn't as prevalent. We didn't have social media back then, either. We know she booked a flight from Gatwick to Hong Kong the day after the warrant for her arrest was issued. She didn't show up for the flight. We alerted all ports but nobody saw hide nor hair of her.'

'And Greenhill?'

'Zilch. And I mean *zilch*. It's my belief both of them either had false IDs – which don't really work any more since Social Security have got wise to all the tricks by now – or they bought newly stolen passports. We froze Flowers's accounts, but that didn't mean she didn't have a million or ten stashed away somewhere, and with lots of money, the world was her oyster.'

He leaned back in his chair, glancing outside. His office was a fair size but the view could have been better since all it faced was the blank wall of another office building.

'I thought they could have rented a boat to cross the Channel, headed to Eastern Europe. It's almost impossible to find someone in Croatia, for example, because you don't need any kind of ID or information linking you to household accounts, like gas or electricity. But if I started looking for them there, I may as well just wander around the streets shouting their names.'

'What about Central and South America?' Lucy suggested.

'Easy to keep off the grid out there,' he agreed. 'And these two are especially slippery. They haven't contacted anyone from their pasts. No calls to Granny or Mum and Dad. They left that world behind.' His gaze turned inwards for a moment. 'I wonder what they're doing now, to make a living.'

'You think they're still together?'

He shook his head. 'I think they're too astute to do that. They would have split, I'm sure.'

'There's a warrant out for Greenhill's arrest too?'

'No. He's a "person of interest", but he was obviously in it up to his neck because of the way he buggered off. He was a weird customer, though. No family at all. Didn't socialise. Few people at the factory ever saw him. We never found out where he lived. I rather assumed he was living under an assumed name.'

'Surely *someone* has to know where they went?'

He leaned down and brought out another enormous file, placed it on his desk. He tapped it as he spoke. 'Friends, family, work colleagues... they're all in here.'

Lucy pulled the file across, flipped it open. Her eye went to a photograph of Helen Flowers getting out of a limo at some swanky event that involved a chauffeur opening her door and some red carpet to pop her Jimmy Choos upon. Next, was a copy of the warrant. She continued turning the pages as Pearson continued.

'There were rumours she went to live in Kentucky, USA. Another said she'd gone to Australia.'

Lucy studied a picture of an industrial building. The sticker on the photograph read *TASS Production Facility.* There was a stack of statements from people who Flowers had worked with at the MoD. People who remembered her from her sales days. Another picture of Helen Flowers and then a passport photograph of a man in his thirties. Strong jaw, dark hair closely cropped. A steady gaze that seemed to go right through her.

Lucy felt the shock of it beneath her breastbone, as though she'd been punched in the heart. She couldn't breathe.

'What is it?' Pearson sounded alarmed.

She took a huge breath of air. She was trembling. She felt sick.

She held up the photograph.

'Who's this?'

'Neil Greenhill.'

But it wasn't.

It was her father.

38

D an hadn't sat around after Lucy left. There was no point. He was hoping the man in the mask wouldn't expect him to react so fast. That he'd expect him to stay at home, scared for his family. Which he was. But he could no more sit at home twiddling his thumbs than stick Jenny's potato peeler in his eye.

'He knows where we live,' Dan told Jenny. 'And yes, if I do nothing, then hopefully we won't see him again. I don't like *hopefully*. I want to know that we *definitely* won't see him again. Which is why I have to find out who he is, and shut him down.'

He took Jenny's hands in his. 'Do you understand?'

'Yes.' Her gaze was clear. 'I do.'

'Thank you.'

He texted his old buddy Max Blake and asked if he could stay. Max was an old friend from when he used to work at MI5 and who had helped fill in many of his memory blanks. Max said he was happy for Dan to use his London apartment. He wasn't there. He was in the country with his girlfriend.

After unlocking his gun safe and withdrawing a handful of items – he left behind the guns, he didn't want to complicate things overly – he put them in a small leather holdall. He kissed

Jenny, kissed the kids. Patted goodbye to Poppy. With his overnight bag packed and in the back of his car he drove to London. Pondering the man in the mask – had he killed Kaitlyn? – he rang Lucy. It went to her messaging service. He asked her to ring him back. At the Chiswick roundabout, he pulled off the M4 and headed to Ravenscourt Park. In Max's pad he unpacked his laptop and chargers. Settled himself in.

Lucy had forwarded him Tomas Featherstone's address in Southwark. Dan studied the sleek, modern apartment block on Google Maps. Searched further to see it had a doorman. Security cameras. How to gain access without alerting Tomas? He needed more information. Names. Material to lull Tomas into thinking Dan was a friend. He tried Lucy again. No luck.

Dan busied himself researching TASS. The factory, the workers. He made a note of the floor manager. No mention of the whistle-blower's name. Impressive it had remained under wraps for so long, and he wondered whether the BlackShark Sniffer's inventor, Helen Flowers, had known who it was. He wondered if they were still alive and made another note, to check.

The third time he tried Lucy, she picked up. She sounded off. Her voice was strained, distant.

'You okay?' he asked.

'I'll tell you later.'

'*Serpico*,' he said.

'*Memento.*'

If she'd said anything else, it would have meant she was in danger and he would have pressed the big red emergency button. Over lunch after Mischa's christening they'd been talking about favourite movies when Dan came up with the idea of a safety code for each of them, using movie titles. Lucy had rolled her eyes, but relented, saying '*Memento*'. She was a sucker for thrillers and when she was ill she'd tuck up on the sofa and watch classics like *Rear Window*, *The Third Man* and *The Conversation* back to back.

Since Lucy had given him the right code, Dan's disquiet eased. 'I need some ammunition so I can gain access to Tomas Featherstone. Any names you know that might be useful to help lull him into a sense of security?'

'Why don't you try Neil Greenhill?' Her voice strengthened, but the wire of stress remained. 'If that doesn't work, try Carl Davies. Let me know if you have any luck.'

'Who are they?'

'If there isn't anything else...'

He hadn't known Lucy to cut him off like that before. Something was definitely off, but with her code word ringing in his ears, he had to trust she was okay.

'Later,' he said.

Dan brought out his phone and looked at Chris Malone's photograph once more. She was attractive, with long wavy hair and a supple body. She could be in her forties but it was hard to tell. CCTV didn't take the most flattering of snaps.

With his leather holdall in hand, Dan made his way to Tomas's apartment block. Walked inside the reception area. Lots of marble. A tinkling fountain. A large chandelier above. Fat red and yellow cushions sat invitingly atop a marble bench should your legs get tired waiting. Security cameras in each corner of the ceiling.

Dan went to the desk where a large man with shiny black skin sat. Muscle and fat bulged against the security guard's uniform.

'I'm here to see Tomas Featherstone.'

The man picked up a phone. Raised his eyebrows.

'I'm Neil Greenhill.'

The guard spoke briefly before covering the mouthpiece with one hand. 'He don't know no Greenhill.'

'Carl Davies.'

The guard blinked, but repeated the name. 'He's coming down.'

'Tell him I'll be outside.'

It was raining lightly when he stepped onto the pavement, a soft mist descending. A few people were about, but none on his side of the street. He moved to the side of the building and into a narrow alley lined with industrial-sized bins. Nobody down here. Perfect. He tucked his holdall to one side down the alley before returning to peer back at the building. When a man appeared, craning his head left and right, Dan called out, and waved. The man came over, his steps cautious. He wasn't particularly tall, around five eight or so, and his build was light. All to Dan's advantage. As he slowed, obviously wary, Dan stepped into view.

'What the fuck?' Tomas Featherstone stared at him. 'You're not Carl.'

'No.' Dan walked forward, hand outstretched. 'I'm a friend of his. He sent me.'

Tomas took a step back. He was studying Dan's face, trying to place it. His first mistake. His second was to raise his hand in a defensive position because Dan simply accelerated and grabbed it, twisting it behind him and ramming it between his shoulder blades.

'Fuck!' Tomas yelped. 'What the fuck...'

Dan hustled him into the alley. When he struggled, tried to kick backwards, Dan simply pushed his hand higher. 'I'll break it,' he warned. He wasn't taking any chances. Not with a man Lucy said was *a bit of a hard bastard*.

Tomas fell still. He was gasping. 'What the fuck...'

Dan grabbed the man's other arm but Tomas tried to twist away so Dan kicked the back of his knees, knocking Tomas off his feet and catapulting him forward. His head hit the pavement with a dull *smack* and in the second he lay there, seemingly stunned, Dan sat astride his lower back, quickly bringing out a heavy-duty zip tie and binding Tomas's hands behind him.

He leaned forward to speak in his ear. 'I just need one thing. And then you never need see me again.'

'And what the fuck is that?' Tomas was trying to act the hard man with his aggressive tone, but Dan heard the panic edging his voice.

Dan brought out his phone. Showed Tomas the photograph of Chris Malone. 'Who is she?'

'No idea.'

'Wrong answer.' Dan leaned across and reached into his brown holdall and brought out a knuckleduster, and then a knife.

'Jesus, fuck, man...'

'Bruises, or cuts?' Dan asked, then, without waiting for an answer, slipped on the knuckleduster and punched Tomas hard in the kidneys. He had to make the man realise he meant business. He had to make him talk.

Tomas groaned. Spittle drooled from his lips.

'Fuck,' he choked.

'There's a lot more where that came from,' Dan told him. 'If you don't tell me who she is.'

'Who *are you*?' he gasped.

Dan checked the end of the street. A taxi drove past, then a bus. A couple of pedestrians walked on the other side of the street but neither looked down the alley. Dan kept an eye on them.

'I'm someone who wants an answer. You see, a friend of mine was murdered recently. A very good friend. Her name was Kaitlyn Rogers. She went out with a good friend of yours called Ricky Shaw. Jog any memories?'

'Shit. You're here about Kaitlyn? I didn't know her. I mean yes, I knew of her. But I never met her.'

'The woman in the photograph I showed you has something to do with Kaitlyn's death. Which is why I want to talk to her. And I can only do that if you tell me who she is. You can do that, can't you?'

Dan leaned over to see real fear rising in Tomas Featherstone's eyes. 'Hell, I'm not...'

Dan picked up the knife. Turned it from side to side as though considering the blade.

'Shit, man. You promise not to tell her I told you?'

'I promise,' Dan lied.

'Fuck.' He squeezed his eyes shut. 'This is not good.'

'No,' Dan agreed.

He waited while Tomas considered his position. Dan saw one of the pedestrians had paused and was peering at the alley. Dan realised he didn't have long and pressed the knife against the back of Tomas's neck. A drop of blood bloomed. '*Stop pissing about,*' he hissed.

'Okay, okay... Her name's Helen Flowers. I don't know where to find her, but the last I heard she was living near Birmingham.'

Dan didn't like his hesitation. 'You wouldn't be making it up, would you?'

'No, no...' Tomas squirmed. 'I swear it.'

'When did you last see her?'

Silence.

'I won't ask again,' Dan warned.

'Last year. In the pub. The King's Arms. On Newcomen Street. She was with a friend of my dad's.'

'Which friend?'

'I don't know.'

'I won't ask—'

'I swear, I don't know! I'd tell you if I could, okay?'

'When did you see her before then?'

'Jesus. Fifteen, twenty years ago? I was about eight years old.'

'Where can I find your dad?'

'In the Nunhead Cemetery.'

From the smug tone that had crept into his voice Dan guessed he was lying. He would have nicked Tomas's neck again to teach him a lesson but he'd run out of time. The pedestrian was crossing the road for the alley.

'Oi!' A man's voice shouted. 'What's going on down there?'

Dan leaped off Tomas's back. He cut the cable ties with his knife, tossed the knuckleduster in his leather holdall and without a backward glance, raced down the alley. At the end, he checked over his shoulder to see Tomas standing upright, swaying a little and rubbing his neck. He was looking after him. His face was like a small, pale moon.

39

Lucy had never been so glad of a phone call when Dan rang her. It had given her valuable time to compose herself. Not to let Colin Pearson see how shaken she was. That she *knew* Neil Greenhill.

She'd taken Dan's call in the corridor and now she was back in Pearson's office hoping he couldn't sense the nausea roiling in her gut, the sweat pouring down her flanks and spine.

'Anything else you know about Greenhill?' she asked. Her voice was nice and even and thankfully seemed to give nothing away about her inner turmoil. 'The car he drove, maybe? Where he was last seen?'

'Nothing. Clever sod.' He flipped through his folder for a while. Pulled out a sheet of paper. 'Last seen 3 November 2001. At the factory. The day we issued the warrant for Flowers's arrest and closed the factory down. We missed him by a whisker, apparently.' His lips thinned. 'I wondered if he'd had some intel to tip him off because if he didn't, it's like he had some sort of sixth sense that kept him just ahead of us.'

Lucy's ears began to ring.

The day after they'd gone to arrest Flowers, 4 November, was the day that her father had supposedly flown to Australia with Tina, the yoga teacher.

Had Tina really existed? Or was she another lie? Where had he gone that day? Eastern Europe, as Pearson suggested? Or had he simply gone to Macclesfield and started again?

Her mother's voice rang inside her head. *He lied about who he was. He told me one thing, and then I discovered he was something else. Our marriage was based on nothing but a lie.*

Her mind leaped further. Perhaps he already had a place in Macclesfield back then? Perhaps he'd had yet another name? Another family? Had he been emotionally involved with Helen Flowers? Had children with her?

Lucy resisted the urge to put her head between her knees. She felt as if her heart had been taken out, leaving a huge dark hole that threatened to swallow her. She forced herself to keep talking, holding Pearson's eyes, terrified if she looked away he'd know. It was like driving across a patch of black ice, skidding in slow motion and praying you'd get to the other side safely.

As they began to wind up, she tapped the file before her.

'Can I take copies of things I think relevant?'

'Of course.'

After Lucy had spent half an hour photographing pictures of warehouse staff at TASS and details of Flowers's old MoD colleagues, her nerves had steadied further and in place of her shock came a slow-burning anger.

Anger at her mother, for keeping this from her.

Anger at her father. Anger at Jaya, who had obviously known all along that Dad hadn't buggered off overseas. Anger at everyone who had lied about Dad, from Tomas to his dad, Stan, Reg the publican and everyone else in between. She didn't care if Mum had threatened to eviscerate them, hang their entrails on Traitor's Gate – a stone's throw from the King's Arms in Southwark – they'd *lied*.

She shook Pearson's hand. Thanked him for giving up his Saturday.

'If there's anything I can do to help,' he told her, 'call me. Night or day, I'll be there with bells on.'

As she walked to the Tube, Dan rang. She ignored him. She didn't want to talk to him. She didn't want to talk to anyone. She could sense her past being rewritten with every step, and felt that if she paused, she'd be a different person, marked in some way but invisible to anyone but herself.

She paused outside the Underground station and looked out at Piccadilly, glittering with shop lights, great neon boards strobing red, white and yellow. Tourists were standing and posing beneath the statue of Eros, smiling, laughing. She wondered when she'd laugh again. It felt like an alien concept, something deep in her past that someone else did.

She had no idea how long she'd been standing there when a man bumped into her, muttering, 'sorry'. She came to. Gave herself a mental shake. *It's not the end of the world that your dad's a criminal*, she told herself. *Perhaps you always knew it, which is why you became a cop.*

Mind filled with oppressive clouds of black and grey, Lucy moved away from the Underground's entrance. Walked along Piccadilly. Past Waterstones. Cafés, sushi bars. She couldn't go back to the office. Not yet. She meandered up and down streets with no thought as to where she was going. She spotted a pub. One of those old ones that had been around since medieval times. She suddenly felt like getting drunk. Absolutely falling-down drunk so she wouldn't have to think, and wouldn't have to see her father's twinkling eyes, her mother's tears falling.

She wanted to put back the clock and never to have asked to work this case. She wanted things to be the way they used to be.

Too late for that, a little voice sneered.

She pushed open the door. Dark wood décor and cask ale. British pub grub upstairs.

'Vodka,' she told the barman. 'Double.'

She drank standing at the bar. Then she ordered another. Drank that. Drank another. She settled on a bar stool. Drank some more. Outside, it started to rain. She could hear it pattering against the windows. People came in with dripping umbrellas. Lots of laughter, shaking clothes dry.

'Lucy?'

She turned her blurred gaze to the tall figure standing at her side and said thickly, 'Go away.'

'No.' Dan folded his arms.

'How'dja findme?'

He brought out his phone and waved it at her. 'Location sharing, remember?'

'But I only... have it wiv Mac.'

'He talked me here.'

'Fuck.'

She stared hazily at the rows of bottles shining cheerfully behind the bar. She'd forgotten Mac installing the app after she'd been kidnapped. It had seemed a good idea at the time, his being able to see her real-time location using GPS tracking, but right now she wished she'd disabled the goddamn thing.

'We were worried. You haven't been answering your phone.'

'Don' care.'

'What happened?'

She squinted up at him. 'Nuffin.'

He sighed. 'Let me take you home.'

'No home.'

'I mean to your mum's.'

'No.' She reached for the rest of her vodka but Dan scooped it out of reach.

'My place then.'

She gazed up at him owlishly. 'Wales?'

'No, Ravenscourt Park.'

'Lundun.'

'Yes, London.'

'You got drink there?'

'Yes, there's drink there.'

'Lessgo.'

He took her elbow and guided her to the door, people parting like fish to let them through. Outside, it was still raining. She raised her head to the rain and opened her mouth, trying to drink it. Dan hailed a cab. Shovelled her inside.

'Sorry.' She sighed. 'I'm pished.'

'As if I hadn't noticed.' His voice was dry.

She made it to Dan's pad without mishap. The last thing she remembered was asking where the bathroom was and praying she wasn't going to throw up on the carpet.

40

Lucy's consciousness staggered awake. She was sweating but she was cold. Her head was a red throbbing balloon of pain and her mouth like a camel's armpit. She realised she was fully dressed and that she was lying on a bed. There was a duvet but it lay on the floor. It looked as though she'd kicked it off. At first, she had no clue where she was and felt a moment's panic. She forced herself to look around. Modern. White walls. Beige carpet. Bedside table, wardrobe, en suite bathroom dead ahead.

She recognised nothing.

She rolled to one side and what felt like a knife stabbed through both eyes and lodged itself in the back of her brain. She took in the bucket that had been placed strategically by the bed and as she looked at it, the urge to vomit rose.

She made it to the bathroom just in time, where she stayed for another half an hour. A box of paracetamol had been left prominently on the sink, along with a glass and a travel pack of toothpaste and toothbrush. Two fluffy white towels. A brand-new pack of M&S knickers.

Finally, dosed with painkillers, showered and smelling of

toothpaste, she stepped gingerly out of the bedroom. Walked through a small sitting room into a kitchen.

'Thanks,' she said to the figure at the kitchen table, who was working on his laptop.

'It's okay,' said Dan. He pushed the laptop away. Looked at her. 'Oh, dear.'

She poured herself a glass of water, then another.

'Coffee?' he asked.

She looked at the machine and decided she wouldn't be able to stand the noise. 'No, thanks.' She went and stood at the window. A grass strip stretched between the building they were in and their neighbours. A blackbird was hopping across it, looking for worms.

'What's going on, Lucy?'

She turned and looked into his eyes, as grey as the ocean, and felt so ill, so emotionally wrecked, that she could sleep for the rest of the year.

'Sorry.' It was all she could manage.

'Okay.' He gave several small nods. 'Will you call Mac? He's worried.'

'Later.'

She walked carefully to the sink and poured herself another glass of water.

'Is it to do with the case?'

Her insides turned greasy. She licked her lips.

Dan held up both hands. 'Okay. No questions. Not until you're ready.'

'I think I'll go now.'

'Where to?'

She didn't know. She wasn't strong enough to face her mother. She certainly didn't want to see Mac, who would drag the story out of her by her fingernails. Her throat began to close. Although she willed them not to, tears rose.

'Lucy.' His voice was gentle. 'Stay here. It's no problem, okay? I'll go and get some newspapers, maybe some eggs and bacon. It's Sunday, remember? And Monday's another day.'

He sat quietly, waiting for her to decide.

'I'll stay,' she said. 'Thanks.'

'I'll go out now. If you fancy a change of clothes, Max's girlfriend keeps some stuff in the wardrobe. She won't mind.'

Lucy spent the rest of the day nursing her hangover and it was only when Dan produced a home-made coffee and walnut cake he'd bought from the local deli, seemingly like a rabbit from a hat, that she felt as though she might get through this.

'It's your favourite.' A crease appeared between his brows. 'Isn't it?'

'Yes, it's my favourite.'

Dear God, she was lucky to have such good friends.

'I'm sorry,' she said for what felt like the thousandth time.

'You'll tell me, one day?'

She looked past his shoulder. Pictured her father picking her up and twirling her in the air when she was a kid. Saw his face beaming at her when they'd met last week. Felt the strength of his hug. His love for her. He was her *dad*.

'You will get through it,' Dan said quietly. 'Trust me. Nothing lasts for ever.'

She remembered Dan's struggle in finding the truth of his past against his unreliable memories, how the revelations had been life-changing – devastating – and how he'd rebuilt his life into what it was today.

He looked at her steadily. 'You need to know something.'

'I do?' She tried not to look as though she was panicking.

'Tomas Featherstone. He says Chris Malone is someone called Helen Flowers.'

Lucy could feel her eyes widen. 'No way.'

'Yes, way.'

'But they don't look alike. I mean like *at all*.'

Lucy fetched her phone. Showed him photographs of the two women.

Dan frowned. 'I'd take them to your police forensic artists. She might have had plastic surgery.'

'If she has, she'd have had a total body makeover. Is that possible?' She squinted at Malone's angles, and then at Flowers's soft outlines. 'But I'll ask, no probs.'

To her relief, he didn't talk about the case any more, which meant she didn't have to tell him she'd been to the SFO. She wasn't strong enough to withstand any kind of questioning. They spent the rest of the day reading the newspapers, snacking, not talking much but when they did, it wasn't about anything in particular.

'I know her.' Dan pointed at a photograph of a strikingly attractive woman on the front page of the *Sunday Times*.

'Don't tell Jenny,' Lucy snickered. 'She's gorgeous.'

'She was a flight attendant on my flight back from Miami.'

'Really?' Lucy scanned the article beneath the headline *One Flight Can Change Your Life.*

'God, aerotoxicity makes you blind? It's enough to put you off flying for ever.'

'You can always buy a mask.' He held up the colour supplement, opening it to a full-page advertisement claiming wearing the BreatheZero mask would protect from aerotoxic fumes.

'Ooooh, how attractive. Do you think it might double as a tiara for my wedding day?'

Dan brightened. Turned to the *Style* magazine. 'Talking of which, I saw something about weddings here... Ah, here it is... "They were setting off fireworks and the bride's dress caught fire".'

'I won't be wearing a dress,' she said stonily.

'Well, that's okay then.' He grinned.

On Monday, when she awoke to a clear bright day with enough warmth in the sun to make you think summer was around the corner, she went for a long walk. Walking had always helped clear her head and for a while, she seriously considered backing out of the case – and let her father keep doing whatever it was he did – but she was in too deep, the questions burning too furiously, so she rang Reg at the pub. After they'd spoken, she knew exactly what she had to do.

41

Isla sat with dread in her heart as she listened to the neurological surgeon. Mr Nurmsoo. She'd been worried that he wasn't a doctor, but apparently doctors in the UK had some strange tradition that male surgeons were always addressed as Mr to distinguish them from physicians. It was, she'd been told, a kind of badge of honour but she'd merely found it confusing.

'Isla, we've had the results back.'

Mr Nurmsoo's voice was grave.

Please God, please please please. *I don't want to be blind for ever.*

Isla held on to Emily's hand a little tighter. Her friend had been fantastic, staying with her every day for each test, every doctor appointment. She owed her big time but she couldn't think about that. Not yet. She had to get out of here first.

'We have good news, and bad news.'

She was waiting for him to ask which she'd like to hear first, *just the good news thanks*, but instead he said, 'The bad news is that you have a brain tumour, the good news is that the biopsy shows it isn't cancerous.'

She tried to swallow but she had no saliva and her throat made a little click.

Emily squeezed her hand. Gave it a little shake.

'The fact you have a tumour explains your headaches, your occasional blurred vision and balance issues. The MRI showed damage to your occipital lobe, hence your loss of vision. I would like to operate on Wednesday to remove the tumour...'

He went on to explain he'd be performing a *craniotomy*, and that the tumour was close to areas of her brain that controlled important functions. Therefore she'd be awoken part way through to allow him to ask her to perform various tasks, like reciting her address or answering a simple mathematical question, during the operation.

'This will enable me to avoid damage to those areas,' he told her. 'The operation will take four to six hours, but could be longer...'

She wouldn't feel any pain, apparently, just a kind of pulling sensation. He was hoping to remove all of the tumour but if this wasn't possible, he'd remove what he could. A small area of her head would be shaved and an incision made into her scalp and a small part of her skull – the 'bone flap' – would be removed.

'All in all, it should be a straightforward procedure,' he told her. 'After a few days, we'll give you a brain scan to see how much, if any, of the tumour remains, and discuss if you need steroids to reduce any swelling.'

He ran through the aftercare she'd receive, the side-effects.

'Will I be able to see again?' Her voice was a whisper.

'I think it's extremely doubtful that we'll be able to restore total vision. The best we can hope for is that you regain partial vision. The worst outcome will be no change.'

After he'd left, Isla cried. Emily cried too. Isla wondered at the quantity of tears a body could produce. Tears of anger, of self-pity. Of grief, weeping for the woman she used to be; carefree, happy.

'At least we know it's not aerotoxicity,' Emily said.

Isla blew her nose. Mopped her eyes. She knew her friend was trying to be upbeat, find something positive, but Isla felt another surge of dread. 'We should tell BreatheZero.'

Emily remained silent.

'Shouldn't we?' Isla's voice was small.

Another long silence.

Finally, Emily said quietly, 'What if we didn't?'

Isla twisted her tissue between her fingers. The owner of the company had visited her last week. She'd been really nice, and incredibly sympathetic. She'd offered Isla the equivalent of two years' salary with Egret Air to become the face of the new BreatheZero mask – which apparently caught any toxic fumes so you could breathe safely. She would also receive a percentage of the sales. When Isla heard the sales projections, what she might earn, she'd been stunned. She wouldn't have to worry about money for a long time.

BreatheZero's solicitor was meant to be coming to the hospital later in the day so Isla could sign a contract. Emily had said she'd read the whole thing out, even the small print, and guide Isla's hand to the page to sign if she was happy with it. But now? She licked her lips, suddenly nervous.

'We can't do that,' said Isla. 'Can we?'

Emily sighed. 'No, I suppose not.'

Isla nodded decisively. 'We'll tell them when they get here.'

'Yes. We'll tell them.'

42

Ricky sat slumped on his bed, dejection oozing from every pore.

'They're going to convict me.'

'Not if I have anything to do with it.' Lucy was brisk. She'd felt her spirits strengthen the second she'd walked into the police station that morning. There was something about carrying on, continuing what she'd been doing before the emotional avalanche had hit, that made her feel anchored.

She still hadn't processed the fact her father was a 'person of interest' to the police. That he appeared to be a criminal. She didn't want to relive her memories of him yet because she didn't want them sullied. Nor did she want to look at herself, who she was, where her genes came from. Better not to think about it for a bit and simply do what she was good at.

Catching criminals.

Before she'd set off to see Ricky, she'd gone to a police forensic artist and shown him the photographs of Chris Malone and Helen Flowers. 'All I want to know,' Lucy said, 'is whether they're the same woman.'

'Well,' said the artist, 'I have to say at first glance, no.'

'Not even if she'd done the *Swan* thing?'

'You mean extreme plastic surgery? Like on the TV?'

'Yeah.' She'd watched an episode where a woman who was judged to be ugly was given an 'extreme makeover' that included a dual facelift, liposuction, rhinoplasty and breast augmentation. The woman had had her brow and her ears reshaped and £25,000 of dental work. Today, the woman looked nothing like she had before the surgery.

'There are various things you can't change,' the artist told Lucy. 'Like the size and shape of your eyes. I'm ninety-nine per cent sure they're different women but I'll do some measurements and stuff if you like.'

Now, Lucy sank onto the chair opposite Ricky. 'Sorry I couldn't bring you a coffee. They're really strict now.'

He shrugged. 'Doesn't matter.'

'Ricky.' She waited until he looked at her. 'In order to get you out of here, I need you to be honest with me.'

A hint of wariness crept into his eyes. 'Hmm.' The sound he made was noncommittal.

'I've got some questions to ask, but if you don't answer them honestly, it's likely I won't find Kaitlyn's killer and that you'll spend the rest of your life in prison. Is that what you want?'

He shook his head decisively. 'No.'

'Okay.' She took a breath. 'First, I need to know how Jaya got my father's telephone number.'

'From Reg.' He didn't hesitate. 'At the pub.'

'When I called Reg this morning he told me he never gave my dad's number to Jaya. He couldn't because he doesn't have it.'

Something cautious crept into the back of Ricky's eyes and sat there, watching her.

'I'm thinking she got it from you, Ricky. Am I right?'

He sat quite still but his eyes were flickering fast as he thought.

'Ricky,' she snapped.

He jumped.

'I'm right, aren't I?'

He opened and closed his mouth.

'I'll take that as a "yes". Next question, how long have you been my dad's accountant?'

'I'm not.' His voice was weak.

'Are you sure about that?'

He nodded but it was so irresolute, Lucy didn't believe him. And although she desperately yearned to grab his throat, demand to know precisely what his relationship with her father was, she didn't want to go there. She wasn't ready. Not yet.

'How come you're in touch?'

'We're not.'

'So why do you have his phone number?'

He spread his hands, shrugging his shoulders, widening his eyes in a parody of *How should I know?*

Lucy decided to let it drop for the moment.

'Okay,' she said smoothly, 'let's move on and talk about Helen Flowers.'

Before, Ricky had looked anxious, now he just looked plain scared.

'You know who she is?'

He gave a jerky nod. 'I've never met her. Just heard the stories. You can check all my files, my books, a thousand times to see she's not a client. Never has been.'

'She's a criminal,' Lucy stated.

'So I've heard.' The fear remained.

'Do you know what she did?'

He pinched shut his lips. Fixed his gaze to the floor.

'She sold defective bomb detectors. She put countless soldiers, police and innocent people at risk from Afghanistan to Iran and

Indonesia. She sold a consignment to Morocco. Do you know what happened next?' Lucy leaned forward, waiting until he finally looked at her. She wanted to make sure she had Ricky's full attention. 'A bomb was put on flight EG220, out of Marrakech.'

At that, Ricky's eyes widened.

'Out of two hundred and fourteen people, only thirteen survived.'

He was staring at her, transfixed.

'One of them was Kaitlyn Rogers.'

For a moment she wondered if he'd heard her, and then he doubled over, clutching his stomach as though she'd punched him in his midriff. 'No,' he whispered. 'No, no...'

'Kaitlyn was trying to find Flowers,' Lucy continued. 'She wanted justice. You can understand that, can't you, Ricky? Imagine you've just turned sixteen, and were returning from a beautiful holiday in Morocco with your parents and little brother, and the next instant your aeroplane explodes mid-air and Mum and Dad are dead and your brother brain-damaged, needing full-time care until he dies. Then you discover the crash would never have happened if the Moroccans hadn't been sold *fake bomb detectors*.'

Ricky's skin had paled. His mouth was trembling. He looked close to tears but Lucy didn't stop. She wanted to keep up the pressure.

'Kaitlyn's search for Flowers led her to you.' Lucy decided not to belabour the fact he'd been a mark, he could work that one out for himself. 'What I want to know is what she learned from you, and why it got her killed.'

At that, his head shot up. 'I never talked about work. Not *ever.*'

Lucy narrowed her eyes at him.

'I swear it. And she never asked...' His expression turned

distant as he accessed his memory. '*Never*. We talked about her horses, her motorbikes. Travel. Where we might go.'

Clever Kaitlyn, reeling Ricky in. Kaitlyn had been waiting until he was hooked, and then she'd get him to do anything she wanted, like get him to show her his books, a list of his clients, a lead to Helen Flowers. She'd rented the Airbnb with that specific goal in mind, Lucy had no doubt.

'Whether you told her anything or not, it doesn't change the fact that someone knew who Kaitlyn was and what a threat she posed.' Lucy leaned back on her chair and crossed her arms. 'I wonder who that might be?'

Ricky opened and closed his mouth. 'I don't know.'

'Come on, Ricky. You can do better than that. *Think*. Who knew you'd met Kaitlyn? Who did you tell?'

'Nobody.' His eyes were wide. 'Seriously, I didn't tell anyone.'

'Ricky...' she warned.

'Oh.' His face cleared. 'Except for Tomas. He's my best mate.'

She just looked at him. Waited for the penny to drop.

When it did, he was horrified. 'Not Tomas. No way. He was happy for me! Jesus, Lucy. Your mind is so twisted–'

'If it wasn't Tomas, then *who*?'

His eyes narrowed in the folds of his fleshy face as he began to think. *Really* think. Lucy kept quiet, giving him the space he needed to process everything she'd said and assimilate it into what he knew.

The minutes ticked past while Ricky concentrated.

Then a horrible look went over his face. Really horrible. He stared at Lucy as she stared back.

'You've just thought of someone.'

He dropped his eyes. Shook his head.

'Yes, you have.' She leaned forward again. 'Tell me.'

'No,' he whispered. His tone was panicky.

'You'll go to jail for them? Serve their sentence? For

Chrissake, Ricky! They killed the woman you were falling in love with! They slashed her throat with a knife!'

He closed his eyes. He began rocking back and forth.

'Tell me.' Lucy gentled her tone. 'Tell me, and we'll get justice for Kaitlyn. I promise.'

At that, he raised his head. Met her gaze. After a long while, he said, 'I'm sorry, Lucy. I just can't.'

No matter how much she cajoled, begged and bullied, it had no effect. He refused to say another word.

43

Lucy spent the rest of the morning going through Ricky's client list and Tomas's known businesses to find no mention of her father anywhere. Nor of Neil Greenhill, person of interest to the police, aka Carl Davies. She still couldn't get her mind around the fact that they were both the same person and that they were both *Dad*.

As she queued at the sandwich shop, she considered Helen Flowers and Neil Greenhill. She found it easier imagining Greenhill as another man and not her father, and it didn't take long until she started looking at the case with less emotion and more brainpower.

Back in the office, egg mayo sandwich to hand along with a double-shot cappuccino, she reread the pages she'd copied at the SFO. With all the information laid out and streams of musing blue humming through her mind, she turned to the internet. God, she loved Google. All those newspaper reports from years ago; comment, views, quotes. She kept digging, absorbed in the past, Helen Flowers living the high life, Neil Greenhill a wraith of smoke behind her. Then a headline caught her eye.

Proceeds of crime recovered.

Helen Flowers, the evil woman who provided our British forces
with fake bomb detectors in Afghanistan, has been convicted
by the court in her absence. All her assets have been seized by
the police and are now up for sale.

Apparently Helen Flowers's factory, where the fake bomb
detectors had been made, had also been for sale along with her
Bentley Continental, Porsche, jewellery and mansion in
Cheshire. The government had made a tidy £4 million but the
Daily Mail reported that this sum was a song, and that the
mansion alone should have cost its new buyers at least that
amount.

Lucy dug further to find the mansion had been bought by a
Mr and Mrs Fielding and the factory by HBS Property
Developers, owned by a Mr S. Featherstone.

Her breathing faltered. *You've got to be kidding.* Stan
Featherstone? Tomas's father? Her dad and Stan had been
friends years ago. Had Stan really bought the factory?

She picked up her phone. Dialled Tomas. She was surprised
when he picked up. After the way he'd left the pub, tense and
angry, she'd thought he might blank her. At least now she knew
what he'd meant when he'd warned her to be careful. *You dig too
deep, you might not like what you find.* Wasn't that the truth?
Seemingly out of nowhere a dagger of anger speared her lungs,
so sharp she nearly dropped the phone. Had everyone known
about Dad? Did the whole sodding community know he was a
criminal?

'DD!' He greeted her cheerfully.

'Hey, Tomas.' Her voice was scratchy with a combination of
rage and humiliation. She cleared her throat to try and dispel it.
'How's things?'

'Muddling along, same as usual. A little bit of this. A little bit of that. You know how it goes. What can I do for you?'

Lucy decided not to beat around the bush. 'I wanted to know something about your dad. Whether he bought the factory where those fake bomb detectors were made, outside Watford. I'm talking fourteen years ago now. I gather it went for a bit of a song.'

There was a huge silence, but Lucy knew they hadn't been cut off.

'Yes, he did.' Tomas's tone was cautious. 'Why?'

'Oh, just something that popped up in a file I'm reading.'

'Care to share what file that might be?'

'I can't do that, Tomas. Sorry.'

'Can't blame me for trying,' he responded cheerfully.

'Sure.' Her voice was dry.

'Ah, DD,' Tomas sighed. 'I didn't want to leave the pub like that, you know. I like you, and I was rude. I'm not normally rude to people I like.'

'You were conflicted.'

'Yeah.' She heard him sigh. 'That's the word. Conflicted. I want Ricky out of jail, right? And I want you to do the best job you can for him. Find the fucker who killed his woman. But there's other stuff going on that I can't talk about. And that's what makes me... conflicted.'

'Tell me where to find Chris Malone.'

'Sorry.'

'Ricky's going to go to jail,' she said warningly. 'Can you imagine what's going to happen to him? He's soft, Tomas. He'll be nothing but bait. You're going to really love visiting him, witness his destruction. You will visit him, right? Until he either dies or commits suicide?'

Another silence. Then he sighed.

'Look, if I give you a tip, will you do me a favour some time?'

'No, Tomas.' She was firm. 'I am not open to bribery.'

'Ah, shit.'

She could practically see him rubbing his forehead in frustration.

'I really can't... I mean, I don't want...' He was breathing hard into the phone, obviously tormented.

Lucy kept quiet, hoping he'd give her a lead, but if she was honest, she'd didn't expect anything. He hadn't helped the last time they'd spoken, so why would he now?

'Try 22 Hobgate Road,' he blurted. 'Wolverhampton. And don't, for fuck's sake, tell *anyone* I gave you this otherwise I will track you down and... oh, fuck it, Lucy.' He suddenly sounded weary. 'Everything's fucked, isn't it?'

'It doesn't have to be.'

'Ah. Lucy Davies, always the optimist.' He gave a wry chuckle. 'Promise not to call me until Ricky's out?'

'You know I can't do that,' she responded, but her tone was light as a stream of green joined the blue flowing through her mind. Confidence and hope. She had a lead! 'But thanks, Tomas. I really appreciate it.'

'I have the feeling I might regret it, but in the meantime, I'll just say it was my pleasure. Just don't blame me if it comes back and bites you on the arse.'

It already has, she thought.

After they hung up, Lucy googled Hobgate Road to see the area held several manufacturing companies that produced anything from snacks to soft drinks, carpet tiles and gift cards. Number 22 was also a manufacturing company. With a name she recognised.

BreatheZero.

She clicked on the website.

Immediately a photograph of the beautiful Isla, Dan's flight attendant who had lost her sight, filled her screen. She was smiling, her vivid blue eyes warm beneath her uniform cap.

Want to fly safely? Want to breathe clean air?

As we now know, aerotoxicity is a real health hazard. Isla lost her sight overnight thanks to an acute poisoning. Her aircrew colleagues also suffered severe symptoms, and are still in hospital suffering from chronic fatigue and a dangerous decrease in lung function. These debilitating symptoms can remain not just for days, but *years*.

BreatheZero was founded by Professor Gerald Dunsfold, a graduate of Oxford University. After finishing his degree, Gerald moved to Australia, and after falling ill after each long-haul flight from Australia to the UK, he began to realise he wasn't suffering from jet lag, but aerotoxic syndrome.

Lucy studied the professor's photograph. He was beaming into the camera, teeth white, eyes shiny. He didn't look old enough to be a professor. She skimmed the rest of the intro and flicked to the next page.

We use carbon filters, as used by the British military and sewn into the masks, which eliminate 99 per cent of toxins caused by contaminated air in a jet aircraft.

She clicked on the big blue box *Buy a Mask.* A variety of masks filled her screen. There were red masks and blue, tartan masks, green polka-dot masks, florals and checks. There even a Hello Kitty mask for girls and one with dinosaurs for boys. Each cost £25 and had names like Commandant, Boss, King and Princess.

A creeping sensation came over her as she explored the

remainder of the website. The technology, the blog, the press reports, FAQs, everything fired up warning colours of purple and red in her mind. Was the site legitimate? It appeared to be, but who knew? She looked up Professor Gerald Dunsfold, read his latest social media messages.

> The scale of the issue of aerotoxicity, a problem that's claiming the lives of literally thousands of flyers around the world every year, is horrendous. It is aviation's darkest secret.

Lucy researched aerotoxic syndrome to see that yes, it really was a problem. She returned to the BreatheZero site. Then she called Dan. Filled him in.

'I'm going to go to Wolverhampton tomorrow. I want to check out the factory,' she told him. 'Make sure it's above board.'

'If you do that, then I'll go and see Isla. See what intel she can give us about the company.' He paused before adding carefully, 'Will you be staying tonight?' He didn't mention her hangover yesterday, or ask if she'd called Mac. He just waited for her to answer.

'Would you mind?'

'Let's eat out. There's a great tapas bar around the corner.'

'Perfect.'

When Lucy arrived at the tube, she picked up a copy of the *Evening Standard* to see Isla was front-page news. The inside pages were filled with the scandal of aerotoxicity. When she checked the BBC News website, Isla was there too, along with a politician saying, *The public have been deprived of the right to know they are being poisoned mid-air.* Scientists were getting involved along with lobby groups and aerotoxic associations.

It was enough to put you off flying, Lucy thought. Unless you had a BreatheZero mask, that was. Maybe she should grab one when she was at the factory. Just in case.

44

Tuesday morning, and Lucy was on the train to Wolverhampton trying to get in touch with Mac. They'd played phone tag all last night thanks to his murder case going ballistic and now she thanked God for texts because at least he knew she was alive and kicking as well as where she was staying. Not that he'd been impressed. He'd managed to convey cold disapproval with barely three lines, which she thought was pretty impressive. He seemed convinced that by staying with Dan she'd trebled her safety risk and she'd been highly relieved that he'd signed off with an emoji of a heart.

And what about Mum? She'd barely turned a hair when Lucy didn't return to stay. She was, Lucy guessed, glad to put off the moment when she'd have to tell Lucy that her father was a criminal. Poor Mum. How awful to have hidden such a rotten past and for so long. But it still hadn't been right, lying to Lucy all that time. She could see that her mother wanted to protect her, but at what cost? She would much rather have known the truth from the start. What really rankled was the fact she hadn't given Lucy a choice. Mum had decided what was best for her daughter, no discussion, no debate, and that was that. How they were going to patch things up was anyone's guess, but Lucy reckoned it would take more than a bottle of Chardonnay.

She gazed out of the window. Hedgerows showed a faint dusting of green and the flashes of yellow – daffodils nodding in the breeze – cheered her in the knowledge that spring was around the corner. New beginnings, she thought, but how her peers and colleagues were going to react when they found out about her father, she could only guess. She sighed. More notoriety was guaranteed.

She arrived at Wolverhampton Station just before midday. Caught a cab to Hobgate Road. The driver wore a turban the colour of tangerines and sported the longest, most luxurious beard Lucy had ever seen. It didn't take long to get there. They passed a primary school, an MOT station. A church. Blocks of dismal grey concrete flats. Just after a recycling centre, the driver pulled over in front of a factory's gates emblazoned with a silver sign. *BreatheZero.*

'Could you pick me up in an hour?' she asked.

'Just text me, love, when you're ready.'

Lucy climbed out into a chill wind laden with rain. Pulling her collar up, she walked across a forecourt busy with delivery vans and lorries collecting boxes from a loading bay. Half a dozen cars were parked on the left, all fairly ordinary, a mix of bog-standard sedans and the like, but one stood out. A gleaming blue Jaguar E-Pace. It was parked in a space labelled *Director. No parking.*

Was that Amina Amari's car? She'd spoken to the woman earlier, pretending to be a freelance journalist and asking for an interview. Amari hadn't been particularly interested until Lucy mentioned she was hoping to sell an article about the BreatheZero masks in the *Daily Mail* weekend colour supplement. Lots of quotes, lots of photos. It had been Dan's idea, and he'd even supplied her with a press card, complete with her photograph, made from Max's plastic ID card and badge printer sitting in the corner of the living room.

'I really shouldn't use this, Dan. If my boss finds out...'

'Just keep it on you,' he said smoothly. 'Just in case. It might help get you out of trouble. It's certainly helped Max from time to time.'

She raised her eyebrows. She'd never met Max, but now she was intrigued. Dan saw the look on her face. 'Don't ask.' His voice was dry.

'Careless talk costs lives?' she suggested.

He didn't say anything, just passed the card over, expression neutral and giving nothing away, which she took to mean Max was probably an old spook buddy of Dan's. Thanks to Max, today she wasn't DC Lucy Davies but Alex Catell, freelance journo.

She pushed open a side door, as she'd been instructed by Amari earlier. Inside was a small hall. A door stood ahead of her, another on her left, a third on her right. She pressed the buzzer on the wall, also as instructed. Faintly, she heard a bell ringing somewhere inside the building. Twenty seconds later or so, the door on Lucy's right opened. 'Alex?' a woman's voice said. Warm, melodious. 'You've made good time. I hope your journey was okay?'

Brown dress, brown boots, dark wavy hair. Honey-coloured skin. Gold belt, gold accessories. Sinuous, confident stride with a slight hitch, favouring her right leg slightly.

Lucy froze inside.

It was the woman from the custody suite CCTV. The woman who'd given Ricky a sandwich with peanut butter inside it. Chris Malone, who'd tried to kill him.

Fuck, fuck, *fuck*.

'It was fine, thank you,' Lucy said. Her voice was hoarse and she hurriedly cleared her throat, searching in her handbag for her press card to cover her shock.

'Amina Amari,' the woman said, putting out her hand.

Lucy pulled out the card with her left hand and took Amari's hand in her right, praying the woman wouldn't notice how damp her palm had become. 'Thanks for seeing me.'

Amari's gaze flicked over Lucy's jeans, boots and down jacket. She held Lucy's eyes. Frowned for a moment. 'Have we met before?'

The words sent a shard of fright through Lucy. Anyone involved with Kaitlyn's murder might have been following the police investigation and seen her on TV, at the press conference.

'I don't think so.'

'Strange.' Amari studied her more closely. 'You look familiar.'

'Maybe I look like someone you know.'

'Maybe.' She shrugged. 'At a press junket or publicity something or other. We've been to enough of them.'

Lucy was struggling to get her brain into gear. 'Me too.'

'We're so pleased you've come to see us.' Amari smiled. 'I have to be honest, we're really very excited about being in the *Daily Mail*.'

'That's if my editor goes for it,' Lucy said, gradually regaining her composure. 'Nothing's guaranteed, as I said before, but I'm confident.'

Amari beamed. 'Let me show you around.'

Lucy followed the woman on a tour of the manufacturing plant. Apparently, the company also made smokeless ashtrays and three-sided flip phones.

'We're always looking for the next big idea. We've just started making levitating desk lamps.' Her expression brightened. 'You must take one with you when you go. They're really cool.'

'Lovely,' said Lucy.

Lucy learned about respiration, dust and military grade carbon filters. How the masks were designed to block particulate pollution from jet engines, but they could also block viruses too.

'The masks filter air through four different layers. It will filter ninety-nine per cent of viruses as well as bacteria. So when you fly you won't just be protected from bled air, but you won't catch any nasty coughs and colds either.' Amari's expression was alight. 'With all the publicity about aerotoxicity, we can't make masks fast enough. We've just signed a lease on a larger factory nearby. Business is booming.'

She swept through the packing area, past the distribution hub and into a neat office with three desks. 'Most of our business is through the internet. Mail order. This is our sales director, Adam Mason.'

'Hi there.'

Lucy took in the man rising from his desk, the grey speckles through his hair, his face lined with laughter.

Her mind was swamped in hissing white light. Her stomach swooped. Her ears were whistling. It couldn't be possible. But it was. It was Dad.

45

Her father was smiling, exuding bonhomie, but then he saw her. The colour drained from his face. He was wearing a suit. Nicely cut, expensive. A blue tie with little yellow racehorses galloping all over it. Shiny, expensive-looking black leather shoes.

'I'm Alex Catell,' Lucy said. She found her press card and held it up so he could see, praying he'd go with it, unsure what the fuck was going on, why he was here, but instinct screamed at her not to let Amari know she wasn't who she said she was.

'The *Daily Mail*?' he said. And then he was walking towards her, his face open and friendly, his colour returning in a rush.

'I'm freelance, but yes. I'm hoping to sell the article to them.'

He took her hand in his. Warm, firm. Slightly sweaty, like her own. 'Nice to meet you. And thanks for thinking of us.'

'No problem.'

'I've given her the tour,' Amari said. 'It's over to you to fill her in on whatever else she wants to know.'

Her father raised his eyebrows. 'Any questions spring immediately to mind?' His tone was, to her horror, almost amused.

'Oh, lots,' she replied lightly. 'So many, in fact, I hardly know where to start.'

'Why don't we go and get a coffee,' he suggested. 'Talk in comfort.' He glanced at Amari. 'I'll take her to the meeting room, okay?'

'Sure. She's all yours.' Amari shook hands with Lucy once more before moving to sit behind one of the desks, her attention already on her computer screen. She didn't look at them as they walked outside.

Lucy was opening her mouth to say something, probably *What the fuck?!*, but her father held up a hand. 'You've seen the assembly line?'

'Yes.'

'And the carbon filters being fitted?'

'Yup.'

'We have a very high number of filaments,' he told her, 'that are woven into cloth, making the speed of absorption really fast. It's also easy to breathe through...'

He spouted guff about the masks as they walked down a corridor. He opened a door to the right, still talking, but the instant they were inside and he'd closed it behind them, he spun around, taking Lucy's upper arms in his hands and shaking her.

'What the hell are you doing here?' he hissed.

She stared at him, his face contorted, anxious, fearful.

'I might ask the same,' she bit back, her tone like acid.

'For Chrissake, I'm undercover. If you blow this I'll...' He ran a hand over his head. 'Shit, *shit.*'

'Undercover?' she repeated blankly.

'Jesus, Lucy. I'm a cop, okay? I've been after this lot since kingdom come, and I am *so close* I can't tell you. Please do *not* fuck it up.'

'You're a cop?'

'Yes.' He closed his eyes. His hands were on top of his head in a position of despair.

He wasn't a criminal? She looked him up and down, the smart suit, the gleaming shoes. Nausea sat in her belly. Then she heard Colin Pearson's voice, the SFO intelligence officer as if he was standing right next to her.

I wondered if he'd had some intel to tip him off because if he didn't, it's like he had some sort of sixth sense that kept him just ahead of us.

'Which police force?' she managed.

He dropped his hands. Opened his eyes. He suddenly looked exhausted.

'Only three people know about this, and now it's four.' A flick of humour crossed his face. 'I hope you can keep a secret.'

His words sent a shiver through her.

'Dad... The SFO are looking for you. They think you're someone called Neil Greenhill.'

Another flash of amusement. 'I know.'

She searched his eyes, and then something inched into her heart, a brief flurry of fear.

'Who is Carl Davies?'

He looked away.

Oh God, oh God, oh God.

'Is it your real name? Carl Davies?'

Long silence.

'Shit. Does this mean my name, Davies, isn't real?'

At that, his head switched around. 'Of course it's real. It's on your birth certificate, isn't it?'

'But it's not your real name.'

'What's in a name?' He gave a weak smile. 'You could be called Dorcas Tarantula and I'd still love you.'

Suddenly the penny dropped. 'Jesus Christ, Dad. Are you saying Mum didn't know you were a cop when you married her?'

He didn't answer. His gaze was fixed to the wall. His skin had turned strangely waxy.

'Oh God.' She suddenly felt dizzy. 'No wonder she threw you out.'

He closed his eyes.

Lucy put a hand against the wall to steady herself. 'What's your real name?' she whispered.

Again, he looked away. He was clenching and unclenching his fists.

'*Tell me!*' she suddenly yelled.

'You should go,' he snapped. 'I don't want my sodding cover blown.'

'You shit.' She was incredulous. 'You won't tell me?'

He glanced at the door. Made dampening motions with his hands. 'Christ, Lucy. This isn't the time, okay?'

'Why won't you?' She stepped close, peering up at him. 'What are you afraid of?'

'It's not that, it's–'

'You lied to Mum. She thought you were someone else, for God's sake! And you lied to me. How could you?'

'It was work!'

'But we're your family!'

He looked as though he wanted to tear his hair out. 'You know how dangerous it is being on a long-term undercover assignment. If my targets found out, they'd go for you and Mum, no hesitation. Can't you see?'

'Plenty of undercover officers have families who know what they do. What makes you so different?'

'I was dealing with people who were killers, don't you get it? If they got a whiff that I was a cop, you and Mum would have been in the firing line. I did it to protect you! There was no other way!'

'That's pathetic,' she spat. 'There's always a way. You caused immeasurable damage and you call it *work*.'

She went to the door and yanked it open. Before she stepped outside, she looked at him standing there, a combination of misery and defiance in his stance.

'I hate you,' she said.

He gave her a sad smile.

'That's exactly what your mother said.'

46

Dan was shocked when he saw Isla. Gone was the smart, bright and confident young flight attendant and in her place was a diminished, frightened woman. He'd been surprised how easy it had been to gain access to her ward, especially since the media coverage of her and BreatheZero, but he'd simply given her name at ward reception, said he was a friend, and he was directed to her room, where she was sitting with her friend Emily.

Emily was also American, a vivid Californian blonde with freckles across the bridge of her nose and green eyes that reminded him of Kaitlyn. Kaitlyn, who come hell or high water, he was going to avenge.

He introduced himself, saying that Isla had looked after him on the Miami flight eleven days ago. He wasn't surprised that she couldn't remember him. She had to have met dozens of business-class travellers over the past month alone.

'I wanted to talk to you about BreatheZero,' he said.

'What about it?' Her tone was cautious.

He couldn't very well say that Tomas, a criminal friend of Lucy's, had given them a tip-off that might help them find a woman who was suspected of trying to kill an accountant called Ricky Shaw, so he settled for: 'I'm working with the police. We're investigating BreatheZero.'

At that Emily's eyes widened. 'No way.'

'Shoot.' Isla's features became animated. 'Why? What have they done?'

He prevaricated. 'It's part of another investigation. I'm sorry I can't say exactly what. You could say I'm information gathering.'

Emily leaned forward. 'What do you need to know?'

'Just a few basic things. Like how they approached Isla in the first instance.'

Isla glanced in Emily's direction. 'Shall I tell him?'

'I can't see why not.'

Isla spoke. 'It was a journalist from the *London Herald* who came and saw me. Nykko. He was doing a story on aerotoxicity. Apparently, I was on the front page of his newspaper.' She plucked at her blanket. 'But I knew nothing of it until a woman from BreatheZero came to see me.'

'What was her name?'

'Amina Amari. She was really nice, wasn't she, Em? And the professor too.'

'Yeah, he was really cute.' Emily nodded. 'And his accent! So British! I could listen to him for–'

'Em...' Isla's tone had a smile in it, but it was also warning. 'Mr Forrester doesn't need to hear about–'

'So I made a date with him!' Emily flung up her hands. 'Where's the harm in that?'

Silence.

'Would you be talking about Professor Gerald Dunsfold?' Dan asked. He'd just returned from Oxford this morning, where he'd been researching the professor who was, apparently, the founder of BreatheZero.

Emily glanced at Isla. Gave a sheepish nod.

'What did they want?' Dan asked.

It was Emily who replied. 'Amina wants Isla to be the "face" of their company. To help her sell more masks and save more lives from being ruined by breathing bled air in jet aeroplanes. She's convinced we'll all be multi-millionaires before the year is out.'

'She brought in a contract,' Isla said, her voice small.

Dan raised his eyebrows.

'No, we didn't sign it,' said Emily.

'No.' Isla looked dejected. 'I don't have aerotoxicity, you see. I have a brain tumour.'

'Oh, Isla.' Dan's heart went out to her. 'I'm so sorry.'

'Yeah, it's really crap.'

They talked about the operation that was going to happen the next day, her terror of staying awake for the four- to six-hour operation, and then Dan returned to the subject that had brought him here.

'Isla. About BreatheZero. Did you know that your face is already on their website? And that you're being shown in their ads?'

'*What?*'

Emily sprang to her feet. Isla sat bolt upright.

Dan brought out his phone. Showed Emily the ad Lucy had seen in the weekend papers.

'They're quoting Isla too,' he added.

Emily read out what some of what Isla was supposed to have said. 'Protect your pregnancy... think of the tiny baby inside you, growing and changing day by day... there is great potential for the toxins to pass through the placenta and be absorbed by your unborn baby...'

'But I didn't say any of this!' Isla cried.

'How *dare they*!' Emily strode to the window and back, her hair almost crackling with fury. 'No contract, no money, but they're using you anyway! What a shitty thing to do. And I am certainly not going to see Gerald fucking Dunsfold for that drink now, am I? Bastard. He can sit there all night for all I care.'

Dan's interest pricked. 'Where were you meeting him?'

'The Hollywood Arms. It's just around the corner.'

'What time?'

Emily checked her watch. 'He suggested an afternoon cocktail at four o'clock.'

'If he contacts you in the meantime, don't let on you won't be there, will you? I'd quite like to meet him.'

Emily's eyes gleamed. 'You have my permission to do your worst.'

47

Dan arrived early at the Hollywood Arms, taking up position at the far end of the bar where he had a clear view of the door. Already it was busy with affluent-looking thirty-somethings. Suits stood alongside jeans and sweatshirts drinking cocktails out of large balloon-like glasses. Stripped floorboards, velvet-covered chairs, friendly staff. Jenny would like the shabby chic, professional atmosphere if not the prices, but then it was in the heart of Chelsea, one of the most expensive areas in the world.

Dan nursed a sparkling mineral water, mulling over the conversation he'd had with Lucy on his way here. She'd sounded so strung out, he'd asked for her safety code again to make sure she hadn't been kidnapped or worse. He didn't like the fact he'd had to ask her for this twice in as many days. It meant that things were potentially thickening, getting dangerous.

'I'm fine,' she'd said. 'I'm not being held or anything, promise. It's just that I saw someone today. It's personal, and it's doing my head in.'

'Want to tell me? I'm a good sounding board.'

'I know you are.'

When she didn't say anything more, he let it go. She'd tell him when she was ready.

Lucy filled him in on the BreatheZero factory and that she'd met the CEO, Amina Amari. 'She's Chris Malone. She gave Ricky that peanut butter sandwich.'

'Ah.' Things were beginning to hang together. Dan told her about Amina Amari using Isla as the face of BreatheZero. 'Isla hasn't signed a contract, but Amari's exploiting her all the same.'

'Nasty.'

'Very.'

'I've followed her to her house. I want to see where she lives. If she has a partner, children…'

Dan made a note of the address she gave him. 'Be careful.'

'That's why I'm ringing. So you know where I am.'

'You've told the SIO where you are?'

There was a pause, then she said, 'No.'

'I see.'

'You're the only person who knows where I am.'

'Okay. If I don't hear from you, say, in an hour–'

'Call the cops.'

Dan took a sip of water, glad she'd told him her plan. However, he didn't like the fact she was going off-grid and without the investigative team behind her. She'd better keep safe or Mac really would kill him this time. Tapping his foot against the wooden bar panel he checked his watch again, knowing he'd be on edge until Lucy next rang in. Meanwhile, he had Gerald Dunsfold to think about. He'd spent a long time looking into the man, his degree at the University of Oxford, his PhD, his professorship, and when Dunsfold arrived at the bar, Dan studied him, intrigued. He was a good-looking man, thick dark hair, shiny white teeth. Well dressed, confident. He was looking around for Emily, and when he didn't see her he went to the bar, placed an order.

Dan watched Dunsfold sink his fancy cocktail and order another. The man kept looking at his watch, gazing around the ever-increasingly busy bar, checking his phone every other second and getting more irritated by the minute. When he'd nearly finished his second cocktail Dan casually moved to stand next to him where he ordered a whisky sour.

When the cocktail arrived, Dan asked the waitress if she'd seen a pretty dark-haired woman looking for him. 'She's my date. She was meant to be here a good half an hour ago.'

The waitress shook her head. 'Sorry.'

Dan pasted a gloomy look on his face. He let his gaze drift to Dunsfold. When their eyes met, Dan raised his eyebrows in a vague query as if to say, *Have you seen her, maybe?*

Dunsfold grimaced. 'Sorry, pal.'

Dan sighed. Turned back to the waitress. 'I'll have another, then. Just in case she's running late.'

When Dunsfold gave a snort, Dan said, 'What?' He kept his expression open, non-confrontational.

'It's my bet she's not running late.' Dunsfold's tone was dry.

Dan gave another sigh. Rested his elbows on the bar. Both men watched the waitress mix Dan's drink. As she poured it into a glass, Dunsfold pushed his now empty glass towards her, saying, 'Another Negroni, love.' He glanced at Dan, obviously hacked off. 'It looks as though we're in the same boat, but mine was blonde.'

Dan smiled ruefully. 'Women. Can't live with them–'

'Can't live without them.'

When the Negroni arrived, they chinked glasses.

'Here's to our dates getting their comeuppance,' Dunsfold said.

'Hmm,' Dan agreed neutrally.

'I thought mine was a shoo-in,' Dunsfold went on. 'Little bitch, leading me on like that. You?'

'Just someone I liked.'

Dunsfold pulled a face. 'That's when the trouble starts. Treat them as they're meant to be treated. Then they know who's boss.'

Keeping his dislike of the man hidden, Dan moved things into a general conversation. He learned Dunsfold was a science professor and in town to promote his company, BreatheZero. 'You've heard of aerotoxicity, right?'

Dan said no, he hadn't, prompting a lecture on the subject and another cocktail for both of them.

'And what about you?' Dunsfold eventually asked Dan. 'What do you do?'

'I don't pretend I'm an Oxford graduate with a professorship in science.' His gaze was flat.

'What?' Dunsfold's eyes popped.

'You could say I'm into research too. But my subject isn't science, it's people. You never went to Oxford, let alone got a professorship. Where did you go?' Dan's tone was conversational. 'Oh, that's right. Australia. Where they didn't check your fake degrees.'

Dunsfold's mouth opened and closed. His skin had taken on a sickly sheen. 'What the... who are you?'

'That's for me to know and you to worry about.' Dan tapped the side of his nose. 'Have a nice evening.'

He walked outside into a soft drizzle. He was smiling. It wasn't often he got revenge without bloodshed. Dunsfold wouldn't be able to sleep now his secret was out. Emily would be pleased.

48

After Lucy had left the BreatheZero factory, she'd walked to the next street, where she called the Sikh taxi driver, and showed him her warrant card.

'I want to follow a man who works at BreatheZero.'

He squinted as he thought. 'It's not dangerous, is it? I've got four kids.'

'I just want to see where he goes, that's all.'

'All right. I suppose it's more interesting than dropping commuters home.'

'He might not leave until late,' she warned.

'My meter's running.'

'And I'm on a strict budget.'

'Forty quid an hour.'

'Thirty and not a penny more or I'll order an Uber.'

He sighed noisily. 'Don't you cops get expenses?'

She just looked at him.

'Oh, I get it.' He sighed again. 'Public money and all that.'

Lucy got him to park where she could see the office door across the forecourt. She hadn't seen a rear exit during her tour and crossed her fingers that there wasn't one or she could be waiting a very long time.

In the back of the cab, she called Dan – who'd apparently just seen Professor Gerald Dunsfold, who wasn't a professor at all – then she rang Mac but he was interviewing so she sent him a text. A quick look at the news websites showed that aerotoxicity, an *unforgivable scandal*, according to a prominent government official, was gaining traction. Just about every news outlet had a variation on the headline Lucy had read at the weekend: *One Flight Can Change Your Life.*

She wondered if the media would have taken to the story quite so fast if Isla hadn't been so beautiful. Clever BreatheZero to use her but not so clever since, according to Dan, Isla hadn't signed a contract and apparently wasn't going to either. Would she sue? Good luck to her, Lucy thought, except if Amina Amari was as ruthless as Lucy suspected, Isla had better watch her step.

Leaning back in her seat, she gazed at the steady flow of delivery vans toing and froing through the BreatheZero gates like worker bees. Was her father really undercover? It made sense, especially since Colin Pearson had talked about Neil Greenhill – Dad – as a *weird customer. No family at all. Didn't socialise... We never found out where he lived.*

Had he really lied to protect her and Mum?

The sick feeling in her stomach increased when she realised he hadn't answered when she'd asked which police force he was attached to.

Steadily, the minutes ticked past. The taxi driver made a couple of calls. Switched on Radio 5 Live. They chatted a bit. Lucy learned his name was Teg and that he supported Birmingham City FC.

It was just after five when the flow of vans ceased and the factory workers started leaving. Lucy's senses sharpened. Teg turned off the radio when the first car left the factory. She watched as people began leaving, climbing into their cars, driving away. An hour later darkness began to fall. Amina Amari was walking outside. Lucy's father was with her.

She stared at him, the face that she knew and the child in her loved. He lied to protect us, she told herself. He's on a job. He's working. *I've been after this lot since kingdom come, and I am so close I can't tell you.*

She watched as her father climbed into the driver's seat of the Jaguar. Amina Amari took the passenger's side.

'He's in the Jag,' she told Teg.

'Okeydokey.' He started the engine and when the Jag pulled out into the street, followed them. As they drove out of Wolverhampton, Lucy switched on Google Maps and followed their journey along Compton Road and onto the A454 to Bridgnorth. Traffic was heavy with commuters and short queues of cars where people were turning off the road. Barely half an hour into the journey the Jag turned right, signed to the village of Worfield, but when they came to a fork in the road, it switched right again. Teg's headlights showed a much narrower road. It was unsigned.

Four hundred yards further, the Jag slowed down, indicating left. Teg slowed with them. When Lucy saw the start of a driveway, she said, 'Drive past them. I don't want them to know they've been followed.'

As they passed, Lucy saw a pair of tall, wrought-iron gates already beginning to open onto a drive with little LED lights glowing on each side of the gravel. At the end stood a house, also artfully lit. From the briefest glimpse she could see it was huge. Absolutely massive. Half-timbered above a red-brick base... and then it was gone, swallowed by the encroaching darkness.

'Pull over,' she told Teg.

He slowed the taxi, coming to rest half on the verge, half off.

Quickly, she rang Dan and told him where she was. He was obviously sensitive to her tone because he asked for her safety code. God, the man was canny. She'd thought she sounded completely normal but obviously not. When she put her hand on the car door Teg said, 'I thought you just wanted to see where he went?'

'I won't be long.'

She climbed out of the taxi and walked back to the gates, checking out the laurel hedge for any weak spots. She passed the gates, which were now closed, and kept walking. There! Well below eye level, really low, was a gap between the trunks. Not for the first time, she was glad she was small. On hands and knees, she scrabbled through the hole, grazing her wrists and muddying her jeans, but she was through. Swiftly she jogged alongside the drive. Skirted the house. It was pitch dark but the house was ablaze, lighting the swathes of lawn. She smelled wood smoke, indicating someone had lit a fire. She heard a door open somewhere and shrank behind a low wall covered in ivy.

'Out you go,' a woman said. 'Have a pee before dinner.'

Lucy's worst nightmare had just started. She knew that tone of voice. She knew pets got fed when their owners returned home. *Please God it's not a Rottweiler or a German Shepherd.* She started to back up, already turning to run for the road, when the dog trotted into view, ears pricked, tail alert.

Small, white and fluffy, it came straight to her, obviously expecting to be petted.

'No,' she hissed. 'Go and pee.'

But the dog remained, tail wagging, little button black eyes shining.

'Go away.'

No such luck. She'd have to ignore it.

'Just don't bark, okay?'

Lucy walked around the back of the house, the dog tagging

along. Slipping from shrub to shrub, she spied through the windows. An enormous living room. A study with big leather chairs. She didn't see anyone. Then a door opened. A slab of light lay on cobblestones. A woman sang, 'Bertie! Dinner!'

The dog tore off.

Lucy moved to another window. This was the kitchen. Huge. Copper pots and pans hung from the ceiling along with bunches of herbs and wine glasses. Amina Amari was there, tossing back what looked like a tumbler of whisky. Who was the woman who'd called the dog? It couldn't have been Amari, not unless she could teleport.

Lucy's father, Carl, was also in the kitchen. No drink. He was unsmiling, his expression grim as he spoke. Amari listened for a while but then Carl said something that made the woman's eyes widen. She looked stunned for a second then she slammed down her glass so hard whisky slopped over the edge. She strode to Lucy's father, stabbing her finger in his face. She was shouting but Lucy couldn't hear the words.

Her father stood his ground but his face was set. He was shaking his head and Amira was pointing behind him, yelling fit to burst. It looked as though she was shouting, *Get out!*

Lucy watched as Amari suddenly stopped yelling, as if she'd been slapped. Although Lucy couldn't see anyone, it was obvious someone had appeared from the body language of Amari and her father. Was it the woman who'd called the dog? Both Amari and Lucy's father were staring at the same space. Both of them were motionless, frozen in a state of... what? Fear? Dismay? It was hard to tell but both looked shaken.

Then Amari spun on her heel, grabbed her drink and downed it in two quick swallows. Lucy's father walked out of the room. His shoulders were stiff with tension.

She'd seen enough. She had to ring Jon Banks. Tell him she'd found Chris Malone. Cautiously she began to backtrack.

She was halfway down the drive when she heard an engine start. Quickly she took cover behind a tree trunk. As the car passed, she had a quick peek to see it was the blue Jag. Just one driver. Her father.

She broke into a run, flying for the gap in the hedge, for Teg and his taxi. She wanted to follow her dad, see where he was going. More scratches, more mud on her clothes, and then she was racing down the road. She piled into the back of the cab.

'Did the blue Jag come this way?' she gasped.

'Yup.'

'After it!'

'If it comes to a race, you know we're gonna lose, right?'

'I just want to see–'

'Where it goes, okay.'

Although Teg floored his taxi, driving as fast as he dared – or so he said – along the narrow road, they didn't catch up with the Jag. Lucy had just told Teg to give up and drop her at the railway station, when her phone rang. *Unknown caller.*

'Yes?' she answered.

'You can stop following me now, okay?'

49

'Dad?'

'The one and only.'

'What makes you think I'm following you?'

She felt Teg's eyes snap to her in the rear-view mirror and ignored him.

'Because that's what I'd do. It's what a good cop would do. I pegged the taxi straight away, you know.'

'What's going on? I mean, I know you told me–'

'You asked me which force.'

'Yes.'

'I think you can probably guess. But it's Special Branch. My handler is Geoff Hanmer. If you get in touch, he'll deny I exist. So give him my code name, *Black Rainbow*.'

A little bubble of hope rose inside her. Perhaps he was a cop, after all. Please God, it was true.

'Ring him.'

'Okay.'

'Do you want his number?'

'I'll find it.'

'You don't trust me.'

'How can I?' she snapped. 'You fucked off when I was eight years old and now I find you're consorting with a woman who tried to kill Ricky.'

'What?' he sounded shocked.

'You heard me. We've got CCTV of her. He nearly *died*.' Which was an exaggeration but she wanted to hit him hard.

'Christ almighty.'

'Why should she want to kill him?'

'I take it you're talking about Amina?'

'Yes.'

'I don't know.' He swallowed audibly. 'But it could have something to do with the fact Ricky's her accountant.'

She hadn't seen BreatheZero in Ricky's client list, and said so.

'That's because it's owned by a holding company.' Suddenly her father sounded tired. 'Look, Lucy. Could you just ring Geoff? Because if you don't, we're going to be at loggerheads and I don't want that. I want us both to be working from the same page. Okay?'

'What were you rowing with Amari about?'

'Not now, Lucy.'

She gritted her teeth. 'Amari is wanted by the police. I have to tell my boss that I've seen her.'

'No.'

'Hey, you can't just–'

'It's not the right time,' he snapped. 'I will bring her in myself, okay? Now, go and call Geoff and ring me back once you've spoken.'

He hung up. Lucy stared at the phone. She was trembling with a combination of anger, panic and confusion. She desperately wanted to ring the SIO, tell him where he could find

Chris Malone, aka Amina Amari, but the kid in her quailed when her father's voice snapped at her: *Please do* not *fuck it up.*

Lucy rang Special Branch. Thanks to it being after seven now, she was presented with a selection of out-of-hours options, forcing her to leave a variety of messages. Dammit, she wanted results *now*. She put her phone back in her bag as Teg pulled up outside the railway station. She paid him. Gave him a generous tip which made him grin.

'It was fun,' he told her, sounding slightly surprised. 'Ring me any time you're back in town.'

On the platform, a chill wind biting her wrists and neck, she called Mac.

'Hello gorgeous,' he answered.

'Do you know anyone in Special Branch? I need an "in" to get some info.'

'And hello to you too.' His tone was dry but before she could snap at him – *I don't have time for this!* – he said, 'Hang on a mo...'

Lucy heard voices in the background.

'Paul Gray.' Mac was back. 'He's a pal of mine, so be gentle with him. Here's his mobile...'

She could have thrown her phone onto the train track when yet another automated voice asked her to leave a message. Didn't anyone answer their phones any more? At which point, her phone vibrated. Dan. Shit, she'd forgotten to ring him to tell him she was safe.

'Dan, I'm sorry. I'm fine. I've just been busy.'

'That's all I need to know. Will I see you at the flat later?'

'Actually, I might stay with Mum tonight.'

The train began to approach, engine rumbling. Dan obviously heard it as he said, 'I'll let you go, then. Speak tomorrow? I've got some interesting stuff to share.'

'Me too,' she said feelingly. She still hadn't told him she'd found her father. She would, though, when the time came, and when she actually knew the whole truth, whatever it was.

Since she had more phone calls to make, Lucy didn't take a seat on the train but took up position in a passageway and where she hoped she wouldn't be overheard. Watching the suburbs of Wolverhampton merge into Birmingham's outskirts, she tried Paul Gray again. This time she got through. Alleluia! Quickly she explained who she was and what she wanted. Gray said he'd check with Mac and if she was ridgy-didge – his words, not hers – he'd pass the message on to Geoff Hanmer.

'It's extremely urgent,' she repeated. 'Tell him to ring me day or night.'

'Will do.'

Next, she rang Mac back. 'Sorry about earlier. I was in a hurry.'

'So I gathered. How's things?'

She yawned so widely tears collected in the corners of her eyes. 'I'm knackered.'

'Where are you?'

'On a train, heading back to London.'

'What gives?'

At that moment, she realised she had to see Mac, and tell him about her father. He'd help her through this. Help her to make the right decisions.

'I saw my dad again.'

'Really? How did it go?'

'I don't know. It's just... really complicated.' Out of nowhere her throat caught. She suddenly felt like weeping.

'Oh, my love.' Mac had obviously heard the emotion in her voice. 'I'm sorry. I wish I was with you.'

'Me too.' She braced herself against the wall as the train gave a lurch. 'I need your advice like nobody's business. I'll come down tomorrow. Stay the night.'

'Great. I'll make sure I'm all yours.'

They talked about his case for a bit, then he moved the conversation away from work to everyday things, like his sister hosting a baby shower for a friend where nobody turned up.

'What, not a single person?'

'Nope.'

'God, that's rude.'

'Everyone texted afterwards with their excuses, but she's still really cross about it.'

'I'm not surprised. I'd be furious. I'll ring her later.'

'Thanks.'

She stood staring out at the shiny wet buildings flashing past. Mac had, she realised, tried to interject some normality into their conversation. God, she was lucky to have met him. She was thinking how to start telling him about her dad when her phone rang. *Unknown.*

Thinking it might be her father using another number, she answered cautiously. 'Hello?'

'DC Davies?'

'Yes.'

'Superintendent Geoff Hanmer.' His tone was clipped and businesslike. 'Paul Gray tells me you want to speak to me, and that it's extremely urgent.'

Lucy stood upright, her attention sharpening. 'Yes. It's about an officer of yours...' Quickly she checked to make sure she couldn't be overheard. '*Black Rainbow.*'

There was a stunned silence.

'How do you know that name?' The man's tone turned wary.

'Through a case I'm working on. He told me his code name so that I could check his legitimacy with you.'

Another silence.

'I haven't, ahem... heard anything from him for a long time.' The superintendent cleared his throat noisily. 'How is he?'

'Er...' Lucy felt wrong-footed. 'Fine. I mean, really fine.'

'I see.'

A pause fell.

'You do realise,' Hanmer said, 'that only three of us know who he is. You are now the fourth. I hope you will take great care it stays that way.'

'Absolutely,' she said fervently. Her grip on the phone was slippery with sweat. Could she ask the question that was burning in her heart?

'What I wanted to know was, er... his real name.'

'If you don't know it,' he said icily, 'then it's certainly not for me to say. If, however, it is in his best interests, then you will have to apply to this station in person and give your reasons why.'

'Actually, I'm hoping he'll tell me himself,' Lucy admitted.

'He's a deep swimmer, DC Davies,' Hanmer warned. 'Unless he trusts you a hundred per cent – and I don't know of any SDS operatives that ever did that – you'll never know.'

After they'd hung up, Lucy stood gazing outside. A deep swimmer was an undercover operative who immersed themselves in their role, sometimes for years. They were officers who lived a secret life among their targets, becoming so intimately acquainted with one another's lives that in the end they could become closer than brothers. But it was all a sham.

The SDS, the Special Demonstration Squad, had been established by Special Branch and disbanded ages ago. They'd been notorious, using the names of eighty dead children to create false identities for their operatives. She guessed her father had been transferred to another undercover unit when the SDS finished. This was why he was investigating BreatheZero. *I've been after this lot since kingdom come...*

Lucy felt like crying for her mum. It must have been awful,

discovering she'd married an undercover cop without realising it. No wonder she'd felt betrayed.

What was Dad doing with Amina Amari? He'd seemed genuinely shocked to learn she'd tried to kill Ricky. What was he involved in?

She spent the rest of the train journey trying to work out what she should do next.

50

D an was still smiling at Gerald Dunsfold's expression of horror. Having duped so many people for so long, the man had probably started to believe he really *was* a professor. He'd actually gone to Sheffield University, where he'd been awarded an exit pass for completing the first year of the degree course, but that was it. His PhD didn't exist either, but that hadn't stopped him from creating a successful career in the sciences. Why didn't employers check potential employees' credentials? All Dan had done was ring Oxford University – Christ Church College – and ask for verification of Dunsfold's supposed first-class honours degree, and he'd immediately been alerted that Dunsfold wasn't what he claimed.

Dan shook his head at the fallibility of humans as he walked back to Max's. Three miles or so, but he didn't want to use public transport. He loved London, loved walking its streets and inhaling sounds and sights that were far removed from his remote country lifestyle.

On the next corner, he passed a vibrant-looking Italian pizzeria and restaurant. Since Lucy wouldn't be joining him tonight, he decided to stop and get something to eat. He ordered a beer. A pepperoni pizza with extra chilli. He rang Jenny and Aimee, checked in. All was well.

After a coffee he paid the bill, resumed his walk. It was dark, but light shone from windows on either side. People were at home, unwinding after a day at work, putting their kids to bed. He could smell suppers cooking and was glad he'd eaten.

He was on the corner of Redcliffe Gardens, pondering whether he and Jenny might ever move back to London, when something began tapping his consciousness. He didn't look around immediately, but slowed his pace, pretending to fiddle with his phone to see if anyone slowed down with him. He then put his phone away and started walking briskly. Behind him, the man who'd slowed when he had also speeded up. Probably not a professional or Dan might not have noticed him so quickly.

Dan turned left at the next street and paused in front of a shop window, sliding his eyes left. He wasn't surprised to see Gerald Dunsfold appear around the corner. He was just yards away, and the second Dunsfold realised it, his face turned panicky and he bolted back where he'd come from. Dan almost laughed, the man looked so comical.

What to do about him? Dunsfold wouldn't have known Dan had pinged him and would no doubt continue to follow. He didn't want to lead him back to Max's flat and supposed he'd better lose him. He started walking down the street towards Fulham Road, planning to jump on a bus and then catch a tube. From there he'd continue to dry clean until he was sure Dunsfold was no longer behind him, but he doubted he needed to be so assiduous. Just catching the bus should be enough.

Halfway down the street, he heard a car behind him, watched it sweep past. A van followed, pulling over just ahead of Dan and stopping. Automatically Dan switched to cross the road but to his astonishment, the back doors of the van swung open and two men in dark clothes, faces obscured in balaclavas, spilled out. They came straight for him. Both held weapons.

For one horrifying moment Dan was frozen, unable to believe it, but then instinct kicked in and he turned and ran.

Dunsfold had friends. Nasty friends, whom he'd called. They'd responded fast. Dunsfold had power, or knew someone who did. Someone who didn't like it that Dan knew their precious professor was a fraudster.

He had to get out of the neighbourhood. These men might not have come alone.

Footsteps pounded behind him. Just the two men. No Dunsfold.

He ran at full throttle. Hurtled down the street. He needed to get to Fulham Road and its bright lights, cars, buses, people. His breath was hot in his throat, his heart pounding.

Was he gaining on them?

Just ahead, someone opened the front door of their house, spilling light outside. Dan pelted straight for it and whoever was there. He had to get to the house, leap inside and slam the door shut on his pursuers. Then he could call the police.

Dan veered into the front garden and at the same time the door closed. Had they heard his pounding footsteps? Please God they hadn't locked their door...

He was halfway up the path, powering for the door, when he felt an electric rolling wave travelling up his body and into his groin. His body exploded into unbearable pain.

His body stiffened, every muscle contracting into a penetrating cramp.

His legs locked.

He dropped like a stone, sprawling across the path.

'Police!' Dan tried to shout. 'Call the police!'

But all that came through his lips was a wheeze.

Suddenly, the pain went. Vanished. He knew what had

happened. He'd been tasered, with 50,000 volts. But the electricity had stopped and he could now function again.

Dan forced himself to get to his feet and *run*.

'Get down,' a man said.

Dan powered forward, every cell, every vein leaping, reaching for the safety of the house.

A blistering pain felled him again. He couldn't crawl, couldn't move.

'Yeah, grab him. Quick.'

He felt hands on his arms and legs. He tried to lash out, but his legs wouldn't work. Bodily, the men hauled him upright. Dan tried to fight but his limbs were soft, his head lolling uselessly to one side.

He was shouting, yelling, but his throat was jammed. He didn't make a sound.

The pain stopped once more. He braced himself to fight against his captors. Began to unwind his muscles from their tension, their shock.

He uncoiled as hard and fast as he'd been trained all those years ago. Grabbed one man's hand and snapped it straight backwards. Heard the crackle as it broke. The man screamed. Dan kneed him savagely in the groin. He didn't wait for the man to topple but flew for his other opponent.

Another blast from the taser.

He went down like a stone.

His hands were fastened behind his back. His ankles trussed. Only then did the blow come. It seemed to take the skull off his shoulders. As he sank into unconsciousness, he thought he heard someone saying anxiously, 'Is everything all right?' The person from the house, no doubt. Too late, he thought. I'll be long gone by the time you put two and two together.

51

When Lucy reached Southwark it was past ten and she was soaking wet. It had been chucking down as she'd exited the tube and as she walked up her mother's little front path she was glad lights were on, indicating Mum was still up and that the heating would probably be going flat out. She was frozen.

'Hi, Mum,' she called out.

'Hi, love. I'm in the living room.'

'I'll be with you in a minute.'

Dumping her handbag on the kitchen table Lucy went to the fridge, pulled out a bottle of wine. Poured herself a large glass. She downed half of it before she trotted upstairs and dried her hair, changed into a pair of sweatpants and fleecy top.

Downstairs, she joined her mother in front of the TV.

'Hi, lovely.' Her mother raised her face for a kiss.

'Hi.'

Lucy settled on the sofa to see that *Newsnight* had two experts talking about aerotoxicity. BreatheZero was even mentioned, reminding her of what Amina Amari had said.

We can't make masks fast enough… Business is booming.

'How's things?' her mother asked. 'Are you any nearer knowing who killed that poor woman?'

But Lucy didn't want to talk about Kaitlyn or Ricky. Instead, she downed another slug of wine. 'I saw Dad today.'

Her mother stilled.

'He was looking really smart. Suit, tie, shiny shoes.'

Lucy glugged some more wine. Cleared her throat. 'He told me...' She took a breath, exhaled. 'That he was undercover when you got married.'

Her mother closed her eyes. 'What else?'

'That Davies isn't my real name.'

'Yes, it is.' Her mother was stout.

'You know what I mean,' Lucy said wearily.

Both of them fell silent.

'Do you know his real name?' Lucy asked.

At that, her mother turned to meet her gaze. Her expression was sad. 'No. He never told me.'

'Oh, Mum.' She leaned her head back. 'I can't imagine what it must have been like. I spoke to someone in Special Branch who said only three people know the truth about Dad. Now, I'm the fourth.'

At that, her mother's eyes widened. 'You spoke to Geoff?'

'Yes.'

'He was best man at our wedding.'

'Really?' Lucy sat upright.

'He and your dad met at cadet training. They spent two years in uniform before they joined Special Branch. Tight as ticks they were. But of course I didn't know any of this. I just thought your dad and Geoff went to school together. That your dad was a salesman and Geoff a lorry driver. I met your dad at a protest march. I really believed he *cared* about racism but it was all a sham. He was spying on us, giving the police information on us *all the time*. He said he was preventing riots, averting unrest and violence in London – what a load of *bollocks*.'

She was breathing deeply, trying to keep control. Lucy kept quiet.

'Can you...' Her mother swallowed audibly. 'Can you understand why I threw him out?'

'Yes.' Lucy reached over and took her mother's hand. Gave it a squeeze. 'It must have been horrible. Not just a shock but the *betrayal*. How did you find out?'

'He told me.' Her mother gave a strangled laugh. 'Can you imagine it? He actually thought I'd forgive him, forgive him for spying on me and my friends, swallow all his lies, and carry on as though nothing had happened. He was *unbelievable*.' Her face flushed at the memory. 'He thought love would conquer all but nothing could be further from the truth. He was a stinking, rotten *liar*. I hated him.'

Lucy squeezed her hand again. 'Why did he tell you? Why didn't he just keep on lying?'

'He would never have come clean if he hadn't been forced to.'

'Forced, how?'

Her mother's hazel eyes rested on her reflectively. Gradually, the pink in her cheeks lessened. Her voice was quiet when she spoke.

'I think you should ask him that yourself.'

'I will,' Lucy promised. She closed her eyes. 'What about his family? He always said he was abandoned as a baby and fostered all through his childhood. Does this mean I have grandparents? Aunts and uncles?'

'Darling, I have no idea. He refused to tell me.'

'How awful,' Lucy said but inside she was saying, *What a complete shit. Didn't he trust Mum?*

'I went mad.'

'I'm not surprised.' Lucy wriggled across the sofa and hugged her mother. 'I'm sorry I was so unforgiving about it. But I didn't understand. I wish you'd told me.'

'He did some terrible things. I didn't want you to know.'

'What terrible things?'

Her mother was silent.

'Mum?'

'It's for him to tell you. Not me.'

They didn't say much after that. Lucy knew they'd talk more about it, but for now they were at peace. When Lucy went to bed, she slept as though felled. No sleep, no dreams. And when she awoke, the first thing she did was ring her father.

'If you don't bring Amina Amari in by midday today,' she told him, 'I'm going to my SIO.'

52

Dan was woken by someone telling him to sodding well wake up. He opened his eyes and his brain exploded into pain. He lay still as a kaleidoscope of colours trembled across his vision. He listened for a voice, any sign someone was with him, but all he heard was his own rapid breathing.

He tried to take stock of himself. His feet were ice-cold and he was aware of the sweet smell of engine oil. He instinctively tried to raise his hand to check his head but his hands were behind him, locked together. So were his feet. That was why they were cold. He looked down at his body to see his knees were tucked against his chest. Instinctively he tried to stretch out his legs but a sudden, shocking pain roared through him, making him scream.

He lay there, gasping, panting, waiting for it to ease. His muscles were begging to be released. He wondered how long he'd been like this, and guessed quite a while. His body was stiff and sore, aching with stasis.

'You're awake.'

It was a woman's voice. Behind him.

He blinked. Tried to turn his head to see her.

'You want to be let up.' It was a statement, not a question.

'Yes.' His voice was scratchy. He was incredibly thirsty.

'I will untie your legs but first you have to answer me. Who are you?'

'Michael Wilson.' Dan gave her the cover name he'd used when he'd been at MI5 in a past lifetime. He also gave her the cover address for good measure. No harm in hoping she might keep her word and release his legs.

'And why is Michael Wilson asking questions about the qualifications of an eminent scientist?'

'I was curious...' He tried to lick his lips but he had no saliva. 'How someone could invent such an audacious deception and get away with it.'

Above him shone a fluorescent light. No furniture that he could see, just a red brick wall, shining with condensation.

'You spoke to Emily Petersen and Isla Hanson, didn't you?'

Dan opted for silence.

Behind him, he heard footsteps on concrete. Then his hands were pulled hard and the pain shrieked through his muscles. He tried to master the agony rocking him but she pulled again and again until he was half-screaming, half-sobbing, 'Yes, yes I saw them.'

'That's more like it.' She sounded satisfied. 'Tell me, what brought you to Isla?'

'Her picture in the paper,' he panted. 'She was my flight attendant last week. I recognised her. I felt sorry for her. I wanted to see if I could help.'

He'd always been told that if he had to lie, to try and keep it as close to the truth as possible, and now he began to fabricate his story.

'Help, how?'

'Loan her money, be a support. I have a friend who's an eye doctor.'

He waited for the woman to ask the doctor's name and was surprised when she moved on.

'What made you go to the Hollywood Arms and confront the scientist?'

Interesting she never said his name, Gerald Dunsfold. Perhaps it wasn't his name at all?

'I was angry for Isla. She'd been led up the garden path by a company who'd promised her everything and done nothing but use her.'

'She has a contract.' Defensive, snappy.

'Which she hasn't signed.'

'She has now.' Triumph laced the woman's voice.

'If it's proven that Isla was under even the smallest pressure it will be null and void.'

When he heard the footsteps walk away and not return, he wished he'd kept his mouth shut.

53

Lucy spent the morning attempting to research BreatheZero but her mind wouldn't settle. She kept looking at her watch, the clock on the wall, waiting for midday to arrive so she could come clean with the SIO. Or would her dad turn up with Amina Amari and turn her in? Anxiety ran across her synapses in waves of orange and red and when her phone rang at eleven forty-five she pounced on it.

'Yes?' she barked.

'DC Davies. Superintendent Hanmer.'

'Oh. Hi.'

'I'd like to see you, please.'

She blinked.

'Before you go to your SIO.'

Her brain locked. He knew what she'd said to Dad?

'My office. New Scotland Yard, Westminster. In half an hour. Please don't be late.'

She unstuck her tongue from the roof of her mouth. 'On my way.'

Lucy caught the Circle line to Westminster. Was her father working with Geoff Hanmer to arrest Amina Amari? She hoped to God he was, or she'd be up shit creek without a paddle if her SIO found out that she'd sat on the fact she'd found Chris Malone and not told him.

An icy wind was whipping off the Thames as she approached New Scotland Yard. Traffic roared along the Embankment, and on the other side of the river the London Eye gleamed in the pale spring sunshine.

Superintendent Hanmer came and fetched her from reception. He was medium build, medium height, no outstanding features. Dark eyes, watchful, intelligent. She could imagine him blending into any crowd without a problem. He shook her hand – firm and cool – and ushered her to his office. No offer of tea or coffee. His expression was flat. Grim. Her heartbeat picked up.

'What's this about?' she asked.

'Your father.'

'He's been in touch?'

'Yes.'

'Oookaaay.' She drew the word out cautiously.

Hanmer suddenly took a deep breath, let it out. Ran a hand over his head. 'Take a seat.' He was curt.

She did as she was told. He, however, stood by the window, looking out.

'I've known your father a long time,' he said. 'Thirty-two years, to be precise.'

She wanted to say, *you were best man at his wedding*, but decided to keep quiet. See what the man had to say first.

'A lot has happened in this time... I've been promoted. He's been... well, he's...' He rubbed the space between his eyebrows, obviously struggling with what to say next.

Lucy didn't help him. She sat in silence, waiting.

'Carl.' The detective cleared his throat. 'Was an excellent undercover officer. He distinguished himself during cadet training – where we first met – as well as through his two-year probation. We both joined Special Branch after two years in uniform.'

Her hands had turned cold, but she didn't rub them. She sat quite still.

'I don't know if you know it, but the day you join the SDS, you have a huge leaving do. Absolutely massive. Everyone gets royally drunk, goes a little crazy.' His gaze turned distant. 'It's because you know you won't be seeing any of your police friends for at least five years. Your only official link to the Met is your payslip.'

Someone knocked on the door, stuck their head inside.

'Not now,' Hanmer barked.

'Sorry, sir.' The man cringed. 'Didn't know you had someone with you.'

The door closed.

Hanmer looked out of the window once more. 'You've probably heard about how SDS officers chose their new identities?'

Lucy felt sick. There had been a huge scandal when it had been made public that an officer had applied for the birth certificate of a child who'd died and used this to create a cover story.

'That's where Carl got his name. Carl Simon Davies.'

Lucy was trembling inside but she kept her gaze steady and level. *You can get through this. You have to know the truth.*

'It also got him a flat, a vehicle and a life story that he made his own. His role was to target subversives and prevent disorder in London. For five years he lived a double life seven days a week. He settled in comfortably with his targets. He enjoyed their company enormously. There was a genuine bond. But if they found out what he really was... well, we were under no illusion about what would happen to him.'

He turned his head and looked at her, as though to check she was listening. She kept her gaze neutral, totally flat as she looked back.

'People liked him, trusted him. He became Treasurer of an anti-racial organisation. It was thanks to Carl that we learned about a large, violent protest that had been planned against the BNP. They were planning on trapping them at a party meeting in their headquarters and burning them to death.

'As a result of his intel, we prevented some of the most violent, most bloody riots London might have seen. Carl was commended by the commissioner.'

Lucy watched as Hanmer rested his palm against the glass.

'The commissioner said Carl had done enough. That it was time for him to come out of the field. Your father refused.'

She opened and closed her mouth, thunderstruck. *He refused?*

'He couldn't get out of his role. He couldn't leave his undercover persona behind. He was no longer the same person. He said he hated being a cop, everything about it. He wanted to stay where he was.'

The detective turned away from the window to face her.

'He enjoyed being with his contacts so much that he was willing to give up his police salary and everything that went with it in order to stay with them.'

She stared at him.

'He married one of his targets.'

Her voice was hoarse when she spoke. 'My mother.'

'Correct.'

A long silence fell. Lucy's ears were ringing, her fingers tingling. Her mind was a smooth, weirdly coloured lake of slate and sand.

'After Carl,' Hanmer went on, 'every SDS officer was visited at home to ensure they were married before they went undercover. It was to make sure they had something in the real world to return to.'

'You're saying he's not a police officer any more.'

'He hasn't been one for over twenty years.'

She was glad she was sitting down or she might have fallen, her body went so weak.

'Why didn't you say anything when we spoke before?'

'I needed to know more of what was going on. He was a good friend and I didn't want to endanger him. I know it's a long time since he's lived in Southwark, but if anyone finds out what he used to be...'

She could imagine Jaya's face. She'd eviscerate him. And what about Reg and the gang at the pub, Tomas and his father? Sweet Jesus. No wonder Mum had thrown him out and refused to countenance his name in the house. She'd suffered a massive betrayal but she still wouldn't have wanted his death on her conscience.

'When did you speak to him?' Lucy managed.

'This morning. He asked me to tell you.'

'Why couldn't he tell me himself?'

His face lengthened.

'He told me to say that he loved you very much, and that he was sorry, but he had to go.'

'Where?'

'He didn't tell me.'

'What's his real name?'

'He told me he wants to tell you himself.'

'Do you know what he's involved in at the moment?'

A look of surprise. 'No. Is it relevant?'

'You said you had to see me before I went to the SIO.'

'That's what your father told me to tell you. He said it was the only way to get you here.'

'He didn't mention the case I was working on?'

'No. You should understand I'm purely acting as an old friend of his.'

'Do you know *anything* of what he's been up to since he refused to come out of the field?'

Hanmer didn't answer at once. He was gazing outside.

'The last I heard, your mother threw him out. I thought he'd gone to Australia. The first I knew of his return was when you rang, asking about *Black Rainbow*. His old code name.'

'You didn't give him tip-offs when he was working with TASS?'

'TASS?' he repeated.

'It's to do with the case I'm working on.'

Hanmer shook his head wearily. 'I've never heard of TASS and I never gave him any tip-offs. The last time I saw or spoke to him was on 3 November 2001.'

The day her dad had, supposedly, buggered off with Tina the yoga teacher.

'You do realise he's used you.' She found it hard not to sneer.

'Yes. But he was a good friend. He saved my life once. I owed him.'

Long silence.

Then he drew himself tall. His shoulders went back, his chin lifted. He turned to her and the world-weary friend of her father's had gone. In its place was a determined-looking superintendent with a gleam in his eye. 'I think my debt's been repaid, don't you? So let's knuckle down. I want you to bring me up to speed with it all. And please, don't leave a single thing out.'

As Lucy finally left his office, she promised to keep the superintendent informed. She strode outside, drawing all her knowledge together from Kaitlyn's murder to Ricky's arrest, TASS and Helen Flowers who sold the fake bomb detectors around the world and Colin Pearson at the Serious Fraud Office.

A cape of sorrow mingled with regret and weariness settled over her shoulders and seeped into her heart.

Her father had been involved with TASS. He was a 'person of interest' to the police. He was in business with Amina Amari, who'd tried to kill Ricky. He hadn't been an undercover cop investigating BreatheZero. He'd lied. He was a criminal after all.

54

The hours passed drearily. Dan tried to occupy his mind by thinking about Isla's operation which was scheduled for today, Aimee's smile, Mischa's hot-red cheeks from teething, but it didn't lessen the endless pain.

When he heard a door open and a woman's footsteps behind him, quick and light, he almost cried out in relief.

'Untie him,' she ordered.

Someone with a heavy tread came over to Dan. One of the men who'd snatched him, no doubt. Dan tried not to make a sound but couldn't stop the involuntary groan when the man jerked his limbs to sever the ties.

'Get him up.'

Dan rolled his head to see two men standing one on either side of him. Both wore balaclavas. They put their hands under his arms and heaved him upright but Dan couldn't stand. He slumped to the floor. Lay quietly as he felt the blood rushing back into his arms and legs and feet, pumping and circulating normally again. Pins and needles fizzed on an industrial scale.

One of the men pushed at Dan with his foot. 'Get the fuck up.'

Dan groaned in return.

He showed Dan his taser. 'You want some more of this?'

Slowly, he shuffled to the wall and, with his palms against the damp brick, staggered upright. Stood swaying. It wasn't difficult to pretend he was in a bad way.

The two men stood on either side of him. They were in what appeared to be a mechanic's garage. Enough room for four vehicles. There was a pit in the middle of the floor and industrial-sized trolleys, tyres, shelves of tools lining two walls. Two plastic chairs stood to one side.

'Sit.'

The woman pointed at one of the chairs. He sat gingerly, rotating his hands and feet to encourage his circulation.

'I need some water,' Dan said. His voice was raspy.

The woman clicked her fingers. One of the men walked to the corner of the garage, to a shelf containing a kettle, mugs, a jar of coffee, a big box of Tetley tea bags. He shoved a mug beneath a five-gallon water dispenser and turned the tap.

'Two mugs,' Dan said.

The man glanced at the woman. She said, 'Do it.'

Dan gulped both down. Pushed them back. 'More.'

After he'd drunk what he guessed to have been a litre of water, he wiped his mouth with the back of his hand and leaned back. Surveyed the woman opposite him.

Around five foot six, her figure was disguised by a heavy boiler suit. She also wore gloves and sneakers, and what raised his spirits further was that she wore a latex mask. With her men wearing balaclavas, he hoped they had every intention of letting him go, safe in the belief he'd never be able to identify them.

Her eyes were brown with little yellow flecks. Hazel. One man had blue-grey eyes, the other brown, which downturned at the edges.

'Mr Forrester.' Her tone was polite. 'If you recall, you were told not to pursue the subject of flight EG220.'

He wondered which of the men had worn the latex mask when he'd delivered the note to his front door four days ago, reminding him that Jibran Bouzid's hand reached beyond Morocco's border.

'Do you really want Naziha to die in that horrible way?'

She gave him a long look, one he couldn't read.

'He's only a little boy,' she went on. 'And what about Khatabi's daughter, Naima? Do you really want their lives cut short because you insisted on sticking your nose where it wasn't wanted?'

Dan could picture Naziha's bright expression, the way he hopped and danced down the street like a happy sparrow. Naima tapping her fingers on Khatabi's car, waving her red-lacquered fingernails at the Commissaire. Her beautiful smile.

He didn't answer.

'Khatabi will never forgive you,' she went on. 'He'll probably come over personally to kill you if we don't do it first.'

As the water he'd drunk started to seep through his system, his head began to clear. Things began to make sense. Gerald Dunsfold, so-called science expert at BreatheZero, had called this woman to tell her Dan knew he was a fake. Jibran Bouzid, the Defence Minister who'd warned him off in Morocco, had obviously told her about Dan. Until now, Dan hadn't connected TASS, which produced fake bomb detectors, with BreatheZero.

It was at that moment he realised that it was this woman's fake devices that had almost got him killed in the plane crash. He stared into her eyes again, a burning rage inside his heart.

'I take it you're now producing fake anti-aerotoxicity masks,' he said just as politely. 'I can't see you manufacturing anything that might be legitimate with your track record.'

Something flashed in the woman's eyes. Malignant, cold.

'You have no idea of the damage you've done.'

Good, Dan thought with satisfaction, but then his mind slipped to Lucy visiting the BreatheZero factory yesterday and he felt a surge of alarm. He hoped she was okay.

'But we're recouping with what you might call a salvage operation.'

Not so good, Dan amended, guessing that he was part of the salvage op.

'What I want to know is: who else knows about our professor?'

Dan raced through the options. If he said nobody, then she could kill him and throw his body in the Thames and nobody would be any wiser. If he said several, she might want names so she could deal with them too.

'Just two of us,' he confessed.

Her eyes narrowed. 'You and Lucy Davies?'

The shock of Lucy's name made him flinch inside. He had to hope she hadn't seen it.

'No, me and my work colleague, Dennis Potton.' If she rang his office asking for Dennis, whoever answered the phone would know Dan was in trouble. His paranoia in creating code names and code words throughout his world was proving a godsend.

'You don't know Lucy Davies?'

He allowed a crinkle to appear between his brows. 'No, at least I don't think so.'

'You're a remarkably good liar.'

He widened his eyes.

'You were on that case together last year. I saw it on the news.'

Not for the first time, he hated the notoriety which that case had got him. It had made him far too vulnerable to be of any real use in any secret world.

Dan leaned forward. 'She doesn't know anything about my looking into the flight disaster.'

'Another lie. She's investigating Kaitlyn Rogers' murder, isn't she?'

Dan put his head on one side. Held the woman's gaze. 'Did you kill Kaitlyn?'

The hazel eyes looked at him, impassive, uncaring. 'What if I did?'

Images flashed like lightning through his head.

Kaitlyn's ripped jeans, red tassel top, bangles on both wrists. Auburn hair twisted into a knot. Her affectionate exasperation for her brother.

Josh drooling over the children's colouring books and crayons. His clumsy efforts to colour in the spaceship.

The devastation of the plane wreckage. The little girl still strapped to her seat. The charred remains. Suitcases, shoes, magazines, clothes. Entrails, body parts everywhere.

But it was the image of Josh that stayed with him.

Dan could count on one hand the amount of times he'd lost control. A rush of heat, of red and black, raw and animal clawed from his heart into his throat and with all his strength Dan thrust himself forward, driving his lowered head into the woman's chest. They fell together, Dan on top, bringing back his fist to punch the coldness from her eyes. Smash her face into oblivion. But before he could strike a blow, a penetrating pain, shrieking through his muscles, felled him onto the cold stone floor.

His hands and legs were shackled again but this time, they beat him until he fainted.

55

After she'd left New Scotland Yard and Superintendent Geoff Hanmer, ex-SDS operative and best buddy of her dad, Lucy went straight to Jon Banks, SIO, and told him everything. *Everything.*

He made notes as she spoke. He was incisive and efficient and asked pertinent questions that meant he had pretty much the whole story from her in under twenty minutes. She could see why he'd been made SIO.

When she started to apologise for not reporting Chris Malone the second she saw her, he held up a hand. 'Later,' he said. 'We are where we are. We need to crack on right away.'

She followed him to the briefing room where he ran the team through the case. That Adam Mason was a false name for a man called Carl Davies who used to be an undercover operative, but who was now a 'person of interest' to the SFO, whereabouts currently unknown. That Amina Amari was suspected of trying to kill Ricky Shaw.

'I want both of them brought in for questioning. Harris,' he pointed at a sergeant, 'get West Midlands Police on the blower for me. I want BreatheZero under wraps as well as Amina

Amari's mansion, her car, her cleaner, her fucking dog. Same goes for Carl Davies, aka Adam Mason.'

He snapped a finger at a constable. 'Find out where Mason lives.' He didn't look at her as he spoke. She could have hugged him for not telling everyone that Mason was her father. That would come later. When she was stronger. Right now she felt dizzy and off-balance, as though she was coming down with flu.

'You.' Another snap of the fingers. 'Find this faux professor. Bring him in. Apparently, there's a contract which he's signed. It might have an address on it...'

Lucy watched as the SIO doled out the tasks. It was a major operation, bringing in the SFO as well as the Birmingham and Wolverton cop shops.

'And what about this Helen Flowers?' he asked, tapping a blown-up photograph stuck on the wall showing a woman with doughy features and small, sharp eyes. 'There's still a warrant out for her arrest so keep your eyes peeled, please, and if you see her, take her down.'

The energy in the room crackled and as people began to move, the SIO barked, 'You.' He was looking at her. 'My office.'

Predictably, he told her she had to go home. Just as predictably, she refused.

'You can't stay here, Lucy.' He was firm. 'I know it's unbelievably tough, but it's protocol. I will keep you informed, okay? But you have to go home.'

'Can't I just sit in the corner? I won't get in the way, I'll–'

'No,' he snapped. 'Out, now. And if I see you anywhere nearby, I will have you suspended.'

She knew he was only doing his job, but even so. She glared at him. He held her eyes unrelentingly. 'Go,' he said, slightly more gently. 'Then I can get on with the job.'

She nodded, picked up her handbag, and went to her mum's. She thought about heading to Bristol and Mac, where she was supposed to be going tonight, but she wanted to be near the action in case she was needed. Kensington was where Kaitlyn had been murdered, and where the core of the case dwelled.

It was one of the most tortuous afternoons she could remember. She spent most of it pacing through the house. She kept calling Dan, but he wasn't answering his phone. She didn't try her father, or attempt to warn him that the police were after him. She'd thought she might be tempted, but no. He was nothing but a cheating, low-life, shitty criminal who was hanging out with cheating, low-life, shitty criminals. He deserved what he got and should she ever feel guilty about it, she'd deal with that when the time came.

She rang Mac. Filled him in.

'Jesus Christ,' he said. 'That's crazy.'

'I know.' She leaned against the kitchen wall, kicking the bin in a steady, small and angry rhythm.

'You want me there? It won't take me long to charge up the M4.'

'No. I'm better on my own. I'll just drive you nuts.'

'It's not a problem. My case is just about wrapped up.'

'Mac, I'm serious.' She stalked to the window. Looked at next door's washing hanging damply above a scattering of crocuses. 'I really *am* better on my own.'

'Okay.' He sounded startled. 'That's fine. Just let me know how it goes. And if you need me…'

'I'll holler.'

After she'd hung up, she prowled some more, relentlessly checking her phone, the news. It took a massive effort not to ring the SIO. If she didn't hear anything by five o'clock, she'd ring him, she decided.

The afternoon dragged by. As the second hand ticked to five o'clock, Lucy rang Jon Banks.

'Any news?'

'They've gone.'

'Gone?' she repeated stupidly.

'Cleared the office and buggered off. Same for the mansion. The dog's gone too. Your... Adam Mason is nowhere to be found either.'

She sank straight down to the floor. 'Shit.'

'Yeah.'

'I didn't tip him off, I swear it.'

'Don't worry, Lucy. I don't think you did. But someone did.'

She recalled Amina Amari shouting at her father. His grim expression. What had he said to her? Had he mentioned her, Lucy? That she was a cop?

'We've got an all ports out for them. We'll get them, Lucy.'

When her mother got home, Lucy told her the lot. Her mother fetched a bottle of Chardonnay but Lucy couldn't drink. She was too anxious, too wired. Plus, she wanted a clear head in case she was needed.

'This is what I was worried about,' her mother said. Her shoulders sagged. She looked every one of her forty-eight years. 'Carl dragging you into something horrible.'

Lucy wanted to say that if she'd known the whole story from the start, she might have been better prepared, but she held her tongue. As the SIO said, *We are where we are.* No point in backtracking.

Her mother made a simple Gujarati sweet potato curry that Lucy pushed around her plate. They watched *The Ten O'Clock News* followed by *A Question of Sport* but Lucy didn't take anything in.

When her phone pinged with an incoming text message from the SIO, she leaped on it.

Still nothing. Sit tight.

Midnight ticked past. Finally, despite her tension, she yawned.

'Darling,' her mother said. 'Go to bed. You can't do anything tonight.'

While her mother turned out the lights, Lucy reluctantly headed upstairs. Brushed her teeth. Climbed into bed. She didn't expect to sleep but she hadn't taken into account the emotional rollercoaster of the day and before she knew it, she was out like a light.

Lucy was in a deep sleep – no dreams – when her phone rang. She fumbled for it, knocking over the glass of water she'd brought to bed and making her curse.

''Lo?' she answered. Her mouth was thick and furred, her head muzzy.

'Lucy.'

One word and she snapped awake.

'Dan?'

'Yeah. S'me.'

He sounded drunk.

'Are you okay?'

Silence.

'Dan!' Alarm rose. 'Where are you?'

'Dark. Bashe-ment. It's–'

His voice vanished. She heard sounds of his phone being moved about.

'DC Davies.' A woman's voice. Lucy's senses went into freefall.

Amina Amari.

56

'What have you done to Dan?'

'Nothing that he doesn't deserve. But you should know that although he's strong, he's in a lot of pain. So you'd better listen up.'

Lucy swung her feet to the floor. Fumbled for the bedside light, switched it on. Her mouth had gone dry.

'I want to exchange your friend here for your father.'

It was so far from what she'd imagined, Lucy said, 'What?'

'You heard.'

'I don't have a father.'

'Don't lie. You were creeping outside my house on Tuesday evening. Or didn't you see the CCTV cameras? And there was I thinking you were a reasonably smart policewoman but you're not. You're like the rest of them. Thick as shit.'

Lucy opened and closed her mouth.

'I bet you thought I didn't recognise you when you came to the factory, but I did. I saw you on TV, you see. Clever cop Lucy Davies joining the team to try and find Kaitlyn Rogers' killer. And then you come waltzing up to Wolverhampton.' Her tone turned puzzled. 'I still don't know what brought you here.'

'Thick as shit cop finds clue all on her own,' Lucy said. She had no intention of dobbing Tomas in.

'I'd like to know.'

Lucy didn't think it wise to tell the woman to *fuck off* and remained silent.

Amari gave a dramatic sigh. 'Well, if you're going to be like that...'

Dan gave a terrible groan. It was the drawn-out, agonised sound a wounded animal might make.

Lucy went light-headed.

'Stop! For God's sake, stop!'

'Well?'

Sweat sprang all over her skin as Dan continued his tortured groan.

'Paperwork,' Lucy lied. 'I found a holding company in Ricky's paperwork that connected to BreatheZero.'

'Fucking Ricky,' she snapped. 'I wish he'd died.'

At least Lucy now knew why Amari had tried to kill him. It was as she'd guessed. He knew too much.

'Did you kill Kaitlyn?' Lucy asked.

'Whatever for?' The woman sounded surprised.

'She was on your trail.'

'I doubt that very much since she didn't even know I existed. Now, get on to your beloved Papa, would you? I'm struggling to make contact with him because he seems to have gone rogue. All thanks to you, his darling daughter. Whatever did you say to him?'

Since Lucy didn't have a clue, she remained quiet.

'Or was it because we had a fight over you?' she mused. 'I had plans for you that he disagreed with. I had no idea he felt so strongly but there you are. Blood will out, I suppose.

'Now.' Her tone turned brisk. 'I shall ring you on the hour, every hour until you're both primed to do the swap. You should know that it'll be near London, okay? So wherever he is, he'll have to get his fucking backside to the capital pronto. But I wouldn't be too long. Your friend's feeling rather poorly. And no police. I don't want all those plods cluttering up what should be a simple exchange.'

'Okay,' Lucy agreed.

'I'm already in place and patrolling the area with drones,' she warned. 'If you don't keep your word I'll vanish and you'll never see your friend again.'

Amari hung up.

Lucy redialled the number immediately but it rang out. She guessed the woman would have discarded the phone.

Fingers trembling, Lucy rang her father but he didn't answer. She left a message that started reasonably coherently but soon degenerated into a panic-stricken monologue. 'Ring me, Dad. Just bloody *ring me!*'

Next, she rang Jon Banks, the SIO. Amari had said *No police* but even with a hundred drones at her disposal, who was she kidding? Lucy could no more ignore the greatest resource at her fingertips than stick a needle in her eye. Surely Amari must know that?

Banks answered his phone on the second ring.

'Sorry it's so late, sir, but it's urgent.'

'I'll call you straight back.'

This was normal procedure. It meant Banks could get out of bed and stumble around trying not to wake up the household while he got his head together. Her phone rang barely a minute later.

'Go ahead.' He was crisp.

Quickly, Lucy filled him in. His calm demeanour steadied her. Her heartbeat began to settle.

'I'll get a team together,' he told her briskly. 'See you at the station.'

Yanking on some clothes she tore around the house, grabbing her handbag, her phone.

'Lucy.' It was her mother, standing at the top of the stairs in her dressing gown, hair awry, expression taut.

'It's Dan. He's been kidnapped. They want to swap him for Dad.'

'Oh God...'

'I'm on it. I'll keep in touch.'

On the street it was raining but she didn't notice. It was quiet. Nobody was about. She ran to Marshalsea Road, looking for a cab, but couldn't see any. Belatedly, she checked the time: 2am. The night tube didn't run from here. She'd have to jog to Waterloo Station and hope she'd find a taxi en route. Waterloo wasn't that far. A mile maybe?

Lucy settled into a steady run, her handbag slung across her body and thumping against her hip. She decided to go via the Cut – there *had* to be a taxi there, surely – and as she ran, she thought about what Amari had said, and what she hadn't.

What did Amari mean when she said her father had gone rogue? What had Dad done? Perhaps Amari had discovered her father used to be an undercover cop and she wanted to swap Dan for him so she could... what? Kill him? And what about Kaitlyn? Was Amari telling the truth that she hadn't killed her? Was Amari so accomplished that she could lie spontaneously like that?

She'd been jogging along the Cut for what felt like half a lifetime when she saw the bright yellow light of a vacant taxi. She flagged it down. Told the driver where to go. Told him to step on it.

They were barrelling along Grosvenor Road, the River Thames oozing inky black alongside, when her phone rang.

'Lucy. What is it?'

A rush of relief. 'Dad, oh thank God. They've kidnapped

Dan. He's my best friend... I'm godmother to his baby son – that's how much he means to me. Amina Amari has him. He sounds awful. I think he's being tortured. She wants to swap him for you.'

Silence.

'Dad? *Dad*?!'

'Quiet,' he snapped. 'I'm thinking.'

She had to swallow the scream that wanted to emerge. 'Think fast,' she hissed.

The taxi passed Chelsea Bridge, yellow lights twinkling against the dark and glimmeringly reflected in the black river.

'Where's the swap?' he asked.

'She's going to ring on the hour and tell us.'

'Where are you?'

'On my way to the Kensington cop shop.'

'Pick me up on the way?'

'Where's that?'

'Rockington Street.'

'You're in *Southwark*?' She couldn't believe it.

'I'm staying with Stan,' he added.

Teflon Tomas's dad. Jesus.

'I'm in a taxi. On my way.'

57

Lucy got the taxi to wait outside Stan's block of flats while she went to press the buzzer. She'd barely said her name before she was buzzed inside. Stan was on the top floor but she didn't take the lift – she didn't trust it not to break down halfway and royally fuck everything up – but ran up the stairs. Eight floors.

She was panting when she arrived but she didn't slow down. She jogged along the exterior balcony. Banged on the second-to-last door. Waited. Banged again. *Open it, for Chrissake!*

Finally, the door swung open. Stan was there, hair sticking up, faded dressing gown belted around an expansive middle.

'Sorry, love. I was on the bog.'

'Where's Dad?'

'He's gone to see your mum.'

'What the–'

'Said he'd see you there.'

'*Fuuuuck!*' Briefly she clutched her head. 'Why the hell did he lie about where he wanted to be picked up?!'

'He's buying time, love. But trust me, he'll be with your mum.'

'When did he go?'

'Straight after you called. Look, if you need a hand–'

'No. Absolutely not.'

She didn't want Stan involved. It was bad enough knowing her father was a criminal without adding more dodgy characters to the mix. She spun on her heel and tore back down the balcony, down the stairs. Leaped into the taxi. Gave him her mother's address. En route she called the SIO, filled him in. No holds barred. She didn't want to be seen giving her father any special treatment. She would bring him in like she would any other cunning, conniving fraudster.

They were turning into her mother's street when Amari called, bang on the hour.

'You have him?' she demanded.

'Not yet. But I know where he is. I'm going to get him.'

'How long?'

'An hour and a quarter or so,' Lucy lied. She wanted to keep a time buffer in place.

'You wouldn't be bluffing would you? Your friend's in such a lot of pain...'

'No. No, no, I swear it.' Panic edged Lucy's tone. 'Please don't hurt him any more. *Please.*'

'I'll ring you in an hour,' Amari purred, obviously satisfied that Lucy was dancing to her tune.

Her mother's house was ablaze with lights. With the taxi sitting outside on a meter, she ran up the path, her hands already holding the house keys. She let herself inside, bracing herself for shouts, screams, accusations, pots and pans flying, but it was utterly silent.

'Mum?' she called.

Nothing.

'Dad?'

Nerves prickling, she tiptoed down the corridor. Glanced

into the kitchen. Empty. She eased her head around the corner of the living room. Her heart caught. Standing in the middle of the room were her parents. Her father was holding her mother, rocking her gently in his arms. His head was against hers. His eyes were closed. He had tears pouring down his face. Mum was clutching Lucy's dad as if her life depended on it and sobbing quietly.

'Ahem,' Lucy coughed.

Slowly, they raised their heads. They didn't look at Lucy, but at one another. Her mother reached up and touched her father's face with her fingers. 'I never stopped loving you,' she said. 'I never stopped hating you either.'

'I know.' He took her mother's hand and kissed the tips of her fingers. 'I know.'

Only then did they turn to face her. Her mum and dad, together. And in that second Lucy felt the years pour away and she was eight years old again, seven, six, and her parents loved each other *so much* and they loved her with all their hearts and she was running to them, her eyes filling with tears, her soul brimming with emotions so fierce, so elemental, she had to be in their embrace where she was safe and adored and loved absolutely.

Nobody said anything for ages. They simply stood and hugged in a family knot, Lucy weeping, her dad kissing the top of her head, her mother stroking her hair. As an adult she hadn't felt as though she'd needed her father, but having him here, holding her and Mum, it was as though she'd been walking for a very long time and had just arrived home.

Gradually, Lucy's storm of weeping eased and she stepped back a little, wiping her eyes. 'So, you've made up then.'

'Hardly.' Her mother gave a snort, flicking a narrowed look at Carl. 'Shall I tell her?'

He nodded.

'He did his usual. Spun a wild tale that he might be dead by this time tomorrow and that he had to see me one last time.'

'It's not a wild tale,' he protested. 'It's true!'

'You know I can't believe anything you say any more.' Her voice turned hard.

'Lucy,' he said wearily, 'tell her.'

'Mum already knows about the kidnapping.'

At that, her father looked at her mother appraisingly. 'You didn't say anything.'

'Why should I?' She held herself tall. 'I don't owe you anything.'

'Aside from this house,' he said, waving an arm around the room. 'And a monthly stipend that helped Lucy through school.'

Her mother coloured and said savagely, 'I didn't touch your dirty money.'

He blinked. 'So what have you done with it?'

'It's in a separate account. You can have it back if you like.'

Her father looked shocked. 'You didn't use *any* of it?'

'No.' She raised her chin proudly. 'We didn't need your help.'

'For God's sake, I worked like hell for–'

'It was *wicked* what you and Helen did with those fake detectors. Unforgivable. Now, I want you to leave. And I don't want to see you again.'

Her father seemed to shrink. 'But I thought that–'

'You were wrong.' Lucy watched her mother standing strong, uncompromising. 'I know you're putting yourself in danger tonight, but at least you're not doing it for yourself. You're doing it for your daughter.'

At that, he looked at Lucy. He looked haunted, and very, very tired. 'Yes.'

'And for that ...' Her mother turned and held his eyes. 'I thank you from the bottom of my heart.'

'You love me,' he declared.

'I hate you too.'

He nodded, gave a wry smile. 'Well, it's just–'

He stopped mid-sentence, his eyes widening. 'Was that a siren?'

Lucy listened. She couldn't hear anything.

'It's a sodding siren.' He shot her an urgent look. 'Did you tell the police where I was?'

'Er... well, actually–'

Grabbing Lucy's wrist with one hand he spun to her mother and scooped her around the waist, sweeping her close for a smacking kiss on the lips. 'Love you, babe. Always have, always will.'

And then he was hauling Lucy through the kitchen, the utility room, and out of the back door, Lucy yelping and trying to slow him down but unable to. It was like trying to stop a charging polar bear.

'Dad, Dad!' she panted, trying to break free. His grip was like iron.

He pushed open the door at the end of the garden. Dragged her into the rear alley where he dropped her wrist and stood over her, chest heaving.

'You want to save your friend?' he asked fiercely.

'Yes, of course, but–'

'Then we do this my way.'

'But the police will be able to protect you! They'll cover us and–'

'They'll fuck things up. They don't know what they're dealing with, but I do.' His expression was hard, unyielding. 'Either you're with me and we save your friend, or I will vanish and your friend will die. Your choice.'

She didn't hesitate.

'I'm with you.'

58

They were lucky enough to catch a taxi near the Tesco Express on Harper Road.

'North,' her father told the driver. 'Just head for the M1.'

'Nice one,' the driver said. He was stocky, running to fat, with a genial expression. 'I live up that way. I can drop you off then go home.'

'Why the M1?' Lucy asked her father, but he didn't reply.

There was a silence, then her father leaned forward and closed the safety barrier between them and the driver. Checked the speaker was off.

'Amina's her hired help. She's ruthless, you know.' He spoke as though he was in the middle of a conversation, glancing out of the window, nodding to himself. 'It took me far too long to realise just how cold-blooded she was. Cunning, too. Clever, manipulative. Far cleverer than I ever could be. She always had me wrapped around her little finger.'

The cab overtook a recycling lorry before turning right towards Waterloo.

'It's my guess she abducted your friend,' he went on, 'because she didn't dare grab you, being a police officer. Dan

Forrester was the next best thing. She wanted to know how much you knew, start damage limitation, but when she learned what I'd done, she turned the kidnapping into a hostage negotiation. She wants me so badly, she can taste my blood already...'

'What did you do?'

'I took all the money out of the company and hid it.'

'BreatheZero?'

'And the rest.' He gave a dry laugh. 'It's a surprising amount when you add it all up.'

'How much?'

'You'll know it when you see it.' His laugh increased. 'I should have done it years ago. God, I've been such a fool, but life was such *fun*.'

He turned to her, suddenly animated. 'We had such a good time, back in the day. You have no idea what money can do... It opens the most amazing doors. We owned two racehorses, can you imagine it? We dined at the Savoy, hired private jets, flew to Monaco for the Grand Prix, sailed through the Caribbean...'

'You're talking about Helen Flowers.'

The light in his eyes vanished. 'Yes.'

'Where is she?'

'I can honestly say, hand on heart, that I don't know.' He rested his hand on his chest, but she didn't believe him. She could never believe him after all his lies.

'You sold fake bomb detectors.'

He looked away. 'It wasn't my idea.'

'But you still *sold them*!'

When he began to spread his hands, to tell her another lie or two no doubt, she said, 'Are you Shaitan?'

At that, he looked incredulous. 'God, no. That's *her*. She made up the name to keep people scared. And bugger me if it didn't work like a dream. You breathe that word in a place like, say, Morocco or Libya, and they practically shit themselves.'

'You did her dirty work out there. Because they wouldn't deal with a woman, you represented her.'

He looked as though he wasn't going to respond, but then he nodded.

'All for money.' She looked at him with an expression of disgust.

'Don't be so sanctimonious, Lucy. You've never been so hungry you've had to eat dog food out of a can. So thirsty you'll drink out of puddles. You have no idea what it's like to be poor.'

'That is no excuse for flogging a fake device that's ended up killing innocents all over the world!'

Carl shook his head. 'You sound just like your mother.'

'Don't you have any remorse?' she hissed.

He seemed to reflect for a moment, then he shrugged. 'I suppose so. But I didn't think that far. I just saw the opportunity to sell something and make a bloody fortune.'

'Are the BreatheZero masks fake too?'

He shrugged again, which she took to mean *yes.*

'Jesus.' She fell quiet with the enormity of it all. The depths of her father's greed. His Machiavellian personality. Dark and light, he was both of those. No wonder she and her mother loved him but hated him too.

'Why did you become a cop?'

He was silent for a moment, then he turned his head to hold her eyes.

'My final foster parents were in the police. They wanted something steady and safe for me, with a good pension. They knew my moral lines were a bit blurred and did their best to put me on the straight and narrow. I liked being a cop, you know. But it wasn't half as interesting as being an entrepreneur. Nor did it pay half as well.'

The taxi cruised along the M1, past Brent Cross, then Edgware.

'Dad.'

'Yes, sweetheart?'

'Did you kill Kaitlyn Rogers?'

At that, he turned and looked in her eyes. 'I may be a bit on the edge business-wise, but I have never, ever, killed anyone in my life. And that includes poor Kaitlyn.'

Did she believe him?

Lucy was nibbling her lip, wondering if he could be a killer, when her phone buzzed. Amina Amari. It was, Lucy saw, bang on the hour: 4am.

Lucy answered by saying, 'He's with me.'

'Excellent! Put him on.'

Lucy passed over the phone. Watched her father as he said, 'Yes, I thought you might. We're already on our way. Yes... yes...' He glanced at his watch. 'An hour. Yes.' His expression was stony when he hung up.

'What did she say?'

'She's given me the rendezvous.'

'Which is?'

He leaned forward and tapped on the Plexiglass divider. The driver snapped a section back. 'Yep?'

She listened to her father giving the driver an address in Imperial Way, Watford.

'Not TASS's old factory,' she said disbelievingly.

'The one and the same.' He snapped shut the Plexiglass divider once more. 'I guess she feels comfortable there, knowing the area.'

Lucy put her hand out for her phone, wanting to check the area out on Google Maps, but her father put it in his jacket pocket.

'Hey! Give it back!'

'I'll give it to you later. I don't want you ringing your cop friends and messing things up.'

'They might save your life!'

'They'll throw me in jail.'

'And I won't?'

He held her eyes. 'I'll have to risk that, won't I? But I'd rather it was you than some spotty constable with bad breath and an attitude.'

Lucy twisted her hands in her lap. She hoped she wouldn't have to arrest him. The ignominy! She'd never get over it. She had to pray something else turned up during the handover, like a passing patrol car, but since they didn't exist any more she'd do better to rely on a simple miracle from God Himself.

He leaned back in the seat and closed his eyes.

'I wish I'd been a better father.'

'Me too.'

They sat in silence for a while.

'I saw Superintendent Hanmer,' Lucy told him.

'He's a good man, Geoff.'

'He stuck his neck out for you.'

'Yes.'

'He didn't know you were involved with TASS or BreatheZero.'

'No, of course he didn't.'

'What about Colin Pearson?'

'Ha! Don't make me laugh. The SFO? They couldn't find their arses from their elbows. We were long gone before they even sneezed in our direction.'

'It's not a joke now, though?' Her voice turned vicious. 'With Kaitlyn dead and my friend, Dan, kidnapped.'

His jaw flexed. They didn't speak until the taxi slowed, began winding its way through an industrial park. Builders' warehouses, tool stations, van rental centres. At 4.20am the area was deserted.

'It should be a simple swap,' her father said. 'Him for me. But if anything goes pear-shaped, run like hell, okay?'

The knot in her stomach tightened.

'She won't really kill you, will she?'

'Put it this way,' he said drily, 'she won't want it known that she's been hoodwinked. Not least by her business partner.'

The taxi turned off the road and came to a halt in front of an engineering company. Orange street lights lit rows of parked cars, a skip.

'We're meeting around the back,' he told her. 'In the car park. We're to walk there.'

He turned to her, expression bleak.

'I love you, dearest daughter,' he said, and she heard the tremor in it. 'Which is why I'm doing this for you, nobody else.'

59

'Dad...' Lucy's emotions were a jumbled mess. In her mind, she saw a picture of her father making blueberry pancakes one Sunday morning. She was at the kitchen table colouring in her pony book, her mother pottering amiably around the kitchen. All of them without a care in the world.

He pushed a twenty-pound note at the taxi driver. 'Wait here. We won't be long.'

'Hey...' The driver began to protest.

'You'll get the rest when we get back.' He was curt.

As her father climbed out of the cab Lucy took a photograph of the taxi ID number before showing the driver her warrant card. 'I expect you to wait, okay?'

'Okay, okay,' he said irritably. 'I've got the message.'

'And if I need to, I will requisition this taxi.'

'No you fucking won't.'

'Nice to know you're happy to do your civic duty.'

Lucy stepped out of the cab and into the chill early-morning air. Her nerves were tingling, her stomach hollow, a precursor to an arrest, a bust. Rivers of pale crimson ran through her mind that she knew would thicken into red when the action started.

She followed her father as he walked around the building. They came to the corner. He peered round. 'They're here.' He put a hand on the brick wall beside him. Closed his eyes briefly.

'Dad…'

'Let me do this.'

He put his shoulders back. 'I go first. You stay here. You watch. I will walk to them and your friend Dan will walk to you.'

With that, he strode out of view.

Lucy hurried after him to see a large car park ablaze with security lights. Rows of industrial rubbish bins lined the wall to her left. Three lorries were parked at the far end. It was empty aside from the two vehicles a hundred yards away. A bright red Range Rover Sport and a blue panel van.

Please God, Lucy prayed. *Don't let Dad die. Don't let Dan die either. Protect them both.*

A buzzing sound made her look up. A blinking red light hovered above her. A drone. It came to drift above her father, paused, then hovered over Lucy before moving slowly away, scanning the area. Although it was a clever move, even a drone couldn't be in two places at once. Could she capitalise on this? With an exit road at the other end of the car park Amina Amari and her gang would easily be able to escape.

She watched her father walk twenty yards or so, roughly halfway to the vehicles, then stop, his hands spread. He was obviously waiting for Dan to appear.

Lucy saw the van's rear door open and two men began manhandling someone outside. Dan. He was staggering, struggling to walk and obviously in pain, but at least he was moving. The men propped him between them and lugged him to the front of the van, where her father could see him.

Slowly, her father took several steps forward. Stopped.

Nothing happened for several seconds.

The Range Rover's passenger door opened. Amina Amari stepped out, her heels clacking on the tarmac.

Lucy felt all the air in her lungs vanish.

Amari was holding a gun. A pistol with a long snout. A silencer. She held it steadily in both hands, aiming it at Lucy's father.

'Carl, you fucker!' she yelled. 'You think we're going to let him go first so you can bugger off again?'

Infinitely slowly, her father inched forward. His face was grey in the street lights.

'How can I trust you not to grab me and keep him?' he shouted back. His voice was scratchy with fear.

'We don't want him! We want *you*!'

At that, her father started walking. Really walking for them. And that was when Lucy knew that unless she did something, he was going to die.

60

Dan almost didn't see Lucy when she emerged at the far end of the car park. He'd been scanning the area, the solitary man walking towards them, the drone floating above, the Range Rover on his right, the van behind him, and then there she was, peeking around the corner.

He let his gaze drift over her, but his heartbeat rocketed. Were there more police? Teams of negotiators? Marksmen, watching their every move? The drone hadn't seemed to have spotted anything untoward.

He had no idea who the man approaching was, just that he was called Carl and that it was obviously a hostage exchange. Dan decided to do as he was told for the moment, but be ready for Lucy's lead, whatever it was.

His body ached and throbbed. There didn't seem to be a single inch of him which didn't hurt, but there were no broken bones and he was upright and functioning. If he had to burst into action, adrenaline would see him through.

'Amina, let Dan start walking,' Carl called.

'Not until I've got my hands on you, you fuck, and you've told me where you've put our money.' Amina didn't wear a disguise or a latex mask, which worried Dan almost as much as the fact she held a pistol. It meant she didn't care he'd seen her. And who was in the driver's seat of the Range Rover? He could see a shape sitting there but whether it was a man or a woman it was impossible to tell.

'Where's Lucy?' Amina suddenly asked.

'What do you mean?' Carl said. He looked around. 'She's behind me.'

Amina yelled, 'Lucy! Show yourself!'

Carl was looking over his shoulder expectantly.

'*Lucy!*' Amina roared.

The drone started flying busily about but Amina wasn't waiting any longer. She stalked to Dan and thrust her pistol against the side of his head. 'I will kill him if you don't *show yourself!*'

Lucy stepped into view. Her hands were open, her arms wide.

'Walk towards me!'

Slowly, Lucy came forward. Came to stand five yards or so behind Carl.

'Let Dan go,' Lucy said.

'Not until I've got my hands on your fucking father.'

Dan did a double take. He was Lucy's *father*? Hell. He didn't know what was going on, but he couldn't let her dad fall into the hands of these thugs.

Carl walked infinitely slowly to Amari who was following his every move with her pistol. 'Get in the car,' she commanded. 'Front seat. And keep your fucking hands raised!'

He did as she said. But as he opened the door, a bundle of white shot outside and tore across the car park.

Carl paused.

323

'Fuck the dog, get in the fucking car!'

He climbed inside. The dog, meanwhile, was peeing against one of the wheelie bins. Dan watched it scamper to Lucy who bent down, he thought to pet it, but instead she put her hand on its collar and hauled it up.

'Whose dog is this?'

'Put the dog down.' Amari sounded weary.

'Let Dan walk.'

Amari looked at the two men. 'Do it.'

The moment the men's hands fell from him, Dan walked forward, towards Lucy, his body tense, ready to sprint or fight. There were three of them: Carl, Lucy and him. And just four of them on the other side. The men weren't much. They may have tasers but they were nothing more than a couple of hired heavies with more brawn than brains. However, Amari was another matter. She had the gun. And what about the person in the car? Carl had left the door open but all Dan could see of the driver was a shadow.

'Let the dog go!' Amari yelled at Lucy.

Lucy was dangling the fluffy bundle high. 'Not until Dan's here.'

No time to think how laughable the situation was. No time for anything but what was happening in the moment, right now. Dan knew the pistol Amari was holding. It was a Beretta. It had a fifteen-round magazine which, if full, would be useful. He glanced at the thugs over his shoulder. They were standing there, feeling good that the guy they wanted was in the car and that Dan was walking away. Everything was going according to plan. He could see they were already relaxing, probably thinking about having a smoke, a bit of a laugh to release any vestiges of tension.

As Dan passed Amari, she didn't look at him. She was

distracted by Lucy and the dog. She was agitated, the gun wavering between him and Lucy.

Perfect.

As the gun returned to fix on Lucy, Dan yelled to Lucy: '*Run!*' and at the same time he planted his left foot hard on the ground and spun for Amari.

61

As fast as a snake Dan was upon Amari, snapping the pistol from her grip, pushing her aside so violently she flew to the ground. Keeping his posture low, legs spread and firm, Dan swept the gun smoothly to the two thugs. Fired twice. Swung back to Amari who was scrambling to her feet, screaming.

The two thugs were on the ground. Lucy had dropped the dog and was sprinting hell for leather back where she'd come from.

Dan pointed the pistol at Amari. 'Shut up.'

She fell quiet but her eyes were alive with fury.

'Carl,' he called. 'Come out.'

'Can't. I've got a gun on me.'

Dan grabbed Amari and put his left arm around her throat. Pulled her close against his chest. Pressed the gun against her temple. She was whimpering.

'Throw your weapon out,' he commanded. 'Or I will shoot her.'

Nothing happened.

'Don't think I won't do it because she's a woman.'

Amari wriggled and he tightened his grip, making her choke.

'You don't know who I am,' Dan called. 'You don't know my history, who I was before I became a civilian. Because you don't know this, you get one more chance before I shoot this woman and come after you.'

Dan waited three seconds. He knew he had no choice. Not if he was going to save Lucy's father.

He twisted Amari to the left, pressed the barrel of the gun against her arm and fired.

She screamed. A single, long drawn-out piercing shriek of shock and pain.

He held her tightly as she doubled over, clutching her arm, half-screaming, half-sobbing.

One of the men, he saw, was crawling away. The other lay still. Blood was seeping from his chest. No sign of Lucy, thank God.

The Range Rover's engine started.

Amari fell absolutely still.

Carl pulled his door shut. The vehicle engaged gear and surged forward. It was driving for the dog, Dan realised, which was trotting towards the vehicle.

'What the fuck?' Amari said.

When the car door opened to let the dog in, Dan pushed Amari aside and sprinted for the vehicle. The dog was now inside, all doors shut, and as he heard the roar of the engine, the driver pushing their foot on the accelerator, Dan ran as hard as he could. Then he stopped. Took up a classic shooter's stance. Steadied himself. He sent his gaze down the barrel of the pistol. Held his breath. And began firing.

One, the near rear tyre.

Two, the far rear tyre.

Three, the far front tyre, which was just visible.

Four, the rear windscreen.

Five, to the right of the rear windscreen, to try and hit the driver.

Six, ditto.

Seven, ditto.

The Range Rover veered wildly to the right and slammed into a row of wheelie bins.

Six rounds left.

Dan raced over. He saw Lucy out of the corner of his eyes and yelled, 'Stay back!'

Crouching low, he pulled open the passenger door. Carl lunged outside. He was white-faced, shocked.

Dan grabbed him, shoved him away from the car. 'Go to Lucy.'

He heard the man stumble away.

Both hands on his weapon, Dan crouched beside the passenger door.

'Throw out your weapon.'

Nothing.

'Throw it out, or I will shoot you. You've got three seconds. One. Two...'

A pistol came flying past him. Clattered to the ground.

'Lucy!' he shouted. 'Grab the gun, would you?'

62

Lucy stuck a finger in her father's face. 'You stay here and you *do not move*.'

He nodded.

She jogged to the Range Rover, where Dan was crouched, weapon at the ready in case the driver did something stupid. Like launch themself from the car, shooting with a backup gun.

Lucy grabbed the gun from the ground. A Glock. Easy to use. No fiddling about with having to cock hammers or anything. You just pointed it and pulled the trigger.

'Come out,' Dan commanded the driver.

The click of a latch and then the driver's door swung open.

'Cover me,' Dan told Lucy. He moved to the other side of the car while Lucy took up position by the passenger door.

Her adrenaline spiked when she heard him yell, '*On your knees! Hands behind your head!*'

There was a brief silence and then Dan called, 'Lucy.'

Lucy walked to the back of the car to see Dan was standing behind a woman, gun aimed at the back of her head.

'This is the woman who held me. The one who... questioned me.'

The woman who'd tortured him.

She was medium height, medium build, middle-aged. Her features were soft and bland. No freckles or moles. She was older than in the photographs Lucy had seen of her but she was definitely the same woman.

Helen Flowers.

The inventor of the BlackShark Sniffer. The person who had sold the fake bomb detectors to the Moroccans. The person responsible for flight EG220 blowing up. The person Kaitlyn had wanted to bring to justice.

'Lucy,' Dan said. 'I need you to bring Amari here so I can cover them both...'

But Amari was already stumbling towards them. She was clutching her arm and shouting at Helen Flowers. 'You bitch! You fucking bitch!'

'Stop there!' said Dan but it was as though he hadn't spoken. As though Lucy and Dan weren't armed. Amari stormed past them and lashed out at the woman on the ground, kicking her in the ribs.

'You were going to fucking leave me here!' Amari yelled.

'Baby, I would have come back for you. That was the plan. I'd never leave you.'

'Don't "baby" me!' Amari roared. 'You let this fucker shoot me!'

'Lucy,' Dan said urgently. 'Find something to bind them with. Quick smart. Have a look in the van.'

Lucy ran to the van. Found a handful of plastic cable ties. On her way back, she saw her father had captured Amari and had imprisoned her in a bear's embrace. Together, Lucy and her father forced her to the ground, where they tied her hands together.

'I should never have trusted you,' Amari spat at Helen Flowers. Her voice was shaking with rage. 'You got me to try and kill Ricky so it was *me* caught on CCTV. You got *me* to be your frontwoman so you could stay in hiding. *I loved you.*'

'You loved the lifestyle, you mean,' Flowers said. Her tone was cold. 'You would do anything for money, remember?'

Dan tied Helen Flowers's hands behind her back. Hauled her to her feet. Turned her around. She looked Lucy up and down.

'You're prettier in real life.' She sounded surprised.

Lucy was taken aback.

'John's always showing me photographs of you.'

'John?' Lucy repeated dumbly.

'John Flowers,' she said. 'Your father. My brother.'

TEN DAYS LATER

Lucy stood at the bar in the King's Arms waiting for Tomas. He was late but at least he'd sent a text message apologising. He'd be here soon. Reg had given her a bottle of wine on the house, which she was working her way through. He hadn't said why, but she guessed it was a form of apology for never coming clean over her father.

Everyone in the area had thought they'd known Carl Davies. They'd seen him as he'd portrayed himself when he'd been under cover: a genial man, popular, fun to be with. A salesman who was an anti-racist activist in his spare time. They'd swallowed her mother's story that she'd kicked him out for being faithless and Lucy thanked the heavens that it wasn't going to come out that he used to be a cop informing against them, or he'd never survive jail. Someone, somewhere would know someone else, and he'd end up dead in the shower block, the exercise yard, and nobody would know who'd done it but they'd feel it was justified.

As it was, everyone knew Carl as Carl with the gift of the gab, who was everyone's friend and who ran on the wrong side of the tracks. From Stan Featherstone to his son Tomas, to Ricky and

Reg, Carl was one of them. Which was why they'd kept their mouths shut when Lucy came asking questions.

Lucy had asked her mother if she'd encouraged her to become a police officer.

'Not at all. You just saw that patrol car at school, heard the radio crackling away, and you were hooked. Nothing to do with me but I was ever so proud.'

Perhaps she'd subconsciously known her dad was a cop? Or had she realised he was dishonest, and had wanted to redress the balance? As far as her dad was concerned, he didn't care, and nor did he have any desire to self-analyse. When she'd visited him in jail, he'd said simply, 'I loved your mum, I loved you. I wanted the best for you.' Then his eyes gleamed. 'Checked your bank account yet?'

She hadn't, but after her visit she'd looked on her phone to see her current account held an amount with so many zeroes she felt a bubble of shocked laughter erupt. Dear God, if she was caught with all this she'd be thrown out of the police! Straight away she reported it to the SIO who then arranged for it to go into an escrow account until the court decided what should be done with it. Dad, she thought, shaking her head in a combination of disbelief and exasperation. Honestly.

She'd asked him what led him to choose the criminal world and he'd shrugged. 'It wasn't a conscious thing,' he said. 'I do remember trying to help my sister out, though. When I was in the police, I found myself tipping Helen off, trying to keep her safe. When she got chucked out of the MoD for stealing, she came up with this idea of how we could get really rich. It just seemed so easy...'

'What about your childhood?'

'I came into care at the age of six months. Through child endangerment and neglect, I've been told. Not that I remember it...' His gaze was distant. 'Helen's four years older but she's never talked about it. We both had multiple foster homes. Although I remained in touch with Helen while being raised in the system, I only really got to know her when we were placed together as teens. Our last placement was with those two police officers who were determined to see us right. That's when she joined the MoD, me the cadets.'

But where Lucy's father had made an effort to go straight, his sister hadn't seen the point.

'She's different from me.' He sighed. 'She's smarter. More quick-witted. Ambitious. She's determined too.'

Lucy had visited Helen Flowers once. She couldn't think of the woman as her aunt. She had a coldness about her that Lucy didn't like or trust, as well as the dead eyes of a fish. She'd confirmed the story Lucy's dad had told her, that they'd been brought up by a variety of foster parents.

'Not all of them were nice,' Flowers told Lucy. 'Some of them just wanted the money the government paid them for supposedly caring for us. One household gave us dog food to eat. Another used us as drug couriers.' Her expression intensified. 'It made us resilient. It also gave us a hunger for money. We could never have enough. Can you understand that?'

Lucy nodded, not because she condoned the woman's rationalisation – she'd known far worse-off children who hadn't turned to crime later – but because she wanted to create a sense of connection between them.

After a while, Lucy began honing her questions.

'Don't you care about the people you've endangered by selling fake products?'

'Of course I do.' She sounded affronted but the expression in her eyes didn't change. 'But I don't let my feelings get in the way. I mean, I'm as warm and caring as the next person, but let's face it, it's a big bad world out there, everyone's trying to get one over you... You've got to look after number one, right? If someone messes with you... maybe tries to undermine you, rip you off... well, you take care of it. Do whatever needs to be done.'

'Including hurting people?'

'Sometimes. But that's business, isn't it?'

'What about John?' Lucy wanted to know if her father shared the same sociopathic behaviour.

Flowers stared at Lucy, unblinking. 'He's more squeamish. I didn't tell him the half of it, believe me. He's a fantastic salesman, but he just didn't have what it took to be at the top.'

'You're Shaitan, aren't you?' Lucy asked. When Helen Flowers didn't respond, Lucy said, 'It's okay. I'm family. You can tell me.'

Flowers leaned back with a sigh. 'They're so stupid, the Arabs. They actually believed I was a djin, can you believe it? All we did was tell a couple of stories and they swallowed it, hook, line and sinker.'

'And when Kaitlyn Rogers left Morocco, Jibran Bouzid contacted you and told you she was a danger.'

'She was going to ruin *everything*,' Flowers hissed. 'She'd already targeted Ricky, the fat slob. She'd even been to Southwark, poking about, trying to find John. It was only a matter of time before she did irreparable damage.'

'You killed her.'

The fish eyes gave nothing away but Lucy felt her skin crawl. Her aunt was a killer. No doubt about it.

Now, Tomas was walking towards her with Ajay at his side. Ajay bumped fists with her but Tomas greeted her with a kiss on the cheek.

'Wish you weren't getting married, DD,' he said, bouncing on his heels. 'And to a cop! What a waste.'

'How's Ricky?' she asked Ajay.

'Very grateful to you, man. 'Cept he's not so happy 'bout all the interest in his bizniz affairs, thanks to you too.'

'Any blowback on you?' She arched her eyebrows at Tomas, who shrugged.

'It's all above board, DD. I swear it.'

She gave a snort. As if she believed *that*, but Tomas and his lot were so slippery she doubted if the police would find anything to pin on them.

They talked a while, about the case, its ramifications not just in the UK but abroad, until Lucy put her head on one side and said, 'I've just got one question, Tomas.'

A guarded expression rose, but he nodded.

'Why did you give me the BreatheZero address? Without it, I may never have made the connection.'

He picked up his beer, took a couple of gulps. Exhaled. 'I thought what they'd done, what they were *doing*, was disgusting. Selling fake stuff like that... it really made me sick. Dad told me all about it, see. How that aeroplane got blown up. How everyone knew about Carl and what he was up to with that cold witch of a sister. Your mum didn't know, mind you. She only discovered he was selling fake detectors when a warrant was issued for his arrest. That's when your mum threw him out. That's when he disappeared.

'Nobody was too sure about him running off with another woman, but Dad and his mates let your mum put the story about. They were pretty sure she was disgusted with what he was doing too.'

Lucy studied Tomas, thinking over his dissembling to Dan. He'd said the photograph of Chris Malone was of Helen Flowers. He'd wanted Flowers to be found. Wanted her to face justice.

Tomas may be a criminal, but he had his own code of right and wrong. She knew exactly where he would have got that from.

She turned her wine glass around. When she spoke, her voice was low. 'Your dad was the whistle-blower, wasn't he?'

He sighed. Met her eyes. 'It's not something he's proud of, ratting on a mate. But he thought what they were doing was so bad, someone had to put a stop to it.'

She nodded. 'He did the right thing. Both of you did.'

'Yeah. But look where it got you.' He looked gloomy.

'Hey, it's not all bad. I've been offered a book deal!'

'No way!' His face lit up. 'What's it going to be called? DD's big exposure?'

She slapped his arm. 'Enough of the DD. Call me Lucy, please?'

'Sure, sweetheart. But you'll always be Delicious to me.'

Lucy wasn't going to take the book deal. She was notorious enough, thank you very much. Mind you, the look on Magellan's face made it all worth it. She'd made sure she'd been there when he learned that Ricky was innocent. Magellan had sent her a look of such poison she'd had to force herself not to break into a wild celebratory dance of some sort. Instead, she'd sent him one of her most beatific, beautiful smiles, her mind running torrents of blissful vivid green while he glowered malevolently back.

She'd been wondering if she should consider a career elsewhere, but quite what, she wasn't sure. Mac had told her not to do anything hasty, but when she'd mentioned it to Dan, his eyes had glinted.

'You remember that job I suggested to you when we first met?' he said. 'They'd love to have you.'

She laughed so hard tears came to her eyes.

'I'd make a crap spook,' she said.

He shook his head. 'You'd be terrific.'

She hadn't told Mac. She'd simply stepped into his arms when she arrived home and let him lift her, and carry her to bed.

EPILOGUE

Dan was sitting in the sun on the garden bench half watching Aimee play with Poppy the dog, half reading the BBC news on his phone, when Khatabi called him back.

'It is done,' he said.

Dan hadn't realised how tense he'd been until he felt the muscles relax from the top of his head down to his feet.

'Thank God.'

'*Alhamdulillah.*' All praise is due to God alone.

It was thanks to Lucy's father's love for her that he'd turned witness against his own sister, otherwise known as Shaitan. John – also known as Carl – had given the police everything they'd needed to wrap up two fraudulent industries as well as give Interpol enough information to liaise between the British and the Moroccans and bring Jibran Bouzid, the Defence Minister, to justice.

'He has been arrested,' Hafid Khatabi went on. 'He will never be released. He will die in prison.' He paused before adding fiercely, 'You did it. I knew you would.'

'I nearly didn't.'

'If you had no doubts, you wouldn't be the man you are.'

'How is Naima?' Dan asked after Khatabi's daughter.

'She is getting married!' He sounded delighted.

'Congratulations.' Dan was pleased for him. Khatabi was a good man who'd been caught up in something dark and dangerous by trying to do the right thing, and now he could put it all behind him, and walk ahead, into the light.

They talked about Mehdi and Mohammed, who sent their best and their deepest thanks to Dan for freeing them from the tyranny of Bouzid, and then as the conversation began to wind up, Khatabi said, 'Oh, Daniel, wait. I have someone here for you...'

'Hello!' a bright voice greeted him.

'Naziha?'

'Yes, it is me!'

'How are you?'

'I am very well. I am studying very hard at school. I am going to be a lawyer!'

'That is excellent news indeed. I am so glad.'

'Commissaire Khatabi is sponsoring me.'

'He's a very good man. He will be a great mentor.'

'One day, I will come and visit you in England.'

'I shall look forward to that very much.'

After Dan had hung up, he went and picked some daffodils, and brought them into the kitchen. He was wrapping them in brown paper when Jenny came into the room.

'You're taking them with you?'

'Yes.'

She went and fetched some ribbon and made a pretty bow for them. 'Are you sure you don't want me to come too?'

He kissed her lips. 'You stay with the kids. I won't be long.'

He put the flowers on the passenger's seat, next to the urn. Drove down the hill and to the bridge. Crossed the River Severn, sluggish and brown in the spring sunshine.

He thought about Isla as he drove, who he'd seen last week. Her tumour had been removed, and her sight partially regained, but not enough for her to be independent.

'I can get a guide dog,' she'd told him. 'I love dogs,' she added bravely. 'So that's a positive.'

Isla had helped with the case against BreatheZero. 'Amina Amari seemed so *nice*, but she wasn't, was she? And nor was her friend, Helen Flowers. She was the one who got me to sign that contract by threatening to tell the airline I'd called that journalist myself. She even admitted she wanted to scare everyone to death over aerotoxicity so she could sell millions of masks. What an evil woman!'

Lucy had called him yesterday to tell him that Amina Amari had decided to direct her venom onto Helen Flowers, turning against her ex-lover for a lesser sentence herself. Fine by him. Like Bouzid, Flowers could die in jail as far as he was concerned for her role in the EG220 bombing. The same went for so-called Professor Gerald Dunsfold, who had also been arrested. Good riddance to the lot of them.

Dan parked his car next to a grey Vauxhall. A cop's car. He climbed outside into a stiff wind. He saw Mac and Lucy waiting ahead, and the bulky figure of Ricky too. Mick and Julie from Mick's Motorsport were there, along with Jon Banks, Lucy's SIO, and Sergeant Karen Milton.

All there to pay their respects.

They walked with Dan as he carried the urn to the circuit. He put down the flowers and unscrewed the lid on the urn. Checked the wind direction. Then he upended Kaitlyn's ashes on the corner of her favourite racing bend: Tower.

He wished Josh could have been here too but it wasn't possible. He and Jenny had taken on the role of Josh's guardians, for as long as they lived. It was the least they could do.

'She used to blat down here,' Mick said, looking down the track. 'God, she was fast. Crazy girl on her crazy motorbike.'

'We loved her,' Julie added. 'She was incredibly special.'

'She was beautiful,' Ricky choked.

'Courageous.' This from Lucy.

Dan looked at the flowers in his hand and then into the sky.

'I wish she was still here.'

THE END

AUTHOR'S NOTE

I finished this book during the Covid-19 lockdown in the UK. Personally, I found it very odd working on a thriller during such calamitous times and for a while, I stalled. How could I write a contemporary thriller without mentioning coronavirus? I didn't want to dwell on the pandemic or second guess how things might pan out, so I decided to set it the year before everything kicked off.

Before I send the manuscript to my editor, I normally walk the areas where I've set the book. Thanks to lockdown this wasn't possible and I had to rely on memory (never particularly reliable) and Google Maps. Any errors will be mine!

I got the inspiration for this story when I read a book with a similar title to mine: *Scared to Death: from BSE to global warming, why scares are costing us the earth*. Before reading it, I'd had little idea how 'scares' have become one of the most prominent and damaging aspects of our modern world, or how much they cost us. It showed how a small public concern – like a UK health minister claiming there was salmonella in British eggs – can balloon practically overnight into a full-blown scare that can dramatically change people's behaviour.

It got me thinking. Who would orchestrate such a thing? Who would have the gall? And how would they profit from it? The ramifications were huge, and launched me straight into the story.

Like a lot of novels, this one has many elements of the truth, including a fake bomb detector seller who was jailed for ten years in 2013. He is thought to have made £50 million from sales of more than seven thousand of the fake devices to countries including Iran, Thailand and Saudi Arabia.

Aerotoxic syndrome is as I describe it in the book, and although many in the aviation industry are adamant that it doesn't exist, there are others who believe it is responsible for long-term sickness, and even death.

Thanks for your interest in my book, and I hope you'll return to enjoy further adventures of Dan Forrester and Lucy Davies!

A NOTE FROM THE PUBLISHER

Thank you for reading this book. If you enjoyed it please do consider leaving a review on Amazon to help others find it too.

We hate typos. All of our books have been rigorously edited and proofread, but sometimes mistakes do slip through. If you have spotted a typo, please do let us know and we can get it amended within hours.

info@bloodhoundbooks.com

Lightning Source UK Ltd.
Milton Keynes UK
UKHW010639200621
385805UK00002B/354